Doris
Whisper your story...
May

Sonnish

... whispers through time

MARY CAPPER

 FriesenPress

One Printers Way
Altona, MB R0G 0B0
Canada

www.friesenpress.com

Copyright © 2022 by Mary Capper
First Edition — 2022

All rights reserved.

No part of this publication may be reproduced in any form, or by any means, electronic or mechanical, including photocopying, recording, or any information browsing, storage, or retrieval system, without permission in writing from FriesenPress.

ISBN
978-1-03-914681-5 (Hardcover)
978-1-03-914680-8 (Paperback)
978-1-03-914682-2 (eBook)

1. FICTION, WAR & MILITARY

Distributed to the trade by The Ingram Book Company

Dedicated to my darling Patricia—my Emily.

Lest we forget

Chapter One

"**H**igher, Gramma Beth! Higher!" she pleaded between fits of infectious giggles. I felt the warmth of her on my hand as it found the flat of her back, and I pressed her gently higher. Long strands of her auburn hair floated back toward me, kissed with gold in the glistening sun. She squealed with joy, and I thought my heart would explode.

The motion of the swing and the warm summer air were mesmerizing, and I was happily exhausted. "My precious girl, will you remember this day, I wonder?" It was a question said aloud for the universe to hear and not meant to elicit a response from the little four-year-old child. *When the day comes when all she has are memories of me and our rare days together, will she reminisce fondly?* As though having heard my thoughts, she looked back at me with a joyful smile and pumped her legs towards an ever-higher adventure. She was fearless.

I searched my memory for tender thoughts of my own grandmother, but very few came to mind. I had spent a considerable amount of time with her as a youngster, but our relationship had been cool and distant. She had, however, been on my mind in recent days, ever since I had taken notice of the rather large box of her belongings in my garage. I wasn't eager to wade through it; I had dismissed it as simply another item on my ever-growing to-do list. I cringed at the thought that Sara might dismiss thoughts of me one day quite as easily.

She was ready to move on. "Down now, Gramma."

"What shall we do now, sweetheart?" She was away before I finished the phrase, already climbing the steps on the slide. This was our special day; she could do whatever she liked.

I had been excitedly planning it for weeks, and so we'd begun in the early morning with tiny pancakes wearing blueberry smiles. We'd made a game of picking up paper napkins with our sticky fingers, her infectious high-pitched giggles taking up permanent residence in my heart. Those same sticky fingers had rifled through a treasure box of toddler-friendly costume jewellery, and then with strands of beads and bangles hanging around her little neck, she'd determined that it was "Gamma's turn to dress up"—sometimes the "R" was there and sometimes it wasn't. With the promise to be very careful, Sara had poked through my jewellery box and pulled out a gold heart-shaped locket on a chain that I hadn't seen in years. It was dented and dull, and although we tried, we could not pry it open. Still, she'd insisted that I must wear it. I'd clasped it around my neck as she clapped her approval. Deep in the box, she'd found an old pendant fashioned from glass, now cloudy and dull with a little hint of green in the centre. *A leaf or a piece of clover*, I thought. It hung from a leather cord, brittle with age, and I'd bent my head once again so that she could place it around my neck. As she'd begun to finger more expensive items, I had steered her attention to a tickle trunk full of costume bits. Moments later, adorned in a princess dress, which had started life as an eyelet-lace white cotton nightie, and cinched with a silver belt, she'd danced and twirled around in front of the mirror, singing and performing without so much as a hint of inhibition.

The day was a fine one, and so we'd set off to check each item off our play-day agenda. We'd gone first to the beach with buckets and shovels and all the necessary accoutrements. Hours later, sun-licked and still gritty with sand, we'd proceeded to the ice-cream parlour for a much-deserved treat. A ring of chocolate still framed her mouth as we'd made our way to the playground structures. Upon reflection, I probably should have taken time to tidy her up, but we were having too much fun to worry about such trivial things. I felt a pang of guilt for having spent so much time and energy on keeping up appearances with my own children, as though their dirty faces would reflect badly on me as a parent. The fallout from having been born a child of the fifties, I suppose. No such mistake today. We'd kicked the ball around the park before heading to the swing-sets.

"Watch me, watch me, Gramma!" She waved from the top of the slide and then landed with a thump; her wide-eyed expression turned into a hearty giggle each time she slid down, as though the finale was a surprise. My energy was waning even as hers seemed endless, but she didn't fuss when I suggested that it was time for a snack and a story. There was a special event going on in the park that Sunday afternoon, and the musicians playing in the bandstand had drawn a crowd. The benches and picnic tables were all occupied, and so we skipped and sauntered until we found refuge under a huge tree away from the noise and confusion. It was a grand old weeping willow tree, and as we swept apart the curtain of leaves and leaned against the sturdy trunk, I felt a wave of childhood memories rush past me. A proper *déjà vu* moment.

Sara played in the carpet of fallen leaves while I set out a little picnic on my beach towel, and we sang along to the distant sound of the band while we had our animal crackers and juice. She settled on one of the storybooks that she had tucked away at the bottom of the beach bag, and we cuddled together on the damp ground. With one thumb in her mouth and the other tiny hand wrapped around the tacky necklace at my neck, she nestled in close. My voice was animated at first, as I pointed to the pictures, but at each new page, her little body became heavier against mine. I lowered my tone until her head nodded stubbornly one last time before slumping into my lap. The frayed cord in her grip gave way, and I reached down to retrieve the pendant from the ground where it had landed. I stroked her hair for long moments, relishing the feel of her quiet breathing. It was hauntingly quiet; even the sounds from the bandstand were subdued. The tree offered a familiar sensation of calm, the ache across my shoulders melted away, and in no time, I felt my own breathing settle into a slow sleepy pattern. The tiny leaves rustled in the breeze, and the distant sounds of the music disappeared completely. I thought perhaps the concert was over.

It was a gentle whisper that woke me from my replenishing nap, and I looked immediately to see if Sara had awakened. She was sleeping soundly, wet thumb resting against her chin. The breeze came up a little, and long strands of leaves danced all around us. I watched them glisten in the sunlight for a moment, feeling warmth on my skin even beneath the shadow of the great tree, and I shifted my bottom on the uncomfortable ground to stretch out a crampy calf muscle. Feeling blissfully content, I rested my eyes again and inhaled the day.

I was startled awake again by a hushed voice nearby. Had I dreamed it? I thought so, until yet another brushed past my ear. I had not imagined that one. It sounded as though someone was saying *"she,"* and this time, I turned my head to see if there was someone standing nearby. I expected to find a child playing a silly trick, but there was no one there. I felt almost embarrassed for having looked around, the way you do when you trip over nothing on the sidewalk. But another breathy whisper unsettled the hairs on my arms, and had it not been for the sleeping child in my lap, I would have jumped to my feet in search of the culprit.

The whisper was clearer now, not louder but more fervent. *"She"* it repeated, and the word sounds lingered in the air, soft and breathy: *"Shhhhhheeeee . . ."* A stronger breeze rustled through the tiny leaves, and my heart raced, my breaths quickened and became shallow, and I realized I had been pressing the little pendant deep into my palm. In my struggle to shake it off, whatever "it" was, I leaned back deeper into the gnarled wood of the tree. It steadied my nerves a little, and I closed my eyes only to find an image of my grandmother waiting there. The whispered *"She"* hung in the air more subtly now and further away. The breeze settled, and all was quiet except for the distant guitar sounds emanating once more from the bandstand. I could barely breathe. I opened my eyes and inhaled a lung full of air just as the sleeping babe began to wriggle and complain. All my attention went to consoling and distracting her sleepy, tearful question:

"Where's Mommy?"

It was time to go home.

In the quiet aftermath of our wonderful day, I revisited the whispers in my mind and tried to convince myself that I had simply let my imagination run away with me. The logical and organized part of me heard my scientist father say, *"Everything has its place, and everything has an explanation in science or mathematics."* The whispers were just the sounds of the breeze in the leaves—nature playing tricks on a peacefully sleepy gramma. But the niggling feeling that there was more to it just would not leave me alone, and I spent a sleepless night reviewing the events of the day. The details were vivid. I had not imagined the whispers; I was sure of it. *"Sheee."* I heard it again every time I tried to close my eyes. More haunting even than the whispers were the physical sensations: The hairs on my neck still vibrated with anticipation. It was like hearing that penultimate chord in a piece of music, just before the resolve, with your nerves standing at attention waiting to be told "at ease." That was the kind of electricity that I still felt hovering around me. Little wonder I couldn't sleep. Why had Milly come so clearly to my mind? I hadn't thought much about the old battle-axe in years. What an awful thing to have called your grandmother, but that was exactly what we'd called her. Never within earshot mind you.

As I finally drifted into sleep, a cascade of memories and images danced behind my weary eyes like soda bubbles breaking the surface of a glass. A very long time ago, there was Milly, a great willow, and the haunting power of those intense physical sensations.

I was only a child when I had my first encounter under the massive, stately old weeping willow tree in Milly's front yard. Well, it had felt massive to me at the time. It was the centrepiece and crowning jewel of her property. The cascading branches hung like a waterfall of greenery that hovered just above the ground. There was something magical about it—fairy-like. Milly used to tell tales of a great snake that lived beneath the tree. One can only wonder why she would want to frighten her grandchildren with a story like that, but it was enough to keep me from playing near that tree for a long time.

On that particular day, however, an exception was hesitantly made. It had been over a week since I had seen my parents or slept in my own bed. I was feeling sad and lonely and a little guilty. I just wanted to find a quiet hiding place to have a good cry. I approached the great tree, held apart the branches ever so slightly, and peeked through. No snake that I could see. I held the curtain of leaves apart a little further and went through as though stepping out onto a great stage. I walked around the circumference of the trunk, checking every inch of the ground for signs of slithering and then upwards into the umbrella of branches. Satisfied that I was alone, I leaned back against the gnarled, rough wood and slid down until my bottom hit the mossy ground with a thump. Nestled in, eyes closed, it only took a moment for my fears to subside and become one with the quietness of the place. It was as though a giant cloche was lowered over us—me and the tree.

The property was on a corner, so there were always street noises and usually people out and about, mowing their lawns or talking to neighbours. At the very least, I should have heard birds chirping. I crawled over to peek under the branches, and sure enough, the usual sounds were there, but back beneath the tree, all was silent. It rattled me a little, but not enough to coax me from my sanctuary. I leaned back against the trunk and closed my eyes once again. It was peaceful and soothing at first, but the more I relaxed I became, the more I became disturbingly aware of my own breathing and the laborious workings of the heart muscle in my chest. The hairs on my arms took on a life of their own, and I could feel the exaggerated movement of my pulse at my wrist and in my neck. All at once I was calm and nervous, tearful and joyful, cool and warm. It all became too much. Too many sensations were overlapping, and I had the overwhelming feeling that I was not alone. Again, I scanned my surroundings in search of the snake. I didn't see him, but I was spooked enough to scurry out from under my hiding place and save my good cry for another day. I decided instead that the fervent desire to murder my grandmother was a forgivable sin, and my self-flagellation would keep.

It was another year before I finally summoned the courage to venture back beneath the willow. From small child to late teen, I returned often and grew to appreciate rather than fear the heightened sensitivity and creativity I found there. I was drawn to it like a drug. My sister confessed that she too found solace under those branches and occasionally did some writing, but she was never able to sit in one place for too long. She was happiest expending energy, doing gymnastics and tumbling in the furniture-free zone that was the rec room. As I entered my early teens, I was less resistant to spending a weekend at Milly's, in fact, I felt compelled to go even though I spent little or no time with "the old battle-axe." I sat beneath the willow with drawing pads and charcoal pencils and plucked out simple melodies on my guitar. Every now and again, I would catch a glimpse of her watching me from the big picture window, and I resented her fleeting intrusions. I blossomed in that small space and felt inhibitions fall away like dead skin. I found my singing voice there and shrugged off any concerns about who might be listening outside my willowy cocoon. Bit by bit, my willow helped me nurture a little bud of confidence. My willow—and I did believe it was mine—had given me a gift.

That was ever so long ago, I reminded myself upon waking. Still, I mourned the passage of time that had allowed me to forget those mystical days. Perhaps, those memories are meant to be tucked away with all the fantastical stuff of childhood, but I was sad to have forgotten them so completely. How tragic it seemed that the clutter of everyday life should diminish the sensations that were possible when my mind had been quiet and open and young. Now, all these years later, the clandestine connection with nature that had spoken to me as a child was speaking to me again. I felt compelled to listen. A few days later, I went back to the park—back to the tree.

Eyes closed and mind as open as I could manage, I allowed thoughts of my grandmother to wash over me. I acknowledged, with a modicum of remorse and with only a gentle mental flogging, that this was the first time in many years that I had considered her at all. Life was busy, and I had been absorbed in the business of living it, raising a family of my own and surviving a divorce. *Who had time to reminisce about an old lady?* She had always been that to us: an old lady and a cantankerous, miserable one at that. We never thought of her as anything else. She was Grandma, a one-dimensional old battle-axe who looked as though she hated us but insisted we come to visit. Her past and personality were well hidden behind wrinkles and scars and were of little concern to us.

I doubt that we were unique; most children perceive their elders the same way, like black-and-white images on a television screen, each with a role to play. He was Dad, the one who went out to work every day and read the paper from cover to cover with his glasses balanced precariously on his nose. Mom, with her hair pulled back in a French knot, cooked the meals, did the shopping, and ensured that we were always sufficiently pressed and primped for the next family photograph. We neither knew nor cared that these stick figures, essential to our existence, had once been young, vital beings and carried with them stories of a life already lived. My heart hurt at the thought that Sara would only know and remember me as an old shadowy stick figure, and I suddenly felt the part. Speaking to the tree, I admitted, "Age certainly changes your perspective on things."

It had been three decades since a broken hip, agonizing pain, and finally pneumonia put an end to Milly's long life. I'd seen her a few hours before she died. She had been ready. She wanted to go. In her sad eyes though, there had been an expression akin to a plea that I had not understood. I'd just wanted her to let go, and so I'd dismissed her longing glance as fear. She was so frail and broken, her agony palpable, and I ached for her to close those tortured eyes and never wake up. She may have needed something from me in that moment, but I hadn't taken the time to ask or to listen. *"Listen."* Now that was a word she'd used often when I was a child. I couldn't recall specific instances, but the word had held importance beyond the usual *"shut up and pay attention to the adult in the room."*

I tried to remain focused, wishing now that I had spent more time at yoga class, learning to meditate and clear my mind. I gave myself a little shake, realigned my body, and tried to summon a happier, less tormented image of my grandmother. Instead, my mind wandered into a minefield of excuses for having so callously abandoned all thought of her. I wondered if my sister felt the same, if she ever had occasion to consider the old girl. I knew the answer and decided to grant us both absolution; ours were reasons and not simply excuses.

Life had gone on since Milly's death. Not only had we been busy raising our own families, my sister and I had spent twenty years dealing with a high-maintenance mother who (to be fair) was twice widowed and had not had it easy. Both Dad and her second husband were loving, attentive men who had idolized her and treated her as their delicate china doll. She was petted and spoiled, and in turn, was a doting and devoted wife who morphed into the personality of the current man in her life. She took on his likes and dislikes, from food to sports, and transformed herself into the perfect partner. She enjoyed lavish vacations, wore furs and jewels, loved to entertain, and was tremendously proud of her home. They'd left her, and she'd been devastated. That's how she perceived it: They hadn't died; they'd left her.

While the term "cancer survivor" certainly has a more positive ring, it would be more accurate to say that Mom spent nearly thirty years dying of cancer. It became her identity. She always enjoyed being the centre of attention, and in fact, demanded it, which in later years left her bereft of friends when she needed them most. There were, of course, a few stalwart companions who stayed the course, and thank God for them. They were her day-to-day soldiers. Her two daughters, on the other hand, were left to battle the guilt over how much we could physically and emotionally do for her. It was an exceptionally long, hard-fought war for all of us.

When Mom died, I'd been in the process of a move across the country. Most of her household goods and belongings were sold, but there were some boxes of items that had required time to process—time I just did not have.

Those boxes had become building blocks in the wall of moving crates that lined my garage like some Lego nightmare, a project for another day and some extra muscle.

Now, lingering beneath the willow and aware of the retched dampness seeping into my bones, I chided myself for not bringing a blanket. I should have grabbed the one from the beach bag that still sat at the front door. Even the musty towels that I had neglected to unpack would feel good beneath my bottom right now. I had been sitting there for God knows how long, meandering through memories, hoping for some miraculous apparition or revelation, but I had not felt empowered by my surroundings in the least. There was no electricity; the hairs on my arms remained docile. There were no whispers and no profound answers. I was a bit disappointed, but mostly, I felt ridiculous. I grabbed my purse and made it to a standing position after two failed attempts, aware that arthritis and extra pounds are better suited to daydreaming in a La-Z-Boy chair.

Errands completed, I proceeded home and mindlessly pulled into the driveway, reaching above me to pull down the visor and fumble for the garage-door opener. The door lifted slowly as I manoeuvred the car into position. Parking was never my strong suit, and the task was made more difficult with the multitude of boxes still lining the walls of the small garage. They were neatly stacked and simply labelled: HOUSEHOLD OUTDOOR ITEMS, WINTER CLOTHING, MOM'S STUFF, MOM'S PHOTOS, and of course, MILLY'S STUFF. I was more curious than before, but that was one Jenga piece that would have to be extricated from the puzzle on another day. A hot cup of tea and a heating pad for my behind were a far greater priority in that moment. I made my way inside.

It had been a long day, and it was good to be home with time to unwind before starting supper. I was comfortably seated in my reclining chair with the television on, cradling my steaming mug, when my cell phone rang. "Oh blast," I muttered under my breath, still observing my New Year's resolution to clean up my potty mouth. Begrudgingly, I pressed the little button on the side of the chair, comforted by the familiar whir as it inched toward the upright position but a bit annoyed at the pace. I rifled through the purse that I had left sitting at the top of the stairs but couldn't find my phone. The ringing continued, and I realized it was coming from yesterday's beach bag, which was still propped up in the corner by the front door. I made my way down the stairs, unzipped the pocket on the front of the bag, fumbled for the buttons on the phone, and said, "Hello," only to hear the familiar click that told me a telemarketer was about to pick up and annoy me even further.

"Jesus, Mary, and Joseph."

Well, so much for that resolution. I sat down on the bottom step to sort through the now musty beach bag but immediately regretted that I hadn't taken it outside. Sand, cracker crumbs, and leaves spilled out all over the floor as I pulled each towel from its damp grotto. I imagined the vacuum cleaner laughing at me from the laundry room as I pulled out the damp storybooks and the empty juice-box containers. There were dead leaves about an inch deep at the bottom of the bag, which Sara had collected, and I reached my fingers down for a final rummage before taking the bag outside for a good shake, grasping the frayed cord of the necklace and its sad little glass ornament, which I'd found in a corner of the bag's damp bottom.

And there they were: The sensations that I had hoped for and even expected to find in the park that afternoon were buzzing electric all around and through me. With fingertips tingling in anticipation, the tiny dancing pins made their way up each arm and across my shoulders until the hairs at the nape of my neck stood at attention. The air was alight with shiny dust particles, twirling and blinking like fireflies in the night sky, leaving little golden jet streams in their wake. The sweet fragrance of hollyhocks drifted past me, although the blooms were many metres away at the end of the lane, and the pungent aroma of bacon lingered in the air from yesterday's full English breakfast. I could see shiny dewdrops forming on my skin with goosebumps rising beneath; I felt sun-kissed and warmed from within, but my toes and fingertips were icy cold. It occurred to me that all the sounds of the house had disappeared as though the power was out. I basked in the quietness of it for a time, imagining the luxurious peacefulness of log-cabin living with no running refrigerator, no air conditioner, and no computers chugging their unharmonious background noises.

On the tip of my tongue, I tasted a hint of my favourite sour-cherry candies but wasn't able to recall when I'd had them last. I felt energized enough to sprint up the stairs but had no desire to move or risk breaking whatever spell I was under. There was no fear. I was awake; I was certain of that and cognizant enough to know that I should be apprehensive at the very least, but instead, I felt safe and somehow comforted, even embraced. I glanced down at my hand, and still cradled there was the unassuming glass bobble, which looked fractured from within like ferns of frost formed on a cold window, and as I wrapped my fingers around it, I knew it to be the source of this magical experience. Warm now in my hand, I held it there for long moments, and when I opened my fingers, I knew there would be clarity. The frost flowers were gone; the glass was clear enough to see that suspended inside was the tiny green leaf of a willow tree.

Chapter Two

Willow

It is a willow when summer is over,
A willow by the river
From which no leaf has fallen nor bitten by the sun
Turned orange or crimson.
The leaves cling and grow paler,
Swing and grow paler,
Over the swirling waters of the river as I loath to go,
They are so cool, so drunk with the swirl of the wind and of the river –
Oblivious to winter,
The last to let go and fall into the water and on the ground.

WILLIAM CARLOS WILLIAMS

Exploring the mysteries of the willow was my new obsession, and I dove unabashedly into books and stories that I found at the local library and spent countless hours online to learn all that I could about its links to folklore and mythology. I enjoyed the process; it had been a long time since I had studied much of anything. I read that goddesses and water spirits, in almost every culture through the ages, were associated in one way or another with this magical tree, and that its powers were linked to fertility, grief, and death among other things. Farmers for centuries believed that it held the power to bring prosperity in the land (and fruitfulness in the womb). I knew that, throughout history, botanicals and herbs had been used medicinally, but I didn't know that, in ancient times, the bark of the willow had been used for its pain-relieving and fever-reducing qualities, and that it boasts the same properties as the aspirin we take today. I was surprised to learn that the Greeks placed willow branches under the mattresses of infertile women and in the coffins of the departed.

I was reminded of Milly and her snake when I read the stories of serpents playing such a significant role in the myths surrounding the willow. While in most cultures snakes were demonized, the Celts believed that a snake beneath the willow offered protection to the spirits of the departed. Young willow saplings were planted on top of graves in the belief that the spirit would rise up into the new tree and retain the essence of the departed. I saw photos of cemeteries throughout Britain, particularly those situated near rivers and lakes, that are still lined with willow trees, and I wondered if Milly had lived near a place like that as a girl. I wondered a lot about her.

The Greek and Roman mythology was interesting, but it was learning more about the Celtic relationship with the willow that really struck a chord with me. It was known as the tree of dreaming, inspiration, enchantment, and spiritual rebirth. Either fresh cut from the tree or newly fallen, willow wands were made and used for a deeper connection to intuition, dreams, and visions. Celtic people believed that their poetry and creative imagery were enhanced by its powers and that the willow brought them a deeper understanding of emotion. They also believed that the sound of the wind through the willow had potent and inspirational influence on the mind and offered the gift of eloquent communication. Their interpretation of dreams was a revelation. They believed that deep unconscious thoughts speak to us through our dreams in vivid and meaningful ways, which inspired them to place willow branches beneath their pillows while they slept.

I came to the realization that the glass pendant was an amulet of some kind. Whenever I held it close, a kaleidoscope of images floated past my closed eyes, my grandmother most often among them. The mystical little bobble seemed to wink at me from beneath the strewn covers and the stack of textbooks surrounding me on the bed. It held far too much meaning now to be considered a tatty little ornament and although unpretentious in its nature, it seemed to dangle proudly on its shiny new silver chain. The amulet would be going under my pillow again tonight. With a little shiver of anticipation, I wondered if I was the first to feel its magic. I wagged a finger at it. "Well, my pretty friend, I expect you think I'm an arrogant so-in-so. You've been whispering to folks for a very long time, haven't you?"

I drifted to sleep still trying to conjure an image of my grandmother in my mind. Instead, I drifted back to the day I first sat beneath Milly's great tree.

The old battle-axe clomped around in the room above, thunderous in her enormous sensible shoes while we cowered below in the damp and rank of the dungeon, plotting her death. It may be my most vivid recollection of Milly. My collaborator, at the tender age of five, was my sister Julie. Banished to the bowels of the house for having behaved like children for the third day in a row, we resumed deliberations and hypothesized that a simple nudge at the top step would send the old girl plummeting to her doom.

"Wait! What's that?" Stealthily, I moved to the bottom step.

Timid, Julie responded in a breathy whisper, "I didn't hear anything."

"No, silly, take a sniff." I inhaled deeply. "Pork chops, smothered in onions, right?" It wasn't really a question. Little else made my mouth water like those scrumptious medallions of wonderful.

"Yeah, I think so, maybe."

I lumbered toward her with hands raised into threatening bear claws and growled, in my best grizzly imitation, "Do you suppose the beast will feed us?"

Julie, who was not always good at the play-acting part of the game, sulked. "She always feeds us. Now stop that; you're scaring me."

The dungeon, as it happens, was a wonderful place to play make-believe and had been strictly off limits until recently. So often, we'd been warned of the many dangers beyond the door to the beneath of the house; however, details were vague, and so it was left entirely to our vivid imaginations to fill in the gaps. It was Dad who'd swung open the gates of hell when he donned a tool belt and made it his mission to convert at least part of the old girl's cellar into a completely unnecessary rec room. It was yet another failed attempt on his part to elicit some spark of enthusiasm from Uncle Ian. "Rec room." Now that's a moniker that congers up images of parties and amusement—not activities generally associated with Milly's house. The dingy space remained dingy even with the addition of panelling and ceiling tiles, but the subtle changes were sufficient enough to dub the area a "playroom" and get us out from under Grandma's feet.

The steep, narrow, and previously forbidden staircase was now ours to descend; our proud papa gave us a tour of the newly finished area to the left of the stairs, pointing to the little table and chairs as though Disneyland could not hold a candle to it. "Girls," he said, "you must not go in there." He pointed toward the bi-fold doors to the right of the staircase. "Now, I mean it. It's no place for children." Thankfully, he neglected to elicit any promise, and we did not offer one. Honestly, what was he thinking? To a child, this was like issuing an engraved invitation, and so at our first opportunity, we went beyond the doors to find a dungeon worthy of the name. In retrospect, he may have been daring us to seek an adventure.

Creepy, dark, and foul-smelling, it was the best of all forbidden places. The uneven floor was part cement but mostly dirt with sink-hole grates that spoke in low haunting echoes and emitted a noxious rusty odour. There was soft green moss, slimy in places, that inhabited the back wall along with sinister implements of death—corroded garden tools for those with no imagination. Once we survived the labyrinth of mouldy boxes, we discovered monsters with relentless arms and legs and gaping hungry mouths—an old wringer washer and a past-its-prime furnace. We inched our way toward an old trunk with an enormous latch that gave way to a plume of musty, mildewed air. We hesitated, certain we would find the bodies (or at least the bones) of the dead and a little disappointed to discover only a stack of horrid-looking dresses with miles of yellowed crinoline from the olden days. Beyond that though, on the far wall, we stumbled upon the headless soldiers, which was the ghostly impression given by mangy old uniforms hanging on a wall with hats hovering above them on metal hooks.

Every opportunity to explore this new square footage offered an adventure in what was just another visit mired in absolute boredom. Like randy teenagers, Mom and Dad needed their together time, and so every second weekend, we were packaged up and carted off to Grandma's house like misplaced UPS parcels. The colouring books in our overnight bags didn't go far in filling the time. There were no toys or children's books at her house, no swings . . . nothing that would indicate to passers-by that grandchildren were welcome there. She didn't stock up on sweets or kid-friendly cookies, and there were no cartoons on the TV. Neighbourhood kids, if there were any, never dared venture near the cranky old woman's house. We were never told we were special or pretty, and hugs were a rare commodity. Overall, a trip to the dentist was nearly as much fun.

On this occasion, our customary and tolerable overnight stay turned out to be an interminable three-week purgatory. We'd been rifled out of bed in the middle of the night amidst a flurry of activity as Mom packed suitcases, wrote notes to the school, and searched for passports. Our paternal grandfather in England had fallen gravely ill, and Dad hoped that he and Mom would get to see him one last time. (Sadly, they were too late.) It was after week one that Julie and I began formulating a plan for Milly's demise.

Everything in that house was accomplished with military precision apart from bedtime, which was pretty much up to the discretion of the individual. Morning reveille was at eight a.m. Beds were made. Housework began after a breakfast of raisin toast and tea sweetened with a ridiculous amount of sugar. The furniture was spit-polished, floors swept, glass shined, and crevices in the rubber runners on the hardwood stairs manicured with a toothbrush. This routine was followed by an inspection; a positive critique may have been rewarded with a Fig Newton, depending on her mood. What came next could have been called any number of things (playtime, alone time, don't-bother-me time) but simply meant we were left to our own devices. The TV went on at precisely four p.m., and not a pin was allowed to drop while Grandma's play was on. I grew to hate every actor on *General Hospital,* and God save the person on the other end of the line if the phone rang during that hour.

Supper was at six p.m. sharp. The military rule book went out the window at this point as we were all encouraged to draw up our individual TV tables and watch the news while dining. Milly wasn't a bad cook, come to think of it. Just as they were at our house, meals were usually meat and potatoes of some description; goodness knows foreign foods like pasta never made it into the pantry. I was well into high school before I ever tasted spaghetti or pizza. Her meals were simple, but she was a deft hand at seasoning, and everything tasted good. Her specialty was pork chops baked in the oven with dried onion flakes and butter; the onions turned a caramel colour as they roasted, and oh, how I loved those sweet crunchy bits. As with everything else that she cooked, butter was a major component.

Perhaps my happily awakening taste buds had less to do with her skill and more to do with my mother's lack of it. Mom's culinary handicap was Dad. He was a ferociously fussy eater, and to be honest, had it not been for Milly, I suppose I would never have had the opportunity to try new and wonderful things like spinach. To Dad, a green vegetable was a pea. That's it; that's all. There were no other green vegetables. Everything else was either a tree or a bush or a leaf. Lettuce in a salad was tolerable, but tomato and cucumber were the only allowable partners in that relationship. Cucumber, of course, was a white vegetable after the skin was peeled off. Milly's salads were much more adventurous. Apples and bananas were permitted to accompany the lettuce, and everything was bathed in copious amounts of Thousand Island dressing. After supper, dishes had to be washed, dried, and put away before the first notes of the *Coronation Street* theme song started to play. Okay, so Milly got this one right. She is solely responsible for my incredible fifty-year relationship with "The Street."

The evening was spent in front of the TV, watching all *her* favourite shows, with *Perry Mason* and *The Lawrence Welk Show* at the top of the list. Her snack of choice was black olives. She ate them one after the other straight from the can. Disgusting. Just before the eleven o'clock news, we were set to task preparing more raisin toast with unsalted creamery butter and sweet, sweet, sweet tea. Once you were flying high on all that sugar, bedtime was suggested but never mandated. Some strange and scary movies happened at that time of night and seemed splendidly vivid in what I perceived to be colour even though it was a black-and-white TV.

The dungeon notwithstanding, I quite liked Milly's house. It had charm, if not warmth. It was on a pretty corner lot with wonderful trees and flower gardens. I think she must have been an adequate gardener in her younger days. Tiny pink blossoms fell from a magnificent flowering crabapple tree at the top of the short driveway. A rickety stone walkway and steps led to a tiny vestibule via the back door. No one ever used the front door, although the glass in it was spit-polished daily just in case. You entered the kitchen first. It was a small version of a country kitchen with a retro Formica table set and oilcloth flooring. There was a small dining room to the left, housing a proud Duncan Phyfe table, a tidy china cabinet (which displayed Milly's few prized possessions), and a bookshelf for her Harlequin novels. Sneak peaks into these little treasures would serve me well after puberty. From the dining room was the first in a series of French doors that ushered you to and from each tiny room in seemingly grand style only to let you down by the dowdy spaces beyond. Case in point was her uninspired living room with its beige furnishings and the few unexceptional looking tidbits on the mantel of the phoney electric fireplace. Each of the French doors was bejewelled with a crystal doorknob, and although I bristled at most of our routine cleaning tasks, I took considerable pride in polishing the shiny door accessories. They always seemed out of place somehow, like diamonds hanging from a hemp bracelet.

The steep, narrow stairs to the second floor started just beside Uncle Ian's chair. At the top was a wide, short cupboard and to the right was Uncle Ian's smoky bedroom. To the left was the other gabled room, which was dedicated to our visits. It could have been described as a guest room, but Milly did not have other overnight guests. There was a tell-tale remnant of pipe smoke in that room, which surprisingly didn't bother me as much as cigarette smoke did. Mom and Dad were both smokers, and I dreaded being in the car with either of them, especially on long road trips. The room had once been occupied by a gentleman border named Mr. Kemp. I have a vague recollection of him being included in family outings before we girls were old enough for sleepovers. I don't think he had any family of his own, and when he died, Dad had inherited his shiny red Plymouth. The closet at the top of the stairs was far too short for hanging clothes but housed Uncle Ian's shoes and a few uninteresting-looking boxes.

Uncle Ian was a fixture in Milly's house, much like any other piece of furniture. Mannequin-like, he was able to stay in one position for hours at a time without even moving his eyes. Eerie really. As children, we were told only that he had been damaged in the war. When we were older, the term "shell shocked" was used, but it held no meaning for us. He was odd, a loner who rarely conversed. He and Milly had a working relationship within the house, each with their own roles to play. He went to work every day at a factory job and contributed funds toward room and board. Milly ran the household, cleaned constantly (with or without our help), and prepared the meals. Before bed every night, she packed his lunch and set the table with everything he would need for breakfast in the morning. He came home, had a shower, ate a hot meal, and plunked himself down onto his chair by the stairs to watch TV before hibernating for the night in his smoke-filled room, all without benefit of conversation. Oh, there were the occasional few words or phrases exchanged but mostly just grunted answers to a specific question. He did little to help around the house or the property, much to my mother's chagrin; his only contribution was a financial one. Grandad Daniel had died when I was a baby and left Milly with very little income. She'd sold off small pieces of the property on either side to pay off the mortgage and managed on her small pension and board money from Uncle Ian, and from Mr. Kemp until he died.

Although you could set a clock by their day-to-day routine, Ian also had bouts of unpredictable behaviour. He would disappear without a word, often just overnight but sometimes for weeks on end. He must have had a very understanding employer. On one occasion that I can recall, my mother received a frantic phone call in the middle of the night from Spain, where Ian had managed to lose his passport and wallet. He took planned vacations and travelled alone quite extensively but very often had to be rescued from one situation or another. He was an easy mark and made some questionable choices. Once, he had been taken in by a Hare Krishna group at the airport. Milly kept her composure during his unscheduled sojourns, knowing that upon his return Ian would quietly present her with a gift, "For you, Ma," by way of an apology.

My mother behaved less like a sister to him and more like a mother or caregiver, and it was clear that Ian trusted her. There was an unspoken fondness between them. My dad tried, bless him, to make friends with his brother-in-law but was never terribly successful, hence the rec-room project and many others. Dad was no quitter. He was something of a photography buff and attempted to get Ian interested in that as a hobby but to little avail. The slim, handsome, empty shell of a man had no focus, and sadder still, no interest in life. He had never married, had no family, and had not so much as a girlfriend of whom we were aware. Although I do recall Milly making a snide comment during one of his overnight disappearances: "Uncle Ian may have found a lady friend for the evening while he was shopping downtown."

One hot, humid summer day, I saw him without a shirt for the first time and observed the horrible scars on his back and left shoulder. I had a new appreciation for the physical damage that he'd suffered during the war, but I was still ignorant about the rest. It was an awfully long time before I began to understand the dark hidden scars that ran far deeper than those we could see.

On the main floor and to the right of the kitchen were Milly's bedroom and the only bathroom, with its tiny pedestal sink, a mirror that was smaller than your face, and a little shelf dedicated to her blue and white bottle of Milk of Magnesia. Her bedroom—beige like everything else—had a long, low bureau that ran the length of the wall; her bed ran parallel a few feet away. It all looked very pristine and militaristic, but just inside the door to the right was a wonderfully ornate vanity dresser. It had a tall oval mirror suspended on either side with large wooden finials and a sumptuously tufted bench sitting at the ready. It looked so out of place. I loved to sit there and preen in front of the grand mirror on those rare occasions when Grandma was out of sight. It was fit for any princess.

One day when Grandma was busy chatting on the phone to some old crony, I sat at the vanity and dared to rummage through the drawers. The one on the top left was being stubborn, and so I gave it a little tug. It slid out completely. Thankfully, I had a good grasp on the handle, or it would have landed on the hardwood floor with a clunk. I looked toward the door, a little rattled, but thankfully had not drawn any attention. In my struggle to align the drawer back on to its groove, I noticed that it seemed too short for the space. I balanced it on my lap and bent to peer into the dark cavity, immediately noticing a little brass nob. I reached in, hooked it between my fingers, and gently pulled out the little wooden box that it adorned. The concealed box, which was about ten inches wide and six inches deep, had a groove on the bottom that slid snugly along the drawer runner. Oh, what a find! It did not appear to have a locking mechanism, but I couldn't lift the lid. I gave it a little jiggle to size up the contents but there was no sound. I turned it over, and on the bottom, burned into the wood was an odd-looking symbol. I had been in the room longer than intended but was too curious to stop now, and so I tried once again to lift the lid. With a little pop, the top shifted, and I opened it ever so slightly only to confirm what I already knew: It was empty. Disappointed, I slammed shut the lid.

"Find anything interesting?" asked a voice from the doorway.

My heart skipped a beat, and I scrambled to return the box to its hiding place only to have it lifted from my hands. "I'm sorry, Grandma. I was snooping."

With a cool tone, she responded, "So I see."

"I thought there would be treasure, but there's nothing in it." I pouted.

Leaning in, she held the box close to my ear and gave it a little shake; it rattled and clattered as though filled to the brim with jewels and coins. I could feel my eyes widen, and she grinned down at me as she laid it back into my hands.

I gave it another jiggle, no sound; I peeked inside, and it was still empty. "How did you do that? Is it magic?"

"I suppose it's a sort of magic," she said in a low voice, with just a hint more accent than usual. "This box is filled with whispers. They are the story of my life, my greatest treasures. In the old country, we called the whispers, '*Sonnish*.'"

Excited, I asked, "Why can't I see them?"

She tucked the box back into its dark home and simply said, "They aren't your treasures, and my story isn't finished."

She didn't scold me for snooping, but as she reached the doorway, she turned and said, "Perhaps, if you learn to listen very closely, you will hear the '*Sonnish,*' and one day, these treasures may belong to you."

"Grandma, what is the symbol on the bottom of the box?"

"Oh, that's the three-legged man. He guards the whispers and all those who speak them."

"Does he have a name?"

"Triskelion," she replied before giving me one last look that spoke volumes. The conversation was over, the room was to be vacated, and I was to find something quiet to do.

It was a riddle that kept my attention for a brief time but was never discussed again. Stealthily, I took many opportunities to re-examine the puzzling little box, but it always remained empty, and eventually, I became bored with its lacklustre magic. Still, I always referred to it in my mind as the skeleton box and took considerable pride in keeping knowledge of it entirely to myself. "Triskelion" was far too complicated to remember, and "skeleton" seemed much more synonymous with hidden treasure.

Sometime later, Grandma's bedroom grew to be much less inviting. It was in the early seventies (I think) when both Mom and Milly entered wig mania. It was the new fashion. Mom became a blonde, because they have more fun, and Milly happily cancelled her regular permanent-wave appointments. The top of Milly's long dresser looked like a freak show from *Dawn of the Dead*, with a seemingly endless row of white Styrofoam heads in various stages of undress. Had they been made of wax, Madame Tussaud would have felt right at home. The first wig in the row was newly washed, another combed out and ready for curlers, and the next looked like a cat that had stepped too close to an electric fence, teased and sprayed within an inch of its life.

The last was coiffed and ready for its premiere tomorrow. There was always one bald head, serene and alarming (today's wig had to have somewhere to spend the night). There were no two wigs exactly alike, but Scotland Yard would have been hard pressed to pick one out of a lineup.

Awake and feeling refreshed, I reached beneath the pillow until my fingers found the amulet. With vigour, I clasped it close to my chest and embraced its energy. I could feel Milly near me, smell her perfume, and taste those marvellous pork chops. Every vivid moment of my dream remained clear in my mind, and I felt as though I could reach out and touch her. I climbed out of bed and sat down at the computer desk, not bothering to tidy up or take the much-needed detour to the bathroom. Minutes later, after clicking on this and that and waiting for the virus scan to allow me into my own files, I found the photo gallery that I had meticulously scanned onto the laptop several months ago. Tired of lugging shelves full of heavy photo albums with me when I moved from place to place, I'd made a project of scanning each and every snapshot and creating digital files both for me and my children. It was a huge undertaking made greater still when I'd inherited all my mother's albums, but it had paid off in the end, quite literally, as moving companies charge by weight!

With my bladder about to burst, I had almost given up, and then there, in all her glory, was Millicent Cynthia Aspinall Pearse. She lit up the screen like some grand and ghostly silent-film star, statuesque and stately with an air of upper-class snobbery. She was taller than a Victorian era woman had a right to be, with big hands and features. The scars on her cheeks, never explained or discussed, were barely visible beneath the layers of pancake makeup that she always wore in the company of others. She could not be described as pretty or beautiful with her aristocratic British nose and her too-small mouth, but she had dark flashing eyes and was generally pleasant to look at. There was a presence about her.

I rolled the chair away from the desk but left her photo glowing on the screen; her eyes followed me around as I busied myself with preparations for the day. I really didn't mind her scrutiny. I recalled our childish plots to do her in and chuckled to myself. Understanding that she may well be reading my thoughts, I turned to address the image on the screen with a brazen "Sorry 'bout that." She gazed back at me through young eyes, both foreign and familiar. I had no recollection of seeing this or any photo of her as a young woman. She had always been the antique that appeared in family portraits—miserable and stoic like a character holding a pitchfork on a box of Corn Flakes. This youthful creature, in a uniform of some kind, was slim and fit and wore her intelligence proudly. There was a soft gentleness in her expression. Milly was in there, but she was well disguised.

I scrolled through to find a snapshot of Grandma as I remembered her and found a much more familiar image of her in a Legion uniform at about age seventy. For us, Milly was more like a great-grandmother. She was older than a grandma should be (or so we thought). Mom, we were told, had been a "change-of-life baby," which had meant absolutely nothing at the time. Extremely proud of her longevity, Milly volunteered information about her age to anyone within earshot and long before a listener had a chance to ask. She was a plus-sized woman, and I was certain that she was born in her Eaton's size-twenty-two all-in-one girdle. Oh, those dreaded trips to Yorkdale to buy a new one!

"Now, there's a memory I could have done without, thank you very much," I muttered while wondering if speaking to the computer screen was becoming a habit. Outside of the house or in the company of visitors, her neck was traditionally adorned by a three-strand pearl choker with a faux-ruby clasp, and indoors, she was buttoned up to the chin in a zippered housecoat. Spit-polished sensible shoes, mid-calf-length dresses, and hats were the norm; although, as I recall, she did go through a polyester pant-suit phase. While girdle shopping was beyond horrific, trips on the bus and lunch at the mall were a diversion and certainly preferable to our frequent visits to her corn doctor. Milly always travelled by bus or streetcar. I don't ever remember her driving a car and could not imagine her behind a steering wheel.

Her ear was tuned to all things British. Whether in the mall, on the bus, or awaiting her turn at the doctor's office, she would immediately engage in conversation with anyone who had a smattering of a British accent. She would ask, "Where in the old country are you from?" I'm sure it never occurred to her that the "old country" could mean anything other than Britain. She was devoted to the royal family and took trips back to her birthplace whenever possible. She was not what you could call a kid person, but she liked babies and took pleasure in entertaining infants on the bus by clicking all five digits on one hand in succession. It sounded like a rapid-fire machine gun to me, and grated on my nerves worse than squeaky Styrofoam, but always seemed to astound and quiet a fussy baby.

There were those oh-so-rare occasions when she would consent to travel by taxi, usually due to poor weather or when the corn doctor had been overly ambitious with her feet. This was a huge extravagance for her. She would begrudgingly pry open the metal clip of her coin purse to find the exact change, never considering the option of a tip for the driver. We thought she was cheap. It was embarrassing. Mom or Dad would have given the nice man a gratuity, of that we were certain.

My sister Julie and I were baby boomers, brought up in a middle-class, relatively affluent household, where doing without was something of a foreign concept. We were not what you would call spoiled. We had everything we needed, not wanted. There were no brand-name labels, our clothing was bought on sale, and winter coats were put on lay-away at the discount store. A product of their time, Mom and Dad were careful with their money, but not as frugal as Milly. Dad was a chemical engineer, making a good wage at Canadian General Electric, and Mom worked so that they could take extravagant holidays together—holidays that did not include us, as they were meant only for the perpetual honeymooners. While Mom and Dad were away on "honeymoon," we were left at home under the gentle care of Mrs. Shaw, my best friend's nana. Now there was a lady who looked and acted like a grandmother should, like the ones we'd come to know on television. She was a good egg, and I did not mind at all being left with her. She was a big lady with a sizeable appetite who allowed me free reign in the kitchen and enjoyed any concoction I produced. She was easy-going and taught me how to play canasta; games often went on into the wee hours. Bedtimes, even on school nights, were loosely managed. This arrangement was far preferable to the torturous alternative of a two- or three-week stay with Milly. At least we had our friends, our playthings, and of course, no interruption of school. More's the pity.

Of course, I know now what I clearly didn't know then: Having lived through the great depression and two world wars, Milly knew all about doing without and was, to say the least, thrifty. Saving and storing for another day was in her nature. There were exceptions, of course. It was little wonder I suppose that when sugar was finally in abundance, she treated herself to several heaping spoons full of the sweet stuff in every cup of tea and at every opportunity. This kind of extravagance rarely found its way to her grandchildren, however, and as kids, we neither understood nor appreciated why she was so tight with her wallet. It was after a morning of bus travel, and a grotesque shopping excursion to Eaton's for a new size-twenty-two all-in-one girdle, that we asked "politely" for pocket money to buy a treat. She'd promptly reminded us about the quarter she had bestowed earlier in the week and sniped something about candy and sticky fingers.

Then she had grumbled, "I'll think about it tomorrow after we're finished at the corn doctor's office." Oh God, I still have an aversion to feet. And that was it: the tipping point. I whined and Julie fussed until the old battle-axe fulfilled her promise to banish us once again to the dungeon. Once there, our mission was clear. We firmly agreed that our subterranean summit meeting must not end until we had a decisive plan for murdering Grandma.

We'd been quibbling over the "You do it" ... "No, you do it" part when the door had opened, and the enticing aroma of those marvellous pork chops had drifted down the stairs.

"Come on, you two. Supper is ready." And she was saved.

I caught myself in a wide grin and flipped back to the earlier photo of the young woman I had never known. I admired the spirited face with its strong, determined jaw and wondered at the circumstances of life that must have occurred to snuff out such a wide-eyed and hopeful countenance. "I wish you were here to ask."

She stared back at me.

Chapter Three

With the willow research set aside, and the photo gallery in sleep mode, I turned my attention to the garage. With some assistance from the young fellow next door, I managed to rearrange the boxes and remove the one labelled "MILLY'S STUFF." The movers had been careless with all my belongings, and this carton looked to be no exception, now a bit battered and worse for wear. I felt even more obliged to handle it with gentle reverence.

Waiting until I had the house to myself, I sat on the laundry-room floor with a pillow wedged under my bum for comfort's sake. With the hefty box looming in front of me and knife in hand, I hesitated for just a moment in deference to what may or may not lay within. I felt a sneaky chill on my skin and checked behind me to be sure that the connecting door to the house was closed. I rested my hand for a moment on the amulet hanging around my neck. The hairs on my arms stood at attention, and I addressed them with a deliberate, defensive shiver.

"Shake it off. You're getting carried away." However bizarre it seemed, logic or no, what I knew for certain was that Milly had found a way to be heard. She had never been the type to go unnoticed or be ignored, and it was my experience that, when she commanded, you did as you were told. It was clear that she was determined to take me on a journey, and I felt completely safe going along for the ride.

I carefully sliced through the packing tape and folded back the first flap. As I lifted the thin protective sheet of Styrofoam, an overwhelming wave of sadness came over me. I was not expecting fanfare or the Holy Grail, but the underwhelming sight of mounds of wadded-up scraps of newspaper unsettled me just a little. Here was Milly's life. Unceremoniously wrapped in old newsprint and stuffed in a box. I hesitated before unravelling the first of her treasures, waiting for an invitation that never came.

"This is ridiculous. These things belong to me now," I declared to an empty room. I wasn't sure if I was trying to convince myself or hoping to summon a response, but I startled myself into submission and charged ahead. Picking up one crumpled mound of paper, I made a start. The first was a figurine that I remembered having held a place of honour on Milly's mantel, and then there were a few mismatched pieces from a set of china that I'd loved as a child. I remembered it making such a cheerful-looking table with its clean white background and bright-yellow daffodils. The teapot was missing, but the cream and sugar vessels were intact, and I gingerly set them aside, determined to make use of them. There was a tiny pair of crystal salt cellars and a ceramic Toby mug bearing the face of a bulbous-nosed drunkard wearing a peaked cap.

Next, I unwrapped the pale-yellow canister that had adorned Milly's small china cabinet. It was painted with flowers and pheasants and had a bamboo handle. I tried to imagine what purpose it must have served; it was too small to have been a container for sugar or flour. Next was a green Royal Winton fruit bowl with a small chip on the base and an interesting little box containing six vintage coffee-bean spoons, so named for the little orange-glass bean-shaped ends on each silver spoon. I had learned about those one evening while binge-watching *Antiques Roadshow*. Wrapped separately were two ornately engraved fish knives with bone handles, similar to those I had seen at an antique market. A tattered-looking makeup bag was home to a sparkly collection of costume jewellery that I assumed she had used on stage at her Legion shows. Among the items were a pretty two-tone-blue rhinestone brooch and an ornate-looking necklace with green and blue rhinestones. The latter, I thought, would have been quite striking in its day worn as a collar on a crisp white blouse. Of course, everything old is new again and antique pieces like this were back in fashion.

Beneath some of the other more unremarkable items was a little plastic packet that contained a few more expensive pieces. Among them a topaz ring that had often-adorned Milly's gargantuan hand. I tried it on, but it was far too big for my size-five finger; I made a mental note to have it fitted for my daughter as it was her birthstone. I smiled at the beautiful silver-and-marcasite bird-in-flight pin that I determined would look lovely on my black dress. I had a clear recollection of Uncle Ian giving the pin to Milly following one of his disappearances. "For you, Ma." (And all was forgiven).

Tucked neatly into the side of the box was a slender leather case, and as I pulled it out, I noticed that this was just the first of three identical cases stacked one on top of the other. The tiny brass clasp on the first case opened with a snap and revealed a royal-blue interior with a neat row of military medals all clasped to their velvety bed. There was a faded label pinned to the underside of the lid, which simply read "Daniel." The second identical case was similarly labelled "Ian," and the third bore Milly's name. As I opened hers, a single tiny item that had become dislodged in the case fell onto my lap; it was her Legion pin. I rolled it over in my hand and pictured her marching smartly up to the cenotaph on Remembrance Day in her Legion uniform. She could recite the "Commitment to Remember" without script or prompting even into her very old age:

> *They shall grow not old,*
> *As we that are left grow old;*
> *Age shall not weary them,*
> *Not the years condemn.*
> *At the going down of the sun*
> *And in the morning*
> *We will remember them.*

Milly's involvement in the Great War was part of the fabric of our family history, but as with most veterans, she said little about her service or about the war for that matter. I knew her only as a devout and passionate Legion member who said nothing to dissuade my decision at age sixteen to enlist in the Canadian Armed Forces. Once again, of course, war is back in the news, and as the images of broken soldiers returning from overseas flash across the TV screen every evening, I am reminded of my good fortune to have served only as a peacekeeper. The array of medals in front of me signified horrors that I could only imagine. While I felt a deep sense of pride, I was also ashamed of my apathy on the subject. Why had I not asked more questions? For too long, I had been content with what little information had been passed down, and now I was anxious to begin researching what I could of our family's military history.

To the left of me was a pile of crumpled newsprint, and all around were Milly's treasures. Most were trinkets that offered snippets of memory from my childhood, but I had yet to reach the bottom of the crate. Beneath layers of paper were items that I had never seen before. The first was a faded and worn leather-and-canvas box that appeared to be military issue. It housed a delicate-looking antique camera made of wood and brass, with glass plates nestled into their own canvas compartment. It was exquisite—the kind of heirloom that should be displayed proudly. Where had this beauty been hiding? I could not recall ever having seen it at Milly's house. I nestled the camera back into the felt-lined bed and put it aside for further inspection. I felt quite sure that there would be identifying marks or numbers that might explain its origin. Beside it was a heavy brass container with a lid, which was oxidized a dark green on the inside and decorated with engravings all around the exterior. "1915" was chiselled on the bottom; I was certain that I was holding in my hand an artillery shell from the First World War. I was transported, for just a moment, to the gloom of the battlefield and the cries of the wounded. I tried to imagine what circumstance would induce someone to commemorate the moment with a trinket such as this.

At the bottom of the crate, no doubt put there as cushioning for all the rest, was a faded and worn carpet bag that had obviously been well used over a lengthy period of time. The handles were threadbare, and as I peered inside, I half expected to see a Mary Poppins lamp rise upward. Instead, I found a single Simpson manila envelope, which I chose to put aside for later. There was a small rolled-up bundle of khaki-coloured canvas held together with ties that were attached at each end of the roll. Inside were tiny little pockets and pouches that housed all that a soldier might need to sew or repair his uniform: a button and some thread, an extra swatch of khaki fabric, and a pair of sewing needles. It had been one hundred years since the war and still this little bundle remained intact. I was besotted.

My attention then shifted to the two remaining pieces hibernating serenely in the bottom of the tattered bag. I was struggling against an emotional response; my body grew tense and my breaths shallow. I swallowed hard over the growing knot in my throat as I traced my fingers around the "skeleton box"—the vessel with the groove along the bottom that slid so neatly into its hiding place behind the drawer in her vanity dresser. The little box filled with secret whispers—the *"Sonnish."* Childlike, with eyes tightly closed, I lifted the box to my ear and gave it a gentle shake. There was no sound at all, and as I tentatively lifted the lid, every fibre of my being was just as certain that the box would be empty. Her story might be finished, but these were not yet my treasures. I remembered the day she had stood in the doorway of her bedroom and said, *"You must learn to listen."*

Tears flowed freely as I reached into the carpet bag once again and gingerly grasped the three-strand pearl choker with the faux-ruby clasp that Milly had worn nearly every day that I knew her. I felt my body slump back against the washer/dryer as I held the choker in one hand and balanced the little box on my lap. I would never be able to explain the wave of emotion that came over me; I could not understand it myself. Milly (Grandma) had never been one of my favourite people. She had not been endearing or affectionate; she was cantankerous and obstinate. The "old battle-axe." I suppose I'd always known she'd had some impact on my life, but I'd never considered her a mentor or even someone to admire. She had been here and then she was gone. I wished that I could say that I had missed her, but in truth, I hadn't.

Why this? Why now? For whatever reason, she was back, and I felt her hug me for the first time.

And so began the journey of piecing together the fragments of Milly's life into a narrative that I hoped would give us both peace. Christmas deliberations had forced me to set the undertaking aside for a time, and I was grateful that Milly's whispers took a deep breath and waited silently. With the clutter of the holidays stored away for another year, the time was ripe to begin my research. What began as a project quickly turned into an obsession with trips to the library, conversations with antique dealers, and hours spent in front of a computer screen. I began by studying the meticulously organized medals, marvelling at the weight and feel of each one, and learned that, while some were medals, others were commemorations. Each one signified a place or an event and summed up a moment in history. I met with one of the curators at the National War Museum, who was extremely helpful in identifying the World War I field camera.

"The markings identify an 1891 Bausch and Lomb lens," he said enthusiastically, "and it's particularly important to know that this is the original case." He was happy to share his vast knowledge of the war but a little long winded about the ordeal photographers faced with censorship. "The brass were concerned that battle images would undo propaganda and incite outrage at home," he said, nodding continuously. "Only official military photographers were authorized, but some soldiers smuggled in small cameras of their own. It was actually a crime to have one." His head nodded its own punctuation as though each tidbit of information should be accompanied by an exclamation mark. He continued. "However, there were commanding officers who looked the other way because they wanted their regiments to be memorialized on film."

He went on to say that a camera such as mine was indeed official, but because they were cumbersome and photos were limited to the number of glass plates one could carry, most shots had been staged for propaganda purposes.

He asked if I had any photographs that may have been taken with this camera, and more specifically during a conflict. I confessed that I had yet to review all the items left in my care and promised to share with him any photos that might be of interest.

He was pleased to see the brass canister that I had mentioned in my preliminary email and confirmed that it had indeed been made from an armoury shell in the Great War. "Trench art," he proclaimed. "Soldiers found many ways to occupy their time between conflicts, and there were huge quantities of shell cases available for the taking." I was insulted when he described my treasure as a poor example. "This is very crudely done by comparison to the many elaborate examples we've seen," said the prig.

I could feel the hairs on my arms wrestle with the impulse to smack him and expected Milly had something to do with that. He guided the way to a display case that housed amazing examples of trench art carved with extraordinarily intricate designs. Some were fashioned into vases or candlesticks and others into lamp bases. Having thanked him for his time, I returned with my treasures to the car, determined to return to the museum after I had taken the time to assess all the information in my possession. Once all my ducks were in line, I was certain that the massive amount of information the museum had to offer would come into better focus for my purpose.

I made copious notes about my conversation with the curator and then turned my attention to the manila envelope lying unopened on the desk. I had been tempted to tear it open many times in the weeks since I had recovered it from the crate. But each time, I'd resisted. I'm not sure why, except that it felt like an invasion of privacy. Still, it was time. I unravelled the string that curled around the clasps and tipped everything out onto the desk. Unleashed, the confused jumble of documents and photos stared back at me with an expression of hopefulness. I took time to peruse each one, cataloguing the information into my ever-growing notebook and feeling incredibly grateful for the organizational skills that usually drove my family crazy. Carefully, I sorted documents into two piles: Milly's British birth and Canadian citizenship certificates in one and those that referred to Grandad Daniel and Uncle Ian in the other.

Some of the work was tedious, but then there were the little treasures that broke the monotony. I held in one hand the photograph of a young handsome WWI soldier, and in the other, a snapshot of the same face (though much older and weary) in yet another uniform. Bringing the two images closer together, I was saddened at the thought that this man had spent most of his life at war. Grandad had died when I was only a baby, but I recognized his face from photos I had seen in Mom's wedding album. Next was a photo of a remarkably handsome Uncle Ian in uniform before the war had damaged him. He looked so much like his father. There was tenderness and a sparkle in his eyes that I had not seen before. What a waste. So many of the documents were war related: military discharge papers, certificates of appreciation for war service, a Great War Veterans Association membership card, and a postcard with a caption that read, "H.M. Hospital Ship *Araguaya*." Daniel's first war discharge was printed on faded and worn canvas fabric, its edges slightly frayed. I marvelled that it had survived for one hundred years and took a moment to insert it into a protective plastic sleeve, hoping to preserve it for my great grandchildren in the next century. I flipped through faded family photos that I had not seen before and set aside some interesting-looking paper money that appeared to be German, though I wasn't sure.

I looked at the clock. It had been hours since I'd sat down at the desk. Finally, though, I'd reached the end of the paper trail. There were a few pieces of old sheet music bound together with an elastic band, under which was tucked a postcard. The black and white image showed a group of men and women posed in costume. Looking more closely, I could see that the group was made up entirely of men, some of whom were elaborately made up and costumed to look like women. The caption simply read, "Dumbells." The photograph looked professionally done. This was no motley bunch of war buddies. There was more to learn about this skillfully disguised group. I clipped the postcard to the cork bulletin board in front of me for inspiration. I closed my weary eyes for just a moment, and the image of Milly's basement came to me as clearly as though I were standing there. Perhaps it was simply the smell of the musty paper, but in my mind's eye, I could see her big trunk full of costumes and the stack of sheet music that lay beneath them. A hearty sneeze brought me back into focus, and I looked around at my tidy mess, not sure how to proceed. I need not have worried. Milly led the way.

She visited often in my dreams during the weeks that followed, and each morning, I woke refreshed and content that I was able to remember each vivid detail of our encounter. It was a very new experience as my dreams usually faded away before my eyelids fluttered back to consciousness. Like a home movie long forgotten on a dusty shelf, each dream was a walk through my own memories, and although I wasn't learning anything new about her, we were becoming reacquainted. Little moments, dismissed as a child and forgotten, took on a different, more mature perspective. I began to realize that she had indeed made a significant impact on my life.

Singing was my first love, and although I had no illusions or any great ambition, I did crave acknowledgement that I had some ability. I did not get that at home, but Milly, in her cool and dispassionate way, found an avenue. She was enraptured by *The Sound of Music* when it came into theatres and made me her companion on each of the seven times she went to see it. There was something about the film that brought emotion from her as nothing I had ever seen before. I loved it too, but not in the same way. Careful not to invade her private thoughts, I watched out of the corner of my eye as tears spilled off her chin each time the movie ended, and I marvelled that she could quell all evidence of it by the time the house lights went up.

She found ways to incorporate the songs and imitate the costumes in the biannual Legion productions, which by that time were her pride and joy. She was the entertainment chairman at the Thistletown Branch and took the job very seriously. Now and again, she took me along. I was told to sit quietly in the back while she orchestrated the rehearsals, but on occasion, would let me sit with the pianist at the end of the session, while she was busy wrapping things up. She would holler back, "Doris, give 'Edelweiss' another try. Mary will sing along with you." At the time, I thought she was trying to keep me out of her hair, but instead, I think she was offering me an opportunity. Did she have an influence on my life? Perhaps more than

I had given her credit for. While singing had not offered me a career, it has played a huge role in my life and my very salvation at times.

My research continued during the long and arduous winter; I was grateful for a project to occupy my mind in the comfort of a cozy room. As the months progressed, however, the organized chaos of books and memorabilia took on a life of their own. Every time I learned something new, ten more questions arose, and all I knew for certain about Milly was that I knew nothing at all. The bulletin board was cluttered with Post-It notes and photos, and on the table was a long sprawling sketch of a complicated-looking family tree. The greatest obstacle in researching her life was simply that there was no one left to ask. I had waited too long, and the importance of the photos on my storyboard were abundantly clear. They were all that I had left. She loomed large, like a giant jigsaw puzzle with hundreds of missing pieces. I felt that I had enough military clues to warrant another visit to the war museum, and so, on my return visit, I spent hours roaming through the galleries and passages. There was a special exhibit called "Women at War," which illuminated the momentous role women had played both in the military and on the home front during each world conflict. Although this exhibit was appropriately slanted to the Canadian perspective, I could imagine that much of it related to Milly's life experience as a British subject.

Each gallery depicted facets of a particular war, from weaponry to the human toll, and were both impressive and horrifying. With the information gleaned from the medals in my possession, I was drawn to the maps, photos, and even models of those specific conflicts in which my ancestors fought. I walked through the amazing replica of a trench that was akin to one of the thousands of trenches occupied by soldiers during the Great War. As detailed as they had tried to be, it was obviously impossible to reproduce the horrors those men endured. I looked through the telescopic lens, much like you would find on a submarine, which rose above ground level so that trench soldiers could watch for snipers. There were many props set out to add realism to the display, but by far the most poignant, sitting on a make-shift shelf in the dirt wall, was a lone helmet pierced by a bullet. A strategically placed lantern shone a gloomy green light on the bullet hole and stood as a solitary symbol of all those who had lost their lives in this all-too-opportune grave.

It gave me a cold shiver, and I felt my flight response kick in as the walls of the make-believe trench began to close in on me. I was grateful that a group of rambunctious schoolchildren forced my speedy exit. Deciding that enough was enough for one day, I was making my way through the labyrinth toward the main lobby when I stumbled upon an exhibit describing the many concert troupes that had sprung up to entertain the soldiers at the western front. Chief among those described was a highly esteemed Canadian troupe called "The Dumbells." The massive poster before me was almost identical to the postcard still clipped to the bulletin board at home. I read about their antics and their bravery and wondered if Milly or Daniel had actually seen them perform. Surely the postcard meant something. It was important enough that she had kept it safely tucked away all this time.

With a few more tidbits to pin to my ever-growing storyboard, I decided once again to tackle my family tree. I purchased a membership on one of the ancestry-search sites and spent hours poring over names and dates, adding and subtracting bits and pieces into the ever-expanding tangled mess that I assumed should have resembled a tree. Long ago, I remembered Milly saying, *"You children have no idea who your family members really are. Everybody, including the damn next-door neighbours, are 'Aunty this' and 'Uncle that.'"* She wasn't wrong. We'd been brought up to give honorary kinship to all the adults who came into our lives. I suppose it was meant to be inclusive and respectful without the formality of mister and missus. Our parents were simply trying to expand our very small family circle, contrived as that might have been. Most of our family lived in England, and so our holiday table, unlike most of my friends, had only six chairs around it—we four plus Uncle Ian and Grandma Milly.

I didn't know the names of my British relatives except for Grandad Patrick, Gramma Annie, and Dad's two brothers, Gordon and Paul. As I wound my way through the ancestry site, my paternal lineage seemed straightforward. I was able to go back six generations on Dad's side of the family. The road to and from Milly, however, led to more questions than answers. She was my mother's mother. *Should be a doddle,* I thought. The information on her birth certificate gave me a starting point. I discovered that she was the youngest of seven children born to William and Mary Aspinall. I was surprised. I would have imagined her to be the bossy older sibling. Her only sister was Alice, who was twenty years older than Milly, and between them were the five brothers. In a 1901 census, I found it curious that Milly, at age six, was living with Alice, and I wondered if her parents had died, but I found her in a later census living with her mother and father once again.

More curious still was the fact that Alice's married name was Simpson, and although I had to check my facts, I was fairly sure that Annie, my paternal grandmother, was a Simpson *before* she married Grandad. *Quite a coincidence,* I thought. My head was starting to ache behind my tired eyes, and the whole endeavour was becoming a bit tedious. I removed my glasses and rubbed my temples for just a minute without much relief. I was about to pack it in when a notation (a little leaf) popped up over Milly's name. It led to her maternal line and seemed to have a clear path going back five generations.

I stretched out my legs and ventured to the kitchen to brew a pot of tea. Two Tylenol later, I was back at the desk, learning all that I could about the women in my family who hailed from the Isle of Man. Geography had never been my best subject in school, and so I dusted off Dad's big, fabulous atlas and visited with my new best friend: Mr. Google.

I found the Isle of Man (just a tiny fleck on the map) floating in the Irish Sea near England and Ireland but closest to Scotland. The isle's history, deeply Celtic at the core, had riotous roots that you could almost imagine reaching serpent-like in all directions beneath the sea, connecting her to the land masses in the distance. Still, over the centuries, her persona remained unique. I felt her roots reaching out to me, and I felt comforted by her. Shivers followed a path up and down my arms.

As I read further, I felt at home. Learning about my heritage was somehow validating. It seemed little wonder that I had always been drawn to the sea. I'd lived most of my adult life on the east coast of Canada and never felt quite as rooted as I did there. As military families do, we moved often and made our house a home wherever we went, but I always felt my heart skip a beat when I knew we were to venture east again. My most favourite place, Prince Edward Island—the gentle island as she is called—is where I'm certain my soul will journey to in the end. She too has deep Celtic roots, especially in the music heard at kitchen parties *(ceilidhs)* all around the Island. I could almost smell the sea air and feel the salt on my skin as I read further.

I learned that the ancient people of the Isle of Man developed their own language, a version of Gaelic that was unique to them. Both the people and the language are called "Manx." I scrolled through some text and came upon an image that I recognized immediately as the symbol on the bottom of my skeleton box. The "triskelion," it said, is an ancient symbol consisting of three legs that radiate from the centre and are reputed to mean "whichever way you throw, it will stand." In the Manx language, it's called *"Ny Tree Cassyn."* The symbol is found on the Isle of Man flag.

There had been much written about the Viking history of the island and the centuries of fighting over its ownership, but it was the description of the people that resonated with me. *"A profound belief in the power of magic was one of the characteristics of Goidelic peoples,"* it said. I tried to remember the word that Milly had used all those years ago to explain the whispers in the skeleton box. Whenever she'd spoken of the old country, I'd assumed she was referring to England, but now I wondered if she was also referring to the island of her ancestors.

What was the word? I was annoyed with myself for having forgotten. Certain that it would prove to be a word in the Manx language, I began to type: *"What is the Manx word for whisper?"* And there it was. *"Sonnish."* The muscles across my chest unravelled. I had not realized how tense I was. I relaxed my shoulders, breathed deeply through my nose, and opened my mind to the possibilities. Taking a step further, I wondered if I might have misinterpreted the word that had come in the whispers of the willow that day in the park so many months ago. I typed in *"She"* and the Manx dictionary responded with *"Shee,"* meaning spirit and peace.

Perhaps, tonight, Milly would come to me in dreaming. She did.

"Shuyr my chree," she said. "Sister of my heart."

Chapter Four

The End of May

The fragrant air is full of down,
Of floating, fleecy things
From some forgotten fairy town
Where all the folk wear wings.

KATHERINE LEE BATES

I embraced the first days of spring, grateful for nature's gentle reminder of rebirth. It never ceased to amaze me that what had been buried six feet beneath snow and ice could survive, waiting patiently, and then peek through the ground in search of the sun. A resurrection. It occurred to me that Milly was attempting to do just that. In body and mind, I felt myself emerge from hibernation, leaving in my wake a confusion of scraps and fragments of a life researched but not fully understood. I had run the gamut in my homework with emphasis on further study about my Manx heritage and about the generations of women who came before me. I could feel the strong feminine energy reaching out to me with Milly leading the charge. Oh, how I wished I could talk to her. Really talk. Sit with her in that dowdy front room, sipping a cup of diabetes-inducing sweet, sweet tea, and hear all about her life. How else was I to complete the pages of her story? That was the question I had asked in dreaming the night before. She had responded, *"Spring, when all life is stirring in the depths and the moon is full, that is when the spirit and the willow will be at its most powerful."* If there were insights to be gained, I would find them there. With a more open mind and greater focus, I waited for the full moon and ventured back to the tree, confident that I would hear the *"Sonnish."*

The park was deserted but for a few energetic souls on the jogging trail.

The ground was still a little squishy underfoot, but I made my way toward the far corner, still too far in the distance to see from this vantage point. I carried with me a basket containing a blanket, a flashlight, and the skeleton box, which remained silent and empty. It had never been far from my thoughts or my line of sight, perched on the top shelf in my room. Like King Tut's tomb, I coveted an invitation to the secrets within but respected its divine right to privacy and reverence. I hoped by now I had earned some rite of passage, and so, I carried it with me in the hopes that Milly would grant me access. The amulet, cool against my skin, bounced gently in time to my footsteps, and Milly's pearl choker weighed heavily in the pocket of my jacket.

The rain from the night before had left the air fresh and fragrant; I inhaled the colour green. Resplendent in its rebirth, the park was lush, and I could feel the loving heart of the earth beating beneath my feet. The chatter of birds filled the air with tales of their journey home, and a sweet-smelling gentle breeze propelled me forward, although I felt no desire to hurry. The grasses along the path were in their infancy, struggling upward to exceed last year's height, and their fern cousins were still a mass of curled and tangled serpents. I had never noticed before just how many shades of green there are. I too had experienced an awaking it seemed, a greater appreciation for my surroundings, and a kinship to the energy that connects all things. It had always been there; I simply had not listened. My mind wandered blissfully, and I watched the opalescent blue of the forget-me-nots dancing freely against their verdant cousins. I stopped a moment to pluck one dainty little bloom from its cozy bed. "Forget me not." The significance was not lost on me.

As I took my next step toward the willow, now within view, I felt my knees buckle just a little, and the breath catch in my throat. My body needed a deep inhale, and I panicked for just a moment. There was a pleasant sensation of warmth that started at my toes and lingered on my fingertips as though I had slipped slowly into a steamy bath. My lungs filled with replenishing air. When I found my centre again, the surroundings changed, like an entirely new canvas. I hesitated to move another step, afraid to break the spell but excited to take it all in. The vibrant splendour of the scene was exhilarating; the subtle hues of green were suddenly alive with a festive spectrum of vivid colour. The grass on both sides of my path was a blaze of bright emerald-green, with edges illuminated in radiant yellow, and dotted all around were amethyst-violet sequins. Beyond that, and for as far as I could see, the ground was aglow in deep amber. The fragrance of apple blossoms drifted in the air, and tiny white petals tinged with pink danced and floated to the ground, laying a carpet before me.

There was a pearly mist hovering just below a ghostly sky, sparkling opalescent mauve against the deep purple of the trees. Magic was all around me. Nature was silent. I could see birds flitting about, soundlessly nattering to each other. A cornflower-blue butterfly fluttered to a stop on the network of shimmering grasses to my right. She lingered there, taking the time to visit with the flower fairies peeking out modestly beneath the ferns. She had been invited of course by the delicate fragrance of the lily of the valley and the gentle jingle of her tiny bells. The willow waited in the distance. It boasted no colour. Luminous and glistening, it twinkled as though it were home to a thousand fairy lights. I was not concerned about curious onlookers, and I was not compelled to look behind me. This effervescent wonderland was inviting me. Only me. Her branches beckoned, and I gratefully accepted the invitation, each step cushioned in anticipation.

We met as old friends do, her gentle strands of foliage parting as though I had paid admission. The kiss of the warm wind kept me comfortable despite the chill of the hard damp ground, and I felt the pulse from her mighty roots. I watched her tendrils frolic playfully with the carpet of forget-me-nots beneath and hoped she would find no reason to weep today. *"If you listen carefully, the silence has a soul,"* Milly had promised. I cradled the skeleton box in my lap, gently wrapped my fingers around the amulet, and closed my eyes. Within moments, I felt her hand slip into mine. It was a young hand, not at all the withered frail bones with the prominent veins that I remembered, but still, I knew it was Milly. Before she was Grandma, she was just Milly. Her story unfolded.

The Gift

See! I give myself to you, Beloved!
My words are little jars for you to take and put upon a shelf.
Their shapes are quaint and beautiful,
And they have many pleasant colours and lusters to recommend them.
Also the scent from them fills the room with sweetness of flowers and
crushed grasses.
When I shall have given you the last one,
You will have the whole of me,
But I shall be dead.

AMY LOWELL

Chapter Five

Millicent Cynthia Aspinall was a big name to fill for a curly headed blonde tyke from Lancashire. From the start, I was a rambunctious youngster, never still. I had only my brothers with whom to play, and so, with skinned knees and frenzied hair, I was not a stereotypical girl child of the late 1800s. I loved to run and play, brandish the wooden sword of the swashbuckler, wrestle, and fish, and I was fortunate to have been born to a forward-thinking mother who didn't insist that I follow convention. I learned to sew and crochet but always with one eye to the outdoors and the adventures I might be missing. Father, who was slightly more traditional, bowed to his wife's proven methods in child rearing and her subtle ministrations of feminism. He was content that I was a keen student who excelled in mathematics and science, and that I was, for the most part, pleasant company. I was rarely given to fits of temper or tearful outbursts, but I did tend to be bossy with my brothers, usually organizing them into some game or sport. I was quite content in my own company, dancing and singing at the bottom of the garden. On his rare days at home, Father watched me through the picture window and smiled beneath his moustache as I twirled and sang.

I did not let on that I knew he was there; I simply put on an extra-special show. Mother was insistent that her girls receive a well-rounded education, which (for middle-class young ladies) also included schooling in the social graces. I found the classes redundant and a little ridiculous; I had only to look to my mother for the perfect example of a lady. Competitive and stubborn, I made my way to the top forms in those studies that I considered to be useful to my future, but unlike many of my contemporaries, I was uninspired by poetry, literature, and classical music. Making friends did not come easily to me. My strong opinions were all too often aggressively delivered, and in many ways, I was awkward and shy. Some of the girls at the school were from wealthier families and looked down upon my independent nature and absence of style. I quarrelled with a classmate over the need for girls to go to school at all; the little princess provoked it.

"What good are maths to us anyway? I plan to marry well and have babies."

I was incensed. "I will have a profession and a family," I boldly announced to the smug girl who continued to denounce my ambitions. "I see no reason why one should exclude the other." My outbursts were not rare and made me unpopular and lonely, although I would never admit the latter.

Father, a master cooper by trade, was a successful business owner in Warrington, which put the family comfortably in the category of upper middle class in the Edwardian era, but he never forgot his working-class roots. He took pride in offering fair wages, reduced working hours, and sickness benefits to the workers in his factory long before such reforms were mandated by the government. His employees, in turn, were hard working and loyal. He was open to innovative ideas and welcomed what he considered to be an era of change. Three of his sons were involved in the business, and he was happy to have me lend a hand during half term and holidays.

"Automobiles and planes are only the beginning for this bright new century, my dear Milly. Before long the factory will run itself," he called up to my high perch in the seat of the lorry, which by the way, I had taught myself to drive. I had spent the morning at the loading bay, helping the lads make ready for deliveries and enjoying their easy banter. I dabbled at a bit of everything in the factory, wherever a spare hand was needed. Too often though, I was required to spend hours pouring over accounts in the office—my punishment for being good at maths, I suppose. I far preferred the laborious tasks and working with the lads.

Mother, who was alarmingly efficient, intelligent, and kind, raised our family and ran her household singlehandedly, which was unusual in our circle. Most in our "class"—*oh, how I loathed that terminology*—had at least one servant and a nanny for the children. However, when I was in my early teens, Mother suffered a frightening episode with pneumonia, and it was at that time that she finally agreed to have a housekeeper come in once every week.

Mother was strong and decisive, but her directives were fastidiously cloaked in swaths of cotton, a skill and a concept that was unfortunately lost on me. She was a firm believer in the importance of intellect over appearance, and a quiet advocate of spirituality and enlightenment over religious formality. She was born and raised in an urban environment but was every bit an ethereal child of nature. Like her, the house was a contrast in colour and texture, old and new, oak and parquet, clean lines and chintz curtains, pastel walls and Persian rugs. While father had insisted upon installing many of the new inventions of the time, she preferred the ambiance of gas lighting, and so it remained. Her ancestors hailed from Scotland and the Isle of Man, but she had been born into a working-class family in Radcliffe. Her father was a stoker at Bleachworks, where both she and her mother were employed as cotton weavers. As an adult, she made it her mission to speak on behalf of the poor and the working class and made it her goal to improve the working conditions they were forced to endure. She had proudly married a man who shared her convictions.

She toiled alongside him to build a successful business, encouraged a strong work ethic in her children, and educated us in our civil responsibilities. As a teen, I accompanied Mother to suffrage rallies, fundraisers, women's social and political union meetings, and lectures on workplace reform. Mother was vehemently active in the women's movement and in pursuit of her right to vote as a citizen of her country, but moreover, she was on a quest for equality and basic human rights for all. "Civil rights belong to everyone. Race, gender, and social status have been the great divider for far too long," she'd declared as we approached a meeting being held to establish a Cripples Aid Society chapter in Manchester. The first of its kind had been established in North Staffordshire by the Duchess of Sutherland, with whom I became acquainted at a society tea held in her honour.

I was proud to share the same name with such a distinguished lady. "Meddlesome Millie, that's what they're calling her in the press," I announced quietly, standing shoulder to shoulder with my exquisitely tall mother.

She gave me a sly wink. Her response was calculated: "She's certainly not one to sit idly by."

I was fully aware of my own good fortune. My home environment was one where choice was permitted, and I was happy to be living in an era where choices for women were growing in number. Had my family been wealthier, I might have been destined for the life of a debutante with little ambition other than to be married, and to have been poor would have offered me fewer choices still. I recall sitting in Father's office double-checking the figures on the ledger and contemplating my options for the future: the application for business school still unopened on the desk. *It would be the sensible choice*, I thought, drumming my fingers on the envelope, but the notion of sitting still in a classroom for another two years sent my head reeling. I looked down at my oversized feet; my all-too-sensible shoes were planted firmly beneath the very desk where I had just spent the entire afternoon, and I felt the energy drain from my body. I moved my feet just a few inches.

Is this the view that my future holds? I dreaded the very prospect. Father expected it; the family presumed it. Perhaps, I should have been content with the advantage offered me of an education and a job usually given to a man, but I was young and restless, longing for adventure. Maps in an atlas might have been enough for my stuffy professors, but I wanted desperately to experience the places they had so inadequately attempted to describe.

I spent the better part of my summer working in one capacity or another alongside my father and brothers at the factory amidst the constant murmurings of war. In August, following the assassination of Archduke Ferdinand, it seemed that the most recited word in the English language was "declares." The angry black letters of the headlines shouted: *3 August 1914 Germany declares war on France; 4 August 1914 Great Britain declares war on Germany; 5 August 1914 Montenegro declares war on Austria-Hungary; 6 August 1914 Austria-Hungary declares war on Russia; Serbia declares war on Germany.* The ensuing public response was brash patriotism, fear, and fervour, but it brought me a much-anticipated and sought-after tingle of excitement.

The traditionally calm environment that was our household was suddenly in an uproar. My brothers, their friends, and many of the young men at the factory were anxious to enlist, concerned that they might miss out if they waited too long. It was, after all, "their patriotic duty to fight the noble fight," and the general consensus was that the war would be over by Christmas. Father, who had lost comrades in the Boer War, had a more realistic perspective and argued that the boys were needed at the factory. He tried to see their point of view and compromised by saying, "Perhaps you should wait. If the conflict lasts longer than a few months, there may be a greater need of you at a later date."

Mother, who was a pacifist in every way, could not begin to comprehend the mindset; she despised the mob mentality that had encroached upon her dining room and inhabited her gentle sons. For the first time in my twenty years of existence, I heard my mother raise her voice in anger. She ranted. "Have you all gone mad? Is there not one among you," she pointed a perfectly manicured finger at each of her boys, "who can see that violence is not the only avenue toward resolving a dispute? Be certain of your convictions and that the cause is equal to your enthusiasm! Is it worth the life you risk? Is it worth the lives you will take?" She stormed from the room, leaving a bewildered family in her wake.

By early spring of 1915, my brothers Richard and Harry were overseas, and I was conducting my own covert mission to join the war effort. My applications to the WVR (Woman's Volunteer Reserve) and the FANYs (First Aid Nursing Yeomanry) were turned down because of my age; I lacked parental consent. I had only to approach Mother and Father once on the subject to know that there would be no support from either of them, but it was a conversation that served only to galvanize my determination. I was not rebellious by nature, quite the contrary, but I could not sit idle and allow this opportunity to pass me by. The government remained steadfast in its negative attitudes regarding women taking part in the war effort; even trained nurses from Britain were obliged to serve with the French and Belgian Red Cross. British Army Nurses (QAIMNS), many of whom had served in the Boer War, were the only exception. I knew that there were many ways I could be of service on the home front, but like my brothers, I was resolved to make my way overseas.

Frustrated, I turned my energy to fundraising and committee work, much of it influenced by the women I had met through my mother's efforts in the suffrage movement. Although the two main suffrage organizations had agreed to suspend political agitation during the war, women remained active in their pursuit of personal freedoms and in finding avenues in which to assist the war effort. Through these works, I met many inspirational women who led with great strength of purpose, and I was proud to serve on a committee that raised funds for a hospital in Calais, France, organized by the Duchess of Sutherland (Meddlesome Millie) who had been much in the news. The duchess was just one of several wealthy women who had ignored the British authorities, formed an affiliation with the French Red Cross, and funded their own mission in establishing ambulance units and hospitals in Belgium. As Belgium fell, Duchess Millie and her affiliates had been trapped under German occupation for a brief time before managing an escape back to England. Not to be daunted, she set about raising funds for a return to the battlefields with a large contingent of nurses, surgeons, and drivers, and by the spring of 1915, the hospital in Calais was established with more than one hundred beds.

A member of that same committee was the amazing Cicely Hamilton, an author and playwright whom I had long admired. We spoke often of our mutual desire to make a more personal commitment overseas and hoped that the duchess might find need of our help in Calais. In the course of our committee correspondence, Cicely invited me to be her guest in London to see her new play: *A Pageant of Great Women*. A suffragette and fearsome feminist, Cicely was co-founder of the Women Writers' Suffrage League and wrote the lyrics of "The March of the Women," composed as a theme for the Women's Social and Political Union. On the morning following the play, we sat together over breakfast, discussing her novel, *Marriage as a Trade,* which Mother and I had read, discussed, and debated at length.

There was a lull in the conversation as she poured from the teapot to refill our empty cups. "You've heard of Dr. Elsie Inglis?" she asked. Seeing my blank expression, she continued. "I'm sure you've read about her in the papers. She's a Scot and a damned fine surgeon. She has approached the British authorities about setting up her female-staffed relief hospitals overseas, but they will hear none of it. They condescendingly responded to her, 'My good lady, go home and sit still.' She didn't."

"Maddening," I growled. "Has she had any success?"

"Yes. Turns out that our government may close the door to help from women but the French authorities do not. I've been doing a great deal of campaigning for Dr. Inglis, fundraising and the like, but she knows me well enough to know that I would rather be getting my hands dirty. So, now she's asked if I would be interested in coming to France and serving as an ambulance driver." Her voice was louder and more animated as she continued. "Dr. Inglis has asked me to put together a small contingent of volunteers from among our like-minded associates, only six, including myself. The prerequisite, of course, is some degree of experience behind the wheel of a motor vehicle and a smattering of knowledge about the workings beneath the bonnet."

I held my breath, silently coaxing the next words from her mouth.

"What do you think?" she asked. "Would you like to come with me?"

And there it was.

"Name the day."

Excited, terrified, and naïve, I left home without a backward glance, without parental consent, and without saying goodbye. I departed from Earlestown station with one small suitcase, wearing layers of clothing beneath my coat, and carrying a pork pie in my pocket. I sent a lovingly worded letter to my sister, Alice, explaining my circumstance and goal, asking for her support and pleading that my whereabouts be kept secret until I was well away. Tucked inside the letter was a brief note to my parents, asking for their forgiveness and prayerful consideration. In Manchester, I disembarked to change trains and to rendezvous with the other members of our small contingent. As we five introduced ourselves, I could see that each one was struggling to conceal nervousness in one way or another. Lillian and Dorothy overcompensated with busy chatter, while May and Emily wore a cloak of subdued confidence. I fell neatly in the middle, confident in my abilities but shy in social situations.

Lost in my own thoughts, I had barely noticed the pale creature who had sidled up next to me on the platform as we waited for the London train. "Hello," she said, with such a musical lilt that the word sounded as though it had four syllables. The mousy little woman with the sickly complexion and plain-Jane looks did not appear to be intimidated by her surroundings in the least. She repeated her earlier introduction. "Hello. I'm Emily Vivian Davidson." She dropped the suitcase that she'd been holding in front of her with both hands and reached out with the kind of firm, masculine handshake that I respected and that so few women presented.

Returning it in kind, I simply said, "Milly. How do you do?" Emily remained glued to my side until the train pulled up to the platform. In stature, she barely reached my shoulder but had a resolute quality that helped me feel less exposed. My height was a burden. I was more nervous than I liked to admit, and although usually guarded around strangers, I felt comfortable somehow with my new little colleague. Taking seats together, I was pleased that my perky companion was content to sit in quiet reflection. Emily was a good judge of character and sensed that I needed some space, and so she waited patiently before easing into conversation. It wasn't long before the ice melted away beneath her warm charm and we chatted freely. She was wonderfully funny and didn't take herself too seriously.

"I live in Manchester," she said, "not far from the station. I left the old poops at home, crying on the doorstep. Didn't want them embarrassing me or hanging onto my leg as I was boarding the train." I grinned back at her and explained my own circumstance in as little detail as possible. Emily suspected a "running away from home" scenario but did not push for information. Instead, with impish insincerity, she leaned in closer and murmured, "Imagine us now, heading overseas to manoeuvre about in an ambulance. I suppose I'll need to learn how to drive." I turned to her in shocked dismay and was about to confront the issue, but the girl's expression was priceless. "I had you there for a minute now, didn't I?" Our nervous energy muffled in laughter tore away my defences, and by the time we reached London, the seeds of friendship were planted. It was to be a friendship that would see us through a war.

"I'm an only child," Emily told me. "Mummy died when I was just little." She was matter of fact in her delivery, as though she had made the speech often in her life. "Dad's a doctor, not a rich one, just a good one," she said with a grin. "He was anxious about my plans but didn't stand in my way."

I waffled a little at first but finally said, "I'm of age to make my own decisions, but I was not eager for an argument. My mother will be proud that I'm making a statement as a woman, but she is dead set against the war in principle; my father would be much more eager to have me working for him at the factory. He owns a business in Warrington."

"Is that where you learned to drive?" asked the smaller girl.

"Yes, I've done all sorts at the factory."

Emily offered up further information. "I've been volunteering at the hospital in Manchester, but I also do most of the driving when Dad does his rounds. One of the ambulance drivers at the hospital gave me a few lessons on mechanics because (as he said) 'No point gettin' b'hind th' wheel if you canna fix what's 'neath th' bonnet.'" She had tucked in her chin and expanded her shoulders and chest as she mimicked him. With a naughty grin, she continued. "It took me a while to get used to the foreign language up here." She waited for my response but seemed satisfied with the expression on my face. "We didn't leave Brighton until I was eleven. Dad finished his internship and away to the north we travelled to hang up our shingle nearer to where my auntie lives. You folks do talk funny up here."

The little mouse was needling for a rise in me; it was all in fun of course, but I had no interest in the game. I responded instead with a verbal resume of my mechanical prowess and experience as well as a commentary on the committee work I had been doing. She smiled and said, "Lordy, you must be a lot older than you look to have accomplished all of that already."

I wasn't sure if I was trying to impress her or convince myself that I was prepared for whatever was in store. Remaining serious, I summed up my thoughts: "I feel as though we—women, I mean—are standing on the precipice of something wonderful and new. Whatever it is, I cannot wait around for it to find me. I mean to seek it out for myself." As though I had put a period at the end of the discussion, we sat back in silence and watched the scenery go by.

At the end of the day, we five stood together with Cicely in her London flat, toasting our future adventure with a glass of sherry.

Chapter Six

Royaumont Abbey, home now to the Scottish Women's Hospital, was run primarily by women under the direction of the French Red Cross and was located about thirty kilometres north of Paris. It was under the command of Dr. Frances Ivens from Liverpool, as Dr. Inglis was busy organizing and setting up further hospitals and clearing stations.

The abbey, for all its original glory in the thirteenth century, was cold and drafty and stank of damp, but by the time our group of six arrived; it had been scrubbed clean and turned into a functioning hospital. The architecture was stunning, and the grounds were quiet and surrounded by parkland and lakes. The colours of autumn shimmered in the trees and the fresh smell of fruitfulness filled the warm afternoon air. It had been a long journey, but once on site, the staff spared no time in preparing us for our duties. We were issued khaki work clothes, coats, and hats, and billeted two to a tiny stark room. Each room was fitted with two metal cots with thin striped mattresses. A bedside table with an oil lamp stood between them; there was one dresser and a wash basin to be shared. Neatly folded on the end of each cot were linens, a wool blanket, and an emaciated-looking pillow. Emily plunked down on her cot, pretending to find bounce in it.

"Comfy," she said sarcastically.

It seemed a long time since our first meeting, but my new friend was also now a roommate. I rolled my eyes in response and set about organizing my belongings. I opened a window to allow some air circulation. The view was spectacular; one could hardly imagine that a war was raging just beyond the gardens. I took a moment to reflect on the preparations that had led us here.

During our three-week stay in London, all five young women and our would-be recruiter, Cicely, successfully completed vigorous training in first aid, organized by the Duchess of Sutherland through the Red Cross. We were permitted unprecedented access to the hospital wards at London General for several hours each day to observe techniques in dressing wounds and splinting limbs. The nursing sisters were reticent and churlish, making it abundantly clear that we were unwelcome in the wards, but the matron, who had obviously been instructed to cooperate, did her best to ensure a level of training had been achieved. The duchess very clearly had friends in high places. A grand total of seventy hours were spent at the hospital, and in that time, we witnessed enough to know that war was anything but glamourous.

Conversations with returning soldiers gave us a glimpse into the ordeals they had suffered, but few of them cared to elaborate. Words were not necessary to convey the torment of those souls who stared unblinking through unseeing eyes; the poor devils who bore the invisible wounds of the mind were the ones that made the greatest impact on me. Though any romantic notions about travel and adventure were long gone before we ever set foot on the boat to France, we remained steadfast.

Each girl, in her own way, was convinced that she could make a difference. Emily was going along as a driver but hoped it would be a steppingstone to nursing. She was simply inspired to offer comfort and to continue her family legacy of healing; she had no greater ambition than to make her father proud. My motivations were quite different. I needed to make a statement, to be taken seriously, and to open doors to personal independence. My convictions were echoed in the nightly conversations we'd had around the fire in Cicely's front room while we rubbed our aching feet, shamelessly sipped whisky, smoked cigarettes, and honed our French speaking skills. Cicely, who seemed against the idea of marriage in principle, was a marvellous orator, and I enjoyed the lively debates that would go on into the wee hours.

I argued, "I believe that a balance can be struck; I was brought up in a household where mutual respect between my parents was achieved. My greater concern is in striving to achieve that degree of equality and respect in the workplace and in society."

Emily contributed little to these exchanges, sitting quietly and taking it all in, and although the other three girls offered occasional comments and opinions, it was primarily Cicely and I who led the charge. I neglected to mention, during those debates, that my enthusiasm toward independence was due in no small measure to my fervent desire to be something other than "the baby of the family"—a label that was limiting by its very nature. No matter the hour we finally turned in for the night, the free exchange of ideas among like-minded women left me feeling charged with a surge of excitement.

Dawn and a new day could not come soon enough for me. We started each morning in the large lot behind the Red Cross headquarters, taking turns behind the wheel and under the bonnet of the trucks and ambulances that were made available to us on any given day. Although we had been selected for the mission based on our driving experience and abilities in repairing the mechanics of a vehicle, we were required to prove our aptitude through a series of skill tests. We left London feeling confident and prepared.

My attention was drawn away from the window as someone at the end of the hall shouted orders in French. Once dressed, we six rendezvoused in the courtyard where we were introduced to the French Red Cross affiliates who would be issuing our orders and to the vehicles that would be our prime responsibility in the months to come.

It took less than a day for us to realize how blissfully ignorant we had been. No amount of training, absolutely nothing, could have readied us for what we saw inside the abbey. In dark contrast to the lush and resplendent grounds were the wards filled with seemingly endless rows of cots laden with an obscene and mangled mess of humanity. Even Emily's hospital experience with her dad was of little consequence. It had not occurred even to her that what we had witnessed at the London hospital were the clean, sterile versions of wounds that had been on the receiving end of sutures and surgery and care. Now we were face to face with the raw realities.

The nurses were too busy to mollycoddle recruits, and there was little time to ease us into our new roles, and so a method of trial by fire was implemented. You either had the stomach for the work or you went home. It was just that simple. And so, as ill prepared as our Victorian era education and prudish upbringings had left us, we marched past the pile of blood-soaked Allied Forces uniforms into a ward filled with naked, shattered male bodies and learned all that would be expected of us when we were not behind the wheel of a vehicle. The introduction was abrupt and shocking, but we had no option but to acclimatize quickly. Five of us did, and one went home.

Before week's end, I had made dozens of round trips to the field units, lifting my bleeding loads into the vehicle and then hurriedly offloading them into wards specific to their injuries. My job description went from ambulance driver to whatever was necessary in any given moment: pumping buckets full of water, mopping blood-soaked floors, swilling bedpans, rolling bandages, and on and on. Emily spent a half day pushing trolleys loaded with sawn-off limbs from the operating theatre to a fire pit at the back of the compound. Someone had to do it.

We ate little and slept not at all during those first few weeks, our senses under continuous assault. Blood was the constant that ran red and left a rusty stain on everything in its path. The smell of it lingered in the air mingled with camphor and ether and the odours of smoke, oil, and latrines; in juxtaposition was the pungent aroma of manure and all that was common to the functioning farmyard behind the abbey. We were unnerved by the relentless trembling of the ground beneath us. Near enough to shake the ancient buildings were the explosive sound of shells bursting and the inter-mittent rat-a-tat of rifle and machine-gun fire, which reminded me of the playful sounds my brothers used to make when they frolicked outside with their firearms made from tree-branches. "Rat-a-tat, rat-a-tat-tat," they would repeat as they dodged between the trees. It brought too close to home an image of my brothers on a battlefield, shooting real firearms at real people and dodging between trees in real fear for their own lives.

Frightening sudden bursts of light indicated a big blast, contrasting the tiny flares that looked like fireflies in the night sky. A steady convoy of trucks and ambulances coughed and rattled their way to and from the grounds, and overhead was the spectacle of sputtering aircraft. Voices talking and shouting orders echoed around the clock. The overwhelming barrage on all the senses was too much for some, but the five of us remaining girls persevered and in time adapted to most everything in our environment, except for the constant sickening groans and screams of men in agony. Those were sounds that took permanent residence in our ears and minds and could never be adequately described in a soul-cleansing letter home.

From the start, I wrote weekly letters to my family, each one maintaining a carefully penned and upbeat tone as I had no wish to distress them. Mail delivery from England was surprisingly efficient with letters arriving within just a few days, and I cherished each of them. My brother William, who had served in the Boer War, was required to help run the family business but wrote as often as he could. He imparted news of the many boys from the factory who had enlisted and expressed his sadness over the fates of those who would not be returning home.

I shared with him my feelings after just one month in France, writing, *"It's all such a terrible waste, but you know that. I am resolved to stay and serve; I find that I am quite fond of the discipline and order of life here. It suits me. I miss you all, of course, but I feel needed and useful."*

My father, still angry at my decision to leave home, wrote occasional brief and businesslike notes, often offering up a guilt-laden summons: *"Milly, do you not think it is your duty to be here to help your parents cope? It is very difficult to maintain a business and a home in these uncertain times. Your mother frets about your safety, and I fear she needs you more than she lets on."*

I could almost hear the tone of his voice, seeping off the page, and I had no doubt that his concern for my mother was honest and heartfelt. I knew also that she was stronger than he gave her credit for. I replied with long thoughtful letters, which always ended the same: *"I love you, Papa. I will make you proud."*

Two of my brothers, Richard and Harry, were serving in the Mesopotamian campaign, and although I rarely heard from them directly, I was grateful to receive news of them from other family members. Another brother, John, was found medically unfit to enlist due to the effects of scarlet fever, which he'd suffered as a youth, but he was doing his bit for the war effort as a volunteer in a munitions factory. Upset and depressed that he could not follow his siblings, he turned his frustration and anger on me. His little sister was serving in what he considered a man's role overseas, and he could not reconcile his feelings about it enough to correspond. I penned short notes to him in the beginning but desisted after a time, afraid to rub salt in the wound.

Mother shared tales of her grandchildren, local neighbourhood news, and her continued work on behalf of women's liberties. She had not been at all surprised by my departure nor my pursuit to serve overseas. We had a special relationship that transcended the need for apology or explanation. She began every letter with the same term of endearment:

My Dearest Darling,

We feel, on occasion, the vibration of the guns that are on your doorstep, and I can but imagine the terror you must endure. The zeppelin raids continue to create much fear in every county in England, and we are fortunate to have been spared their assault. The concern over further food shortages has turned many of our respectable neighbours into a scurry of squabbling squirrels, hiding their cache of provisions and looking about in either direction to be sure no one has witnessed their hiding place. One takes risks just moving through the market these days. Alice and I have begun work with the Red Cross sewing parties. She's volunteered to sew pyjamas out of the fabric donated by her customers, but even with all her skill, I wonder how she finds the time. I've been busy knitting socks for the care packages and can only hope that the young men who receive them will forgive my poor workmanship. We have had letters from the boys who send you their love and seem to be well enough for now; they both expect to have leave before Christmas. I will close for now. Take great care to be safe in body and be diligent in finding quiet moments to minister to your spirit. It too needs your special attention in these challenging times. I will keep you close in my heart as always,

Mother

Letters arrived from a few of my associates on the suffrage committees, and I was always excited to receive mail from Annie, my fourteen-year-old niece. Her notes were full of upbeat banter about school and friends, and she made it her mission to chase away the gloom of the war for her aunt Mil. Annie was strikingly attractive, almost exotic, with deep chestnut-brown eyes, an alabaster complexion, and shiny auburn hair. She talked about the cinema, her favourite music, and about sport. In her most recent letter, she'd written, "*Dearest Aunty Mil, Mum says you are very good at Maths, so you must come home soon to help me. It is not at all my best subject. The mistress says it isn't as important as improving my needlepoint, but Mum insists she's wrong. She was quite upset about the comment, come to think of it.*" I grinned, imagining the look on my sister's face and her outrage at such a narrow-minded comment from a teacher.

Best and most frequent were the letters from Alice, my only sister and oldest sibling. Although busy raising a family of her own and continuing her work as a seamstress, Alice made the effort to write at least once a week. Ours was more akin to a mother-daughter relationship, which was understandable considering our twenty-year age difference. I so loved and admired my graceful sister. Whenever I saw her handwriting on the envelope, I would tuck the letter into my apron and await the perfect quiet moment to sit alone in the lounge. By the light of the candle glowing in the mason-jar lantern, I inhaled each delicately penned word from the page and felt her essence beside me. At the age of six, the baby of the family, I had been sent to live with Alice during the scarlet fever epidemic that had invaded our household. Two of my brothers had been stricken with it. For me, it had been like a wonderful holiday. I enjoyed having my young nieces to play with, and there had been a new baby to fuss over. Alice just nuzzled me into the nest with the others as though I had always been there, and for the first time, I enjoyed the perks of being the oldest child in a household. Sadly, the holiday went tragically and horribly wrong when my brother George succumbed to the deadly illness. I was too young to understand the grief hanging over my parents and was happy to be left in Alice's care.

In one of her letters, Alice confessed that she'd had a difficult time with the recent birth of her seventh child and that the doctor had impressed upon her that there should be no more.

I wrote back, *"I have a hard time imagining you without a baby perched on your hip. There's been one there for as long as I can remember. I do hope, my dearest sister, that you will heed the physician's advice and perhaps find some healing time to spend at the garden."*

Four months after our arrival at the abbey, Emily and I were transferred to a casualty clearing station (CCS) sixteen kilometers closer to the front lines. Dressing stations, CCS, and hospitals of all kinds dotted the landscape; many of them moving from one location to another as the front shifted and the imaginary line on the map moved with the fighting. Battles were becoming fiercer, and the brutality of winter in the trenches was filling the wards with as many sick as wounded. CCS locations were struggling to keep up, and although volunteers were arriving more steadily from Britain, more experienced personnel were preferred for positions at the front. I was astounded to be referred to as experienced after such a short time, but both Emily and I had proven our abilities not only as drivers but as nursing assistants, and we were grateful to be held in high regard at the hospital. We were not going far and would be returning to the hospital often, which made our goodbyes much easier.

Cicely saw us away with a wave. "Keep your heads down, lassies. I'll have a good bottle of Scotch waiting when you get back." She was the last of the group of six remaining at the abbey; the other two gals, Dorothy and May, had been transferred to another hospital that Dr. Inglis had opened recently.

It was only in letters to Alice that I was able to convey the brutal truth of my life at the back of the western front. I described living in tents and makeshift barracks, through dysentery, biting cold, rat infestations, and lice. I mentioned Emily too, but was deliberately vague knowing all too well that even personal letters were scrutinized. I proudly wrote to Alice often about my friend.

Alice,

We've had to cut our hair very short. "The ignorant little buggers are impossible to get rid of when you've got a tangle of hair. Poor Emily. She's not the prettiest of creatures, looking more male than female when she's in her driver togs. She is lovely though in every other way; jokes about it herself. Oh, Alice, I do so want you to meet Emily. I am most grateful to have her as a friend, and I know you will love her as I do. She's one of us. I'm sure of it. A kindred spirit. Well, you know what I mean. Em has an impressive work ethic, and her previous experience around a hospital ward has been invaluable; it doesn't hurt that she has a personality that charms and endears her to the strictest of nursing sisters and makes her a favourite with the patients. I seem to benefit simply by association. We've made an oath to stick together through this if there's any way at all to manage it.

Milly

The weeks turned into months, and after a long bone-chilling winter, I was despondent when I put pen to paper in a deliberate attempt to lighten the load I carried in my heart.

My dearest Alice,

Winter here has been like some gruesome blood-red ice-skating rink,
and I thought perhaps my fingers would never thaw, but now I think
that spring is crueller still. In the field beyond I can see daffodils and a
bed of wildflowers, and on the hillside I can just make out green buds
on the trees, but here in camp there is nothing but an endless murky
quagmire of mud. You sink into it up to your ankles, and it makes a
hellish bumpy ride for my lads. I have always thought of them as my
lads, until now, getting to know them a little and talking to them of
home. On one of my rounds to the trench dressing station last week,
I picked up young Jimmy. He was one of several lads that I picked up
on that run. You remember, he's Ivy's boy from the factory? He and
I spent many a day together taking inventory and going through the
waybills. Papa thought he was a little too brazen and good looking and
always kept a keen eye on him, which of course, made it even more
fun to misbehave. He had been hit in the thigh; his skin flayed open
to the bone. He lay surrounded by bodies, half buried in the mud and
a pool of his own blood, for a whole day before anyone could get to
him. The medics did their best to clean the wound, but he was so mud
soaked that I did not recognize him when I lifted his stretcher into the
vehicle. Even in his tortured state, he winked at me and said, "Well now,
mistress, imagine meeting you here." I followed his care closely, making
a nuisance of myself at the British Red Cross hospital up the road, but I
took every spare minute to drive over and sit with him. He asked about
Papa and the factory and how our lads are making out. His spirits were
good, although he was tormented about his comrades. The surgeon did
everything he could, but gangrene set in, and on the fourth day, they
had to remove the leg. Still, Jimmy kept his good humour and made
me promise I would dance with him at the next work's party. When
he woke from the surgery, I was there holding his hand and even the
morphine could not diminish his feisty grin. By the end of the week, he
was dead. I pulled up to the compound, and the career army nurse, who
served during the Boer campaign and was usually a sour old melon,
met me at my vehicle. The expression on her face told the tale. "The
infection spread," she said, "and there was nothing that could be done."

She actually hugged me, and they rarely do that, saying how sorry she
was for my loss. I was paralyzed at first. I had not prepared myself. I
was sure he would be going home—missing a leg, but still going home. I
have watched hundreds of men die here, but this was different. Perhaps
it was just too close to home. Too real. Isn't that ridiculous? I went out
into that lovely field surrounded by forget-me-nots and wept until there
were no more tears. I will not, and I cannot, put myself through it again.
I will do my job and do it well, but I will not get close to anyone again.
It is just too hard. They're not my lads anymore.

Yours always, Milly

In May, we were offered leave but only for a week, not enough time
to make the journey home worthwhile, and so we set out instead for
Paris-Plage, where we were billeted at the convalescent home for nursing
staff and female volunteers. Em and I were accompanied by Cicely and
several other girls from the abbey who were also in need of a few days'
rest and relaxation by the sea. It was an eerily quiet journey with little
conversation or banter, as though we were all in the same desperate need
of a few hushed moments of personal reflection. We spent the first evening
at a corner café, savouring fresh fish and sipping brandy. The gulls gliding
and swooping overhead was all the entertainment we needed. In the days
that followed, the rejuvenating tonic of good food, fresh air, and sunshine
brought a healthy glow back into body and soul. We took long walks in
the countryside, shopped in the small town along the way, went to bed
early and slept late, and before week's end, the heaviness was lifted, and
we once again engaged in convivial chatter.

Upon our return, Emily and I were reassigned to the abbey; we were both
grateful to have a respite from tent living at the CCS. The work was steady
but not insurmountable. Most of the wards were transient, a man was either
able to return to duty or he was transported to a hospital in Britain or to the
south of France for convalescent care or further treatment. The sick ward
was always full of influenza, pneumonia, trench fever patients, and a few of
those were on the DIL (dangerously ill) list. There was a ward for prisoners
of war, the surgical units, and the ever-expanding gas ward. With the warmer
weather, the convalescent units were spilling outdoors. For those unable to

walk, beds were wheeled into the sunshine. Dr. Ivens was a great proponent of fresh air as the best medicine.

A restless atmosphere was the precursor to a big push, and every member of the staff would independently scurry about without need of specific instruction in preparation for a large influx of wounded. But between skirmishes and major offensives, there were days when the hospital seemed still. The usual routine of scouring floors and beds, and delivering meals and meds, seemed calm in the wake of the mass-casualty chaos. I relished those moments, especially when they coincided with one of my half days when I could walk through the gardens to the river for an afternoon alone.

My darling Alice,

I have discovered a way in which to carry the garden with me, and it is a project that keeps my fingers busy and my heart full. It came about during a relatively uneventful week when my vehicle sat idle for several days—perfectly tuned and buffed of course. Several of the nursing sisters were offered leave while those of us remaining took on duties as we were needed. I had occasion to work several night shifts in one of the convalescent wards with Sister Marceau, a kind and gentle soul who ministers to the boys with great tenderness and has become my friend. The ward was quiet except for the boys who suffer night terrors, but they were easily settled. I was filling the time with needlework while Sister sat reading, and I noticed a pink blossom pressed into the pages of her book. I commented on it, and she gently flipped through the pages to show me several other colourful blossoms. On the table beside her was another volume in which she'd pressed an array of herbs, exquisite leaves in hues of green all suspended perfectly between the pages. They were quite lovely, and I thought I might do the same. Later that week though, when I was helping out in the gas ward, I discovered a way to incorporate her hobby into one of my own. There, in a crate at the end of the hallway, was a tangled and broken mountain of discarded eyeglasses removed from boys who would no longer need them for one reason or another, or simply found ownerless on the field or in an ambulance. I received permission from Matron to help myself to the materials, and so I began. Enclosed, you will find the first of my little creations; a talisman of hope

and wellness to keep us close in these dark times. I hope that you will
carry it with you and think of me.

Yours always, Shuyr my chree (Sister of my heart)

I worked on my creations during quiet times, on duty and off, and by
lamplight in my room, but my favourite by far were those so-infrequent
and glorious half days. I carried the necessary materials in a basket together
with a stick of bread, a chunk of cheese, and a flask of tea. I wandered the
same path past the great oaks and the chestnut trees that offered fatherly
protection to the dancing willows that lined the riverbank, and there I spread
my blanket. Sorting through the pieces of glass, I found two that fit together
as though mated and sanded them gently into an oval shape with the fine
sanding file that I'd bartered from a local carpenter along with a tiny pair of
needle-nosed pliers. It had cost me a carton of cigarettes, but it was worth it.
I reached up into the tree, plucked a perfectly formed leaf from the willow,
and pressed it gently between the two pieces of glass, running a fine thread
of casein glue around the edges. I encircled the piece with a double row of
wire taken from the twisted tangle of eyeglass frames, twisting it tightly into
place around the glue. Then I integrated a third small piece of wire, weaving
it in at the top and crafting it into three sister spirals to crown the delicate
piece. I sat back against the tree trunk and appraised my work. The willow
leaf took on a green milky hue beneath the glass, reminding me of the mist
that hovered beneath the great trees at the bottom of my garden in England
just as the dawn broke into day. The spiral embellishment was an homage
to the triskelion, a symbol of my Celtic ancestry. Happy with my creation, I
harvested a few tender leaves from the tree, pressed them into a notebook
for future use, and gathered the rest of my belongings. I had promised Emily
that I would return to the abbey in time to share the evening meal.

Emily, as it happened, was to receive the second of my creations some
time later. Many of the volunteers and nursing staff had fallen ill with one
thing or another but none as desperately as Emily in the early summer.
Her symptoms were much like that of trench fever, but the doctors were
hesitant to diagnose it as such. Her temperature spiked so high that they
feared for her life, and I seemed the only one who could quiet her delirium.
She was immersed in cool baths, wrapped in cool towels, and I made it

my responsibility to see that she stayed hydrated. The nursing staff made no argument about my ministrations; they were confident that Emily was in good hands and equally confident that I would not neglect my other duties. On the third day, and during an episode of particularly disturbing delirium, I climbed into the bed beside my friend and cradled her as a child, humming gently. The screens around the bed proved ineffective in keeping the matron from witnessing this breech of hospital decorum, but she said nothing. Cicely popped her head in to check on us, but she too tiptoed away without a word. Once Emily quieted and drifted into sleep, I returned to the chair beside the bed and reached into my pocket to retrieve another of the little willow talismans that I had created. I slipped it gently beneath the pillow and leaned over to kiss my friend's clammy forehead. "I hope my gift will bring peace to your spirit." More quietly still, I repeated the phrase in Manx: *"Shee da'n annym echey."* I remembered only a few phrases from the ancient language of the Isle of Man. I spoke them rarely and only to those I loved deeply.

The fever broke the next morning, and within a week, Emily was returned to light duty; she carried in her pocket the willow charm that she'd discovered beneath her pillow. She knew that it was my gift and understood that it held great significance. She did not ask questions but chose to always carry the talisman with her.

Sitting with Cicely over a light cold supper, as it was a torturously hot day, Matron approached the three of us. In her guarded and broken English, she said, "I'm happy to see you are feeling better, Miss Davidson." She broke into a wide grin and then said to me, "You, Miss Aspinall, are not to climb into bed with a patient in future, especially with your shoes on." With a swish of her skirt, she moved on. This was the first Emily had heard of the episode, and we were both surprised when Cicely chimed in. "Yes, quite a sight you were too, with your spindly legs hanging off the end of the bed."

Illness and injury were not exclusive to those in the military. In the early months of the war, the German invasion of Belgium sent thousands of refugees fleeing in every direction. Emily was tortured by the reports of human atrocities on Belgian women and children by German soldiers as they made their way through the country in their "race to the sea." They'd considered the neutral country of Belgium an easy corridor through which to invade France and had been certain they would march through unscathed in a matter of weeks. King Albert and the small Belgian army rallied, declaring, "We are a country, not a thoroughfare!" They held them off as long as they could, allowing time for Britain to intercede as was their duty under the 1839 Treaty of London. Still, the country was ravaged and overrun, pushing multitudes in search of safe haven. As the battle lines fixed along both sides of the Somme River, local farmers and families were driven out of their homes. I was haunted by the sight of the Mertens family arriving at the hospital in the middle of the night by horse cart. Their farmhouse had been torched, burned to the ground. Mr. Mertens, beaten and wounded, had managed to run into the flames to save his five children; they were all severely burned. He collapsed into my arms as he climbed down from the cart and stared up at me through tears of anguish; his wife had not survived the blaze. He died in my arms. The children, the four that survived, underwent painful debridement treatments and were eventually transferred to a hospital in Britain; safely aboard the hospital ship, each one carried a willow charm in the pocket of their robe. I wondered what would become of them but had little time to contemplate the matter. The infrequent moments of stillness were over. The gates of hell were opened wide, and the horror flooded in.

On July 1, 1916, the earth began to quake, and the massacre began. I had no way of knowing that the Battle of the Somme was to last until November at the cost of 420,000 casualties for the British Army alone. That first night, over three hundred men were treated at the abbey, but in total, sixty thousand were wounded during those first hours in what the *Times* would call "90 miles of uproar." It was ten days before I slept for more than four hours in a stretch; my ambulance was constantly on the move. The frenzy of activity at the hospital went on for weeks with wounded evacuated to England daily to make room for hundreds more coming in from the front—men with multiple wounds, gas-attack victims, bodies with missing limbs, and whole bodies whose minds had been lost somewhere on the bloody fields along the River Somme. I gave up a few precious moments of sleep to prepare a note to Alice.

Dearest Sister,

I don't know how much you have heard of the state of things here, but I can't imagine the press could find adequate words to describe the misery. I hesitate to share my anguish but do so knowing that most of what I write will be scrutinized and struck out. Although, I expect the authorities are far too busy at present to be greatly interested in my perspective. I should first say that I am well, in body at least. The scene, as described to us from the wounded at the CCS, is akin to our childhood nightmares of Hades. Corpses already buried have been blown from their graves; the pock-marked muddy ground is littered as far as the eye can see like some ghoulish quilt of crimson and khaki. The steady bombardment isn't enough to drown out the screams of the wounded, and the men in the trenches shout and curse in an effort to survive the din. The dead lie everywhere, eyes open in stunned surprise and terror. The ratio of medical help to those in need has drastically changed and requires a constant movement of staff between wards but also between the hospital and the nearest CCS. Both Emily and I have been required to alternate between the two posts, two weeks forward, two weeks back, but we are told that replacements and further volunteers will arrive soon from Britain. During these desperate endless days, every available pair of hands is needed to perform nursing duties even in the surgical ward. We return from an ambulance convoy having already performed the duties of a medic only to be handed an apron in preparation for tasks usually assigned to skilled nurses and orderlies. Emily believes that she has learned more in the past month than she could have done in two years of internship at the London General. We are no longer merely drivers. I am told that I have some natural ability in the wards, but truth be told, I wouldn't mind being merely a driver again.

Mil

In September, the matron called me to her office. Emily and Cicely received a similar summons. She stated her purpose immediately and without emotion. "Your contracts have been fulfilled, and the French Red Cross authorities have asked if you wish to stay on here at the abbey. You need not respond immediately; you have until the end of the week." We left her office in retrospective silence but rendezvoused in Cicely's room that evening to discuss the matter.

The telegram I wrote to Mother simply stated, *"Coming home."*

Chapter Seven

We three women were of one mind, and the journey home was filled with purposeful discussion of our future service. Each of us planned to spend some time at home with family, but in the New Year, we would return to France through one of the new volunteer service organizations. The British government had come to the conclusion that recruiting women to serve in specific roles would free up many more men for combat roles. A woman serving in the war effort had been considered a ridiculous notion in the beginning, but as the war marched on so much longer than anyone expected, and as more young men were needed to fight, necessity won out. Cicely pulled from her pocket a crumpled, dog-eared poster sent to her from a friend in London.

"These are going up all over England, looking for volunteers," she said. "This one was snatched from the wall at Piccadilly Station." She unfolded the recruitment circular, which boasted a picture of a woman in an army great coat and felt hat, smiling and waving to someone in the distance. The bold red and white lettering read:

Women urgently wanted for the W.A.A.C, Women's Army Auxiliary Corps. Work at home and abroad with the Forces. Cooks, Clerks, Waitresses, Driver-mechanics. All kinds of domestic workers and women in many other capacities to take the place of men. Good wages. Quarters. Uniform. Rations. For all information and advice apply at nearest employment exchange.

With sarcasm and a perfunctory wink, she added, "And they provide training."

I raised an eyebrow and responded without opening my eyes. "We could teach the bleedin' classes." Clearly the language of the lads had rubbed off on me. *I'll have to watch that around Mother.*

Emily, playing devil's advocate, chimed in. "We could always stay in England and work for the Women's Land Army." She didn't really expect a response; she knew that working on a farm at home, although important and necessary, just wasn't for us. She was, however, interested in learning more about the VADs (Volunteer Aid Detachments). These were run by trained nursing sisters and staffed by volunteers and seemed a logical choice for my friend. Cicely, however, was quick to warn against it as an option.

"The matron at London General is not impressed by nor does she support the recruitment of many of these volunteers. Upper-class young ladies parading themselves as nurses." She snuffed her nose in the air just for effect.

The jostling of the train had lulled me into a blissful surface sleep, but my eyes snapped open then. "Careful now. That smacks of middle-class snobbery."

"No, not at all. Oh, and nice to see you're still with us. I hate the class distinctions as much as anyone, and Lord knows, volunteers are a must as this mess drags on. Besides, it'll do the little dears good to dirty their hands and get out from under male authority in their households. I'm all for it. I've been earning my own way since my father died, and it hasn't done me any harm." She was on a roll and we, her travelling companions, were a captive audience. "You two were brought up understanding the benefit of a good days' graft, and it shows in your work ethic. It'll give you a future too—independence and the means to support yourselves."

Emily interjected, "The more hands the better, as I see it."

"The issue, my sources tell me, is that nursing sisters who have trained for years and worked hard for their positions have suddenly been inundated with trainees who have never done a day's work in their lives; many I'm told are reluctant to take orders. Good luck with that, if they ever get over here. There is also the ridiculous notion among professional nurses that these young intruders are after their jobs; as a result, emotions are running high and creating stressful working conditions for everyone."

She took a momentary respite and then concluded in a more subdued manner. "Don't mean to put you off, Emily. Just be aware. Even with all your experience, you'd be in the middle of it, training and all. Think on. That's all."

It was Emily's turn to close her eyes and mull over the options. There would be no opposition from her father whatever she decided, but she was concerned about the disapproval I might encounter from my family. As much as she hoped to return to France in the role of nurse, she could not imagine going through such an experience without her best friend at her side. Together we watched bright patches of sunlight flash past our closed lids as the train sped along the tracks toward Boulogne and the leave ship that would take us home.

Papers in hand, excited and nervous, we arrived at the quay only to be turned away. "More important that the men going on leave have transport; they've done their duty. You'll get your turn," said one dismissive plunker. I was more annoyed by the timbre of the message than its substance, but I held my tongue. We watched in the distance as patients were lifted by crane onto a hospital ship bound for home, knowing that each of them would be wearing a coloured tag indicating the severity of their wounds. The Blighty tickets had become a science. We waited for the late-afternoon sailing, which was not a terrible hardship except that Emily and I would miss our connections for home and would need to find accommodation in London for the night. Cicely, who had sublet her flat, had made plans to visit the old aunties who had been so good to her and her siblings after their parents had died. Arrangements had been made to pick her up at Victoria station.

We filled our final few hours in France at the Boulogne Hotel Café over a succulent lunch of wine and fresh-from-the-sea delights, and later stepped aboard the leave ship feeling mellow and melancholy. The sky was crystal clear and the Channel crossing eerily calm as though safe passage had been ordered especially for us. In the distance, the white cliffs beckoned with majestic fortitude and demanded patriotic pride from all those who approached her shores. The ship was filled with young men returning home with wounds that would keep them there, and with many others who would visit their loved ones for all too brief a time before returning to an uncertain future on the battlefields of France. We took in the splendour and fought hard against the swell of emotion aching in our throats.

It had already been a long day, and the train from Folkestone station to London seemed interminable. I dreaded having to say goodbye to Cicely at Victoria station. We had been through so much together, and it felt unnatural that we would not be bumping into each other over breakfast in the morning. She insisted that we would be seeing each other again within a few months and that we must not be dramatic. She was the first to cry. The tearful scene was made short, however, by the arrival of an attendant hired to carry Cicely's belongings and whisk her away to a waiting vehicle. Swept up in the bustle of the station, the two of us remaining scurried along with the crowd, bypassing the free buffet offered by volunteers. We glanced briefly at the lineup of uniformed men heading overseas on the opposite platform, each lugging a long bolster and trying desperately to look courageous. Most were barely making eye contact with their superficially brave mothers and sweethearts, dreading the moment when they would have to say their gut-wrenching goodbyes. Emily tugged on my sleeve; she had no desire to linger or to hear the fateful clunk of the train doors.

"Come on, Mil, let's treat ourselves royally. God knows we deserve it."

We secured a hotel room, dove into a fabulous meal, and then found a music hall. We rounded out the evening in style, sipping cocktails and giggling like schoolgirls. Content and exhausted, we returned to our cozy room and melted into the soft mattress and clean sheets. With the gentle rhythm and comforting clatter of noise below on the busy London streets, we fell immediately into a deep healing sleep.

Over a hearty breakfast, we discussed a plan to return to the same hotel for a couple of days before our triumphant return to France, and then, as we sipped the last of our coffee, an uncomfortable silence fell. It was an odd feeling; we had never struggled for conversation before, and I supposed we were both just anxious about seeing our loved ones after so long. Finally, Emily glanced over her cup and said, "Oh, Milly, I shall miss you."

"Don't be daft, you silly bugger. We'll only be a few miles apart. We'll see each other; there are plans to be made."

Emily remained glum, and I reached over to take her hand. "You goof. I will miss you too, and you know that. How about this for an idea? If you can get away in the next couple of weeks, come to Newton. I would love for you to meet Alice. I've written pages and pages about you; I know she'd love it." Satisfied, Emily smiled, but as we said our goodbyes, she held me in an embrace that was meant to last a lifetime.

Chapter Eight

I was warmly greeted by my family, except for Father, who remained guarded and a little cool. My departure had hurt him deeply, and I was determined to win him over before the end of the week. My brother John, whose initial attitude about my departure had softened over time, apologized profusely for not writing in the beginning. We had since then exchanged many letters, and I assured him that there were no hard feelings. Mother was uncharacteristically emotional and cried intermittently for several hours, but then she rallied, pulled me from my chair, and insisted I must have a tour around the house. Without argument, I followed along as she opened cupboard doors to show me the state that rationing had driven them to, and I sympathized as she conveyed the details of their day-to-day hardships. It was difficult to fall asleep that first night in the quiet comfort of my family home. The hot bath and soft, clean nightgown were a blessing, but the stillness was deafening. While London had been a buzz of activity, the streets at home were deserted and dismal with most of the men overseas. I finally drifted to sleep with images of their weather-beaten faces fresh in my mind. Tomorrow, I thought, would be a good day. I would see Alice.

Mother, Alice, and I spent the day sitting quietly at the riverbank beneath the great willow. My sister and I had always had the ability to speak volumes without words. There was a message conveyed in every knowing glance. It was as though we had never been apart. Alice quieted her baby with a gentle nudge of the pram and looked up from the garment she was stitching only to take part in the pleasant conversation. We refrained from talk of war, as though an unspoken decision had been made that the day must be reserved for peace and healing. We were in the right place.

I promised to spend some time at the factory with my father, and in doing so, I began to understand some of the difficulties faced by those at home. As makers of cotton sacks, among many other things, Father's primary customer had always been the Sankey Sugar Works Company, but the scarcity of sugar had made the sacks an unnecessary commodity. The factory had been able to stay afloat thanks to the quick thinking of my oldest brother, who'd secured a contract from the war department. They were to make cotton sacks called "bandoleers" that held one hundred rounds of ammunition; soldiers were to wear them around their necks to keep them dry. They were also contracted to make feed sacks for the horses at the front. While the contracts were a blessing, they were short on employees. Most of the lads had joined up, and many had died overseas, leaving only the old or infirm to fill the orders. Mother had written about the death of my childhood friend Alfred at the Battle of Loos. He had worked in the factory and lived down the hill on Shop Row in Vitriol Square. Like so many others, he was a lovely boy who had thought he and his young friends would beat the Kaiser in a matter of months and come home victorious. I thought about young Jimmy who had died in that gloomy tent in France. His image smiled at me, and I made a mental note to call on his mother.

Sharing an egg sandwich, I looked across the desk at my father's furrowed brow and noticed the deep worry lines around his eyes. He was only in his sixties, and yet he was hunched over like an old man. He'd gone completely bald since I'd left home, and although I teased him about it, I thought it gave him a particularly distinguished appearance. His kind face looked weathered, and I was concerned about his pallor. *I must speak to Alice about it.* He was proud to tell me that he had begun hiring women to work in the factory, and by day's end, we had made our peace.

I travelled with Mother to a convalescent home nearby where my brother Richard was recovering from shrapnel wounds that had left him blind in his right eye. We greeted each other warmly and talked about the weather and joked about his "keepers," the nursing sisters who were bossy, by his grim account. We steered away from any mention of the war or of the carnage we had both witnessed. "The surgery went well, the doctor said," was Richard's jaunty response to my questioning of his injuries, but I could not help but notice the intermittent twitching in his limbs and occasional chattering of his teeth. He answered "No" every time Mother asked, "Are you cold, dear?"

I knew the symptoms all too well but refrained from comment. My brother was suffering what I had seen hundreds of others go through. In France, they called it "shell shock." His symptoms were mild compared to many, but I was still concerned. I stopped in as often as I could in the weeks that followed, and on each visit, brought him something new to occupy his mind and his hands. I spent the better part of one day teaching him to crochet and watched triumphantly as his tremors subsided. I spoke to the nursing sister on the ward, explained my experience, and asked if I would be permitted to offer a massage to my brother. I had seen great strides made with patients just like him when the correct therapies were administered. I was denied. Once again, I determined to speak to my own sister, certain that if Alice were to visit, she would be less likely to take no for an answer.

Every day was filled. I visited with my nieces and nephews and dropped in to pay my respects to neighbours and friends who had been tragically touched by the war. Alice mended and made alterations to my clothing, noting sympathetically that I'd been reduced to skin and bone. Mother managed to make something out of nothing at every meal and fill my plate to overflowing. She was a marvel. After only a brief time though, I decided I must speak to them honestly about my intention to return to France in the New Year. My announcement came as no surprise, nor was any objection offered; in fact, shortly thereafter, Father arrived home with a package.

He nonchalantly placed it in front of me and declared, "You'll be needing those," before making a quick exit from the room. I lifted open the lid of the box to find a new pair of highly polished sensible shoes. I dreaded the painful breaking-in period but appreciated the sentiment and the extravagance. I slipped them on to show Mother and then made my way into the front room. I bent over Father's chair and planted a tender, lingering kiss on his shiny bald head.

I had not heard anything from Emily and presumed that the poor girl was unable to escape her family, but I missed her and was growing anxious to formulate a plan. On a clear sunny Sunday morning, I was sitting quietly on the front porch, listening to my mother singing as she busied herself in the kitchen. Father was reading the newspaper in the front room, his spectacles balanced precariously on the tip of his nose as always. I closed my eyes and hoped that the tranquility of the moment might wash over me and shroud, even for a moment, the haunting images that followed me even into sleep. I was startled awake by the high-pitched toot of a car horn, and as I watched the vehicle sputter to a stop in front of the house, an eager Emily cranked open the door and vaulted onto the porch. Her enthusiastic hug nearly knocked me off balance, and because of the difference in our height, Emily's head landed firmly into the middle of my bosom, which brought about spontaneous laughter from the gentleman standing by the car.

He made his way up the steps and said, "If you're quite through, my dear, I would like to meet this Miss Aspinall I've heard so much about."

Emily detached herself and said, "This is my father, Dr. Davidson. Daddy, this is my dearest friend, Milly."

A handshake would not do. Dr. Davidson enfolded me in his arms, and said, "It's wonderful to finally meet you. I was beginning to think you were a myth." It was clear that Emily had inherited her easy charm and impish smile from the man standing before me. He concluded his embrace with a kiss on my cheek and said, "I'm grateful to you, Milly. Thank you for taking such good care of my girl."

"It's been a mutual undertaking; I can assure you." Emily was once again by my side with one arm draped around my hip; I invited them into the house to meet my parents. Mother was already waiting at the door and greeted the guests with her usual generous warmth, and as they entered the front room, my father rose from his chair with a hand extended to meet the visitors. Following the introductions, a hearty conversation began over a pot of tea and the sweet scones that Mother had just taken from the oven. One of the perks of being in business with the Sankey Sugar Works was that, unlike most families in Britain at the time, Father was often able to supply the family with a little extra sugar for the pantry. It was, however, reserved for baking, nothing so frivolous as to be stirred into a teacup. Dr. Davidson proved to be the kind and witty character that Emily had so often described; he took such genuine interest in what others had to say that it seemed as though you were the only important person to him in that moment. Individuals skilled in the art of conversation always impressed me, especially those who asked questions and listened to the answers rather than offering up reams of unsolicited personal information. He did tell us that he was spending little time in his own practice, offering instead to work with wounded veterans at local hospitals and hospices. Without going into graphic detail, in deference to my mother, he had been successful in conveying the enormity of the physical damage our young men had experienced. He spoke also about the tragic emotional toll suffered by so many and indicated that there was still a great need for education in the medical field regarding their treatment. I wanted to talk to him about my brother's condition but chose to wait for a more appropriate moment. Mother, who had clearly had enough of war talk, put her arm through Emily's as though they had been chums for a lifetime and chimed in. "You must both stay to tea; I have a lovely joint in the oven."

Dr. Davidson replied, "I thank you very much for the invitation, but I have delayed far too long already. I have rounds to make this afternoon, and if I'm not home in time for Sunday supper, Emily's auntie will be very cross."

No amount of urging on Mother's part could sway him, but Emily piped in to say that she would very much like to stay. "I confess, I hoped I might impose on you to stay a night or two."

"It's no imposition, my dear. There's a bed already made up in the guest room."

I was delighted. "That's brilliant, Em. Alice is coming over to spend the evening, and I'm so glad you'll finally have a chance to meet."

And so, it was decided. The good doctor rose to make his departure and thanked everyone for their hospitality. He paused, and with a hint of dramatic flair, turned to face me, taking me tenderly by the shoulders. "The medical work that is being done overseas on site and under such harrowing circumstances is simply astounding. I've said this to my daughter already. Many of our young men have you to thank for their lives." Emily knew that she had always had his approval but hearing the words in person rather than in a letter was validating. "I am so proud of you both," he said, before pulling me in for another long embrace. I looked over to find Mother wiping the tears that spilled off her chin and my father choking back and blinking away moisture that was resting on his eyelashes. I thanked the good doctor for his kind words, and all the work he was doing on behalf of the lads, and then ushered him toward the door.

Emily said her quick but affectionate goodbye and turned to follow Mother to the kitchen, in search of an assignment. The two men shook hands, and I insisted, "I'll walk with you to your motorcar."

Before we reached the end of the path, I asked if I could have just a moment. He nodded. "Of course."

I explained the situation with my brother Richard and asked if he had any advice. I confess I hoped he might offer to check in on him given an opportunity. He assured me that he would do his best. "That particular convalescent home is not currently in my jurisdiction, but I will look in on him, just as a friend of the family." He nudged my arm and gave me playful wink. "One has to be careful not to step on toes, but if I can offer any insights to the staff there, I certainly will. I will report back to you as soon as I have something to offer, okay?" I was both relieved and grateful.

I thanked him and promised to pay a visit at his home in the very near future. When I returned to the house with the overnight bag that Emily had completely forgotten, I was immediately greeted by the lilting voices of two of my favourite people mingled together in jovial conversation. I decided to leave them to whatever task was at hand and join my father in the front room for a hefty glass of sherry.

A jaunty Emily greeted Alice at the door and introduced herself before I could do the honours. "No introduction needed," said Alice warmly. "I would have known you right from the off." She was too late to share our meal but joined Dad and me in the front room for a nosh while Mother and Emily put away the last of the china. She turned to me. "She is exactly as you've described her; you've found yourself a gem there, Milly dear." It was no surprise to me that Emily had won everyone over from the first moment; it was one of her many great gifts.

It was a fine clear evening, the breeze barely ruffling the leaves on the great willow while we four lounged lazily beneath. Like a snapshot in time from a bygone era, the moment was as casual and carefree as any Victorian scene. I took in every nuance, hoping to engrave it into memory. I watched as Mother casually folded nappies on her lap. She always had a supply of them on hand, while Alice and Emily continued the effortless kind of conversation that kindred spirits enjoy. I had never seen Emily in civilian clothes before and thought how pretty she looked in her pale-blue dress with its tiny yellow flowers. Mother looked like an angel in white, her silver hair glowing pink with the sun setting behind her, and Alice . . . Well, Alice was just beautiful; there was no other way to describe her, with skin the colour of ivory and perfect features framed by auburn hair. It was swooped high on her head with one miraculous comb that managed to hold everything in place except those few straggly tendrils of curl that floated past her ear bobs. She radiated goodness. At that moment, Mother rose from her chair and asked for some assistance at the house. Emily was up and out of her chair before anyone else could offer; she took two steps for every one of her older companion's as they strode together up the steep slope of the lawn. "Short legs." I grinned in Alice's direction.

The evening sky was layered in shades of pink, its reflection echoed in the bevelled panes on each side of the wide kitchen window in the distance. Mother floated in and out of its frame like the little dancing doll in a child's jewellery box. Emily was busying herself and smiling in her oh-so-natural way, and I could see their mouths moving in easy conversation.

I sat with Alice in quiet comfort but caught her watching me in short glances. Without comment, she pulled her chair closer and reached into the pocket of her apron to retrieve the small box that had been patiently waiting there for the perfect moment. "I know that you will be leaving us soon. I don't know when, but I do know that you're anxious to go," she began. She looked up the hill and continued. "Emily must have felt it too; I'm certain that's why she's here." My intuitive sister rarely misinterpreted life's signals. It was no secret that I wished to return to France, but Alice was correct. I was feeling restless. I was still in the process of weighing my options with the different volunteer organizations and had been in touch with Cicely, but I was most eager to hear Emily's thoughts before deciding.

Alice placed the little box in the palm of my hand. "My darling girl, it is my hope that you will carry this with you as you continue your journey." I opened the box and found a dainty gold locket attached to a clasp so that I might wear it as a brooch. I placed my other hand over my heart and was about to speak, but she urged me to investigate more closely. I probed the edge with my fingernail, and it popped open to reveal two tiny photographs; the faded image on one side was Alice and on the other was me.

"I snipped these from the family photo we had taken just before the war started, and hope that when you finally come home to stay, we can have new ones taken." I closed the locket and held it tight to my chest; tears welled up in my eyes as I reached over to encircle her. Before I could say anything, Alice whispered, "Behind the photos are engravings, a talisman to draw you close and keep you safe. 'Ny Tree Cassyn' stands firm beneath my image to remind you of your roots and to ensure you will always land on your feet, and 'Shee' is engraved behind yours to bring peace to your spirit and keep us always connected. Come home to us, won't you?"

We held each other tight for long moments, and I found enough voice to whisper, "Shuyr my chree," and then repeated, "Sister of my heart."

Alice pulled me away and said, "Listen for the *Sonnish*. The whispers of the strong women before us are always near and will bring you comfort in the dark days." Then she lifted out the leather cord that was tucked beneath her blouse. "Sisters of the willow, I am never without my amulet." She gave the little glass pendant I had sent her a kiss and tucked it away again. She looked up into the crown of the tree. "You see, her roots found a way to bind us even at your abbey in France."

I pinned the locket inside the bodice of my blouse and wiped the tears from my face, just as Mother and Emily returned with a decanter of sherry and four tiny crystal glasses.

Emily sat on the edge of my bed, and we tittered like schoolgirls for what must have been hours. The tea that we brought with us to the room was liberally laced with whisky. We were in our nightdresses, swaddled in blankets, and buried beneath my beautiful red-and-white quilt with the colourful appliqué tulips. Mother had made these unique treasures for all her children. The crisp white-linen nightgown that Em wore was beautifully smocked at the bodice and cuffs, and I commented on the workmanship, explaining that I had spent my life around women who were skilled seamstresses. My nightdress was a finer fabric than those we had worn overseas, but still, as was always my style, it was buttoned up to my neck. This one had a little lace ruffle at the collar that irritated my already sensitive skin.

Several glasses of sherry and a few ounces of whisky were enough to sooth my inhibitions, and I happily engaged in the giggle and gossip session. We spoke irreverently about the many characters we had come to know in our travels overseas and chuckled over some of our mishaps. It felt so good to shed the serious overcoats we'd been wearing for so long. Our conversation went from hilarity to tears and back again many times over.

Eventually there was a lull in the banter, and I turned my back to Em for just a moment, unfastening the top three satin-covered buttons on my nightdress and lifting out my new locket to show her. Emily leaned in to see the photos inside and paid all the compliments and praises that one might expect. She fell quiet though, and I sensed a shadow. It was fleeting but still concerned me.

"What is it?" I asked.

She faltered but said finally, "Mill, we've known each other a long time, we've been through hell and back, but still . . . you're so shy that you have to turn away just to undo a couple of buttons."

I felt suddenly wounded, but she continued cautiously. "I've seen the scars on your neck; you don't have to hide them from me."

I was uncomfortable about the abrupt change in direction the conversation had taken, and as always, I was embarrassed about my scars and reluctant to confide something so personal. I looked into the kind and gentle eyes of my friend and knew that, no matter what, I would find unconditional approval in them. Emily had an intuitive sense of timing; she remained quiet and still until I found the strength to concede that trust was an honour she had earned. The tender velvet chain that bound us tugged at me as I unfastened the remaining buttons on my bodice and held open the front of the nightdress to reveal the ugliness of my scars. I watched her face for a sign of revulsion, but her expression did not change. In her eyes, I found only a reflection of my pain and an echo of the affection we felt for each other. I lifted my chin and ran my fingers from jawline down to where the tangle of melted flesh turned into normal skin just below the breastbone. Although faded a little over time, the hideous welts that had been there since early childhood remained silvery pink and shiny. They scarred my soul like a birthmark. Emily reached for my hand and held it to her heart. She needed no explanation; she wanted only to comfort and assure me. I found my heart in the heart of my friend and wept.

"Certain people are sent to us," I said, "by nature or the universe or whatever deity you believe in." She smiled in agreement, and we held each other close.

I explained what I knew of the burns that had torn my flesh. "They are the result of a botched medical treatment when I was very young. Truth be told, I don't remember any details. I have no recollection of my surroundings or the people who were with me at the time. I remember only pain and darkness, sensations that come back in my dreams from time to time. My mother has always rebuffed my questions, insisting that it serves no purpose to quite literally open and revisit old wounds. Alice was the only one who ever spoke to me about it and simply said that I had been an extremely sick wee bairn, profoundly ill with a dangerously high fever and a horrible cough that left me struggling for breath. Mother had been bedridden with pneumonia at the time and was unable to care for me, and so the family was obliged to accept help from a local lady. I don't know if Alice was taken ill as well or just too busy with her own young family to be of assistance."

I must remember to ask her about that. Stoically, I continued, "The mustard plasters that she administered were, as I understand it, left in place for far too long, and she'd neglected to coat my skin with goose grease before applying them." In a failed effort to sound magnanimous, I added, "I suppose she had her hands full, caring for Mother and chasing around after my brothers." With a shudder, I continued. "When the plasters were removed, several layers of skin came off with them; third-degree burns I am told." I felt suddenly exposed, as though my scars were glowing more brightly red by the moment, and I felt compelled to draw closed the bodice of my nightdress. "Alice says that they are evidence that I fought hard to stay alive."

Emily did not cringe or condemn. She sympathized. "I hate that you went through such an abysmal ordeal, and so young. I think Alice was right. You survived, and I for one am grateful for that." She smiled. "Nature and nurture have worked in equal measure to help you overcome those horrifying memories, and perhaps that dreadful chapter is in part responsible for the empathy and care you've been able to share with others." She smiled again and tried to coax a little one from me, finally succeeding.

My wounds were nothing compared to burn victims we had seen overseas, and I was a little embarrassed at my own self-pity. It was time to move on to a new subject. I swung my feet off the bed and grabbed Emily's hand as I moved across the room. I decided in that moment that I could trust this dear pixie with even the most intimate secrets of my family and what had started as a whisper turned into a conversation. I revealed to her the secret compartment—the hidden box in the drawer of my vanity that housed my most prized possessions. We talked about the willow and my female ancestors from the Isle of Man, and I surprised myself at how much I remembered of the old stories and the ancient language. "We are all connected, you know, linked past and present." I struggled a moment to find an adequate example, but it was right in front of me. "Like the squares on this beautiful quilt. Separate and different, they all work together, supported in their connection and with a solid foundation beneath."

I confided to her about the *Sonnish*. "They are whispers that you hear with your heart," I told her. "They only come to those who are still and listen very carefully with a free and open mind. They bring you *Shee*, a feeling of spirit and peace."

Emily sat in mesmerized silence, and I had not noticed her tears until my narration came to an end. As I sidled closer to her, she confessed, "I envy you. I truly do. I grew up without a mother or sisters or any real connection to the women in my history. Dad has done his best, and I have aunties who have cared for me, but I have not experienced the kind of bond that you share with the women in your family. I have a better understanding now of the amulet," she said. "I respected its significance without considering the power that it represents. What was the phrase that you spoke to me at the abbey?"

I wiped her tears with my hanky. "I didn't know you'd heard me; you were quite delirious at the time."

"It was something about sisters. Wasn't it?"

I wrapped my arm more tightly around her shoulder and declared, "You are family to me, Em; I felt it from the start. Another marvellous thread in our tapestry, another patch for my quilt. That's what I said to you when you were so ill, I simply whispered, *"Shuyr my chree.* Sister of my heart.""

Chapter Nine

Alice had indeed read the signs correctly. Within a fortnight, the tearful goodbyes were behind us and a new adventure had begun. In the end, all three friends decided to join the WAAC, although Cicely chose to undergo training in special communications, which would take her in a different direction. Upgraded ambulance and mechanical training was mandated, but we breezed through it. The final step was the interview process, where our significant previous experience was discussed in detail and the documents of recommendation from the abbey and the French Red Cross were read aloud. We were immediately approved for active service and given an efficiency stripe, which was simply a length of scarlet braid to be worn on the uniform to signify that we had more than one year of wartime experience. We were told that it would be a few days before our travel orders were cut, and in the interim, we were permitted leave. So, we decided to relax and see the sights of London.

"Milly, I believe you look even taller in your new uniform."

We sized up our reflections in the store window. "Nonsense. I believe you have lost six inches, my squat little friend," I replied. I draped my arm over her shoulder for effect, and her reflection shrunk under the weight of it. "Okay," I said, "get off your knees. Let's have at it. What shall we do first?"

Without hesitation, Emily responded enthusiastically. "Let's book ourselves a posh room at one of the hotels and carry on from there. I've loads of dosh, and I don't mean to spend it wisely."

We did just that, depositing our cases and stepping out onto the streets of London in search of some fun. We had been in and around the city for some time but too busy with interviews and the like to really take stock of our surroundings. In what might have appeared a choreographed move, we simultaneously turned our heads and swivelled around to get a better look at a group of girls lingering outside a movie cinema, all with short hair and too-short skirts. Most of them were smoking. We nattered like a couple of old hens about the changes in fashion and the behaviour among women since the start of the war. The streets were alive with activity; people on bicycles fought for position around lorries and automobiles. Magnificent signs and placards adorned the brick facades, and crowds of people bustled about; many were in uniform but many more were not. A group of school children followed their teacher, who was carrying a placard that read, "We growing children must have bread and sugar."

News of the war was everywhere. I pointed to a massive poster on the side of a building, and we chuckled about the wording: "Queen Mary's Army Auxiliary Corps. The GIRL behind the man behind the gun." It was much like the poster that Cicely had shown us on the train in France; it conveyed an image of a bright, smiling young woman in uniform.

"Well, I suppose it lived up to its promise," I said, posing like a model for the picture. We were dressed head to toe in the exact uniform advertised on the poster. It consisted of a military-style jacket, full skirt, brown stockings and shoes, shirt, tie, and a great coat. We each wore a soft peaked cap, which indicated that we would be doing overseas service, and a bronze badge on the front of the cap bearing the letters "WAAC."

We happened upon the site of one of the airship bombings where a group of buildings had been laid to rubble, and although we did not know if there had been casualties in this particular attack, we took a moment to pay our respects. In Europe, we were witness to this type of devastation on a massive scale, but it tore at our heartstrings that the enemy had found a way to target civilians at home. I pushed around the rubble with my shoe and uncovered a piece of pottery that had broken cleanly into three pieces. I held them together and decided that a little cement glue would return the little swordfish to its former glory. Emily found a little porcelain figurine and didn't seem to mind that its arm was missing. We were about to walk away when I caught a glimpse of something shiny. Sweeping away some stone dust, I discovered a rosary completely intact with crucifix.

I looked up at Emily, who said, "I know what you're thinking, but it would be impossible to find the owner. You know it would." Nodding in agreement, I tucked the beads into my satchel along with the fragments of swordfish, which I had gingerly swaddled in my hanky.

We made our way to Buckingham Palace and lingered outside the gates, hoping for a glimpse of a monarch who wasn't there at the time. Still, we were enthralled and devoutly proud that our king had been to the western front to show support to his troops. After a bite of supper, we ended our adventure with an evening of entertainment at the Gaiety Theatre, excited to see a musical play called *Theodore and Co.* We loved all the music, and although Ivor Novello's tunes were beautiful, I favoured those written by Mr. Kern. We girls—and we were feeling like girls for a change—sang the melodies as we strolled arm in arm back to the hotel. "That Come Hither Look" was still repeating in my mind as I sank into the pillow and stared up at the ornate ceiling.

Only three days later, we were on our way to Folkestone station to meet the ship that would take us back to France. We had little to say during the first leg of the journey, still savouring the memories of our magical holiday in London, both silently apprehensive.

We reported to the matron in her tented office, and I noted immediately that beneath the hard exterior were kindly eyes in need of sleep. The weight of her responsibility was evident. This was not just a hospital. It was also a military post where once only a man would have played a role in leadership. For medical professionals and volunteers, the lines that were so boldly drawn in the beginning had blurred out of necessity, and in many cases gender roles had become moot. Volunteer Aid Detachment members (VADs) had earned their place, and hospitals had become better equipped and more efficiently designed for mass casualties. I was grateful to see wooden walkways all over the camp to alleviate some of the mud issues we'd experienced at the CCS. Emily and I were billeted in a small tent with two other girls. Its proximity to the wash tent was especially appealing. Beneath each bunk was the mandatory chamber pot and stacked neatly on the end of each metal cot was clean bedding—our first order of business. I shed my coat and set to work making the bed.

"Come on, Em, let's get to it." The matron had given us the remainder of the day to familiarize ourselves, and so we began our tour of the hospital and its surroundings.

The camp was alive with activity. Bustling all around like busy ants on their ever-expanding hill were soldiers, patients, people pushing wheelchairs or in them, nurses and orderlies, VADs and doctors. It was a blur of colour; patients in blue housecoats lingered outside the wards, puffing on cigarettes, while VADs fluttered in and out of the tents in blue dresses with crisp white aprons and white starched collars. Laundry attendants in blue caps peeked around the linens dancing in the breeze, and nursing sisters floated about in muted grey dresses and capes of burgundy or purple, depending on their rank. Everything and everyone else blended into monochrome dreary shades of khaki.

On the ring-road around the camp, and on the smaller roads running through it, was a cavalcade of moving parts: ambulances, cars, horse-drawn carts, motorcycles, and even a few bicycles. "Good Lord, Mil, it's like a city!" exclaimed Emily.

I agreed. "I hope that the fighting doesn't get so close that we have to pack up this lot and move!"

The huts and buildings were strategically placed and clearly signed, and there was the sense that the military had a much greater influence here than it had in our first posting. In many ways, it was more military than medical. The operating theatres were set up in a large building that had once been a school, complete with running water and electric light. We popped in to make our introductions to the quartermaster in the "Great Stores Hut," knowing that this would be a good fellow to befriend. Floor-to-ceiling shelves lined walls laden with everything that had been in short supply at the abbey: clothing, linens, rope, lanterns, canned goods, boots, wire, paper products, and on and on. There was another hut dedicated to pharmaceutical supplies, which was well equipped with stacks of medicines, bandages, and instruments, but the sour nurse in charge had no time for introductions or niceties. Clean linens hung from lines strung behind and between buildings, and rows upon rows of bleached bandages blew in the breeze, almost dry enough to be rolled and reused. We ended our tour in the mess tent for a cup of coffee, having made the deliberate decision to avoid the wards for one more day. We also chose to wait until the next day to present ourselves to the lieutenant in charge of the motor pool.

Just as I was lifting the cup of steaming coffee to my lips, I was jolted by a bouncy girl who plunked herself down on the bench and announced in an all-too-squeaky voice, "Hello, I'm Dotty! We're to be bunkies!"

I heard my brain say, *Of course you are*, and hoped that the words hadn't actually spilled out of my mouth. I shook the extended hand, smiling politely, and turned to introduce Emily but not quickly enough. The squeaky voice beat me to it. "Hello, I'm Dotty!" she had already moved around the table to sit next to Em. "Now, we've just to wait a moment, and—oh, never mind, here she is. Ladies, this is Nora. We're all just going to be marvellous friends."

Nora, who was tall and slender with a dark complexion and sad eyes, took the now vacant seat next to me and looked across the table with an exasperated expression, saying in a rich, deep voice, "Dotty, take a breath. Just slow down, for pity's sake, and take a breath." She didn't sound unkind, just tired and mildly annoyed. Dotty did as she was told without losing her jaunty demeanour. She sat next to Emily, twitching with excitement until an appropriate moment to jump back into the conversation presented itself. Over a second cup of coffee, we four young women became acquainted.

Dotty Hampstead was a relatively new arrival. From Kent, in the South of England, she's been in training to be a ballet dancer when a bomb from a German airship had laid flat her school just outside London. It was at that point that she'd decided to become involved and had signed up for service as a VAD, much to her parent's dismay. The petite blonde girl, with her hair tied snuggly behind her cap, brazenly rolled her tiny shoulders up and back, saying, "Cowards, the lot of them. Crossing the Channel to drop bombs on civilians. I'll show them guts. There's not a one of those blighters could stand on their toes as long as I can." She won me over with that one feisty (albeit squeaky) speech.

Nora Carpenter was a little less forthcoming with her story, but with some prodding from "Squeak" (as we would forever refer to her), we learned a little about the more sullen girl. Two of her brothers had died in the Battle of Verdun and a third was missing in action. When last she'd had word, his battalion was engaged in the fighting on one side of the Somme River or the other, she wasn't sure. She hoped that, by being closer to the conflict, there might be a chance to find him, or at the very least, learn his fate. She had been at the hospital for several months already, and without looking up from the cup cradled in her hands, she lamented, "Every time I bathe the blood and mud from one of our lads, I hope to find Alex underneath it all."

I felt her words keenly; I hadn't received word of my own brother in some time. There was an uncomfortable lull in the conversation, which gave Squeak the opportunity she had been waiting for. In a flurry of movement, she fluffed out the veil on her cap, pirouetted out of her seat, and addressed the table. "Have you seen the barn?"

We followed her out of the mess tent and made our way across the camp just as the sun was beginning its descent on the horizon and the air grew still. We approached a farmyard complete with chickens, goats, and cattle, several small buildings, a hayloft, and a large barn. Beyond that, I noticed a wooded area and a stream that was lined with willow, ash, and poplar trees. My heart fluttered and skipped a beat. Emily linked arms with mine and said, "Perhaps a picnic. What do you think?"

I winked back at her as we lagged behind our would-be roommates and whispered, "Why do we need to see a barn, do you think?"

Before Em could respond, the doors of the building swung open, and my question was answered. In an amazing feat of restoration, the barn had been transformed into a theatre. In front of us was a fine stage with backdrops and painted scenery, props and plants, and even a drop curtain. All along the sides of the gigantic space were stacks of baled hay, and in front were rows of chairs that formed a band pit. Further back were more hay bales for seating. Strings of lanterns hung from the rafters, and tiny stars fashioned from hammered tin dangled above. Nora spoke first with a little more lift in her voice than we had previously heard.

"We have entertainment of all kinds here," she said, "and it's wonderful for the men. We've had plays and skits, juggling acts, and even boxing matches from time to time. There are musical instruments in the back, and the band gathers together from whoever happens to be here at the time."

Squeak piped in. "There's been some big stars come to entertain from Britain. Lena Ashwell was here, before I arrived of course," she stated with a pout. Then she looked up and said, "It's so pretty at night. You can see the moon through the barn boards, and the lanterns dance light on the tin stars that hang there."

"She's quite right," Nora added. "There's meant to be a concert on Saturday, barring any big assault that day. The fellows on staff are good for a laugh, and there are usually a few blokes in the wards who are fit enough for a dance, if the nursing sisters keep themselves busy—"

She was interrupted by the chilling sound of a siren, and the four of us sprinted across the farmyard toward the wooden pathways where only a brisk pace was allowed. We donned the gas masks that were hanging on our bedposts and made our way back to the mess tent to rendezvous with others not currently on duty. The new gas masks were far more sophisticated than the small box respirators that had been issued following the first gas attacks, but even these were heavy and cumbersome. Still, having witnessed what the deadly invisible menace could do, I had no objection to wearing the monstrous-looking gear. I knew that masks would be hanging by each bed in the wards and that the nurses would be scrambling to ensure all their patients were safely accessorized. Standing next to a terrified-looking Squeak, I lifted the muzzle briefly and said, "You think this lot looks frightening, you know they've even developed these things to fit the dogs and horses up on the front line. Imagine that now." Stealthy and silent, the deadly gas was not particular; it assaulted anyone in its path. The all-clear sounded, the masks came off, and the camp was once again abuzz with activity.

By the end of the week, Emily and I had fallen into pace with our new surroundings and routine, but we could feel the eyes of our superiors taking stock of every move we made. I resented having to prove my worth all over again, but Emily, ever the pragmatist, reminded me that the references we presented on arrival were just words on paper. Digging in our heels, we set about proving the integrity of the endorsements we had earned at our last post. It didn't take very long. Several major assaults occurred within days of one another, filling the hospital wards to overflowing and offering us an opportunity to show our mettle.

There were always wounded to be picked up at a casualty clearing station or transferred to a specialty hospital. Daily runs, sometimes hourly, were part of the routine. Snipers and small skirmishes were a constant, but when there was an all-out offensive or a big assault, the hospital would receive some warning about the number of wounded to be expected. I felt pain in the pit of my stomach every time such an announcement was made. It never got easier. I waited anxiously behind the steering wheel of my vehicle, saying a silent prayer to those in the universe who would help me, and then took my turn in the convoy to retrieve the lads—sometimes hundreds all in one night. As soon as our duties as drivers were complete, we donned an apron and lent a hand in the wards, doing everything from transcribing information onto charts to blanket bathing the poor wretched souls.

Weeks turned into months, and we once again earned our place as valued members of the well-oiled machine that was the base hospital. I had to remind myself now and again that I really had no medical training. In the beginning, I'd guided horse-drawn ambulance carts and cared for the animals, drove motorized ambulances, and repaired mechanical issues. Helping to lift a litter onto the vehicle was the only impact I'd had on a patient during those first weeks on the western front, but as time marched on and my aptitude for the work became apparent, I was called upon to help the medics administer first aid and in general offer an extra pair of hands in the field and on the wards. The nursing sisters found my medical instincts to be sound and approved of my no-nonsense character. My inquisitive nature rubbed the doctors the wrong way at times, and once again, I was fortunate to have Emily as both a buffer and a sounding board.

Em affectionately referred to me as "the nose," because I had an uncanny ability to diagnose an injury by its smell. It would never have occurred to her that it also described my rather obvious proboscis. The medical staff was well versed in the odours associated with different wounds, but as a layman, I proved a quick study. I could sniff out infection in my sleep and a case of trench foot from across the camp. Sadly, I would turn to a nursing sister as she lowered a patient into his bunk and quietly say, "Gangrene. I could smell almonds right away." Sadder still, I was most often right. Most amazing was that I could separate those smells from all the other horrendous odours associated with these poor souls. Many, who hadn't bathed in weeks, stank of sweat, feces, urine, vomit, damp, and mould. Their breath was foul from poor hygiene, cigarettes, and bad food.

One night, as I helped in the gentle bathing of the broken body in my care, I watched as the water made tracks through the blood and mud on his skin like gruesome tattoos. He didn't speak. He couldn't speak. I thought of my brothers as I squeezed the murky mess from the sponge and rinsed it in the basin, all the while watching his eyes and knowing that the fear I saw there would not be so easily eliminated.

Emily's aptitude for nursing was obvious to all, and in short order, she was assigned VAD duties and an appropriate uniform. It was a seamless transfer, and I was pleased that my friend was finally serving the role best suited to her talents and personality. While I had some natural adeptness at the technicalities of nursing, I lacked the nurturing gifts that Emily brought to the work, and so I remained content in my duties as driver and medic. I maintained my credo that, to survive in this environment, I needed to remain detached from the personalities in my care, but there were times when it was difficult to abide by my own philosophy. I worked hard and did whatever was needed but tried not to linger on the wards or get to know the boys in the way that Emily did.

"I don't know how you do it," I said to my cherished friend. "You hold their hands and listen to them talk about home, knowing all the while that they will surely die." I lifted my head up off the pillow and leaned on my elbow to look at Emily, lying on the cot across from mine. "I'm glad they have you."

Emily, who rarely looked glum, simply responded, "I'm glad they have you too, otherwise many more of them would die alone on the battlefield. We all do what we do best."

I loved her, and had from the first moment, if I was truthful. Together, we had gone from wide-eyed adventurers to characters in a nightmare all in the span of single day, and neither of us could imagine what it would have been like if we had not met on the train that first day. In the months that followed, we shared our innermost thoughts and fears, cried and argued on occasion, and had become family in every sense. Emily knew my faults and weaknesses without condemning me for them; likewise, I overlooked Emily's few shortcomings. With a rhythm much like that of an old married couple, we finished each other's sentences and found humorous moments in the grim of every day, tittering quietly in our tent about a slip in the mud or a sour-faced nurse before falling into exhausted sleep. We were both fond of our other roommates, but the bond between us was something special.

"Are you alright, Em?" I asked. "You don't seem quite yourself the past few days."

"I just miss you; that's all."

We had not seen much of each other lately. I had been loaned out temporarily to the CCS about five miles from the front, sharing a tent with only one other gal whose name I could never remember and spending about equal time in the two places for the past two months. I pondered at the subtle changes in my friend. I wondered if there had been tensions in our tent during my frequent absences; three women versus four could make for a quite different dynamic. I was loath to enter into a conversation on the subject though, as personality conflicts and melodrama smacked in the face of my desire for order and discipline, and I avoided them at all costs.

Emily was lying flat on her cot with her hands behind her head, staring upward. I tried to lighten the mood. "It's good to be back. What's-her-name snores loud enough to drown out the bomb blasts up there." An awkward silence remained. The candle flickered in the lantern, casting mesmerizing shadows on the tent, and with Squeak and Nora on night duty, there was a calm quietness to be enjoyed. I rested my eyes.

"What's she like?" asked Emily in an uncharacteristically sarcastic tone. "Your new friend."

"What?"

"Is she attractive? Funny? Is she good company?"

"My God, Em, anyone would think you were jealous. Don't be daft. I don't know anything about her except that she's a pretty decent medic. That's all that matters to me. I think you've been hanging about with our wee blonde friend a little too much; it seems that drama follows her like a shadow. Let's not have any of that." Squeak, who was amiable with the staff and adored by the patients, danced blithely from one horrifying day to the next. She could be a ridiculous flirt and was often scolded by the sisters for dawdling outside a tent with the men who were smoking. She had a pretty face and insisted on keeping her blonde hair long, unlike many of us who favoured the common-sense practice of a cropped hairstyle. Her solution to avoiding lice was to pull her hair up into tight braids tucked neatly under a snug cap beneath her veil. The overall effect made her face look taut, as though she was always surprised about something, and her already wide smile seemed to stretch from ear to ear. She was charming and carefree, naïve to the point of embarrassing at times, never quite understanding the joke or innuendo in a conversation, but the fellows were smitten. Those who were able stood patiently in line for their turn to dance with her at the barn.

Em responded. "I know what you mean. She seems forever in hot water with Sister Fitzgerald." She lowered her voice and continued. "She is a singularly sour old curmudgeon, but it doesn't seem to bother Squeak at all. She just smiles and nods and carries on as before. Anyway, you're right of course. She may be leading me astray. I'm sorry. Just tired I guess."

I wasn't convinced. "Are you sure that's all?"

She was still lying on her back, staring at the crown of the tent, and hesitated a few moments before asking, "Do you remember Sergeant Miller?" I shrugged. There were so many men, so many names. "He was the bloke that took our photographs here a couple of months ago."

"Oh right, sure I remember. A real comic. He's around here quite often, isn't he? Quite smitten with you, I think," I teased but did not get a response. "What about him?"

"They brought him in beginning of last week. Gassed." There was a long pause before she said, "Doc says his retinas are too badly damaged. He'll never get his eyesight back."

"Oh, Em, I am sorry. I know you're fond of him." Sergeant Miller was one of many photojournalists who risked their lives capturing the war on film. He would return from the trenches filthy and exhausted, having followed a battalion into battle, but would not rest until his treasured photographs were brought to life. He shared a darkroom down the hall from one of the operating theatres and would remain there until the tragic images were safely sealed in an envelope and sent to the *Daily Telegraph* in London. Once cleaned up, he was most often found on the wards, kibitzing with the boys, but in his work, he was genuine in his desire to pay homage to their sacrifices. Amiable and funny, he charmed the nurses and volunteers, but he was particularly fond of Emily. He commented often that she had a special way with his boys, a "real gift."

When he wasn't in the field, his camera was set up at the hospital to take portraits for the fellows to send home, and on one such a day, he offered to take photos of Emily and me. I remembered how we primped and preened for the opportunity to be captured on film.

I was lost in thought until Emily sat up abruptly and reached under her bed to retrieve a canvas case she had stored there out of sight. She set it on the bed and looked over at me. "He wants me to have it." She lifted out a beautiful wood and brass camera and dusted off non-existent particles. "As usual, he made a joke of it," she said sadly.

After a moment, she continued. "He announced, as though congrats were in order, 'It's of no use to me anymore. Anyway, once they have me fitted for my eyepatches, I'll have my new career as a pirate to keep me busy.'"

Em shook her head slowly. "I assumed the camera was army issue, but he assured me that he had purchased it himself. It was his property to do with as he pleased." She paused, but I knew not to comment. I waited. Finally, she murmured, "I know we're not meant to accept gifts, and I argued the point with him, but he was adamant. I wasn't sure what to do." She reached into a side pocket on the case and pulled out a small envelope, which she handed across to me. Inside was an image of Emily taken seated on a stool in her great coat and hat, and a similar image of me. The best by far was the photograph of the two of us standing side by side. "He was kind enough to make two copies so that we might each have a set."

I held the packet to my chest and said, "I will treasure these, as I know you will. You must tell the matron exactly what you've said to me. It would be too difficult to keep something this size a secret, and I think it's better to be up front about it. Don't you? I'm sure she'll have no objection." I wasn't sure, but it still seemed good advice.

Fortunately, I was right. Matron spoke to Sergeant Miller about it as she pinned a coloured tag to his jacket. She reached for his hand and squeezed it tightly. "Your service here is appreciated, Sergeant, and I expect the images you've captured will be of great historic value. Let us hope they will function as a deterrent for conflict in the future."

Emily wheeled him out of the ward and helped him onto the vehicle that served as a convoy for all those with Blighty tickets who were bound for home. Some would return after a period of convalescence in a British hospital but many like Sergeant Miller were considered unfit to return to duty.

Matron turned to a tearful Emily and said, "Keep your gift out of sight and send it home for safe keeping at your first opportunity. Now cheer up. You will be happy to hear that they have found a replacement for Miss Aspinall here. She's only one more week left at the CCS. Alright then?" Emily's mouth formed a smile as she looked up at me. Then matron snapped, "Now, you're needed in the officer's ward. There are dressings to be changed. Miss Aspinall, what duties are you neglecting at this moment."

"On my way." I was pleased. It had been a tedious couple of months.

Emily remarked later that day, "Thank goodness, you'll be back in time for our rehearsal next weekend. I don't seem to have your flair for rallying the girls."

"How is the act coming along?" I asked, grateful that my friend's mood had brightened a little.

"Not too badly, and the girls seem to be enjoying it, except that Squeak tries a little too hard when she's in charge. I know she's very talented, but leadership is not her strong suit. It really will be so much better when you get back for regular rehearsals." Her confidence in my abilities was always a boon to my ego.

Born from a need to bring light into a dismal time, the occasional evenings of entertainment in the barn seemed to keep the unit together, and the makeshift stage attracted acts of all kinds. If an established theatrical company were in the area, an elaborate show complete with costumes and music would bring joy and laughter for however brief an interval, but in the absence of a "real act," anything would do. Jugglers, sing-a-longs, solo performances, and even poetry readings were well attended and applauded.

On a miserable wet evening following several long days of mass casualties, we four roommates had been sitting over a cup of hot chocolate in the mess tent, commiserating that there were no "acts" on the schedule. I had been listening to the moaning for what I deemed quite long enough, and so I'd piped in, "The problem is that the acts are always male, and the men are transient. We're the constant here." I had looked at the weary and wary faces of my friends and decided to wade in a little further. "Women make up the vast majority of the staff here, and I'm sure there must be more than a few who have talents above and beyond rolling bandages."

"Well, not me," Nora had groaned. "You'll not get me up there, making a fool of myself."

"I'm not suggesting that everyone need be involved, but surely we could put together a troupe of some sort that could entertain when there isn't a specific act on the roster."

"Do you think the lads would be at all interested?" had asked a timid Emily, doing her best to hide under the table in fear of being volunteered.

I laughed. "You must be joking. This randy lot? You know they'd commit murder to see a flash of ankle up on that stage. It won't matter a lick if we have any talent other than that."

Squeak had jumped in. "Give me my toe shoes and a tutu, and I'll show them a hell of a lot more than ankles." We'd twisted around to be sure none of the nursing sisters were within earshot. "Milly's troupe, we'll call it."

I'd shaken my head. "I'm happy to get the ball rolling, but I draw the line at putting my name to it."

Guardedly excited about this new venture, I'd visited the matron, who was busy in her office as usual. Speech prepared, I'd explained the rationale and the idea and asked for permission to organize a troupe and been surprised to receive an almost immediate and positive response; in fact, she'd insinuated that she would join herself if it were not for propriety.

"I don't imagine it would be considered dignified," she had mused. "However, I do think, perhaps, that this is exactly what we need to lift spirits around here." Her radical discourse had been followed by a list of rules that must be followed. Hardly able to contain my excitement, I had shaken her hand, agreeing to take on the mantle of leadership and the hard hat of responsibility. Then I'd begun soliciting the women in all areas of the hospital, putting "No-Nonsense Nora" in charge of the talent list. It had been a short list at first, as many were shy and some were afraid the matron would do an about-face, but before week's end, I had made a start. There would be no auditions for the chorus, but soloists and dancers would have to show me a sample of their work. I had four women who could be called upon to play the piano depending on the work roster, several who played brass instruments, and two violinists.

Within weeks, the troupe started shaping up, and my enthusiasm spilled over during a late-night conversation in the tent.

"I've been hoping to do something like this for a long time."

Squeak responded. "Really, Milly? I had no idea you had such ambitions."

In my current mood, I shared a little more. "I got another letter from Cicely today." Emily and I had spoken often about our previous experiences and about the wonderful women at Royaumont, but letters from our old comrades were rare, and I was especially excited about this one. Before I could continue, Nora reached under her bed and produced the book I had loaned her recently. She piped in with a degree of cynicism in her voice that I recognized immediately as an invitation for a debate; we had them often. Even with all the seriousness of life around us, a good political or philosophical discussion made me feel closer to home. Emily was too passive for such banter, and Squeak didn't seem particularly interested, but Nora proved a worthy foil. She rarely spoke of personal matters but could offer robust commentary about world affairs and life in general.

"Your Cicely certainly has some controversial attitudes. "*Marriage as a Trade*," she said, holding up the book, "certainly lampoons the whole notion of marital bliss, doesn't it? I can only imagine the hackles rising on some of her readers and all of their husbands." With a sly grin, she added, "She's a big name though, especially in certain circles."

I jumped into the debate, although I wasn't sure what she'd meant by her last comment. "In our household, hers was one of many important names and voices in the pursuit of women's suffrage, and I've discussed this book with her. She's not so much anti-marriage as she is pro-liberty for women."

Nora looked skeptical. "She states pretty clearly that otherwise smart women are being damaged intellectually, especially in the British education system, because they're brought up to look for success only in the marriage market."

"Well, I think that's been true up until now, but I believe the war has already changed many old attitudes. We're all doing jobs that 'genteel women' were considered unfit for a few years ago." I snubbed my nose in the air for effect.

Squeak, who had been quietly taking in the conversation, said, "Good Lord, what's wrong with learning to be a good wife?"

We both turned to look at her, but I spoke first. "Not a thing, little one. It's all about rights and choices. The right to a complete education, the right to vote and participate in government, the right to work and be paid equivalent to men, and the right to choose what is best for you as a person. Your achievements as a dancer already meet the criteria for an alternative route to success outside of marriage. Cicely is just one of many who are advocating for social change, and I'm with her all the way." I wasn't sure why I felt the need to endorse my old friend, but once on a roll, I struggled to quiet my enthusiasm. "She isn't just an author; she's also a successful actor and playwright. She put her lucrative career on hold to volunteer at the abbey and worked as we all did through the nightmare of the Somme. Now she's with the WAAC and runs a postal unit over here." I took in a deep calming breath.

Squeak seemed appeased, and Nora apologized for interrupting, asking what Cicely had to say in her letter.

"She reminded me of the entertainment we used to put on for the patients at the abbey, pantomimes and skits mostly. Cicely wrote them." I looked toward Emily for affirmation and got it with a nod. "Even the language barrier didn't seem to matter. The boys—French, Austrian, whatever—they just appreciated the effort." I turned my attention back to Squeak and said,

"Now, she's joined forces with your big star Lena Ashwell and formed a repertory company. She's writing plays and performing concerts at the front for all the Allied soldiers."

Nora, who was sitting up on the bed with her arms wrapped around her knees, spoke up. "Hence, the new enthusiasm about our troupe?" It was more of a statement than a question, but I volunteered.

"I know our little troupe won't be on such a grand scale, but I'm thrilled that we're going to at least try to follow suit. Our intentions are the same, and our hearts are in the right place. I think that's what matters, and I really believe we can do some good here."

Emily was eager to join in at this point in the conversation. "Cicely is really something special, and I believe she'll be proud to learn about our little troupe."

Nora spoke directly to Emily. "You haven't had much to say about dear Cicely's social rhetoric. Any views on those, Emily?"

"I've never found fault in any of her thinking. She's written another book, but we haven't been able to get our hands on a copy. Have we, Mil? I don't remember what it's called, but it's sure to be a dilly." She looked over at me then, almost apologetic. "I didn't have a great deal to add to our evening deliberations at the abbey, but I was a good listener."

Nora turned on her cot to face Emily, and teasingly said, "Sharing nightly rendezvous at the abbey? How risqué!"

The slightly intimidated girl did not respond, but her closed-up body language indicated that she'd had enough of the conversation. An odd uncomfortable veil hovered in the air, with only Squeak remaining oblivious. I had noticed tension between the two women a few times before but assumed there had been some disagreement during my absence. I had no interest in delving into whatever ridiculous drama was going on, nor was I about to let it ruin my good mood. So, I continued. "I've always felt inspired by our Miss Cicely." I glanced at Emily with a smile. "She is the very reason we found our way to France in the first place." The conversation ended soon after, and the candles were extinguished.

The weather turned fine, and "we four" (as we often referred to ourselves) sat at one of the outdoor tables, finishing our steaming bowls of split-pea soup. We had been told there was another big push expected that night, and so the day was spent preparing the wards, the surgical theatres, and the vehicles. As usual, it was a solemn, retrospective time in the hours before the first of the casualties arrived. I broke the silence.

"The will-o'-the-wisp."

"What?" Emily lifted her head from the bowl where she'd been breathing in the steam to help her blocked sinuses. We had all had terrible head colds.

I pointed in the direction of the marshy field just beside the barn, and there in the dusk, dancing on the mist, were the pale-blue flames of the fairies. "The will-o'-the-wisp," I repeated, "that's what we'll call the troupe."

"I like it!" exclaimed Squeak.

"Alluring and misleading," said Nora in the huskiest, sexiest voice she could muster, just for effect. "That's what will-o'-the-wisp means."

"Perfect," I said, "We'll lure them in and mislead them with Madame Tutu over there." We threw back our heads in laughter until the intrusive siren sounded, and the moment passed.

The troupe was organized and in full swing when I'd learned that I was to be shared in equal measure with the casualty clearing station a few miles closer to the fighting. I'd spent as much time as I could with the troupe during those agonizing eight weeks, and when my double duty was finally over, I approached the barn to find rehearsals under way. As Emily had indicated, Squeak was doing her utmost to annoy everyone, which brought about a round of applause at my arrival. I genuinely thanked my little friend for all her hard work in keeping the momentum going in my absence and then asked everyone to take a seat for a moment.

"I checked the schedule," I announced, "and I'm happy to say that we have guest performers signed up for this Saturday." There was a hearty round of applause. "But as of now, there is nothing on the schedule for the following weekend. I suggest we be ready to make our debut at that time, just in time for Christmas." The terrified expressions on their faces told me that these women felt ill-prepared, but I assured them they would be ready.

"We'll meet every chance we get between now and then, and I promise you a standing ovation." I hoped that my outward voice sounded more convincing than the doubtful one inside my head. "Ladies of the ensemble, are you with me?" I shouted with authority. I would have preferred a more resounding response but had to make do with a few muted utterances of agreement. Emily was along for the ride; it seemed that anything I suggested was a good idea to her. She wasn't much of a singer, and stage presence wasn't in her wheelhouse, but she was an enthusiastic and positive influence around the nay-sayers.

Two weeks later, the Will-o'-the-Wisp took the stage for the first time and received the standing ovation I had promised even before they had sung a single note. Doctors, patients, nurses, orderlies, VADs, and visitors were all on their feet more as a tribute to these marvellous women than to any great anticipation of musical talent. The reason didn't matter. The support was there. The result was a jolt of encouragement that inspired the performers to overcome their stage fright and earned unbridled applause at the end of each number. The show went off without a hitch, ending with a stunning performance by our resident ballerina.

Chapter Ten

In 1917, one battle led to another, and the wounded kept coming. The fields were littered with corpses, and the landscape pockmarked with craters, miles of trench, and barbed wire. At the hospital, volumes of horror stories unfolded. With eyes glazed over in shock and disbelief, the wounded who could talk shared the descriptive accounts of the filth and ugliness they had endured, we as caregivers listened, and no-one escaped the nightmare. Many of the wounded felt guilt for having survived while so many of their brothers in arms had not. I held tight to the hand of a man dying of gas gangrene, his sputum green and his breathing laboured. His feet were bound in bloody bandages, and in the next bed, his friend (whose arm was now a stump just above the elbow) said, "Rats. They were eating his feet." A nursing sister tried to calm him, but his tears flowed, and his body shook as though a burden might be lifted in the telling.

He continued. "We were pinned down for two days, bodies everywhere. My arm was gone, and I was caught in the barbed wire. I thought for sure Roy was dead, but when the rats started chewing on 'im, he started to moan. I couldn't get to 'im. I tried, miss. Honest I did."

He wept, and Sister drew closer and rested her cool hand on his forehead, murmuring, "You did all that you could. He'll be at peace soon."

I stayed with my charge until he took his last breath, then closed his eyes and drew the sheet over his face. I looked through his belongings and found his paybook, making a note of his home address. It would be my responsibility to write his family the standard, brief paragraph of lies: "He died peacefully and without pain."

Nora had never given up hope of finding her brother. The matron watched and waited for a long time before finally calling her in for a chat, inviting me along for support. I waited at the back of the cramped space while the two women sat in silence for a few moments. Nora knew what was coming.

"It's time to let him go," said Matron with great warmth and understanding. "I've watched for far too long the torment you put yourself through.

You know as well as I that too much time has passed. He will not be found." Nora knew the truth of it but needed to hear the words and was grateful for the kind delivery of the message.

Matron continued. "Hundreds and hundreds of our young men have died, never to be identified." The despair in her voice was palpable. She held in her hand a pair of identity discs strung on a cotton cord, the first a green octagonal shape and the second round and red in colour. The goal was that the red tag could be retrieved simply by cutting its short string, leaving the green tag with the body; others, subsequently finding the remains, would know that the death had already been reported. The details on the green tag were meant to be useful in preparing a grave marker. "So often, these things are of no use at all," she said, tossing them down on her desk in frustration. The cotton cords broke easily, and the discs were lost during the fighting, or the fibrous material would simply disintegrate in the wet and mud. Bodies that lay for days, sometimes weeks, before being retrieved were impossible to identify, and those with wounds to the head and face were beyond recognition.

"I'm sorry, my dear. Truly, I am. I hope that you will choose to continue your valuable work here." She rose from her seat then; the interview was over, and there was work to be done.

Nora stood and said, "Thank you, Matron. I think I would like to stay a little while longer." As she left, I followed behind with a quick nod to Matron.

I had spent most of the morning on funeral duty, and my hands were still cold when I slipped my arm through hers. Steering her toward the mess tent, I said, "Why don't we go find ourselves a nice warm mug of chocolate? Sound good?"

In a few minutes, we sat silently until Nora was ready to speak. She finally asked, "Where've you been?"

Rubbing my hands together for warmth, I answered. "I took a turn falling in behind the coffin wagon today. There were quite a number of us considering the cold. Still amazes me that they're able to bury these poor devils despite the frozen ground."

"The cemetery is going to grow right out to the coast before long; we'll be burying them in the dunes," Nora stated matter-of-factly.

I waited until I could see the bottom of my mug before asking, "So, are you staying? Is that what you want?"

"For now."

"Right, then. Let's round up the gals and have a chat. I know we can't do anything to take away your pain, but we're here to support you. You know that, right?" She nodded. I reached across the table and rested my hand on her cheek. She smiled back. "Come on," I said. "Let's go find the girls." I had some news to share that I knew would cheer everyone up just a little.

We found Squeak coming off duty in the delousing tent, scratching her head and shuddering. "I'll check in with you after I've paid a visit to the wash hut," she said as she manoeuvred around a group of soldiers smoking outside the ward. They winked and whistled, and she tilted her head and flicked up one shoulder in her usual coquettish salute.

Emily was pushing the tea trolley around her ward, and when I poked my head in, she said, "Best get your face out of here before Sister finds you an occupation. I'll be through here in another hour." I didn't mind the idea of lingering in the warm tent where the stoves were continuously fed, unlike those in our quarters, but I chose instead to follow Nora back to the mess tent.

I stopped by my bunk just long enough to pick up the embroidery hoop and thread I had left on the bedside table and then sat across from Nora, who had a cup of hot tea waiting for me. "You're always busy with something," Nora commented as she watched me poke the tiny needle down through the fabric, completing the last stitch of a tiny leaf before moving on to the next. I rethreaded the needle, holding it up to the light for just the right angle, then pulled the pale-green strand through the eye and rolled the end around between my thumb and index finger, pulling it taut to form a tiny knot.

"Idle hands and all that," I mused. "I've found that it pays to keep my hands busy, and my mouth shut."

"I just don't have the patience for that kind of thing," she said with customary pathos in the tone of her voice.

"You keep busy though, and you're not a gossip. I see what you're like around the lads, always playing draughts or cards, helping them write their letters. They're all very fond of you." There was a silent moment before I simply said, "I'm sorry about your brother."

Woefully, she nodded. "I suppose I knew it all along ... just too stubborn to give up."

"Are your folks anxious for you to come home? I expect they're missing your help around the farm."

The Ladies Land Army had been tremendously helpful to farms in the area, but with all three brothers lost to the war, I'd assumed Nora would want to go home. I wasn't prepared for her cold response:

"I have no desire to go back . . . ever." The period at the end of her sentence was clear. The conversation was over. I looked up from my embroidery into the sorrowful eyes of my friend wanting desperately to console her, but I knew that the girl was not ready to shed her armour; she would share her story when she was ready.

Getting to know Nora had been difficult, she was something of an enigma. We shared a life beneath the canvas of our home away from home, but I really knew extraordinarily little about her. She was strikingly attractive but not what many would call beautiful. She had large, wide, haunting eyes and a voice to match, a gorgeous shock of wavy black hair, and a lovely smile (rare as it was). She wore an air of sullen seriousness but could be witty and charming when the mood suited. She had a wonderful rapport with the patients in the rehab wards, kibitzing and allowing the odd foul word to slip into their lively banter, unnoticed by the sisters on duty of course. Off duty though, she associated only with fellow staff members, and some found her to be abrupt and standoffish at times. I'd learned early on not to be wounded by her curtness. I recognized and appreciated her many other dimensions.

Emily and Squeak arrived in good time, and as the four of us sat over supper, I waited for an appropriate moment to announce my surprise: "We've been granted leave. Four days and transport to Paris." There was stunned silence for a moment before Squeak sprang from her seat, knocking chicken and dumplings into Emily's lap.

"You're not having us on, are you?" Her high-pitched voice found a whole new realm.

"It's all been cleared. Matron is sending us as a group while the lull is on. 'Safety in numbers,' she said. Sister McCreary will be our chaperone. She has a seminar to attend, and she's a good egg. She'll give us some rope." As the war entered its third year, there grew less and less emphasis on propriety; rules of conduct relaxed somewhat as nurses and VADs became more trusting of one another. I suspected that Sister McCreary, who was also in need of much-deserved time away from camp, would be completely disinterested in childminding four grown women.

"When do we leave?" asked Emily, who was beaming across the table at my cleverness in securing such an adventure.

"Day after tomorrow. Just enough time to tidy up and organize a plan."

Nora, who hadn't said anything, interjected, "Could we please, just this once, fly by the seat of our pants and do without a blessed plan?"

I could not imagine life without a schedule, and I feigned injury at her comment. She backtracked a bit, nudging my arm, and saying, "Well, how about half a plan?" It was settled, and the cold, dismal day seemed a little brighter. We talked more (through chattering teeth) in the tent that night. I was grateful for the woollen stockings my mother had sent in a recent care package and more grateful still for the extra blankets offered by the quartermaster who had taken quite a shine to Squeak.

Watching my breath float out before me, I said, "I really don't mind what else we do, but I'm going to see as many shows as I can fit into four days."

"Not the girlie shows that the lads talk about?" asked a squeaky voice in the darkness.

"As long as there's music and dancing, I don't care what they're doing or wearing. Crikey, there can't be anything we haven't already seen around this godforsaken place."

Emily chimed in. "We can buy some new sheet music for the Wisps; it won't matter that the words are in French."

"... and some new soaps and things" added Squeak.

Nora, mimicking one of the nursing sisters, said with a harrumph, "Be sure there are no scents, ladies. The rules of conduct clearly state that there should be nothing that might attract masculine attention."

With a giggle, I blew out the candle.

En route to Paris, Sister McCreary gave the compulsory warning speech about men on leave and the rampant venereal disease epidemic, but she seemed more concerned that we keep our money well hidden from street thieves and put me in charge of ensuring the safety of the group in her absence. She led the way into the hotel and ensured that the rooms were satisfactory before reporting to the hospital for her seminar and settling into the room they had organized for her. As she was leaving, she took me to one side and said, "I'm off then. Behave, and I'll see you at the end of the week." With a wink, she strode out of the building and back into the waiting vehicle. We shared two to a room, and although the hotel rooms were small and cold, the beds were comfortable enough with puffy warm duvets. There was a communal toilet at the end of the hall complete with a bathtub, which I planned to put high on my agenda.

After a quick unpack, we donned our heavy overcoats and made our way out onto the streets of Paris. The city was no longer under immediate threat, as it had been early in the war when the German armies were only thirty kilometres from Parisian doorsteps. The threat was so dire at that time that the government and national assembly had been hastened away for a period of time and masterpieces removed from the museums and galleries. Although the front had moved much further north and government officials had returned to their offices, there remained the fear of aircraft raids and airship bombings as evidenced by a number of shattered buildings and a few massive craters.

Our foursome spent a leisurely late afternoon in a French café called an *estaminet* and dined on a supper of egg and chips with cheap red wine. There was an older gentleman sitting on a high stool in the corner, playing guitar and singing French folk songs. The establishment quickly filled up with soldiers, and in one glance, we could make out uniforms from France, Britain, Australia, Belgium, and Canada. The melting pot included all manner of rank as officers and their men drank together, exchanging stories of their shared experiences. As the room became more crowded, we were obliged to move our chairs closer together to make room for three girls who had just finished work at a local factory. They spoke only a smattering of English, but Nora was quite fluent in French and the rest of us had picked up just enough of the language to get by.

The mood was high and conversation flowed without any great effort. French women, no different than those in Britain, had embraced the challenge of taking on jobs left vacant by men in the military, and conversations about rationing and doing without the basic necessities echoed those from home.

"No pastries, no brioche," one gal announced. They went on but spoke too quickly for me to keep up. Nora explained that butter and flour were scarce and that there was only one type of bread being sold, which was made with heavier, more rustic flour. Another gal wrapped her arms around herself and made a dramatic shivering gesture, saying, "There is little coal. It is mined in the north where the fighting is greatest." I knew that most of the mines were actually behind German lines but chose not to add insult to injury. Instead, I asked about venues where we might see a musical revue and perhaps a few different café concerts, and the girls were happy to offer suggestions. The conversation concluded with an arrangement for all seven of us to meet the following evening for a night on the town.

The guitarist finished his set and thanked the crowd for the few coins that had been deposited in his guitar case. Before he was seated with wine in hand, a trio of singers had taken his place. There was much singing and laughter, and wine flowed freely at a single franc per bottle. There was some innocent flirting and a few playful marriage proposals, but finally the evening wound down and we made our way back to the hotel. Many of the men went in search of licensed brothels, the *"maisons de tolerance,"* where blue lamps indicated officers only and red lamps were for other ranks. These establishments were sanctified by the army because they believed sex to be a physical necessity for their men.

I looped my arm through Emily's. "So many double standards," I said. "We can't use scented soaps, and nurses are never permitted to marry. Little wonder these blokes have to find prostitutes."

The following day, we left the hotel in search of tourist attractions and stepped out into a street that had been dusted with a soft layer of snow during the night. "It's so pretty," said Squeak. "You could almost forget about the war." We scoured through museums and galleries and lunched at the patisserie recommended by our new friends. We finished the day at Notre-Dame Cathedral but were disappointed to see that the stained-glass windows had been removed to safety and replaced with pale-yellow windowpanes that washed the interior of the church with a tepid light. We made it back to the hotel with just enough time to rendezvous with our Paris friends.

The musical revue was all that I'd hoped it would be with bright costumes and exuberant performances. Most of the political satire was lost on me, and the dialogue spoken far too quickly to follow, but my enthusiasm was not altered. "It was marvellous!" I exclaimed as we left the building, my sentiment echoed by one of the French gals: *"Oui, il 'etait merveilleux!"* Together, we sat around a table at a nearby café and drank wine into the wee hours, laughing, singing, and putting the war as far to the back of our minds as possible.

Shopping was on the agenda the following day. Anything (we had learned) could be purchased on the black market if one had funds, and we did. We were paid forty-five shillings per week, with twelve shillings deducted for food, and with little else to spend our money on, we were able to save a fair amount. Some of the wealthier women who had volunteered for service chose to do so without benefit of pay, but we could not expect financial help from our families. We bought a few trinkets and small gifts to send home, as well as toiletries and niceties for ourselves. I stocked up on coloured thread for my needlework, wire, and a new pair of needle-nosed pliers for my beloved amulets, and Squeak found a pair of gently used toe shoes at a pawn shop. The pawn shop proved to be the best find of the day. We combined our coins to purchase a lovely china teapot for the matron as a thank you for permitting our holiday, and Nora helped identify a few good pieces of sheet music before turning her attention to a rack of novels. At a corner shop, Emily stocked up on cigarettes for her pal in the supply hut, and then we turned our attention to supper. The smell of meat pie drew us into the café where we had spent our first evening.

As promised, we were met by our Parisian chums, who (as it turned out) shared a nearby flat. Before night's end, we had frequented three different café concerts. Later, I rubbed my sore feet and waited patiently for my turn in the tub room before sinking blissfully beneath the duvet for an uninterrupted and unheard of eight hours of sleep.

After a late start and a hearty breakfast, we were off again. We bumped into Sister McCreary, who popped in just to ask if we were having a good time and (I suspect) to be sure we were staying out of trouble. She confessed that she had taken the previous day for herself but felt compelled to return to the hospital for another series of lectures. The Grand Palais had been converted to a military hospital and was integral to the war effort as a gathering place for medical professionals to share information and new insights. She waved goodbye.

Nora, who had been quiet through breakfast, suggested that she might stay behind for the day. "I'm feeling a bit off," she said. "Perhaps a little too much of the grape last night."

Emily, quick to respond, had a hand on her forehead before she could move away. "No fever."

"I know. I'm just a bit queasy, and I've got a headache. Too much wine the past few nights. I'm sure that's all it is."

I frowned. "I don't like to leave you if you're unwell."

"I'll be fine." She sounded a little annoyed. "Some peace and quiet away from you lot should put me right." She gathered her hat and bag, without waiting for further argument, and said, "I'll go have a lie down and see you later at the café."

The three of us shrugged in unison and climbed into one of the few remaining taxis in Paris. Thousands of others had been commandeered by the war effort. My feet were grateful for the rest. Some of the museums and cathedrals were being used to house the wounded, but there was still much to see. We finally made our way to the glorious Arc de Triomphe, but as the day progressed, the wind picked up, and the air was icy cold. We made the joint decision to head back to the hotel for a nap before heading once again to the café for an evening of revelry. We were frozen when we arrived, but as usual, Squeak bounced ahead of us down the hall and was at the door to her room just as Emily and I rounded the top step. Before we could get the key in the lock, we were startled by a high-pitched shriek. Squeak was backing out of her room with her hands over her eyes and bawling indiscernible words. I bolted toward her just as the door to her room slammed shut.

"For Heaven's sake, what happened?" I asked frantically. "Is Nora okay?"

She nodded but gave no other response. I reached for the door handle.

"NO!" she shouted.

"Alright then. Calm down." I steered her toward our room. Emily was in the hallway taking in the scene.

I lowered the now tearful girl into a waiting chair and poured her a glass of wine, then knelt on the floor beside her, resting my hand on her arm. "Tell me what happened. Whatever is wrong?"

She stammered and sniffed and finally said, "They were naked on the bed."

"They?"

"Nora and ..." She didn't finish her thought. Instead, a voice in the doorway answered the question.

"Lise."

Nora stood there in her robe, looking dishevelled. She entered the room, closed the door behind her, and sat on the end of my bed, legs crossed and arm extended in anticipation of the wine glass Emily was already preparing.

Lise was one of our new friends from the café, and more than just a friend for Nora it would seem.

She spoke directly to Squeak, in a matter-of-fact tone that belied her rattled appearance. "I'm sorry you were startled. I wasn't expecting you back so soon."

Squeak wiped away tears and tried to find words. "I don't understand."

"What don't you understand?" replied Nora with a tone bordering on annoyance. "Have you really led such a sheltered existence that you don't understand what's happened here?"

Squeak's shoulders rose and fell as she took in spasmodic sips of air. "I thought it was only men who did that." In a whisper, she added, "The queer thing."

Nora lost patience. "For Heaven's sake! There are men who are attracted to men and women who are attracted to women." She took a deep breath and tried to control her volume. "We're all different. All of us. We're all people with different wants and needs."

Squeak gathered her thoughts for a moment and then responded. "Isn't it illegal?"

"For men, unfortunately it is. Women don't seem to be persecuted in the same way, but we're still forced to keep our relationships secret for fear of losing our families and our jobs." She paused then, glancing around. "And our friends."

Up until this point, I had remained silent. Finally, I said, "I admit to being naïve as well. I think I understand now why you always appear so tormented. It must be a terrible burden to keep that part of you hidden away. I wish you could have trusted us."

"I wish I could too," she replied, "but it isn't easy to know who to trust." Then she added, "That's true, isn't it, Em?"

Emily was sitting quietly on the window ledge, and I realized she hadn't offered any comforting words during all the commotion, which was very unlike her. She met my eyes as I turned to look at her, and then I understood.

Nora collected herself and said quietly, "Squeak, I am sorry for your upset. Will you come with me and let me try to explain?" Squeak nodded.

Nora glanced over at me and said, "I think it best we leave you two alone. I expect you have some things to talk about as well." She looked contrite and sad as she set about the task of ushering her little friend out the door.

The room was suddenly devoid of all sound. We seemed to be sitting miles apart in the tiny space.

"Why did you not tell me?" I finally found the courage to ask. My voice sounded loud and harsh after the long silence.

"I didn't know myself for a long time, and I really didn't understand. I was sure it must be wrong or dirty or evil in some way."

"I've never seen you show any interest in any of the women we've worked with." I was scanning my memory for any inkling but came up blank.

She was still staring at the floor. "I don't love any other women. I love you. Have from the first day but didn't know the extent of it." She didn't wait for a response. "I know that you love me too, just not in the same way, and I'm content with the friendship and relationship we have. I'll never expect more."

Words wouldn't come. I was shocked at my own naivety.

Tears were streaming down Emily's face as she continued. "This will change everything, won't it? I'm going to lose you."

I have no recollection of crossing the room, but then I was cradling her trembling body and stroking her hair as we sat together on the window ledge. "Nothing need change." I wiped her tears with my sleeve. "We will always be as we have always been. You are my sister, my cherished friend and companion, but Emily. . ." I lifted her chin, and she forced her eyes upward to look into mine. "We will not be lovers."

Emily nodded. "I know."

We did not go to the café that night. We had a plate of sandwiches and another bottle of wine brought to the room where we sat talking into the wee hours with Nora and Squeak. The conversation was open and honest, questions were asked and answered, and happily, no one judged. Nora explained that she had been caught in a similar situation with a local girl at home and that her parents had all but disowned her. Although searching for her brother had indeed been her purpose in the beginning, a sense of belonging was her reason for staying.

Squeak asked, "Nora, how did you know that Emily is also . . . likewise inclined?"

"I don't know; I just had a sense about it I suppose. I wasn't certain of course until Milly was transferred to the CCS, and Miss Muffet here," she reached over and took Emily's hand, "turned into a brooding old cow. She was miserable and jealous over Milly's new roommate, and when I challenged her about it, we shared an unspoken meeting of the minds." She leaned in to plant a kiss on the smaller girl's cheek. "I am sorry, my friend. I was wrong to share your secret; it was a frightful thing to do. I suppose I just felt exposed and needed to divert some of the attention." Emily gave her hand a squeeze, which implied simply that all was forgiven.

The penny finally dropped for me. "So, that's what all the tension was about that night in the tent? You two had already had words about this. Nora, you were being snide about our friend Cicely at the time. Were you implying that she too is homosexual?"

"Absolutely," she replied. "In all that I've heard and read about her and the subject matter of her own work, I think it's blatantly obvious." She let that sink in for a moment and then asked, "How do you feel about that?"

"Naïve and a little stupid, I suppose. Conflicted too, if I'm honest. I wonder now about my own nature. It never occurred to me before that there is an option. I far prefer the company of women over men. It depends, of course, upon the nature of the woman, but I am more comfortable with my own gender. Is it a matter of choice or is it nature? I spent many happy hours in Cicely's company, sitting in her front room debating the issues, oblivious to her proclivity, proudly standing with her in defence of women's rights, but I never once envisioned us slipping between the sheets. I suppose I've never had any great urge to jump into bed with anyone, but if I did, it seems to me that I would put more stock in my partner's intellect and personality than in their gender." I let that thought roll around in my head for a moment before adding, "One thing I do know for certain is that my future must have children in it. I suppose that puts me squarely in the opposing camp, doesn't it?"

Squeak piped in then. "I love men. I love how they look and get weak in the knees for a deep voice. I love the attention I get when I flirt a little and how I feel when they look at me. Are any of you attracted to men at all?" she inquired. "I mean, how does it work? I've seen all of you spend lots of your free time chatting and playing cards with the lads; you've danced with them. As shy as you are, Em, you never turn a fellow down who asks you to dance."

Emily, who was feeling more comfortable now, said, "I like people. I enjoy spending time with, talking with, and having fun with lots of people. It doesn't matter what sex they are. Who I choose to have a physical relationship with or to love is an entirely different matter. I've never taken anyone to my bed, and perhaps I never will, but I will continue to dance whenever I can."

Nora embraced the freedom of this honest exchange. "I enjoy spending time with the lads, but the dancing is all part of the façade. You have to keep up appearances if you don't want to be found out."

"How horribly sad," I said. "As much as I've always despised class distinctions, I think this is worse. Society dictates what we should wear and how we should behave, and the strong arm of propriety also dictates who we can and cannot love. We shouldn't be fighting for women's rights; we should be fighting an all-out war for *people's* rights."

There are events that change the shape of our lives, and we four left Paris altogether different friends than we had previously been. Sister McCreary did not interrupt our melancholy silence.

Chapter Eleven

Mud soaked and bloodied, he was still the handsomest man I had ever seen. While the medic applied a simple dressing to the wound on his leg, I did my best to quiet him. Sweeping the dark curls from his forehead, I whispered the same words I had said a thousand times: "You're in good hands; you're going to be all right now." I helped the stretcher bearers gently lift him into the ambulance and climbed into the driver's seat to begin the journey back to the unit, while the dam in my throat was losing its battle to hold back a flood of tears. I had seen enough wounds to know that, aside from the gash in his leg and the frostbite to his toes, this soldier— this lovely man—had fallen victim to mustard-gas burns and inhalation. He was having difficulty finding his breath, clawing at the air and talking in painful breathy whispers. There were yellow blisters forming around his mouth.

"Try not to talk," I whispered back to him. "You're going to be all right," I repeated gently. He was one of the lucky ones really; his eyes didn't appear to be affected. So many that I transported were blinded by the gas, some permanently, their eyes sticky and glued shut with painful suppurating blisters. I glanced upward in a silent prayer of thanks that those beautiful eyes had been spared. I always tried to give the boys a smooth ride, but every journey was a new adventure in water-filled potholes and craters. This one was particularly difficult.

Once at the hospital, he reached out for my hand as he was carried toward the triage tent, and I held tight to it until he was lowered onto a cot. As though automated, I went through the motions. I checked his dog tags, printed his name and serial number on the clipboard, took his vitals, and jotted down the information. "Ernest Daniel Pearse," I whispered as I sponged the grime from his face. The nursing sisters were hovering, an oxygen mask was applied, and I was grateful for these new advances in dealing with the deadly gas. His fretful fight for breath eased just a little. I heard Sister Jonah call across the room for Emily, who was beside me in three long strides.

"Come on, Milly. You must come away now. Let the doctors see to him."

His desperate look begged me to hang tight to his hand, and I did just that until he was cleaned up and led away to the operating theatre with my kiss planted on his forehead.

I took pride in my professionalism and made a point of keeping my emotions in check, but this was an exception that everyone on the staff understood. Emily escorted me from the tent back to our quarters, where she unlocked her trunk and retrieved the half bottle of Scotch she'd been hoarding. She put a blanket around my shivering shoulders and sat very close, all the while muttering the phrases one would expect in such situations: "He's being well taken care of. He'll pull through this. You'll see."

I lay on my bunk, eyes open but not awake. Emily gathered the blankets around me and spooned in behind me without saying another word.

It had been several months since I'd first drunk in those sultry blue-grey eyes with their long sweeping eyelashes and felt my heart skip a beat. He had been just another soldier who'd walked out onto our performance stage in the barn, but with curls of dark hair dancing on his forehead, he had stood with quiet confidence and sang in rich warm tones:

> *If you were the only girl in the world and I were the only boy*
> *Nothing else would matter in the world today*
> *We could go on loving in the same old way*
> *A Garden of Eden just made for two*
> *With nothing to mar our joy*
> *I would say such wonderful things to you*
> *There would be such wonderful things to do*
> *If you were the only girl in the world*
> *And I were the only boy.*

I had not been alone in the audience that day, but I'd felt as though he were singing only to me. It had been a wonderful and very professional concert full of jokes, music, political jibes, and satire; still . . . it was his performance that had resonated with me. Our early Christmas entertainment had been provided by a marvellous Canadian concert troupe called The Dumbells. Formed by ten men from the Canadian Army Third Division earlier that year to build the morale of their comrades at the front, they'd taken their name from the division's emblem: a red dumbbell that signified strength.

They wrote much of their own music and material and carried their curtains and costumes wherever Canadian troops were located, and fortunately for us, to hospitals and clearing stations along the way.

Following the performance, the troupe gathered in the mess tent, some still dressed in their women's garb and makeup, where the frivolity and singing continued into the wee hours. Matron, who on behalf of the hospital was thanking them for their time and effort, called me over to their table. "Gentlemen," she said gesturing toward me, "Miss Aspinall here is responsible for our very own concert troupe called the Will-o'-the-Wisp. And a fine troupe it is too, if I might say." I was happy to hear the pride in her voice but a little shy to be hailed in such company as we had just witnessed.

They invited me to sit with them, and I looked around in vain for those mesmerizing blue-grey eyes. "Where is the soldier who sang, 'If You Were the Only Girl'?"

One of the lads answered. "I think he's gone off to visit his pals in the ward. He's not one of our regulars. We pick up local talent from among the Canadian lads wherever we go, just to round out the show and make it unique to each unit. He's sung with us a couple of times. He was here visiting a few blokes from his division who were wounded and agreed to join us." It was difficult to take this man seriously as he pried off his false eyelashes and smeared his lipstick on a wad of paper. The illusion these fellows created with their characters was quite astounding. Some would have passed for women if you didn't look too closely at their five o'clock shadows.

It was only moments later that Private Pearse entered the mess tent and joined us at the table. He was quiet and modestly received the praise lavished on him by his fellow entertainers. I chimed in.

"Your song moved me very deeply, Private Pearse." He thanked me with a timid bow.

Squeak joined us when she finished her shift, and each fellow at the table rose as she was introduced. The conversation took many turns; we were immediately comfortable in each other's company, but in the end, our laughter became raucous and brought negative attention from the duty nurse.

The leader of the troupe, Captain Plunkett, announced, "Very well, friends, I believe that's our cue to say goodnight." One of the fellows took Squeak by the arm, insisting he walk her back to her quarters; she giddily agreed, of course. As I followed along behind them, Private Pearse appeared on my right side.

"It was a fine evening, wasn't it?"

"It was indeed," I said.

We met in passing several times in the days that followed, stopping to converse for a few minutes each time. He asked questions about the Wisps and hinted that he might venture over to the barn that evening for whatever impromptu entertainment was on offer. I offered a lukewarm response in an unsuccessful attempt at nonchalant worldliness: "Perhaps I'll see you there."

As it happened, I was called away that afternoon, and it was dark before my return. Tired and dirty, I decided to go directly from the showers to my bed. Squeak, who had just finished a shift, was having none of it. "Come on, Mil; they've got a lovely little three-piece playing over there tonight, and there's some dancing going on. It'll do you the world of good."

There was no point in resisting once my little friend had made up her mind to something, and so I slipped back into my sensible shoes and followed her out across the camp. She was right of course. There was a lighthearted atmosphere; the small crowd were in good spirits, laughing and dancing. Private Pearse, who by all accounts had been watching the door, wasted no time in taking my hand and leading me onto the makeshift dance floor. He proved as skilled at dancing as he was at singing. The evening concluded with "Let Me Call You Sweetheart," and then he was gone. His three-day pass had expired, and he returned to his unit.

Emily leaned in and whispered, "I believe you're smitten, Miss Aspinall." In the soft glow of the lantern resting on the wooden crate that served as a table between our cots, I could see she was lying on her side, hugging her pillow.

"How do you feel about that?" I asked, a little afraid of the answer.

"I had no doubt it would happen eventually, and as long as you're happy, so will I be." I knew she meant it. It had been months since our leave in Paris and no further discussion had seemed necessary. "We four" had a much deeper appreciation for and acceptance of one another. It was a resilient bond. We became very protective of each other and developed some bad habits: surreptitious smiles and the occasional exchange of knowing glances that others at the hospital noticed but didn't understand. Both Squeak and Nora cherished the amulets that I had gifted them, and although they weren't privy to all that the charms represented, they embraced the sentiment. True to our word, nothing changed for me and Emily, and we did our best to continue as we were before.

"He's beautiful," I said.

Emily snickered. "You do mean *handsome*, don't you?"

I shook my head. "If those sultry grey blue eyes and long eyelashes were on a woman, you'd call her beautiful. I could bathe in those eyes. I'm not sure what to do with these feelings, Em. It's unlikely I'll ever see him again." The winter had only begun, and yet the biting cold and dampness had already leached deep into my bones. On this day though, I was distracted from its icy fingers and didn't realize I was shivering until Emily approached, sat on the edge of my cot, and pulled the covers up to meet my chin.

In the most loving voice, she said, "You'll see each other again." With a wide grin, she mimicked Squeak's colloquialism for premonition: "I can feel it in my water!" She planted a kiss on my cheek just as the rest of the foursome entered the tent.

"What's this now?" inquired Nora, face pulled taught and haughty in a snooty expression. "We can't leave you two alone for a minute." She was carrying four mugs of hot beef Bovril just off the cooker.

"Oh pish," said the little ballerina. "You're just jealous. I'll kiss you good-night if it'll shut you up."

"We were discussing Milly's beau if you must know," Emily responded with a wink. "He left today, and she's feeling a little glum." We sipped at the steamy beverages, and I did my best to ignore their good-natured jibes and sniggers until my dreamy, good mood started to diminish.

"I'm going to sleep. You three can carry on without me," I announced as I reached over to put out the lantern. *Beautiful*, I repeated to myself just as I drifted into a wistful sleep.

I saw him again several weeks later when he hobbled off a transport with a minor leg wound and a nasty case of trench foot. He had already been treated at the Canadian hospital and was on convalescent leave for two weeks. He was given a pass on the proviso that he report to a hospital or clearing station to have the wound checked for infection every few days. Emily had seen him first and made a dash for the transport unit where I was up to my elbows in grease. "He's back," she said.

A little annoyed at the interruption, I said, "What are you on about?"

She repeated with raised eyebrows and a tell-tale smirk, "He's back."

"Oh, Em, you are a good scout!" When I tried to hug her, she pushed me away. I was a little startled.

"Not until you have a good scrub. This is a clean pinny I've just put on." As she toddled away, she looked back and bubbled, "I'll have that hug later. Don't forget."

Oh my God, what a girl! I love the bones of her.

The following week brought with it a clash of emotions. The hospital was filled to overflowing with wounded from all clearing stations in the region. Field and base hospitals were running at capacity, and there was no longer room for allied distinctions or rank separation in the wards. I spent twelve hours a day either transporting wounded from the battlefield to the unit or from the unit to other hospital locations. The vehicles needed regular maintenance, requiring several additional hours of work each day. There was no such thing as off-duty; I caught a few hours of sleep whenever I could, but the wounded kept coming. I didn't really stop for meals but stole a few precious moments at a time to sit over a cup of coffee with Daniel. Even the transient quarters were at capacity, and I knew he wouldn't be on site much longer.

I started my shift the next day delivering newly arrived supplies to the hospital ward. One of the nurses requested that I stay and help to redress a few of the minor wounds, giving me a list of the beds I should see to. Among them was Private Pearse. The shrapnel that had been removed from his leg was sizeable, but the wound was healing nicely. I removed the soiled bandage, cleaned around the area, and coiled clean sterile gauze around the leg. The trench foot was much improved, and I was thankful that he would not lose the foot as so many others had. He was instructed to leave his feet open to the air as much as possible. I gently massaged camphorated oil into the soles of his feet and checked between each toe for any fungus. Beds were at a premium in the ward, and so I settled him into a wheelchair, surrounded him with blankets, and tucked a pillow beneath his still bare feet for a little elevation. Then I wheeled him out into the lovely brisk, clear day for a minute or two of fresh air before returning him to the ward. He would be returning to his unit the next day, and we agreed to write to one another.

In the weeks that followed, I felt a keen sense of relief whenever an envelope arrived with his handwriting on it.

It was the Battle of Arras that brought him back to me. The bodies of Canadian soldiers littered the pockmarked fields at Vimy Ridge and filled our hospice ward. It was dire. Thankfully, Daniel's prognosis had promise, the leg would heal but the gas damage to his lungs remained a worry. It was his flat and impassive countenance that concerned me most in the moment. I sat with him whenever I could, tracing my fingers around the tortured lines on his face and feeling the muscles relax under my touch.

Emily was a good scout. Whenever I returned from a run, she did her best to report what she knew about the health of this particular soldier. His lungs were severely damaged, he was unable to speak due to the burns and swelling on his vocal cords, and there were symptoms of gastrointestinal involvement. It was a vicious cycle; breathing and throat issues were made worse by vomiting, but it was crucial to get some nutrition into the poor emaciated men.

"It will be some time before he'll be strong enough for transfer," she told me. "He may not be able to acknowledge you, but he seems to be comforted whenever you're there."

"Do you suppose he'll ever see active duty again?" I asked.

"No, not likely. Eventually, he'll be returned to England for long-term care. As he is now, it's doubtful he would survive the journey."

The duty nurses knew me well and didn't seem to mind my frequent visits. Still, I felt compelled to make excuses and to be useful. They began finding me one occupation or another and a reason to be there beyond the obvious. Each barked order carried with it a suggestion or a wink. "Miss Aspinall, there are bandages to be rolled and pans to be emptied."

I sat with him for a few minutes at a time, all the while talking in soothing tones about nothing in particular and without expecting a response. After a bad episode of night terrors, Emily came to find me. "Just stay with him for a little while. It may calm him."

I slipped into the ward still in my nightclothes, held his hand, stroked back his hair, and much to the chagrin of a sour old nurse, started singing softly to him. *"Let me call you sweetheart . . ."* Emily distracted the nurse with customary flair, and I continued softly, *"I'm in love with you. Let me hear you whisper that you love me too. Keep the love light glowing in your eyes so true. Let me call you sweetheart; I'm in love with you."*

His eyes moved toward me for the first time since his arrival, and he smiled and blinked a thank you. Always busying myself, I emptied the urinal and returned just long enough to straighten his pillow and coverlet. "I'll stop by to read to you in the morning if you'd like, but you must promise to get some sleep." He blinked and nodded a positive response. I knew that it was a promise he couldn't keep; the night terrors had a life of their own.

After a fortnight, I started to see and hear some improvement. His breathing was still laboured, but his speaking voice was returning, making a pleasant change to the one-sided conversations we'd been having. I suspected that his singing days were over and mourned the loss of such a talent.

I visited Daniel as often as I could, and once he was transferred to the convalescent ward, I was allowed to wheel him out into the sunshine for some much-needed therapy that only Mother Nature could supply. The Canadian field hospital was still filled to overflowing, and so the agreement was made that we would keep some of their wounded with us until they were fit enough for transport across the Channel. It was Nora who shared that bit of good news with me.

Eventually Daniel was able to take short walks, and we talked until he tired. I learned that he was born in Widnes, only eight miles from my home in Earlstown. We were both reared in modestly affluent circumstances and seemed to have much in common. His father was an innkeeper, and while Daniel didn't care much for that type of work, he appreciated the education it offered him. Like me, he'd learned how to keep accounts and manage a business.

"My dad," I told him, "is a master cooper by trade but when wooden barrels fell from popularity in the shipping business he changed gears and eventually opened his own business manufacturing sacks primarily for the Sankey Sugar Works." We shared intimate accounts of our early family life and laughed over the similarities in our upbringing. He too was the youngest in his family, anxious to make his own way and seek his own adventures.

He'd immigrated to Canada in 1913 to try his hand at farming. He lived and worked on a small farm just outside Winnipeg, but at the outbreak of war, felt compelled to fight for his new country and alongside soldiers from his country of birth. He joined the Cameron Highlanders, served in the 43rd Battalion, and had spent the past year in the trenches of war-torn France.

I listened intently as he shared his horrifying stories of life in no man's land and hoped that the telling would help to lift his heavy burden; I had heard many of the stories before but never so vividly as through his eyes. We cried together as he recalled friendships made and lost. On one occasion, I was pushing him in a wheelchair, and he seemed to get lost in his own conversation. "Stand to, each dawn, is the usual time for an enemy attack, and if you survive that, the next greatest enemy out there is boredom. You must keep a keen watch out for snipers while you carry out the usual chores, you know, cleaning latrines, filling sandbags, things like that. You look forward to your daily ration of rum, but after that, there's too much time to think."

I recognized the haunted, far-off look and the fatigue behind it. "Shell shock" is what the doctors called it. The harrowing ordeal of a night spent in the trenches was playing out in his mind, and I decided it best to continue the conversation on another day.

His health was improving, although his breathing was still laboured and shallow. During our conversations, I saw him struggle for tiny sips of air between every fourth or fifth word. I felt my body suck in deep cleansing breaths in an involuntary mission to help him. He was beginning to take in more nourishment but remained thin and frail. I hoped the fresh air would help, but it was mostly an excuse to continue our outings.

I loved our time together and the gentle ease of our friendship. Bit by bit, the bricks crumbled and fell away from the protective wall I wore like armour. As soon as the weather and the soggy ground permitted, I introduced him to my little sanctuary off beyond the barn where a little river flowed that was lined by trees of all kinds. The willows among them were nursing tiny bright-green buds. I brought along a blanket, some crackers and cheese, and a flask of tea spiked with a dram of Emily's new stash of Scotch. It was a fine spring day, and my glorious patch of nature's beauty was calling out to us for attention. It was in dramatic contrast to the vast ugliness all around. One could almost imagine that (somewhere in the world) there was peace.

We arranged ourselves on the tartan blanket, quietly comfortable in each other's company. Daniel opened his satchel and reached in for the gift he had been working on. It was a heavy brass container complete with lid, which he had made from a shell casing, skillfully engraving it. The tiny etched flowers and laurel wreaths wound around the entire object and up onto the lid. He'd begun the project to keep busy against the mind-numbing boredom in the trenches but without the proper tools hadn't been able to complete it. He'd resumed work on it as part of his therapy at the hospital, and the result was a stunning work of art.

"I want you to have this, my Milly," he whispered.

I couldn't respond immediately. He had said, *"My Milly."*

He broke the silence with great tenderness in his still raspy voice. "I can't imagine how I would have survived this if I hadn't found you here." He reached for my hand and cradled it gently between both of his. His skin was rough but warm, and his eyes spoke with great affection. My intuition screamed at me to pull away and put a stop to this, but my heart would not let me. Like the sharp edge of a serrated knife sawing through a crusty loaf, the inner softness that I did not know existed was dangerously exposed and vulnerable to all nature of wound.

I'm unsure if it was impulse or instinct that won out, but I leaned in and placed a lingering kiss on his mouth. He responded with great passion, and the boundary lines were finally crossed. He wanted me and not simply for comfort and companionship as I had convinced myself. I was in unfamiliar territory.

I had no illusions about being beautiful. I was too tall, had inherited my mother's long, aristocratic British nose, and I knew that I looked matronly for my age. The no-nonsense air of authority that had stood me well in most aspects of military life also made me unapproachable. I hadn't paid much attention to my reflection in some time but imagined for a moment the sour, rigid face I might find there. Neither had I thought much about my scars; I had done my best to hide them at first, but makeup was hard to come by in the army. Before long, faced with the hideous wounds and scars on so many of our patients, mine had seemed less and less significant . . . until now. I thought about darling Emily and that lovely day in England when secrets had been shared. She cared enough for me to see past the scars and help me find the person hiding beneath.

My beautiful Daniel moved his kisses to my cheek and then my neck as though he were reading my thoughts. Without hesitation, he caressed down my throat and between my breasts and bent to kiss all that had wounded me.

From that day on, whenever an opportunity for privacy arose, we walked and talked as lovers do. We manufactured reasons and places to be alone, often back to the river and the ever-expanding seclusion of the willow. We talked about a great many things but avoided words like "future" and "home." He did finally ask me how I'd come to have such scars.

"I was afflicted with the measles as a small child," I explained matter-of-factly, "and during an episode of high fever and congestion, I was treated with mustard plasters. They were left on for far too long, and then when the plasters were removed, several layers of skin came off with them." His expression reflected the pain that I still remembered after all this time. "The initial injury was bad enough, but the agony I recall in my nightmares is the weeks of debridement that followed."

The coincidence was not lost on us. Although the delivery systems could not have been more different, our burns were both derived from the same source: mustard.

For many weeks, Em, Nora, and Squeak were all that anyone could ask of friends. They were kind and supportive, made no demands of my time outside of work, and filled in for me at Wisp rehearsals. They were not afraid to speak their minds, but even Nora was uncharacteristically charitable with her words and tone. Beneath the lantern light, on a rare evening when we four were all finished for the day, Emily hesitantly asked, "Does he ever mention her?" She had, in her ever-so-tactful way, addressed her concerns more than once, but on this night, she seemed particularly troubled.

"No, he's never spoken more than a sentence or two about Canada or his life there." I had no reason to feel defensive. We all knew that Daniel was a married man. It was clearly noted on his documents, and I had even delivered his wife's letters to him during those first weeks in the infirmary. I looked around at the faces of my friends and knew that they were not judging or condemning; they were simply concerned.

Squeak smiled. "You were smitten with him from the beginning. There was nothing harmful or shameful about admiring a young man and becoming his friend, now was there?" She paused, vacillated before continuing. "But it's much more than that now, isn't it?"

"A great deal more," I replied. "I know I should feel some remorse . . .

shame even. But I don't. I'm not supposed to want him. I'm not supposed to imagine or hope. But I do. It's the most inexplicable thing. I know there's no future, no tomorrow, but for every moment we have together, I want one more. I want to feel my heart skip a beat just one more time, and I hold on tight each time it happens because it might be the last." I mopped away the tears that spilled onto my chin.

Emily moved beside me while Nora piped in. "I feel for his wife, of course, but it's little wonder that romances happen when people are bound together for months at a time. We are all human beings after all and living through extreme circumstances to boot. Oh, I'm not trying to diminish the hardship that folks back home suffer. Ours is different is all. There's every chance we may not see tomorrow."

In a softer tone, but with the same sentiment attached, Emily added, "Soldiers . . . and we're all soldiers," she scanned the faces around her, "will never be able to adequately explain to the folks back home what we've experienced here. They'll never understand, and it won't be their fault, but in the here and now, we make connections because we need them to survive. We've done it. 'We four.' It's not likely that we would have ever crossed paths or been friends back home, but I can't imagine three other people that I'll ever love more. The lads talk about it all the time. The bonds that they make with their comrades are unbreakable."

Nora agreed. "It's not about choice. It's about need." In an uncustomary overture, she plunked down on the end of my bed and took my hand. "You and Daniel were brought together here for a reason. You needed each other, and I don't believe there can be any place for shame or regret in that."

Feeling a little left out, Squeak sprang from her bed to mine and surrounded us in a group hug.

Emily offered a final thought, and it was a sad one on which to end the evening: "He'll be leaving soon, Milly. Matron said she can't put it off any longer." I knew the truth of it, but the words still stung. "It isn't going to be easy, we know, but we'll be here to catch you." More quietly, she added, "I'll always be your soft place to fall."

I drifted into sleep thinking about Emily's words: *We're all soldiers.* I had not considered that. We were always in the line of danger and witness to every imaginable atrocity that one human being could inflict on another. Many of us suffered trauma and symptoms similar to those that the boys dealt with, but we did our best to hide them for fear we'd be sent home as "hysterical women." I supposed it was possible that shell shock could apply to us as well. Even when I was exhausted, I resisted the shrewd temptation of sleep, knowing that haunting images and night terrors were waiting to find me. We weren't in the trenches and couldn't compare our misery to theirs, but our drivers and nurses had suffered many physical injuries as well as emotional ones. I had, on more than one occasion, spend a terrifying night trapped in no man's land before daylight made it safer to return to the hospital with my charges. As in all things, our sex was denied similar status and therefore treatment. Emily was spot on. We were the female Tommies of our generation.

I opened my eyes in one last attempt to deny sleep. The faint outline of my friend was visible in the hint of moonlight coming through the screened window. Her body rose and fell beneath the covers in a slow rhythm that suggested deep slumber, and I envied her. I had no doubt that she would be there to catch me when the inevitable fall occurred.

And it did. Two weeks later, Daniel was transported to England for further treatment and convalescent care. He would undergo surgery to remove some of the scar tissue from his esophagus and lungs before he would be discharged and returned to Canada. Our tearful goodbyes were said many times in the few short hours we spent together before his departure. A big push kept me occupied away from camp much of that time, but we sought one another at every opportunity, each rendezvous more difficult than the last. We made love one last time without speaking; my senses scrutinized every part of him in a silent promise to remember. When we parted, he handed me an envelope with *"My Milly"* scrolled on the front in his beautiful handwriting. Inside, he had written out a poem:

> *Twilight and evening bell,*
> *And after that the dark!*
> *And may there be no sadness of farewell,*
> *When I embark*

LORD ALFRED TENNYSON

Its meaning was clear; I was not to see him off. It would be too difficult. Hours later, he was gone, and in his pocket was the amulet I had made especially for him with a leaf from our willow.

As promised, Emily was there to catch me.

Chapter Twelve

I heard screams and was surprisingly confused by them. They were muffled and distant, and no matter how hard I searched, I could not determine the source. In the dense mist and fog that enveloped me, I saw my mother's smiling face just as the screams drifted further away. I felt the muscles in my face form a smile and smelled the sausages Mother had cooked for breakfast on that last lovely morning. My mind was swimming with the details, the sounds and textures of that last happy holiday at home. I approached wakefulness, annoyed at the interruption of a voice in the distance coaxing me to swim to the surface. Emily's face emerged in the haze, her voice clearer now. "Come on, Mils. Oh my God, Milly, please wake up. Come on darling, it's me. Just open your eyes … that's a good girl … are you still with me? Oh, please, Milly, wake up for God's sake." My eyes fluttered a moment of acknowledgement before another searing pain tore through my body. I recognized that the screams were my own, and I was grateful for the darkness that engulfed me once again.

I watched the dust motes dancing sleepily in the swath of sunlight peeking in through the door. My eyelashes blinked them away when they came too close, and it took long moments before I could focus again. I recognized my surroundings but couldn't concentrate long enough to explain them. There was a heavy fog all around me; the room was spinning but the pain was gone. I remembered pain. I was in a hospital bed; I could hear voices and activity beyond the screens that surrounded me but had no idea why I was there or what had happened.

I made a concerted effort to shake off the cobwebs and make some sense of my situation. *What is the last thing I remember?*

The fighting had escalated again with the Battle of Passchendaele, and I was in constant motion transporting casualties from Allied forces to our doorstep: British, Australian, and New Zealand lads mostly. We had heard that the Americans had finally entered the war effort, but we had not seen much evidence of them as yet in our corner of the world. Twice in as many weeks, my vehicle had broken an axel on the rutted roads leading from the casualty clearing stations, and were it not for the assistance of the soldiers manning the little straw sentry huts, I might never have made it back to the hospital with my charges. I had a recollection of being under my vehicle, struggling to make repairs to the most recent damage, and thinking, *This poor old fella is getting as old and tired as the rest of us.*

The first pain had struck deep in my pelvis. I was frozen in place and couldn't shift my body on the wooden trolley to slide out from under my tired metal companion. I felt a gush of blood and assumed that my monthly had begun, but the second wave of pain told me there was something more going on. I was one of the fortunate few that sailed through menstruation without discomfort. It was a nuisance of course. Fortunately, French nurses in the early days of the war had realized that the disposable cellulose bandages they used on wounded soldiers absorbed blood better than cotton, which was revolutionary for us. Still, supply was always in demand, and we were forced to wash and reuse. I went to my quarters to check on the condition of my clothes and tidy up when another wave of severe pain overwhelmed me. The space around me began to spin and that's when everything became a blur.

Through a gap in the screens, I could see doctors and nurses bustling about, but no one seemed to be making eye contact with me. I lay there still and quiet, a well-behaved soldier waiting for orders. It was such a relief to see Emily's face peek around the screen; I imagined she was there to rescue me from whatever mistake this was. She didn't sidle up onto the edge of the bed but instead sat guardedly on the chair beside it looking ever-so glum. The seconds ticked by slowly as I waited for her to speak or make some overture while worst-case scenarios played loudly in my mind.

Had I been wounded? I reached down to feel that my legs were still there. Finally, with a long outward breath, she reached for my hand, held it in hers, and brought it to her lips for a kiss. She opened her mouth to speak, but words (although well-rehearsed) eluded her, and she wept uncontrollably. I twined my fingers through hers and waited until she finally gained control. She began her speech with "You're going to be all right. You've been in and out of consciousness for nearly a week, and we thought we'd lost you at one point." She drew out a hanky, sniffed, and carried on to explain in great detail all that had happened since she'd found me unconscious in a pool of blood on the floor of our tent. In the end, the only words I heard were "You'll never be able to have a child." I gasped for air, suffocating and inconsolable. I had been pregnant and had no idea.

So many questions circled. "What woman doesn't know that they're with child?" I chided myself aloud. "How could I not know?" I demanded of Emily. Already on the bed beside me, she moved closer, cradling me in her arms. She repeated her earlier explanation slowly, waiting for me to absorb each account before continuing.

"You suffered a miscarriage. It was an ectopic pregnancy." Again, she waited to be sure I'd heard her and understood the words. My expression told her clearly that I had no idea what an ectopic pregnancy was, and so she explained further. "Sometimes they call it a tubal pregnancy because the fertilized egg never makes it to the womb. Instead, the fetus grows in the fallopian tube until there is no room for it. In your case, the tube ruptured, and that's why there was so much pain and bleeding." She waited and watched for my reaction before continuing. She was exhausted, and I knew that her heart was breaking for me, but she pressed on. "We had no way of knowing how long you had been in that state, only that you'd lost a tremendous volume of blood. The doctors—well, the whole staff really—just assumed it was a normal miscarriage and didn't recognize the severity of it right away." She looked apologetic. "The demands were so great at the time . . . so many wounded, just so much . . ." Her voice drifted off.

I stopped her. "They had little time to worry over a girl who had gotten herself in the family way."

She nodded reluctantly. "They assumed the bleeding would stop in a day or two and that you would come around after a transfusion. But you didn't, and the hemorrhage continued, and your temperature shot up. By the time they'd diagnosed you correctly, the infection had already set in and there was nothing more to be done. They removed your uterus. They call it a hysterectomy." She was galvanized in her commitment to ensure that I understood all the cold clinical details, but her delivery and the expression in her voice was fraught with emotion. Still, she'd confirmed again what it meant for my future.

Walls of darkness closed in around me. Nora and Squeak were among the many friends and associates who visited in the days that followed. They spoke all the appropriate words in a futile effort to lift me from the cell of solitary confinement in which I was trapped. I felt as though I was suspended in cold stark stone, sculpted in relief, and isolated while all around me receded.

I acquiesced to the ministrations and sadistic rituals of the hospital staff. The dressings were routinely changed on my long, ugly abdominal incision, and the drainage tubes were checked for any blockage. Bottles of fluids were refilled, and once every day, a nurse (looking apologetic and embarrassed) administered the obligatory douche of Dakin's solution diluted to half strength. My senses were stifled. Nothing hurt. I didn't cry. I was numb. I watched the doctors and nurses weaving about from my new vantage point. It was a unique perspective that gave me greater appreciation, but I knew that there was no treatment for the invisible agony I suffered. This was so vastly different from the sadness I'd felt at Daniel's departure. I tumbled it over in my mind. For weeks, I had suffered a desperate ache, always on the brink of tears. I likened it to a nasty head cold that I knew I would have to ride out, suffering the symptoms that would surely pass with patience and time. But this was no common cold. This was a cancer.

The nursing matron stopped in on a few occasions to monitor my progress. She might easily have shipped me home at the first opportunity, but the mutual respect that we had developed over time held me in good stead during this ordeal. She reported that *"Lieutenant Aspinall suffered a ruptured appendix and following surgery is healing well. She will be returning to duty in good time."* While most of the nursing staff were aware of the true nature of my internment, a ruptured appendix was the story they were all sticking with. I was thankful for their respect and compassion. I was never shamed. I was grateful.

I searched my mind for solace. I listened carefully for the *Sonnish*, for wisdom and spiritual guidance, but to no avail. My despair was shrouded in guilt and bereft of logic. *Do I deserve this? Is this my punishment for breaking the rules, for ignoring my instincts and loving despite all reason?*

Emily brought a supper tray dressed up with cloth napkin, a china teacup, and a daisy in an effort to disguise the flaccid appearance of my soft diet. I gave her an obligatory smile, and she did her best to make small talk. I was thinking that this was the first time I had felt a disconnect between us when she reached into the pocket of her apron and pulled out my gold locket. She pressed it into my hand. "Your amulet has been under your pillow all this long time, but I thought perhaps Alice might bring you some comfort."

I was wrong. Emily could see into the deepest hiding places of my soul. Alice's letter arrived the next day.

My Chree,

*You have been much on my mind. The wind has carried your torment
to me although I do not know its source. Hold tight, my darling. Tie
your angel wings to mine, and together, we will defeat whatever darkness has befallen you. Do not chide or judge yourself too harshly as I
know you do so often; find instead your reflection in the eyes of all those
who love you. Simply speak my name, and I will come to find you at the
willow where we will weep joyful tears together.*

Always,
Shuyr my chree, Alice

I was still holding the letter when Emily returned that day. "Help me,
Em. Help me open a door."

"The door is open, Milly; you just have to reach out for my hand, and
we'll walk through it together."

In time, the hopelessness diminished, but a light had gone out, and I
could feel that my spirit had changed. On the first opportunity to take me
outdoors, Emily wheeled me down to the river. She sat beside the wheelchair,
patient and caring as always.

"I want to talk about the baby." The announcement surprised me as
much as it did her. "Did they know how many weeks along it was? Could
they tell the sex?"

"They think it was about twelve weeks, but they didn't mention anything
about the gender." Her eyes captured mine and did not let go. She waited.

I tried to trace back through the calendar to find the moment of concep-
tion—the moment when Daniel and I had created another human being.
Still, Emily watched and waited.

"What a waste," I finally whispered. "There was a piece of him that I could
have cherished always. I would have loved that baby so much." She did not
respond, simply nodding in acknowledgement.

This was my first sojourn back to a place that had once felt like a peaceful
haven—a place that I had deliberately avoided after Daniel left. There seemed
little joy in anything without him. The heart of the universe continued to
beat but mine had slowed into a lonely rhythm. I moved through each day

doing all that was expected of me, fighting hard against grief and trying to push him to the back of my mind. He was far away but right beside me. I filled the emptiness with memories, guarding every moment as though it might be snatched away. I felt his essence in the breeze and heard his voice in every note of music while his divine eyes sparkled from the stars.

I broke the silence. "We agreed to make a clean break of it. No letters. No contact."

"That was probably wise, don't you think?" Emily noted. When I didn't respond, she continued. "You have written though, haven't you?" She smiled a knowing smile.

"Volumes and volumes," I said. "Almost every day, I pour my heart into letters that will never be sent."

Never judging, Emily simply said, "That sounds like good therapy. I am no expert on the subject, Mil, but I do believe that in time the loneliness will diminish. Take some comfort in that if you can."

As we approached 1918, little changed in our daily routine. The hospital grew in volume and population, and tents popped up like wild mushrooms all over the landscape. Matron was transferred to a base hospital closer to the coast, and the new matron in chief was a militaristic warhorse with an unyielding temperament.

Daniel was never far from my thoughts. I had heard through the grapevine that he had been treated at the Auxiliary Military Hospital in Preston's Moor Park, and it warmed my heart to imagine him at home in Lancashire, although Preston was far to the north of my hometown. My letters to him were a weekly indulgence akin to a diary, but I remained true to my promise. It was Daniel who yielded. In one lonely postcard sent from the hospital ship *Araguaya* en route to Canada, he had written, "My Darling Lancashire Lass, yours always, Daniel."

I felt the gaping wound re-open in my soul.

Air-raid attacks were ever increasing and sirens sounded around the clock. There was little time or desire for sleep. We pressed on. Nora was loaned out to an Aussie unit not far away, and we missed her rare but infectious smiles, her grit, and her tangy personality. We stayed in touch, of course, and saw her occasionally, making the most of those rare reunions, usually in the barn, sharing a sip from a secreted flask of Scotch. There seemed to be a steady stream of volunteers who occupied her space in our tent, but the only name that stayed with me was "Gertie." She was a funny gal with a lovely temperament, long gangly legs like mine, and teeth too big for the space in her mouth. Hers were the best care packages, and she didn't hesitate to share anything that her family sent—cakes, treats and the like. She had a lovely singing voice and fit in immediately with the Wisps. We were fortunate that the new matron did not object to the troupe or the goings on at the barn. She watched and monitored strictly during her first few weeks to be sure that there was no interference with the work to be done. Satisfied that we were all mature enough to meet our obligations, she conceded that the entertainment was a tangible use of our free time and a good escape for patients in recovery.

Emily, who found something good to say about everyone, made an exception for the matron. Rankled beyond consolation, she stated defiantly, "She's an acidulous old cow." We were in the mess tent where nosy ears were always on the lookout for gossip or rancour.

I hushed her a bit. "Em, keep it down, sweetie. You'll be dropping us both in it." Splinters of anger were stabbing at the air. "What's she done now?" She didn't really have to tell me; I knew that, since her arrival, it seemed that the old bat had made it her mission to annoy Emily.

She lowered her voice. "She's 'keeping me in my place.' That's what. My God, you'd think that after three years of this shit I might have earned some degree of respect. I'm a nurse, God damn it, and a good one, pushing around a tea trolley when there are boys over there moaning in pain and looking for a nurse." It was a little disconcerting to hear her swear, but I was proud and happy that she was finally offering herself a much-deserved pat on the back.

"So, what are you going to do about it?"

"I'm going to march right into her office and tell her how I feel; that's what I'm going to do. Now, what do you make of that?" The speech was incredibly out of character.

I responded carefully. "That's exactly what I think you should do, but I'll believe it when I see it," I said with a grin. "Just for now though, let's go to the tent and pour you a wee nip to calm you down before you storm in there and start another war before this one is over."

True to her word, Emily had a sit down with the matron and came away galvanized to complete formal nurses training at the first opportunity. I had little doubt she would breeze through it. In the meantime, the relationship between the two women changed. There was a mutual appreciation, and over time, a degree of respect.

Tragedy struck in June when an air raid sounded and bombs fell from overhead. The thudding and rumbling were so commonplace that we barely noticed just how close they were until two massive explosions erupted within the camp. The first destroyed the delousing tent and several others, killing two orderlies and injuring a doctor. The second was a direct hit on the barn. There was panic, screaming, and people running about without a purpose. The fire brigade was quick to respond, and litters of wounded were being carried into the triage and surgical units. I was in the transport office, checking the roster and awaiting orders for my shift.

My first thoughts were of my dearest friend: *Em! Where's Em?* I dashed across the compound, heading for our tent, and met her halfway. She was looking for me. It was utter chaos. The smoke was thick, making it difficult to see where the damage was, but it appeared that the wards and the surgeries were intact. Emily spotted it first and pointed a shaky finger toward our lovely theatre. The wooden structure was a tinder box, and flames were leaping high into the air. The fire brigade was losing the battle. "Squeak!" she exclaimed over the din. "She was over there setting up for tonight! I think Gertie was going with her. . ."

Stretcher bearers were making their way up the path toward us, six of them in all. Two of the VADs who had been helping with the new sets were severely burned, and the two lads who had followed them in like puppies were scorched and black. One did not survive. Squeak was on the next stretcher, and she reached for me as they passed. I held tight to her hand and followed with her into triage, letting go only when a nurse insisted kindly that I wait outside. Emily was speaking to the lads who had carried in the first of the litters. "Was there another girl in there?" There was desperation in the words. I watched their faces as they looked at one another and then glanced over toward the path we had just taken. One more litter was being carried ever-so-gently toward us, the body completely covered in a sheet. Gertie was dead.

Squeak had severe burns on all her limbs, but her sweet face was spared. Her right leg had been shattered by a falling timber, and there was little doubt that she would lose it. The surgeons worked on her for hours but made no headway in saving the leg. Morphine was her friend in the weeks that followed, keeping her quiet and comfortable. I was grateful for the gift of unconsciousness it offered her. A special funeral service was held for those killed in the raid, and we cried through the service as we had not done at the myriad others we had attended over the years. The minister, angry and uninhibited, said, "This war—this damnable war—has stolen from us an entire generation of youth." How right he was.

Squeak suffered tortuous debridement and took the news of her leg in stoic silence. We spent a part of every day at her side, and hearing the horrifying news, Nora made the trek to see her several times. Her family was notified of course and informed that it would be some time before she could make the journey home. First, she would be transported to the Paris-Plage convalescent home for further treatment and richly deserved care and comfort. I spent a great many hours with her in the days leading up to her departure and learned that I had never really come to know the amazing woman beneath the giddy façade. More's the pity. We shared many profound and insightful conversations, and I found that I could no longer bring myself to call her "Squeak." The name simply did not fit the countenance of this resilient woman. Even Dotty seemed too frivolous a name for her. She was Dorothy. I'd always understood her to be kind and sweet. Generous too. I was grateful to learn, not too late, that beneath her surface lay an abundance of riches—a soulful depth of character, spiritual insight, and wisdom. Although blind to them, I recognized that I had been on the receiving end of these gifts from the beginning. In one poignant conversation, she spoke of loss.

"We will be leaving a great deal behind us in the soil of France, won't we, Milly?" Her eyes held mine in a vice grip. "You more than me, I think." There was tender sadness in her voice . . . grief not for herself but for me.

Astounded, I asked, "How do you mean?" I could not imagine how she could equate my suffering to hers. She had lost so much. Both a limb and her dreams of returning to dance, as well as her spritely innocence, had been torn from her in one tragic event.

She was thoughtful but not afraid to put into words what was in her heart.

Fond and quiet but speaking with certainty, she announced, "I will see my child dance one day."

I stroked her lovely blonde hair back from her brow. "And, my dear friend, we shall dance together at her wedding." It was a wish more than a promise, but I meant it sincerely.

On the day of her departure, she was carried gingerly to the awaiting vehicle. "We three" held hands in a silent prayer and a mature and serious Dorothy commanded, "We must find and follow new dreams, ladies. And we will." We said our tearful goodbyes. The camp was suddenly cold and quiet. Lonely.

On the eleventh day of the eleventh month, 1918, the armistice was signed, and hostilities ended (for the most part). I was skeptical. The fighting had escalated in recent days with heavy shelling, deafening noise, and countless wounded. How could it all end so abruptly? All around the world, people were celebrating but not here. It was as though, after years of fear and suffering, no one knew what to do next. Moving around in a state of bewilderment, I felt exhausted for the first time in as many months, numb at the prospect of peace. I was grateful that there was still so much to do and so little time to spend with my thoughts. Whenever I closed my eyes, the ghostly images of the thousands of lost lives marched single file through my mind, dragging their fifty pounds of kit, each searching for the little white cross in the graveyard that bore their name. I thought of all those nameless souls who would never find a peaceful resting place.

The hospital was overflowing with wounded and sick. The influenza virus sweeping through the continent was killing as many of our poor lads as the bombs and shells had done. The matron confided that it would be months before most soldiers would go home. She explained to the staff that the process of demobilization on this massive scale was a complicated and lengthy one. Medical examinations were required so that soldiers would be able to make a claim for disabilities resulting from military service, and the sheer numbers of men would make transportation slow and arduous. I was determined to stay the course. I celebrated the armistice, thanked God that the hostilities would end, but unlike many, I was in no hurry to leave. These people were my family, and this way of life was all that I knew. The idea of going home filled me with trepidation.

Emily on the other hand was anxious and motivated to move on to the next phase in her life. Matron had promised her a glowing recommendation and any assistance she could provide in her pursuit of a nursing degree. She was giddy at the prospect of holding a piece of paper that acknowledged her skills and accomplishments. Together with her experience in France, she hoped that a degree would ultimately secure for her a position in a British hospital and the respect she had earned. I was happy and enthusiastic with her and for her.

A month passed; the signatures were dry on the document that had put an end to the war, but we were told it would be months more before an actual peace treaty was signed. At camp, the rules relaxed, and Scotch was flowing freely in our tent on the evening when the penny dropped. Emily had been talking excitedly into the wee hours about her future and about the letter from her father describing the prolific need for nurses back home with more wounded arriving daily. Her animated chatter came to a screeching halt at the sudden realization that, after four years, we would be going our separate ways. My face told the tale; I suspect my every thought was usually written there. I envied her sense of purpose, the firm path etched out before her with a shining light beckoning in the distance. I felt no jealousy. I was immensely proud of this courageous woman: my friend . . . my sister. But unlike her, I could envisage no path, no clear way forward. I had only hindsight. Like the ghostly figures in my nightmares, I saw only dense grey fog beyond my next footfall.

Em was sitting in silence, struggling to find the right words. "W-We'll see each other often back home. Won't we, Milly?" she stammered. "You can come to stay with me in London while I'm in training, and then I'll find a post in Manchester or—"

I stopped her mid-sentence. "I'm not going back, Em. There's nothing there for me. I'm going to stay on here until the hospital is all packed up, and then I'll move on and help where I'm needed. Belgium perhaps. They say it'll be at least a year before the bigger hospitals can close their doors."

Emily's face was ashen, her breaths shallow and quick; I was afraid she might faint dead away. I raced over to hold her, but she didn't move at all. I held her shoulders and gave her a little shake.

"Come on, old girl, it's not as bad as all that." I put on a big comic smile in a futile effort to lighten the mood. It fell short of the mark.

The war was over, but neither of us had considered this moment. We didn't speak, but I could see the gamut of emotions playing out on Emily's face just as they were playing out in my mind, each of us contemplating life without the other. Finally, we dressed for bed and cuddled while watching our shadows dance together on the tent wall in time to the rhythm of the flickering lamplight. *Who would I be without her?* She had been my anchor since the very first day, always sunny and warm, gently sanding around my sharp edges without ever making it obvious even to me. She was my social crutch as well as my friend and most ardent supporter. *How will I survive without my shadow?* I felt physical pain at the thought of saying goodbye. Always in sync, I knew she was feeling exactly the same. I lay my hand on her chest and felt the rapid beating of her heart.

We spent the next few days avoiding each other, avoiding further conversation, and avoiding the inevitable. It wasn't difficult really as we were busy around the clock, but still the tension was unbearable. We struggled through small talk, making meals out of discussions about the weather. It was uncomfortable new territory for a relationship branded in comfortable ease and openness.

We happened to arrive together at the mess tent. Over a plate of stew, we passed the time of day. She started it: the game of "Who will?" It was, as usual, an effort on her part to make everything better for me. "Who will swipe my last piece of bread?" she asked as I reached for her crust, and she slapped away my hand as usual. I was taken aback for a moment until the grin on her face told me we were playing a game.

"Who will irritatingly correct my grammar?" I responded in kind. The game was perfect. She was perfect.

For several weeks, we played, and it kept us amused. *Who will finish the last biscuit in the tin? Who will finish my sentences? Who will laugh at my joke when no one else does? Who will answer my questions even before I ask them?*

We walked through the day of tears in a blur. The transport was waiting to take my precious girl away. "How will I fill the gaping hole where my Emily used to be?" I asked as her bags were loaded onto the lorry.

"Who will love me unconditionally?" she responded.

We held tight for as long as we could, but finally, one of the nurses took her hand and led her to the steps of the vehicle. The ground opened to swallow me, and I raced to her for one last kiss.

"My *Chree*."

"*Shuyr my Chree*," she whispered back.

When Matron called me into her office a fortnight later, I assumed it would be with news of a transfer to Belgium. We had discussed it at length, and she'd had no hesitation in recommending me for the post. Although still skillfully organized, the room looked bare, with books and files crated up for shipping. She sat behind her desk, looking smaller in these stark surroundings, and her usually starved demeanour took on a different appearance as she asked me to be seated. "Miss Aspinall," she began in her customary frosty, professional tone, "I would like first to say that your exemplary work here has been appreciated." Her voice softened just a little as she continued. "You should be very proud of the role you have played in the war effort."

I was astonished by both the words and the delivery, and although feeling quite speechless, I managed to say, "Thank you, Matron. I'm grateful for your acknowledgement and for your leadership." Something in her expression made me feel uncomfortable. *Oh my God, where are you sending me? Africa?* I was quite open to any new adventure, but just wanted her to get on with it and put me out of my misery.

Finally, she opened the piece of paper in front of her and said, "I've received a telegram from England. Milly, your father has passed away." She waited for just a moment, watching for my reaction before reading the message. I was still turning over in my mind the notion that she had just called me by my first name when she continued, reading the telegram:

Dearest Milly (stop)

Papa passed away on Friday (stop)

It was his heart (stop)

Mother is inconsolable (stop)

Please come home soonest (stop)

I need you, Alice (stop)

I would not be going to Belgium. My adventures were over; I was going home, and I knew there would be no coming back. Matron read my mind and rose from her chair. "I am sincerely sorry for your loss, but the time has come to put a period at the end of this sentence, has it not, Milly?" I nodded. She handed me a scrap of paper. "Take this with you to the communication hut. It will give you leave to send a message in response. I will begin making arrangements for your departure and transport. I can make no promises about how quickly we can get you home, but we shall do our very best."

I sent a simple response to Alice, "On my way (stop)," and one to Emily, "Father has died (stop) I'm on my way home (stop)."

Chapter Thirteen

The funeral had taken place long before I made it home. Emily met my train in London, her face like a beacon in the steam and filth of the platform. We could not have predicted that we would be seeing each other so soon, and although our reunion was bittersweet, I felt somehow replenished just at the sight of her. We had just time enough for a quick visit if I were to make my connection north, as she would head back to the hospital where her training had already begun. We sat together in the refreshment room and clinked our glasses of brandy—comforting brandy—in a toast to my father. She was happy to share news of the funeral, which both she and her dad, Dr. Davidson, had attended.

"It was a wonderful turnout, Mil. You would have been so proud. Your dad clearly made a mark in the community and was very well thought of." When I didn't respond, she continued. "Your brother William said the eulogy, and your mother, looking ever-so sophisticated, was stoic through the whole service. Alice told me that she'd been a desperate mess up until then."

Solemnly, I said, "I'll do what I can to support her; that's really why I've come home."

"I know, and she'll be glad of it."

We parted with promises to meet again as soon as her study schedule would allow. It was yet another tearful goodbye.

The weeks passed, and Mother's grief settled into a deliberate return to routine. Father, I learned, had been ill for some time, leaving my eldest brother to run the family business. Those from our family who had served in the war effort overseas had survived, fractured in one way or another but alive, and I was grateful for that. How sadly ironic it was that my father should not live long enough to witness finalization of the peace treaty. Fate. Cruel sadistic fate!

Grief and sadness were put on a shelf to be dusted off from time to time; the British stiff upper lip was in full rigor mortis. Everyone had a role to play except me. Mother continued her committee work. "The Representation of the People Bill passed in February, allowing women over thirty the right to vote," she announced proudly. "It was a tremendous moment for the suffrage movement, which might never have been achieved were it not for the war and the strides made by women like you who proved your merit." She touched my face. "But there is still much to be done. We continue to work tirelessly toward legislation that will give women equal rights to vote; men are eligible at age twenty-one." She also had her grandchildren to fuss over and insisted that the kitchen and the cooking were still her domain, snatching the apron from my hands and pushing me out the door whenever I dared to interfere.

My brothers were all gainfully employed and busy with their own wives and families. Richard had come a long way in his recovery and worked alongside William at the factory as his second in command in charge of the books and finances. They had no need of my help, and for that I was silently grateful. Alice continued her work mending and sewing; she had made it her mission to transform my outdated, oversized civilian clothes, nipping and tucking until the waistline of the garments fit my smaller frame. She had not heeded her physician's advice and was once again in the family way; this would be number seven.

Return to civilian life was not easy. I mourned my father's passing of course but felt the loss of my independence and self-worth even more deeply. I learned that, while I had been overseas, many of the local girls had been working in all manner of jobs left vacant by the men. Our neighbour Francine had worked at the Cunard Shell Works at Merseyside, preparing projectile heads, and another gal had driven a streetcar. Women all over the country had proven their worth working in forestry, delivering coal, and running businesses; the Women's Land Army provided a workforce to run the farms. But the men were home, and it wasn't long before old assumptions resumed: "A woman's place is in the home."

I desperately missed the discipline and order of military life and could not stand the feel of my civilian clothes.

Spring turned into summer seemingly unnoticed, and I coaxed myself out of bed each day, into my fussy clothes, and out for a walk. I was bored and lonesome, immersed in a mood of blank hopelessness; everything and everyone irritated me, so I felt it best to keep my own company. It had only been a matter of weeks, but it seemed an eternity since I'd been content. I desperately needed an occupation. I was persuaded to stroll down the length of the property toward the big wicker chair by the river, and I noticed (for the first time in my memory) that the gardens were unkempt. I pictured my father on his knees weeding and fussing, snipping buds from the rose bushes in his silly straw hat. The garden missed him as I did, but I had found something tangible to do. Much to Mother's dismay, I donned my khaki overalls and an old shirt from my father's wardrobe and began restoring the garden to its former glory, taking especially tender care with the roses.

Each time she passed me, she groaned her disapproval and plunked a straw hat on my head. I tossed it aside as soon as she was out of sight in favour of full exposure to the warming rays of the sun. The perfume of the honeysuckle filled the air, and the fragrant buds of white and purple lilacs shivered with excitement, ready to burst. Each day, I was wooed ever closer to the river and to the willow pavilion that waited patiently there. It had been my favourite childhood hideaway; I could tuck myself away beneath its gracefully dancing branches in plain view of the household and yet somehow secreted. I was the youngest of seven children; my parents were already old (in their forties for goodness' sake) by the time I came along. I always felt that I was underfoot and in the way, except there.

Mother, as usual, had been paying attention. She came out of the house carrying a tray with lemonade and biscuits. "Come along, dear," she said, gliding toward the wicker chairs alongside the tree. It always seemed to me that her feet never actually touched the ground; they just hovered above it under her skirts. I followed her, and we sat quietly together, allowing the sun to lick our skin. She had not yet scolded me about the hat.

"It used to seem so much bigger," I blurted, looking upward.

She smiled. "You were very small when you first found comfort here." I remembered with fondness the day that she had introduced me to the spot. In my mind's eye, I could see that we were dressed in our Sunday best, but I could not recall why. We'd sat close together on a blanket cuddled against the damp, and even at that early age, I had treasured that rare precious moment alone with her.

She broke into my thoughts. "Do you remember the afternoon we spent here? The day that I told you the story of the faeries?"

I nodded blithely and quoted, "'They speak only to those who really listen.'"

"The *Sonnish*," she said, "the cherished voices of those gone before. And what do they bring with them, my Milly?" She was speaking to me as though

I were a child, but I didn't mind.

I closed my eyes. "The *Shee*."

"Spirit and peace," I heard her say, but the tears welling up behind my closed lids were making me feel self-conscious and uncomfortable. She reached over and cupped my face with her hands. "You've lost yourself, haven't you, my dear?"

I nodded, and the tears flowed freely. "I haven't heard the whispers in an awfully long time. I think they are lost to me. I try, but there is no joy, no peace, even here in this beautiful garden. I tread through each day soberly, without wings. I know there are colours all around me, but I see only dismal grey . . . soot and ash. It's stained here and there in the rusty brown of blood. So much blood." I was shivering in the sunshine. As though she knew it would be too much, she resisted the urge to console or wrap her arms around me. She held my hands and waited for the tremors to subside. When I opened my eyes, she was sitting close by my feet, and with her fingers spread out flat on the ground, she was tracing a figure eight with her hand. Her timing, as always, was intuitive.

Finally, she said, "Do you know, Milly, that the trees talk to each other?" She didn't wait for a response. "They do." She continued. "There's a relationship between them, a nurturing interconnected network, a family. They speak their own language and share each other's resources. When one tree suffers a trauma and the roots are damaged, it takes time to heal and grow. It must reach out and seek the others for support." She stopped just a moment to be sure she had my attention; she did. "The oldest and largest sustain the weak because they have greater access to the sunlight, the strength and knowledge to feed those in need."

I acknowledged that I understood her meaning, but she persisted. "I have been witness to the trauma that your brothers have suffered but in particular the horrors of the mind that continue to plague Richard. Milly, I see in you the same symptoms, the same far-off look."

I felt such adoration for this woman who had suffered so much but could still open her heart to feel the pain of others. She was remarkable. "You are right, of course. I'm sorry, Mama. I have not come home to be a burden to you; I know you are grieving still, and I should be taking care of you." She stroked my hand gently and waited while I gathered my thoughts; she did not interrupt them with her own. I composed myself as best I could and continued quieter than before, just a notch above voicing no sound at all. "I have an overwhelming desire not to feel anything again, but instead, I feel shame and guilt for wishing, every day, *If only I could die.*" I watched but her face did not react. "I don't know what to do."

"You've made a start today, simply opening up to me. As it happens, I have already taken the second step on your behalf." She was decisive in her delivery. "Dr. Davidson is coming tomorrow to have a chat with you."

We sat in comfortable silence for a time, each lost in thought; Mother no doubt listening to the whispers, smiles periodically creeping over the corners of her mouth. I watched the branches waving their arms as the wind conducted the music and imagined myself as a child. This had been the place where I came to pretend, where I travelled to the four corners of the round world, and in my imaginings, visited the pyramids and the Orient. I swashbuckled aboard magnificent ships! My fantasies included a life on the stage where, as a world-renowned singer, I had the undivided attention of all around me. I would curtsy, graciously accepting the applause of my appreciative audience and the accolades from the king and queen when they attended my performance at Royal Albert Hall.

After my illness and the painful burns, Mother had brought me here each day, and I'd found some measure of relief beneath my sparkly tree. The sunlight, especially in the early morning, gave the tiny leaves a silvery appearance that twinkled when they danced in the breeze. It was my favourite time of the day and my most beloved place to be. As I leaned back in the chair and watched the glittering dance, I found it difficult to summon those joyful feelings, and yet I was still drawn to this place.

Dr. Davidson had not changed at all. He was as kind and gentle as the daughter he had raised. We talked for hours about important things and about nothing at all. He came by to visit twice that week and again the next; he was patient, did not push, and waited for me to exhale. With that breath, a flood of emotions—violent emotions—were released. I admitted to having suicidal thoughts, always sitting on the precipice but never brave enough to dive over the edge. "There are so many feelings: anger, fear, resentment, helplessness—"

He stopped me from continuing the list, placing a hand on my arm. "Those are not the worst of them. Is that right?" Clearly, he already knew the answer to his question.

"Guilt," I replied. "Guilt and shame." He didn't ask what I felt guilty about. He really hadn't asked about any specifics. I wondered if Emily had betrayed my trust and told him about Daniel and the baby. Then I scolded myself. *Em would never do that.*

"Milly, I've spoken to hundreds of chaps and heard horror stories that keep me awake in the night, and I didn't even experience them. One can only imagine what you've been through. Of all the myriad emotions replaying in your mind, guilt and shame are among the most debilitating. Or at least that's what I have witnessed." He tipped his head slightly to the left as he spoke as though to look at me from another angle. Emily often did the same.

The air in the room was heavy and velvet. Beads of sweat were twinkling on his brow. I knew that Mother would want me to offer him a cold drink, and I rose from my seat to play hostess to this kind man. He pulled me back down into the chair and spoke to me in his clinical voice. "Milly, there is no formula or cure for what you're going through. I wish there were. You can't deny your feelings any more than you can deny the events and the conflicts that you survived, but you must allow yourself time. Be patient with yourself."

I told him about the ghosts and my night terrors, and how I had tried day after day to climb out of this cavernous despair. I looked around to be sure Mother hadn't come home. "As horrific as it was over there, I dreaded coming home. Isn't that horrible when I think of all the lads who wished for nothing else? I honestly do not know how I will cope with this life of mundane drudgery. The monotony of setting one foot in front of the other is more than I can bear." I was on a rant, but he made no attempt to inhibit me. "The whole country is in a state of shock and grief. This household is grieving. Everything and everyone seem to be moving in slow motion, colourless like some insipid painting in shades of grey. I feel lost in it, swallowed up."

He looked intently into my eyes. "Your mother is suffering through the stages of grief, yes?"

"Yes, of course."

"And you show her gentle concern and patience, yes?"

I nodded.

"Milly, should you not then offer yourself the same? Your guilt, I can guarantee, is misplaced, but you must dissect it for yourself. If indeed you have anything at all to feel guilty for, make amends if need be. I hope it will motivate you just a little to know that the people who love you, me included, are grateful for the gift of your survival." The last sentence melted away into silence and with it my heart.

Dr. Davidson promised to come by again in another week but left his contact information should I have need of him urgently. "I miss her desperately," I said as he was leaving. "Emily is very important to me." He caught me in a bear hug and said his goodbyes.

True to his word, he arrived the following week with two surprises for me. The first was a lovely long letter from Emily, which I tucked away in my pocket to enjoy later, and the second a beautifully handcrafted notebook. "I would like you to begin keeping a journal, a daily entry to express your thoughts and feelings no matter how insignificant you may think they are. It is my experience that writing the words will help to reduce the tension you feel and may in time give you some respite from the power they hold over you."

I thanked him for the lovely gift and promised to follow his instructions. He took his usual seat by the window and waited for the conversation to orchestrate itself. He had a deep understanding of all my symptoms. He confirmed what I already knew. "You are suffering from shell shock, no different at all from the diagnosis given the lads. If you open a textbook, you will find it defined as a *'psychological disturbance caused by prolonged exposure to active warfare, especially being under bombardment.'* I would say you fit that description. Wouldn't you?" He did not judge when I explained the guilt that gnawed at me for wishing in my heart that my adventure was not over.

"Does that sound masochistic?" I asked him in earnest.

He shook his head. "You identify yourself in this role; it's become your persona. We all want to feel needed and important, and there is no shame in that. You simply must find other avenues for your talents and open your mind to all that you are and can be."

I admired and trusted this man, and I knew that by holding anything back I would make it all the more difficult for him to help me. "There's something more that I need to share with you Dr. D." My voice quivered hesitantly, but he didn't press. He was leaning back in a casual posture, as usual, with one elbow propped on the arm of the chair, his thumb cupping his chin and his forefinger reaching out to his cheekbone. I was thinking, *How beautifully manicured his nails are; it's such an important thing.*

I was hedging and still he waited patiently, his eyes promising no judgment. I confided in him the story of my ordeal and the burden of shame I carried with me from France. I scrutinized his face for evidence of shock or aversion, but his expression held only concern and sympathy. In a burst of tears, I said, "I do not dare to confide, even to my beloved sister, about my darling Daniel, a married man. I will have to go to my grave with the secret of my pregnancy. I will never marry . . . never bear children or have the future that I hoped for." He was kneeling beside me then, hanky in hand. "My sister is with child again, Dr. D. Did you know that? This will be her seventh. I desperately want to be happy for her. Really, I do, but I cannot bear to look at her for fear my jealousy will spill out into rage. No one can know my story, and neither will they ever understand the depths of my despair. I feel so alone."

"You have me, and I know you have Em. Do not be so quick to discount those around you; I think you do not give your sister enough credit. She strikes me as a woman of great character with a kind and open mind." I know he didn't intend to sound lecturing, but his words came across that way. My thoughts registered on my face as usual because his voice softened then. "You have been left powerless and vulnerable, Milly. You are grieving, and I'm so incredibly sorry for your loss." He meant it. "Why don't you tell me all about Daniel? He must be a very special man."

This was not the response I imagined, but oh, how wonderful it was to talk about my Daniel.

It had been raining in a steady downpour for days and a stroll even to sit beneath the tree held no appeal. Mother decided to visit Alice, who was coming close to her time. I was invited to accompany her but politely excused myself as I had letters to write. I decided instead to brave the elements and go out to do a few errands. I picked up liniment from Boots chemist and went to the grocers to do a shop for tea. I was happy to see that the shelves were starting to fill up with stock. Safely home, I shook off my wet mac, made myself a cuppa, and settled in at the writing desk to start my letters and make an entry in my journal. I finished the last letter, which was to Nora, who had finally written to say she was settled in Australia. Her decision to emigrate came as no surprise; she had enjoyed her assignment with the Aussies a great deal and talked about the possibility each time we saw her. I scoured my mind for news to share and did my best to sound upbeat, but I kept the note brief and signed off with a promise to keep in touch. I added it to the stack of letters to go into the post.

I reached for my journal and sat for some time, coaxing the pen to form words on the page. I looked down at the last entry, *"Grief isn't rational,"* and could find no more to say. I knew I must make more of an effort and was determined not to leave the desk until I had made some headway. I was annoyed by a knock at the door and then another, quite sure that it must be a caller for one of the boys, and since no one else was at home, I chose to ignore it. At the third knock, I reluctantly rose from the desk and moved toward the door.

My spirits were immediately lifted at the sight of my dear Emily on the doorstep swaddled in a bright-red rain jacket and hat. *Colour! Just look at that colour!* She was like a ray of sunshine. We embraced for what seemed a long time, and once settled in the front room, we sat holding hands for even longer. We had so much to talk about but for many moments said nothing at all. There had been letters, of course, but words on a page paled in comparison to an all-out natter with your best mate.

Emily knew that her father had been spending time with me. The content of our conversations was private of course, but I didn't mind sharing them with my friend. She was pleased to know that I had felt comfortable enough to confide everything to her dad and was certain a step had been taken in the right direction. She told me all about her studies and life in London. We reminisced, cried, whispered, and even heard ourselves laughing throughout the afternoon. There was a lull in the conversation, and Emily bounced from her seat, grabbed my hand, and led me upstairs. She snatched up the case that she had left at the front door, and with a huge grin and in her best snooty upper-crust voice, said, "Come on, Jeeves, and show me to my room."

She deposited her case on the bed, looked me up and down, and snickered.

"Hmmm . . . that simply won't do. Put on your best frock . . . Seriously, something that isn't grey or black. We're going out on the town." She followed me into my room, rummaging through my wardrobe. She pulled out a skirt made from a green checked fabric, recently altered for me by Alice, and a white blouse with ridiculous ruffles that she insisted I put on. She crossed the room to the trinket box on my bureau next and found a lovely little cameo brooch, which she secured amongst the ruffles at the nape of my neck. She insisted I do a pirouette and announced, "You'll do!" Then off we went.

"Where are we going?" I finally asked.

"Does it matter?" she answered whimsically. "We're going on an adventure; let's just see where it takes us." She was right of course. It didn't matter at all. I followed merrily behind her, ready for anything.

It was a marvellous evening. We started at my local over a glass of beer, and as usual, Emily made chit chat with strangers seem like the easiest thing in the world. How I envied her that skill. We made our way to the station and boarded a train into Manchester, where we combined our pocket money, reserving just enough for train fare home, and bought tickets to see whatever was playing at the Palace Theatre on Oxford Street. It was a wonderful play called *Sleeping Partners,* but when we left the theatre, we wished we had enough left for a drink before heading home. Arm in arm, we skipped past the Opera House on Quay Street, finding something funny in everything we saw along the way.

"My God, Em. I have missed you so much. This has been the best of all tonics, honestly it has."

"Well, my pet, we've got two more days of merriment to carry on with before I have to return to the land of the all-night nursing rounds. Let's make the most of it."

We did. Mother made us a lovely tea on Em's last evening, and just as we were tucking into the bread pudding (laced with strawberries from the garden), there was a knock at the door. The cheery visitor didn't stand on ceremony but poked his head in the door "Ello? . . . Anybody home?" Mother made a beeline for the door, took the good doctor's hat, and invited him to the table to join us. It was more in the manner of instruction than invitation. She set a place for him and spooned out a portion of pudding while I set about filling his cup with tea.

"I finished my rounds a little early." With a loving glance at his daughter, he said, "I thought you might like a lift to the station."

The company and the conversation were like a charm. I felt almost human for the first time since I had set foot back on British soil. Dr. Davidson sipped on a glass of sherry, from Mother's finest crystal of course, and said, "I have a little news that might be of interest to you, Miss Milly." He was being intentionally cryptic and waited a moment or two for effect before breaking the suspense. "King's Hospital in Blackpool is opening a neurological wing to help those suffering symptoms of shell shock and other neurological disorders. I'm taking up a new post there starting next week." We were all thrilled for him and for the many patients who would benefit from his help, but I felt a pang of sadness and panic that he would be so far away and that our talks might be over.

Emily piped in. "Many hospitals are starting to offer neurological help; it seems the powers that be are finally starting to get it." Mother nodded her approval. Em continued. "They're offering workshops in everything from woodworking to cooking. There are some hospitals offering trades and skills training to help those who are able-bodied return to the workforce. It's wonderful really." Her excitement was on full tilt.

Dr. Davidson's enthusiasm was more muted but nonetheless evident. He looked directly at me. "The best treatment for the countless cases of post-war depression is to keep these individuals busy and give them routine and a sense of purpose." He waited for the right moment and glanced over at my mother before continuing. "Milly, I want you to come with me. There are openings at the hospital for people with your skills and experience, and I would relish having someone with your empathy on my staff." I looked around the faces at the table, each one urging me to take his offer, even Mother.

Emily smiled. "You'd be so wonderful there. A treasure. And I can guarantee that you will find familiar faces among the nursing staff. I certainly have, and it has been such a comfort. It will be for you too; I just know it will." Her words, however unnecessary, were kind and meant to persuade. I was decidedly overjoyed to accept the good doctor's offer.

Within a week, I was seated on the late afternoon train to Squires Gate, Blackpool, having closed the door on my family home for the last time. Of course, it was a dreary grey day. I was dressed in my sensible grey clothes and riding aboard a dismal grey train, but I closed my eyes in anticipation. Hope.

I hoped there would be colour, if not at my destination then somewhere in the near future.

Chapter Fourteen

My Dear Em,

I am in my element, and in just a short time, I have begun to feel alive; perhaps to say that I can embrace life might be an exaggeration, but I do believe I am coaxing a little bud of some kind. Your father, as always, has been remarkable. We continue our chats, weekly now, and on every occasion, his words find their target in meaningful ways. In our last conversation, I told him that the smells associated with the hospital have brought about a flood of memories and emotions. He wasn't at all surprised and said that scents and odours seem to trigger more memories than any of the other senses. I continue with my journal and find that words find their way to the page more easily now. I am sharing a flat with two girls, Mae and Evelyn, but we are rarely in the same place at the same time. They seem nice enough, but we all keep to ourselves.

Must dash,
Yours always, Mil

Darling Milly,

At the hospital here in London, we see a steady flow of patients, and there remains an ever-present sense of need with our vets in for treatments and surgeries. Some are housed in wards for long-term care and others are ambulatory. Clinics have been devised to care for the specific treatment of burn victims, amputees, etc., and many of these wards are filled to overflowing on any given day. I spend most of my shift in the operating theatre, where I am finally permitted to touch the instruments. Bloody bureaucracy . . . lots of one-upmanship. But I am doing my best to charm the pants off the lot of them.

There was, however, an incident recently when we students, and I do mean all of us, were called into Matron's office to be chastised. A lot of bother over nothing, of course; a witness testified to our misbehaviour . . . as though we were children for God's sake. It had been a particularly brutal day as I remember it, and during a supper break, a group of us stepped outdoors for a breath of air before continuing our long shift. There had been a significant snowfall, lovely really, and while we were strolling around the grounds in our ever-so-proper way, it struck me that we resembled a column of penguins, waddle and all. I was the first, I admit it with relish! I scooped up a handful of snow and biffed it at the darling gal in front of me. In moments, we were embroiled in an all-out snowball fight. Such fun. It was just the ticket; freed up all those pesky pent-up frustrations. Matron was appropriately miffed, but the girls did not give me up as the instigator. Good bunch.

Build yourself a snowman, my friend . . . Yours, Em

Dearest Em,

I have news of Alice. She is safely delivered of another girl; Dorothy, they are calling her. I think of our dear Squeak and how pleased she will be when I write to tell her that she has a namesake in my family. They have begun calling the baby "Dolly"— isn't that lovely? Everyone is well and healthy, and I look forward to getting home for a visit before very long.

I continue to pitch in and do a bit of everything here. Pushing wheel-chairs one day and sitting behind a desk working on ledgers the next. I do see familiar faces now and then, nurses mostly but a few of our wounded too. Sadly, in our ward, the wounds beneath the bandages are the only ones that have healed. The battle rages on behind their eyes. Many slouch and drag their feet; it's ghoulish really to watch them wandering aimlessly around the ward in their faded-blue fatigues and red tie. Many continue to wear the Silver War Badge on the lapel to remind us all that their wounds were earned in service. "For King and Empire. Service Rendered."

The most disturbing for me are the poor blokes who are unable to walk or right themselves, as though the entire world is on a slant. Hostile, that's what these wounds are, and onerous for doctors like your dad. Well, at the very least, the thin and emaciated state they were in overseas has improved; they look healthier now with a few extra pounds on their bones.

It seems that hospitals and clinics are springing up like weeds all over Britain; every available building is being utilized in one way or another. King's Hospital was a racecourse before the war. Did you know that? The grandstand was converted to a hospital and became the headquarters for the Royal Army Medical Corp, and now it has 4,600 beds, operating theatres, and wards that treat all nature of affliction, including venereal disease—now that is a particularly busy ward.

The kitchens here are massive as you can imagine and are run mainly by women; nice to know we're still needed somewhere. Does the same hold true in your hospital?

*My brother Richard and his family have moved back into the family
home with Mother, and I am glad of it. They will be good company
for her; I have worried about her rattling around in that big house
all alone.*

Will I see you at Christmas?
Milly

Happy New Year, darling friend,

*It was so lovely to see you during the holidays and to spend time with
your ever-growing family. Baby Dolly is precious, and I was happy to
see that you were so comfortable spending time with her.*
*Darling, I have news that might come as something of a shock, and I am
not sure how to temper the telling of it. So here goes. When I returned
to London after our holiday, I was surprised to find a letter from your
Daniel. I am enclosing it because I feel it best that you see his handwriting and read the words for yourself.*

I have not responded and will await your instruction before I do so.

*I know that this will stir up some demons, and I urge you to find time to
sit down and talk it over with Dad.*

Love you, Em

Dear Miss Davidson, "Emily,"

I write to you today in the hope that you will assist me in finding Milly. I assume that she has returned from France but hesitate to contact her family as I do not know what, if anything, they know of me. I found you quite easily by contacting the Red Cross and hope that you will forgive my boldness. I have returned to England following the death of my wife, Beatrice, in Winnipeg, Manitoba, almost two years ago.

When we said our goodbyes in France, both Milly and I agreed that a clean break would be best; we promised never to reach out to one another, but much has changed since then. I had two surgeries at your hospital in London to remove portions from each of my lungs, and once my recovery was deemed satisfactory, I was scheduled to return to Canada aboard the Araguaya. I broke our vow and sent Milly a postcard just days before my departure; it was a frightfully impulsive gesture and one that I regretted immediately. I hope she did not hate me for the act. On the morning of our sail, I received a telegram explaining that my wife had succumbed to the influenza epidemic that ravaged much of North America. I went from the hospital ship across country to the Manitoba Military Hospital where I was treated for pneumonia and remained there until my military discharge was final. Beatrice was buried unceremoniously and alone as were so many who had left their parents and families in search of new life in America. I have agonized with guilt and grief this long time. When I was finally fit for travel, I sold our modest belongings and returned to England. I have been living with my mother for some months now.

Please understand that I do not wish our Milly any undue distress; I have only a genuine desire to meet with her. I would appreciate any information you can offer about her present situation. Is she well? Is she living with her family, or has she given her heart to someone else? I have no expectation but am fervently hopeful that she still feels as I do. Ours was a sincere and uniquely special "friendship," the kind that comes along all too seldom in life.

I remain, yours very truly,
Daniel Pearse

Dear Em,

I can only imagine how you have struggled with this. And I regret that you have been drawn into this drama. It is a testament to your kind nature that Daniel felt comfortable in reaching out to you.

I am tormented. It feels as though someone has opened the book of my life and cruelly flipped backward through the pages to the place where my heartbreak began; the very sight of his handwriting pierced like a bullet shattering flesh.

I feel so desperately torn in two. His despair leapt out from beneath the words, and I longed to reach into the page to comfort and console him. I feel so desperately sorry for his wife, for Daniel, and for her family. She was so young.

My mind is wandering through a maze, and old wounds begin to ache. I had just begun to dismantle them, make peace with them; I fear the outcome should I begin to pick at old scars. I must set boundaries of protection to respect and care for myself in order to remain in this healthier place.

I cannot deceive myself, Em. This man has lost his wife. He is guilt ridden and still in mourning, a widower. If he were ever to remarry, he would want a wife who could give him a family, not damaged goods, a broken, barren woman like me. I am not as he remembers, and our lives could not possibly be as he imagines. I fear he would grow to resent me, and I could not suffer that. I would rather he remember me as I was.

I humbly ask that you respond to him on my behalf. Offer my condolences for his tragic loss; tell him that I am well but that I have begun a new chapter in my life. That I will carry the past with me on this new journey with loving memories of him but that I must move forward. I harbour no regrets and pray that he finds happiness and well-being.

Thank you, dearest girl. I promise to heed your advice and will sit down with your father later today.

Milly

Dear Milly,

I have written to Daniel making my very best effort to convey your message. It was kindly worded.

I know that you have thought this through, and I understand your fears, but I do worry that you may be making an error in judgement. As always, my Shuyr, I care only that you are happy. There is always a risk in love, I know it all too well, but weighing those risks can be tricky business. You only have one life, my darling; I wish only that you live it fully and bravely.

That now is the totality of my wisdom. I am spent.

I wonder if we might consider for a moment the possibility of a short holiday together. Might do us both good! I know that you and Dad are planning to travel down together in June to attend my graduation, but if you are able to take the time, we could tack on a few days and take the train down to Kent to visit with Squeak. I felt so terrible that we were not able to attend her wedding in the fall, the timing was simply impossible, but perhaps now we could make a go of it.

Give it some thought.
Love always, Em

Dear Emily,

You and your father always appear to be of one mind. Our conversa-
tions, since Daniel's letter, have been mired in discussion about weighing
risks and confronting fears. I admit that there is a huge part of me
that wants to leap into the abyss, open the old wounds, and gamble on
second chances, but as irrational as it may be, fear wins out every time.

In Doctor Dad's words, "Fear resonates in the past and can all too often
exclude any vision of the future. Be careful not to confine yourself in a
cell of your own making—you may have to face your fears and let the
truth be told in order to conquer them. The key to the cell door may be
just within your reach."

Profound, don't you think? He also suggested, cautiously, that pride may
be playing a greater part than I would like to admit. I'll have to give
that some more thought.

In the meantime, I have been granted leave for one full week. Seems
we're going on a holiday. Your dad will return here after your gradua-
tion, and I will follow him back from London after our visit to Kent. I
am so looking forward to it.

Until then, yours always,

Milly

The graduation ceremony at the Royal College of Nursing was splendid. Emily looked taller somehow, holding herself just a little more confidently under the weight of her cap and gown. Dr. Davidson, who was overcome with pride and emotion, held my hand tightly during the entire ceremony. He treated us both to a wonderful meal at the very posh Criterion restaurant and theatre, and I was thankful that my flatmates had convinced me to splurge on a new frock and matching chemise. The dining room was exquisite with plush seating and romantic chandeliers. There were miles of draped fabric and crisp white linens that adorned the waiters as well as the tables. I was astounded by the opulence; ghostly statues gazed down at us from their pedestals and precious stones blinked defiantly from within the Venetian tiles that imprisoned them. My eyes wanted to linger on the artwork that the walls but were drawn instead toward the magnificent gold-leaf ceiling.

We raised our glasses in a toast to our graduate, each making a little speech to let her know how immensely proud we were of her well-deserved achievement. She had maintained a dignified composure throughout the day but squealed with delight at the gifts we presented to her at the table. Her father had bought her an exquisite pearl pendant with matching earbobs, which she donned immediately, and when she made her way around the table to hug him around the neck and plant a kiss on the top of his head, it drew the attention of all those seated around us. While she was up, I slipped a tiny little box wrapped in blue ribbon next to her wine glass. She sat down and smiled as she reached for it, looking at me with the kind of loving expression that stays with you all of your days. She lifted the hinge on the delicate little box and sighed over the tiny gold signet ring engraved with her initials, but when I showed her that my initials were engraved directly behind hers on the inside of the ring, she wept for the first time all day.

The meal began with a consommé so clear that you could see the pattern on the bottom of the wide china plate. We ate white bait, squab, veal medallions, and mouth-watering temptations from a trolley of sweets. It was a most memorable experience, one to be cherished.

The wonderful day was followed by an equally marvellous visit to Kent where we laughed and cried, reminisced, and drank copious amounts of whisky with our lovely friend. Squeak ("Dorothy") was proud to introduce us to her husband, Jack, who worked at the local distillery. He was a delightful man, full of life and equal to the task of keeping up with our energetic friend. We strolled together through the shops in the warm summer sunshine, and I stumbled upon a confectioner who carried my favourite sweets: barley sugars. I hadn't seen any of those since before the war. I picked up two bags for myself and one each to send to Mother and Alice.

We were on the tail end of a memorable week, and I could not wait to put feelings into words in my journal; I would have to consider some synonyms for "happy." I was considering just that during our journey back to London when I took stock of a change in Emily's mood. "Post-holiday blues, sweetie?" I asked. She gave a noncommittal grin but didn't really respond. I watched for some time as she twisted the shiny little ring around on her pinky finger; she seemed more distracted than sad. She had something to say; I had known her long enough to read the signs. I asked if there was something bothering her.

Without looking up, she admitted, "I've been putting this off. I didn't want to spoil our lovely week." She hesitated, and I waited. "But I must tell you that I've had another letter from Daniel." Her expression apologetic, she continued. "Milly, he is desperate to see you. My letter has not put him off. My message was clear, I swear it was, but he is persistent."

"I will write to him, Em. There's no reason why you should be coping with this." I took her agitated hand and kissed the ring. "I'm not sure what I'll say. It may be difficult to convince him of my convictions when I'm not certain of them myself." She nodded, looking relieved, and chose not to offer any opinion or wisdom. We sat quietly as the train slowed toward its destination.

Finally, as though she had been holding back a dam, she blurted, "Perhaps you should tell him the truth."

The conversation ended as we pulled into Victoria station. Our holiday was over.

I put pen to paper many, many times in the weeks that followed but failed to write the letter. I finally approached Dr. D. for assistance, and the man who usually led me down a path toward my own decisions was forthright in his delivery. He believed it was time to speak truths to Daniel. "You can see that he is suffering as you do, can you not?"

He sounded uncharacteristically annoyed. "Every day, Milly, is an opportunity to move forward. Take this path and see where it leads you." His expression softened then. "You share a history with this man, and together you suffered a tragic loss. Shouldn't he be permitted to know about it?" I had not thought about it in those terms; he gave me much to chew on as I made my way to the flat that evening. By the time I reached the door, I had made the decision to brave a step forward.

My heart and soul bled all over the pages of the letter and proved to be both an emotional and cathartic exercise. I spared nothing in the details of the events that had taken place or of my suffering in the aftermath. Although I penned a return address on the envelope, I did not expect a reply. I was conflicted. If he did not respond, I would be angry and hurt, and if his response carried with it a rejection, it would be a bitter, bitter pill.

I went about my duties in mechanical fashion, glum and giving the letter box in the foyer of our building a wide berth. Weeks had passed, and there was no letter. I tried to convince myself that this was for the best, but my mood soured like milk left too long on the step. I dreaded the approaching Christmas season, the inevitable family festivities with giggling children and the portrait of perfect domesticity; it held no place for me. As though to add to my misery, Dr. D. called me into his office to break the news that he would be leaving the hospital in the New Year.

"I believe that this facility will be shutting its doors in the very near future, and I have been offered an opportunity to open two new clinics in London." He saw the injured look on my face and laughed. "Come on now, Milly, I've not shot your dog or anything as sinister as that now, have I?" I had no choice but to smile back at him and laugh at myself. "I will have to wait and see how the land lies before I can make any promises, but if you've a mind to, you might think about joining me there." I felt a little better.

Home for the holidays was something to look forward to . . . or that is what I told myself over and over again. "'Home' is such a big word," I said discreetly to my journal. "It means so little to me. I feel like a gypsy."

My family home was no longer mine; one of my brother's children inhabited my old room, and my current residence was no more than a place to lay my head. I was pleased to learn that Alice was hosting the occasion at her house in Warrington and that Emily planned to meet me there for the first few days. I hadn't invited her; she had volunteered, God bless her. *She always knows just what I need and when I need her.* She promised to meet me at the station.

As the train clattered along, I rehearsed my smile and worked hard to convince myself that it would be grand to see everyone, especially Mother and my sweet Alice. Most of the family planned to make an appearance as it would probably be the last Christmas with my brother John, who had decided to move with his family to Australia. I imagined their faces, each popping into frame before me with the same pathetic expressions clearly thinking, "Poor, lonesome Aunty Mill." *Ugh. Pity. What a useless emotion.*

"Poor lonesome Aunty Milly." The words escaped from my lips causing the passenger seated next to me to turn his head and grunt a response. I could not shake off the dread. Christmas. "Bah humbug," I muttered in Dickensian style while burying my face in the muffler I was grateful to have around my neck. I pulled up the lap blanket that had fallen at my feet.

I envied John his new adventure but coveted the journey that my favourite niece, Annie, was about to embark upon. She had written to tell me her news and looked forward to introducing me to her fiancé, Patrick. I was delighted for her, of course, and excited to meet her beau. I teared a little at the thought of the lovely dark-eyed beauty in the white wedding dress Alice would make for her. I pulled back my chin and adjusted my posture to regain composure and curb any feelings of envy that might reflect on my face.

The conductor announced arrival at the station. I felt conspicuous in the crowded compartment as I donned my coat and hat, my height (as always) a burden. I retrieved the beautiful carpet bag that Alice had made for me the Christmas before from remnants of tapestry fabric. I bumped into another passenger, and for the first time in my life, did not bother to apologize. *I must buck up if I am not to ruin everyone's holiday.* The train bumped to a stop amidst much noise and confusion: whistles and clatter, happy travellers, noisy children, and shouts from the platform. There was some pushing as people edged toward the door with their extra cases and Christmas packages. I made my way down the steps and onto the platform, in no particular hurry. I was, in that brief moment, grateful for my height as I could see above many of the bodies pushing their way toward the exits and connecting trains. I had no doubt that my little chum would announce herself with a squeal of delight at the first glimpse of me. True to her word, Emily was there. She looked a picture in a hunter-green coat and matching felt bonnet and waved furiously to draw my attention.

"Come on, love," she shouted over the din, "let's see if we can't find a seat in the refreshment room for a wee bit before we venture out into the cold; it'll be ages before we can find a taxi." I nodded in agreement and followed her as she cut a zig-zag swath through the crowd. We found a seat near the entrance, and she went to the counter to get us a drink. The place smelled of cinnamon, and my mouth started to water. I hadn't eaten all day, and I could see the tray of Chelsea buns calling to me from the counter but could not catch Emily's attention and did not want to risk relinquishing our seats. My stomach growled in complaint.

She returned to the table with two large whiskys, and we toasted our friendship. The hubbub was dying down a little, and we were finally able to hear each other. "Milly, don't look so glum. I believe we have much to look forward to and that you will have a marvellous holiday."

Always smiling, always positive, my Em.

I submitted to her reverie, and we clinked glasses again. As the din subsided, she leaned in. "Sweetie, Daniel has been to see me," she said unapologetically. The shock registered on my face, but she pressed on. "I apologize for the blunt delivery." There was no remorse in her tone as she continued. "He needed an advocate, a soldier to help him fight this battle." I was still gobsmacked and words would not come. "Milly, he read your letter to me, and together we cried buckets. We spent a whole afternoon together, and I am convinced that he wants you and nothing more. He said that every moment without you feels like a punishment, and he will love you to his last breath."

I was shaking and pulled my coat tighter around my body in a pointless effort to control it. "Why in heaven's name did he not respond to my letter? Why did he go to you instead?"

"He believed that his words on paper would seem hollow and that you would not be persuaded. He assured me that, in one brief meeting, you will understand that he has no desire nor need for anything but you. I believe he is absolutely correct, Milly, and I confess that we have conspired together." She paused for a moment, taking in my bewildered expression. "My motives are noble. I hope you will see that."

Then she was looking toward the door. I followed her gaze, and through the flurry of faces and hats coming in and out of the room, I caught a glimpse of a familiar shock of curly hair. My heart leapt from my chest as the mass of bodies parted just long enough for me to hone in on those exquisite grey eyes. His handsome face wore a tentative, understated smile as he fixed on my gaze and made his way toward us. I rose from my seat and forced the muscles on my face to move into a smile, never glancing back at my friend still seated at the table. He greeted us both with a timid Christmas greeting, taking his eyes from mine just long enough to acknowledge Emily and then repeated fondly, "Happy Christmas, Milly."

I searched for words. "Daniel, I . . . it's so good . . . you look . . . Happy Christmas, Daniel."

The room finally came into focus. I allowed my gaze to take in more of this man whom I adored; he was thin and a little pale and wore a long black mackintosh. *Not warm enough for such a chilly day,* I thought. It was only then that I realized he was not alone. Holding tightly to his hands, on either side of him was a small child. I was suddenly awake. "Oh my! I am sorry. Forgive my rudeness," I said as I leaned down to say hello to the youngsters. "What's your name?" I asked the little girl on his left who looked to be about seven years old.

A surprisingly mature and confident voice responded, "I'm Heather."

I smiled. "Happy Christmas, Heather." The little girl dipped a quick curtsy. Questions floated through my mind, but as I turned my attention to her little brother, who was tucked timidly behind Daniel's coat, I had the answer to the greatest of them. One glance into the eyes of that beautiful face told me that this was Daniel's child. In his short pants, wool coat, and hat, he looked like a tiny replica of the man standing in front of me. Quietly and with trepidation, I crouched down and softly asked, "And you are?"

"Ian," he whispered, shyly.

These were Daniel's children.

Daniel leaned in to kiss me on the cheek, and I melted into his touch. "It appears we have much to talk about, doesn't it?" he said with an air of authority. I was shaken and confused but mindful of the little faces looking up at me. I swallowed deeply past the massive lump that had taken root in my throat and searched for air in my lungs.

Emily was quiet throughout this encounter; clearly nothing about it came as a surprise to her. She rose slowly and deliberately, reached behind her chair for the coat that was draped there, and announced with a grin that she would leave us to talk and meet me later at Alice's. I nodded acknowledgement without words but managed a shy smile to let her know that I understood and appreciated her efforts. She was out the door before I could find anything appropriate to say.

Daniel broke the uncomfortable silence, turning his head in the general direction of the children while keeping his eyes fixed on me. "Why don't we have ourselves a Christmas treat?" He left them both in my care while he purchased an ice lolly for each of them and a much-needed refill for my glass. The children looked pleased if not excited. I had little experience with youngsters but observed a particular gloominess about these two; their sad angelic faces watched my every move. I still struggled to find oxygen, my heart pounding so loudly I was sure it could be heard, but I summoned smiles and an occasional phrase to ease the moment. When the children were content with their treat, napkins tucked neatly under their chins, Daniel and I found an opportunity to speak together in muted tones.

Daniel took my hand and rested it in his atop the table. "Now, let's put this together, shall we?" I was uncharacteristically submissive and sat in stunned silence while he spoke, certain that he could hear my thoughts. I glanced from him to the children and back again. "We are a fearful pair, you and I." He paused and tilted his head to keep my attention. "You," he said, squeezing my hand, "have been afraid that I would deny you because of the ordeal that has rendered you childless." I flinched at the painful memory. "A nightmare that you suffered alone, without me to hold your hand as I do now. I am so desperately sorry."

I was looking down, frantically holding on to the emotion that would erupt from my body if I gave it even one spark of energy. "I too was fearful, Milly, fearful that the love we found together in France would be denied . . . forbidden if I were to tell you about my children. It was not my intention to deceive you. Our situation was unique, and at the time, nothing else seemed real. Every day we were together was a gift; every day we managed to stay alive over there was a gift." He was making headway; I nodded and raised my eyes to look at him. He lifted my chin with his hand and stroked my cheek with the flat of his fingers. "Lots of blokes had love affairs over there, but ours was not that. Honour and duty took me away from you, but love has brought me back."

I leaned my cheek against the warmth of his hand. "I'm not the same girl . . . so much has changed."

Cautiously he went on. "I love you, Milly; it won't matter to me that we don't have a child together. We could be a family." He glanced over to the children. "We can have a life together, if you would consent to being my wife and their mother. He did not take his eyes from mine, but he let moments pass, allowing me to take it all in. My mind was swirling with all the things that I wanted to say but just could not form a single thought. He reached into his pocket and pulled out the amulet I had given him on our final day together in France. "I keep this with me always; it has led me back to you. We have barely scratched the surface of what our lives could be, Milly, if you'll have me . . . us."

A waiter waltzed toward the table with a plate of Christmas sweets for the already sticky children, and I saw in that moment a renewed vision of my future. I looked deep into his eyes then, nodding slowly. "I will be their mother."

As we left the station, I watched fluffy cloud pillows move across the sky, leaving just enough space between them for a glimpse of the sun.

Chapter Fifteen

Daniel and the children spent a day or two with his sister and her family in Manchester before heading back to Widnes in time for Father Christmas to arrive. It gave him an opportunity to do a little Christmas shopping and to allow me a breathing space to gather my thoughts and my wits before engaging in any conversation with my family about this new set of circumstances.

The family was welcoming and excited upon my arrival at Alice's, and Mother was busy as always in the kitchen, I could smell my favourite steak and kidney pie (hers was the best). Emily sat in the wing chair in the far corner of the parlour, listening intently to the ramblings of my brother William who as usual had much to say about both the business and politics. Her posture changed ever so slightly when I entered the room, her back straightening in the chair, but still she remained politely attentive to her lecturer. We shared a brief silent conversation through smiling eyes.

It was a quiet evening, with my older nieces and nephews upstairs minding the youngest except for Dolly, who lay in a cot beside me. At the head of the table was my brother-in-law, Philip, whose roly-poly exterior contradicted his hard-working nature. I believed beer to be the root cause of his inflated belly. He had a ruddy complexion, dark hair, and a bushy moustache that jiggled and twitched when he laughed. I liked him. He had always been like a second father for me, welcoming me as one of his own when I was little. Dashing in and out of the kitchen with items for the table was my favourite of Alice's children, Harry, named for my brother who was spending the holidays in Scotland with his new bride.

"Annie sends her apologies," Alice said. "She's spending the evening with Patrick's family but will bring him back with her tomorrow. She's anxious for you to meet him."

"I look forward to it," I said. *More now than before.* It seemed that my outlook and attitude about everything and everyone had been given a lift. I listened enthusiastically to all the news but kept my own council for the time being. William included me in his conversation from time to time but continued to prattle mostly into Emily's ear; she seemed unperturbed. I glanced around at what was a delightfully serene domestic scene, knowing of course that it was the calm before the storm. The extended family were to arrive in the morning.

After dinner, I asked Em if she would like to take a jaunt out into the crisp evening air. She was grateful for an escape and an opportunity to talk about the events earlier in the day. Before she had a chance to explain or apologize, I wrapped my arm tightly around her shoulder. "As usual, my sweet friend, you had my best interest at heart and your judgement was sound." With a gentle bump of my hip, I added, "Never made you out as the cupid sort . . . and sneaky too!"

She leaned in, fitting snuggly into my armpit and turning her head to look up at me. "I was so worried, not at all convinced of the outcome, but I can see that the end has justified the means. I've never seen you look happier; you're positively glowing."

I described the scene that had taken place after her departure from the station, and she wrapped me in her arms. "It was fate, Milly. Destiny just needed a little push."

I held her closer. "Thank you, Em. From my heart, thank you for all that you are and all that you have been to me. If I haven't told you often enough, I love you so very dearly." We stood in the street, tears of joy flowing freely, unapologetically cascading in blissful happiness.

Her voice took a serious tone then. "I adore you. You know I do, and as long as I can be a part of your life in some way, it's enough for me. Do you think I could be 'Auntie Em'?"

Before I could respond, she stepped away, wiping her nose on her sleeve in a deliberate effort to mock the moment. Then, taking a detour from the sentimentality of it all, swept the back of her hand up against her brow in a dramatic gesture. "I never imagined for a *moment* that I would be embroiled in a *secret* rendezvous with a handsome man in a covert operation to thwart my best friend. It was all very exhilarating!"

Tears turned into laughter as we strolled back toward the house arm in arm. By the time we returned, the children were tucked in for the night, and we joined the adults in the parlour sipping whisky. Chatter grew louder as the drink flowed, but I was content to sit with my own company in quiet reflection. I felt an unfamiliar sense of calm and caught myself smiling covertly from time to time. I noticed Alice was watching me from across the room; I felt her reading my thoughts and heard the *Sonnish* for the first time in a long, long time. The spirit of peace, the *Shee,* washed over me, and Alice beamed.

She gently called for the attention of the room and raised her glass in a toast: "Happy Christmas, my dears. I have a notion the New Year will be a grand one for us all."

The house was filled to overflowing, and so Emily and I shared the small room at the top of the stairs. Finally snug in a bed that had been lovingly made up with crisp white linens, we lay back hesitantly, trying not to wrinkle the perfectly creased pillowcases. We were both tired. Em was quiet. I lay still, reflective . . . afraid to move for fear that I would wake and find that the events of the day were naught but cruel imaginings. I struggled against the unfamiliar, fluttery sensation in my chest but finally relaxed. I was happy, and that was all there was to it. I savoured the moment and replayed in my mind all that Daniel had said and the promises we'd made to each other. The map of my future had changed in an instant.

There was a quiet tap on the door and a voice in soft, hushed tones asked, "Are you still awake?"

I sat up and smoothed out the coverlet, "Come in, Alice."

Em got up to open the door. Carrying a round tray in one hand and manoeuvring around the door without spilling a single drop of tea out of the china cups, Alice swished into the room. Emily gently closed the door behind her and climbed back into the bed, covering the goosebumps that were forming on her legs. Alice rested the tray on the bureau, and without another word, passed a cup and saucer to both of us. She took hers and nestled into the Queen Anne chair beside the bed. We each took a sip while Alice grinned at the reaction on our faces; the hot drink was shamelessly spiked with whisky.

She wasted no time in posing the question that had been on her mind. "So, my pet, you have a fella?" Our conversation was matter of fact at first as I described Daniel and confided that we had agreed to marry. Alice looked affectionately at Emily, who sat in silence, then paused a moment before catching the younger woman by surprise, "And how, my dear girl, do you feel about that?" It was not so much the words but the tone that carried with it a keen understanding of the situation.

Emily found her intuitive candour refreshing and responded simply. "Overjoyed."

Alice turned her attention back to me, and in her big-sisterly way, with genuine warmth, encouraged me to share my secrets. Once I began, the words flowed easily and without fear of reprisal or shame. Our twenty-year age difference melted away; she was no longer my surrogate mother, we were just two women. Sisters. I brought Emily into the discussion when it came to the part about the baby and asked her to share her insights during that period of time. Throughout the conversation, Alice listened and smiled, wept with despair, and cried happy tears. I had always known that she could be trusted with my secrets; it had been pride and shame that had prevented me from pouring out my soul to her. She rested her cup on the bureau and picked up the amulet that Emily had left laying there along with her watch and pearl pendant.

Looking at it, Alice said, "I wonder how many of these you've given out over the years, Milly."

"I have no idea. Dozens and dozens, I suppose."

Emily added, "It's a good question, Alice. I often wonder how many of them came home with the lads and how many others are still somewhere in France."

"I know of at least three that remained there," I said wistfully. "Two belonged to young Jimmy from the factory and Gertie, our roommate at the hospital. The third I buried beneath the willow for my baby." Emily, who was hearing about that for the very first time, sobbed into the hanky Alice handed her.

"Ladies," Alice said, "I am humbled by your resilience and confident that happier times are ahead for both of you." She rose from her chair and tossed us both a kiss. On her way out the door, she said, "Most of all, I am thankful that you have had each other to lean on."

We agreed that there were parts of the story that need not be shared with the family and that I would introduce Daniel to them in the coming days, in my own way, at my own discretion and with her full support.

Emily said her goodbyes in the morning, and I promised to call in at the Davidson home before the holidays were over. Later in the day, the great holiday flurry of activity began with neighbours popping in, children running about, and everyone chatting at once. Wonderful aromas continually wafted out from the general direction of the kitchen. A tray of warm sausage rolls almost made its way past me, but I reached out and grabbed one just in time, causing a burst of giggles from the child carrying the tray. I grinned sheepishly, remembering how I had dreaded this day. I offered to help and pitched in where I could, but Alice and Mother had things well in hand, and I was surprised to find that I was content to sit quietly, responding to conversation as needed and allowing children to bounce on my knee.

The festivities wound down. Gifts had been exchanged and bellies were full. The men were smoking in the front room and discussing a visit to the pub while the women put the house back in order. The children were either napping or happily playing with their new toys. It was a snapshot in time that I would long cherish. I had just settled into a chair when Annie arrived with her charming Patrick. Eager to get ahead of the melee of holiday handshaking, I weaved my way through the room, treading on full-grown toes but mindful not to step on any children.

Reaching them, I gave my precious young niece an affectionate hug. She was flushed and nervous, and while Patrick busied himself hanging coats, I gave her an extra squeeze and said, "If you love him, so will I." And I did. There wasn't anything not to love about the tall, lanky drink of water. He greeted me with an earnest handshake, not the flimsy kind that some men offer to a woman. His kind face with its high forehead and warm smile would have been enough, but it was his unmistakable adoration for my lovely niece that won me over. Like Annie, he was quiet and reserved but loved a good laugh and was obviously wonderfully comfortable with the family and they with him. He sat in the corner chair that I had surrendered, one long leg stretched over the other knee, pipe in his free hand while the other arm encircled Annie as she sat on the arm of his chair. They were happy.

As the women completed their tasks and found places to sit, the conversation turned to weddings and plans for Annie and Patrick. There was no hurry of course and much to settle before taking their vows, but it was great fodder for some fun and lively banter. Some of the jokes and jibes caused Annie to blush, but Patrick kept his composure and gave as good as he got. It was a happy, lively room until one of the older grandchildren seated next to me looked up and asked, "Are you ever going to get married?"

There it was: the dreaded question. And all around the room, the pitiful expressions, the unspoken *"Poor, sad, lonesome Milly."* Many of course had not heard the child's question at all, and the conversation continued uninterrupted, but my perception was that the activity within the room had come to a full stop before proceeding in slow motion. I turned to the child, and in a kind and matter-of-fact voice, replied, "As it happens, Penny, I am indeed." The child was content with the answer and went on to talk to the neighbour sitting on her other side, but Mother had heard the exchange, as had William.

"What's this now?" he asked. I suspect he thought I'd been annoyed by the child and fobbed her off with my response.

Mother, sensitive to the nuance in my voice, was more charitable. She inquired further. "Something you'd like to tell us, Millicent?" She rarely used my full name, and I felt a little like a child in trouble.

"It's true. My beau proposed marriage last week." I embellished slightly. "He's anxious to meet all of you when he comes for me tomorrow." Before anyone could respond, I turned to Annie and apologized. "Honey, I'm sorry for tramping on your merriment. I had no intention of blurting my news out just yet or in this way. I suppose the little one here just caught me off guard." I patted the little blonde head seated next to me.

Patrick was first to his feet. He extended his hand and pumped mine enthusiastically. "Don't be daft," he said. "Good news is just that: good news. We're happy to share the moment with you." He turned to Annie. "Aren't we, love?" She too was on her feet, clapping madly. In only moments, the barrage of congratulations and questions hit me like floodwater escaping the dam.

Mother kissed me gently on each cheek. "I am very happy for you, my dear." Her smile was genuine, but her eyes spoke a little rebuff. "Perhaps you could have warned me. Better yet, it would have been nice to meet this young man before now." Alice and I exchanged a knowing glance and embraced as sisters do. Mother noticed it though; she did not miss much. I explained that Daniel was a wounded soldier I'd first met in France but had later cared for in the hospital in Blackpool. I watched Mother recoil ever so slightly as I went on to say that he was a widower with two small children. My explanation of his wife's death in Canada brought about horrified gasps and a sympathetic moan. I had the attention of the room and quite liked it. It was intoxicating, but I broke the spell to speak once again directly to Annie.

"Like you and Patrick, we will be in no great hurry to get married, and I promise that we will not interfere with your plans." In unison, they shook their heads in a rebuke.

Daniel's arrival at the house the next day was equally exhilarating. All the attention I had enjoyed the day before was compounded by the sensation of standing with my arm nestled through his. Alice was especially warm and welcoming to this stranger among us (she was the hostess after all) and her immediate acceptance went a long way in winning Daniel over to the rest of the family.

As the day drew to a close, we donned our coats and went out for a breath of air. We had not paid any mind to the noise and clamour of the house until we closed the door; the silence was deafening and such a relief, though neither of us wanted to admit it. It took a second to register, but then we turned to look at one another and burst into spontaneous laughter. It was a lovely clear night, and as we strolled along in silence, Daniel reached into his pocket and pulled out a small box wrapped in a silver ribbon. We found a place to sit, and Daniel handed the gift to me. "This Christmas box is a treasure to honour our past. Our future begins tomorrow."

I knew then that it wasn't a ring but could not imagine what he meant. I slid the ribbon off and gingerly lifted the lid. Inside was a tiny bracelet of rosy gold links, the two ends held together with a delicate gold padlock. It was too small to wear; it would barely fit around one of my fingers. Puzzled, I looked into his face as he reverently explained, "For the child we lost."

The sadness and foreboding were gone, and a blissfully warm blanket of love surrounded me. Just before I drifted to sleep that night, I glanced out the window into the clear dark sky and confided my good fortune to the stars. If life were a fairy tale, it might well have ended in that moment. I was filled with hope but still harboured no illusions.

Chapter Sixteen

The day finally arrived. The contents of the house were sold, the years of savings tucked away into Daniel's money belt, cases and trunks packed, and we were adorned in the new clothes and coats that Alice had made for us. Brother Harry alone took us to the Liverpool dockyard and pinned carnations on each of our lapels. All the goodbyes had been said in the weeks leading up to this day, and I was grateful to avoid a teary scene. Nothing was to spoil the excitement of this new adventure.

It was August 1926, and the Pearse family were about to board the SS *Regina*; Daniel was exuberant. The newly formed Canadian Department of Immigration and Colonization, together with the two major railway companies, had been advertising extensively throughout Britain since the war had ended in an effort to bring agricultural immigrants to the prairies. As a Canadian veteran, Daniel was entitled to one the preferable plots of land close to the railway and was further offered a subsidy toward our travel by the British government. He had been in contact with an army friend who had made the move with his family two years earlier and was encouraged to hear that farms in the area of Tisdale, Saskatchewan, were experiencing bumper crops and farmers in neighbouring towns were in good circumstances. Daniel had the paperwork for our homestead in his breast pocket along with the *Dominion Lands Handbook*, which laid out all the rules and duties of a homesteader. After our arrival in Canada, he would have to refer to this document for information on filing a patent on the land and to legalize ownership of the property. We were to have a quarter section of farmland, one hundred twenty acres just outside Star City, Saskatchewan. As proud as any landowner could be, Daniel guided his well-dressed family up the gang plank and aboard the vessel.

S.S. "Regina" Third Cabin Tourists

DINNER

POTAGE DAME BLANCHE

HALIBUT A LA JUIVE

ROAST GOSLING, APPLE SAUCE

QUARTERS OF LAMB, MINT SAUCE

CAULIFLOWER

BROWNED AND BOILED POTATOES

COBURG PUDDING; PARIS CAKES

ICE CREAM AND WAFERS

TEA, COFFEE.

AUG. 8. 1926.

ANY COMPLAINT RESPECTING THE FOOD SUPPLIED,
WANT OF ATTENTION,
OR INCIVILITY SHOULD BE AT ONCE REPORTED
TO THE PURSER OR CHIEF STEWARD.

On our first night at sea, we approached our designated third-cabin-tourists dining room in our absolute best attire and found an easel outside the door on which was posted the menu for the evening, with "White Star Line" printed boldly at the top, above a sepia-tone painting of sailing vessels that was captioned "Cartier's Arrival in the St. Lawrence."

It was a wonderful evening and a great beginning to our journey.

There were, of course, those passengers who suffered traveller's illness, but our hearty family remained well and enjoyed the eight days at sea. Daniel's lingering coughs seemed to quiet with the salt spray and the healing summer sun. The children, who were now twelve and ten years old, enjoyed activities on the deck, and Ian—enamoured with the workings of the ship—was uncharacteristically talkative. We disembarked in Montreal, revitalized albeit with wobbly legs, and watched as our luggage and steamer trunks were loaded onto the train bound for Saskatchewan.

I lay in our cramped sleeper car, lulled by the rhythm of metal on metal beneath me and soothed by its gentle rocking until the train manoeuvred a sharp turn and yet another high-pitched screech cut through the air. I was brought upright from my sleepy haze and watched the moon for a while as it played peek-a-boo through the clouds and cast dancing shadows around the tiny cubicle. It seemed to be following us. I considered all the miles of track that lay before us and the promises it represented, but the moon captured my attention again, and I wondered if the folks back home were watching it too. I nestled back onto the pillow and allowed my thoughts to drift back along the path that had led us here. So much had happened since that memorable moment in the train station when I had been struck dumb at the sight of Daniel with his children. I was astounded by the wisdom of a universe that could align the stars in such a way as to bring us to this new adventure.

I suppose the adventure had really begun in 1923, the year of weddings. Daniel and I were married in July, and the ceremony at the registrar's office in Warrington was quiet and serious with only our two witnesses in attendance. Emily stood proudly with my brother Harry, and they signed the register next to ours. Harry bought the first round of drinks at the local pub following the ceremony, and we were overwhelmed by the turnout of relatives and friends who were waiting there to wish us well. Philip Simpson, with his arm around Alice, made a lovely little speech and bought the second round. Mother paid for the food.

Two months later, Annie walked down the aisle, looking every bit like a china doll in her delicate lace veil, and married Patrick Turner, the love of her life.

Our children—oh my, how I loved saying that aloud—had taken almost as long to accept me as had Daniel's mother. *The old curmudgeon.* I took my time getting to know them all. I was sensitive to the fact that the two motherless children had been left with strangers, uprooted, and passed around; they continued to wear cloaks of sadness. They were understandably wary and clung only to one another. For nearly a year, Ian experienced terrible nightmares and wet the bed more often than not. Heather was distant and defiant even with her grandmother. I was thrown into the role of motherhood, and we all agreed that I was wading out of my depth in the beginning. I was careful to tiptoe into the water ever-so-gently until we were all sure I could swim.

I transferred to a hospital in Warrington and gratefully accepted Alice and Philip's offer of room and board so that I could be nearer Daniel, the children, and the old curmudgeon. Daniel worked at a news agent, and together, we tucked away every spare shilling. We had a future to save for and enjoyed the moments when we could sit with our heads together at the kitchen table, tallying up the accounts for the week. Mother Pearse finally relented, accepted me for my strengths, and in an awkward speech over Sunday lunch, invited us to live with her once we were wed. There were challenges of course, with two strong-willed women running the same household, but we struck an essential balance and found some semblance of harmony.

The children began to thrive and spent most of each day at school. They liked me most of the time. Daniel was an old softy, which left me firmly planted in the role of disciplinarian. Somebody had to be the bad guy. Sadly, my parenting style was born of military training and seemed a little harsh at times, though I tried never to be unkind. We enjoyed family outings and even took a soul-cleansing trip to the seaside. As regularly as possible, we visited with Daniel's lovely sister Sandra and her family in Warrington. Our spotlessly clean home was run with military precision, but it was also filled with singing and laughter. In time, I was relieved and delighted to see that smiles had replaced the dreadful morose expressions that the children had worn at our first encounter.

I continued to work at the hospital until the day Mrs. Pearse took sick. Then one day, I arrived home to find Ian in tears and Mrs. Pearse on the floor. She'd had a severe stroke. Heather was off in search of her father, but by the time they returned, the old lady had taken her last breath. I was sitting on the floor with her when it happened, cradling her head in my lap and stroking her hair, with Ian pressed into my side and his head buried beneath my arm. For the first time since my wedding, I was the lady of the house. The only Mrs. Pearse.

Only weeks after her funeral, a much-needed bright light of good news shone on the family when Annie was safely delivered of her first child. David, with no second name, was her pride and joy and the first of three sons she would have with Patrick. I was overjoyed for the little family and relieved that this petite girl had come through the delivery with a healthy child.

I tidied Heather and Ian in their Sunday best in preparation for a visit to see the new baby and hoped that the outing would put smiles on their faces once again. It had been a difficult few weeks. Daniel mourned his mother, and the children suffered, each grieving in their own way. They were all too familiar with death and sadness. I carefully folded and wrapped the gift that I had been working on for months and allowed Heather to carry the parcel into the house. Annie was delighted with the crocheted pram cover and asked Heather if she would like to hold little David. She gingerly laid the baby in the little girl's lap and sat beside her. I watched Heather's sullen expression transform into a tender smile and was grateful that this was a good day.

Every fortnight or so, when the weather was fine, Mother and I met for a picnic at the willow; Alice joined us when she could. On just such an occasion, Alice brought with her a tiny book of poetry and read to us in soft lilting tones that matched the peacefulness of the day.

I am standing upon the seashore. A ship at my side spreads her white sails to the morning breeze and starts for the blue ocean. She is an object of beauty and strength, and I stand and watch until at last she hangs like a speck of white cloud just where the sea and sky come down to mingle with each other. Then someone at

my side says, "There she goes!" Gone Where? Gone from sight—that is all. She is
just as large in mast and hull and spar as she was when she left my side and just as
able to bear her load of living freight to the place of her destination. Her diminished
size is in me, not in her. And just at the moment when someone at my side says,
"There she goes!" There are other eyes watching her coming . . . and other voices
ready to take up the glad shout . . . "Here she comes!"

HENRY VAN DYKE

She knew. Alice knew because she had the gift of second sight, and Mother, who looked longingly up into the umbrella of leaves, shared that gift. Alice gave me an approving glance and said, *"Cheayll mee sonnish ny marrey."*

I heard the whisper of the sea.

The two intuitive women were well informed. Our plans for the future had begun to take shape, propelled in part by the council who'd informed us we could no longer reside in Mrs. Pearse's house now that she was gone. I had confided in Emily, of course, and also to my brother Harry, but had decided to share our news with the family only when we were certain of the details. There seemed little point upsetting the applecart unnecessarily. I had not considered that Mother and Alice had their own sources for information.

In time, and at a great family picnic in the garden, we announced our plans to immigrate to Canada. "We'll be on our way in just a few short weeks," Daniel proclaimed proudly. Our news was met with enthusiasm by most and awe from others. I looked around at the faces, both young and old. Most were folks who could never conceive of living anywhere else, comfortable in their community and content in the sameness of their day to day routine. To them, in that moment at least, we were the great adventurers . . . pioneers heading off into the wilderness. I suppose we were.

Amid the fervour, I watched as Mother discreetly wound her way through the garden and up toward the house. I followed her. She stood at the kitchen window surveying the happy gathering on the great lawn, and when I approached, she simply said, "Take us with you, Milly."

I wrapped my arms around her waist and dropped my chin onto her shoulder. "Allow us to share your journey, if only in spirit." She turned around and cupped my face with a deliberate pressure that meant I should take heed. "We are the roots to your tree, the source of your river wherever it leads, and there will be days when you need that connection even though you are far away." We stood together for a time, arm in arm, watching the scene below play out like a great choreographed ballet. The willow stood majestically tall as the children danced in her swaying branches, and family and friends mimed in happy conversation moving from one vignette to the next, as it occurred to me for the first time that I may never see any of them again.

Emily's absence from the party was conspicuous, if only to me. I still felt the need of her acutely in these social situations, and I just simply missed having her nearby. I felt that way every day, truth be told, although marriage and motherhood had not put any real distance between us. Nothing could. Daniel commented often that we were *"like twin flames keeping each other alight; if one were to be extinguished, it would surely douse the other."* We spoke often and visited when we could, and although she was unreserved in her enthusiasm about our plans, she also made it clear that she had no intention or desire to say goodbye in any way.

"I suffered one farewell with you, Milly. I will not suffer another. The Royal Mail will simply have to up its game," she'd said playfully and then looked away.

The day wound down and the tidying began, weary families peeling away one by one. In the end, when all the goodbyes had been said and the tearful scenes played out, Daniel took the children for a walk while I made my way to where Alice waited at the bottom of the garden. We would see each other often before our ultimate departure, but I knew that quiet moments such as these would be few. The air had grown hot and heavy, sweat trickled down my back, and my feet ached; I had not been off them the entire day. If Alice felt the same, she did not show it. We stood silently, watching the still water as swarms of midges swirled in and out of the ferns on the riverbank. There were a million things that I wanted to say, that needed to be said, but the words that rolled freely and eloquently around in my mind were harnessed there. Volumes were spoken in that silence, and I hoped that with all of her intuitive powers, Alice had been able to hear the conversation. Just when I thought the tension would overpower me, Alice said, "The water looks so inviting, doesn't it?"

It took me a moment to get out of my own head before finally responding. "Yes, it surely does. I could jump right in, skirts and all."

She turned to look at me for the first time. "And there, my dear sister, lies the difference between us." I didn't understand her meaning. She continued. "Where I might contemplate the idea, hesitate, and perhaps even venture to dip a toe in the water, you would indeed jump in, clothes and all. I would consider the mess and the washing to be done afterward, whereas you would find the adventure in it."

"I would moan and bitch about the mess afterward though," I confessed, playfully bumping her arm with mine.

She smiled a knowing smile. "My dear sister, you are among the bravest of souls, and I am ever-so-proud of you. I hope you know how much."

"Thank you, Alice," I said with my arms wrapped tightly around her, "for today and for all the days that have led me here. I will be lost without you. Lost . . . without the three most important women in my life who have held me up and eased me forward; you and Mother and my dear Em. I confess, I am excited and terrified all at the same time."

"We will be with you. We'll always be with you."

Chapter Seventeen

Daniel's previous experience farming on the Canadian Prairies was a tremendous asset, and I was amazed by his business acumen. He knew how to barter and was able to negotiate the best price on all our essentials. The money that we had so conscientiously saved allowed us to build a three-room house, to purchase a few necessary livestock, a single-furrow walking plow, a buggy, and two incredibly important horses. The remainder of our funds were securely locked away in the newly opened Bank of Commerce.

Breaking the land was the first order of business, and although Daniel had hoped to buy a gas-operated tractor, he chose instead the more economical option of hiring some help. He needed to put away funds to buy seed in the spring and had already placed his order for the early ripening Marquis variety of wheat that he had read so much about. Farming on the prairie, I learned, was a community event. Neighbours helped neighbours to build homes sturdy enough to keep out the vicious blasts of winter, and plows and tools were shared. Everyone had skills to be bartered. We worked diligently on our own homestead through adverse conditions of every kind in that first year. It was all new to me, and while I was taken a little by surprise at the austere conditions, I was completely ill-prepared for the kind of cold I had only heard about—the stories were not exaggerated.

I dug in with as much fortitude as I could muster, determined to make a go of it. At the same time, we toiled alongside our neighbours, and I threw myself into the community to help in any way I could. I baked bread and pies to sell at the general store in town and gained some notoriety for my ability to fix a tractor or anything else with a motor. I felt useful and empowered. Daniel found part-time employment through the winter at the office of the local newspaper, the *Star City Echo*. He was lucky to have made the acquaintance of the newspaper owner at a church fellowship meeting, and the two British fellows had immediately hit it off. Together with our savings and our combined earnings, we survived our first tedious winter.

The children were enrolled in the six-room schoolhouse, and as far as anyone knew, I was their mother. Still, I watched with envy as young women carried their infant bundles into church. The desire for my own baby remained a deep longing—some would say an obsession—that impacted how I mothered the two youngsters in my charge. I worked too hard at it sometimes as though I were in competition with the real mothers. I was firm. I could hear it in my tone some days, and although I was not given to overt demonstrations of affection, I cared for them deeply. Our children were well fed and healthy, scrubbed clean with clothes that were no more threadbare than any of the others at the school. Ian had a growth spurt, and his trousers had been let out as far as they would go, and Heather, who was headstrong and argumentative at times, was going through some physical changes of her own. Our family never missed a Sunday service at the Anglican church, and my size-nine shoes were always first in the door at the ladies' community club meetings.

Dear Em,

Thank you for your letter. It is always good to hear your "voice." I am surprised to learn that in all our correspondence I have neglected to give you a description of my new home, at least one sufficient enough for you to conger a picture in your mind.

Let's see now . . . how to describe the prairies? I suppose my first observation was simply the vastness of the sky. It seems so much bigger and grander here somehow; it's bluer than back home as well. It isn't blocked out by clouds of coal smoke. The stars seem to go on forever, and you can imagine that you are looking at the entire universe in a single glance. The landscape is flat—not just flat but horizontal. Daniel laughed at my banter: "Do you suppose the experts are wrong? Are we sure the planet is round?" I thought perhaps, if I squinted in just the right way, I might see the Rocky Mountains—two provinces and 450 miles away. There is a rugged beauty about this place, earthy, sparse, and weather beaten. It is nothing like England. The air is crisp and clean, and at times, so cold that your nostrils freeze. The roads look as though they were drawn in place with a gigantic ruler, straight and narrow, furrowed between fields of wheat, and ending only when they touch the sky on the horizon. I do miss the curvy surprise of a British country road as you wind through miles of hedges. Our boundaries, for the most part, are unmarked. I suppose they matter less.

Daniel had warned me, and I thought that I was prepared for my first Canadian winter, but the brutal severity of it took me off guard. It is a different kind of cold than we experienced in France. It bites and burns. It is unforgiving and goes on and on until you think you'll never feel your toes again. There were many days when we shovelled and tunnelled our way out of the house, snow drifts upon snow drifts as high as the roof. The wind is unrelenting in its cruelty. There is nothing to stop it, just miles of open space for it to swirl and grow in intensity with a malicious desire to torment.

Homes and buildings are built for a purpose and with the materials at hand. They are strong and resilient, but there is little architectural beauty about them. Even the church in Star City is a simple one-story structure with a tiny steeple and a bell. There are no elaborately stained windows, no great statues or carvings, but there is a warmth and sincerity within its walls.

We are but one ingredient in a great soup pot of humankind here in Saskatchewan; people from countries all over Europe and beyond have come to carve out a better future for their families. Our neighbours are Hungarians, Ukrainians, Norwegians, Swedes, Danes, Poles, and Germans. I confess that I struggled with the latter in the beginning, but I am resolved that we all belong. We work hard together as a community in the hopes that we all make a success of it. If one fails, we may all fail.

I think our arrival during a colourful and temperate Canadian autumn may have lulled me into a false state of euphoria. Since then, I have learned, much to my chagrin, that this is indeed the land of extremes. I am happy, however, to announce that we have survived our first arduous summer. The sweltering heat reached 110 degrees Fahrenheit on our hottest day in August when we were at our busiest in the *fields. Nevertheless, our first crop has been harvested with the help of a threshing crew of twenty-five men who move from farm to farm at harvest season. We sold and offloaded the grain at one of the massive grain elevators in town, and Daniel proudly marched into the bank to top up our depleted savings account. He kept back enough cash to buy the much-needed albeit second-hand tractor that he had seen advertised in the* Echo. *With it, he will be able to break more of the land and plant greater areas of wheat. I will be grateful if it lessens his workload just a little. I do worry so about his health. He stopped at the general store to purchase something special for the children and came back to the buggy with a big box, a present for me: a radio. Imagine that! Ours was one of a few households in the area that did not have one, and Daniel knew how much I missed having music around me. He really has such a kind heart.*

I hope, darling Em, that I have painted something of a picture for you. Write soon ... I miss you so much.

Milly

PS. Please tell your darling doctor dad that I continue to journal, although not every day as I should.

On the following Saturday, we excitedly prepared to attend a celebratory dance at the community centre. I was so proud. The Pearse Family, in our Sunday best, proceeded down Main Street in our buggy and stopped briefly at the church to give thanks. There was much to be grateful for. Star City and its neighbouring towns were growing, and best of all, local farms and families were flourishing. I entered the building with my pan of rolls and tray of biscuits for the potluck supper table, warmed at the sight of so many happy exuberant faces. In such a brief time, those who were strangers had become friends.

There were times during those happy, busy days when I forgot to miss home: Britain. I wrote and answered letters every week, sent birthday greetings and remembered family and friends back home in my prayers every night. The distance between us seemed only a few inches on the map in the children's atlas until one day in November of our second year. I was preparing the supper meal when Daniel drove in from a meeting in town and entered the kitchen looking solemn and serious. He handed me a piece of paper, a telegram:

Dear Milly (stop)
Sorrowful news to share (stop)
Philip has suffered a heart attack and died. (stop)
Alice is bereaved and we are all in shock. Thought you should know. (stop)
Love always, Mother (stop)

I sat clumsily in the first chair at hand, holding tight to the scrap of paper as though it were somehow attached to the sender. Daniel held me close. I pictured Philip's effervescent eyes and the smile beneath his bouncy moustache and couldn't believe that his light had been snuffed out so young at only fifty-three. Together, he and Alice had seven children, the youngest being Dolly. How on earth would Alice manage? Well, I knew the answer to that. She would manage, as Alice always did, with grace and fortitude and with the help of her family of course.

Sweet Alice,

I have no words. I feel your pain all these many miles away and wish there were something I could do to relieve your sadness. It must have been such a terrible shock for you and the children. I want to hold you in my arms and care for you as you have so often cared for me. I knew that this would be but one of the many pitfalls of moving so far away, that sad news of the family might come, but I never imagined that it would come so soon or that it would first be Philip. Cherish your memories, dear heart. He lives on through his beautiful wife and family. You will be strong in your grief (I know you), but please reach out to those around you for comfort and support. I pray for your healing heart.

Yours always, Milly

The next two years saw the farm prosper and grow. Three of the neighbouring farms joined forces with us to purchase a combine, which made harvest time much less rigorous and more economic with fewer farm hands to pay. Always cautious about spending large amounts of money, Daniel had been hesitant, but I was resolute that he should invest with the others. He relinquished the argument when I reminded him of the weeks he had spent in bed with pneumonia during the winter and the doctor's stern warning that he must not overdo.

Dr. Brigham was a regular visitor at farms in the area. He came to call on our children, who suffered the usual illnesses, but Daniel's failing health brought him to our door often. The doctor was well versed in Daniel's military medical history and had many patients who were among the walking wounded. During each visit, I took in the scene as the doctor listened carefully, stethoscope in his ears and head turned toward the wall. He would nod and say, "Okay, Daniel, deep breath. That's it. Again. Now, give us a little cough." Then he would nod and repeat, "Again." He was never alarmist but made his concerns known with a charming friendly manner.

"I'll stop by and check in on you again soon," he would say with a kind smile before mounting his horse and heading off to see the next patient on his list. He prompted his horse, "Tch tch, Sport," tipping his hat as I waved from the door. I know I was one of his favourites. He often stayed for coffee and sometimes a meal. On one occasion, and after a shot or two of whisky, Daniel told him about my contributions during the war, offering what I considered an inflated account of my acumen in the field of medicine.

"She's made of sturdy stuff," he said, "and so cool in the face of adversity."

Dr. Brigham turned to me. "Why did you not go into nursing? I can picture you, with your tall frame, in a nursing uniform and cap."

"And taking orders from a hospital matron," I replied with a hint of sarcasm, tilting my head in just such a way that he took my meaning.

"No, maybe not." He chuckled. I knew he liked me very much and the feeling was mutual.

Daniel wasn't through. "Do you know what they used to call her? ... *The Nose*. Yep, she could identify ailments and infections by their smell. Honestly!"

The doctor smiled back at his enthusiasm. "So, Milly, would you consider helping me on my rounds? When you have time, of course. I can always use an extra pair of hands, especially 'sturdy' ones." He grinned.

"Happy to help if I can," I replied, not sure when I would ever find the time. But I did. There was always time to do what you loved, and above all, I loved feeling useful.

That was also the year the alarm bell sounded, and every man within earshot was rallied to help extinguish a fire that broke out on Main Street. We could see the glow in the sky and knew, before our neighbour drove in the yard, that there must be something terribly amiss. Despite all efforts, and the new fire engine with its water hose and pump, the buildings along the east side of the street were engulfed in flame and could not be saved. It was a terrible tragedy for the town, but with God's grace, as the minister reminded everyone on Sunday, no lives had been lost in the fire. There were a few individuals who sustained nasty burns though, and I made myself as useful to the good doctor as I could. At a town hall meeting in the weeks that followed, Dr. Brigham announced, to the resounding approval and appreciation of all in attendance, that he would donate the funds to rebuild a portion of the street in cement. He simply stated, "It'll not burn down again. That we can be sure of."

The following year was another boon for wheat farmers, and we were proud to read in the *Reader's Digest* that Saskatchewan was being referred to as the "World's Granary." With money in the bank, many of our neighbours were buying additional parcels of land and better equipment, but Daniel was content with what he had. He had seen fortunes come and go when people overextended themselves, and he was not going to make the same mistake. I was grateful that he was not a gambler and that we had sufficient funds to hire some help.

Dearest Mother,

How excited we were to receive your astounding gift. When we received word from Tisdale that a large crate was waiting for us at the train station, we could not have anticipated what it might be. The vanity dresser now stands proudly in our bedroom, and my little treasure box has been rescued from the shipping trunk, where it has been secreted since our arrival here, and is now nestled safely back into its home and hiding place. The set of daffodil dishes that I so loved as a child are on full display in a cabinet that Daniel built in the front room, and they

make me smile each time I walk by. The fruit bowl and the canister
will be put to good use but with great care. I am amazed that all these
fragile treasures survived the journey, and I thank you with all my
heart for your generosity. Lastly, we all send our thanks for the beautiful
knitted garments; the children will wear them proudly to school. I can
feel the warmth of your handprint on each one, and there is still a trace
of your scent about them. They bring me closer to you.

My best love to all, Milly

I dared not tell my mother that her beautiful Royal Winton fruit bowl
had arrived with a tiny chip on its edge, or that the bevelled mirror (now
reattached to the vanity) had suffered a hairline crack at the top left corner.
In that tiny flaw, I could see myself in two reflections. *How profound.* One
reflection seemed to be peering toward the window, recalling and secretly
longing for the comfort of life in the bosom of family. I closed my eyes a
moment and saw a hearty young woman sitting beneath the great willow,
longing for adventure. The opposing reflection stared directly back at me,
thin, weary, and lonesome—another note for my journal.

It did my heart good to have a few special (some might even say frivolous)
trinkets around me. The little swordfish that I had discovered in the rubble
during my stay in London rested next to the treasures from Mother. The
house was serviceable, and I had no complaints. The previous year, we had
built an additional bedroom and expanded the front room, but our world
was all about function. Spending money on the household, even to make
life easier, came last. The operation of the farm was always the priority. We
continued to haul water from a well and bathed in a galvanized tub set in
front of the fire, repurposing the water to wash clothes and bedding. Nothing
was wasted or taken for granted.

We were among the fortunate families who had electricity, but there was
no other heat source besides the wood stove in the front room. We spent
much of the winter huddled in front of the fire, listening to all and sundry
on the Westinghouse wireless radio. Hockey games and our own Famous
Farmer Fiddlers were always entertaining, but we also paid attention to the
grain quotations and could at times pick up broadcasts from as far away
as Chicago. Our one great extravagance came about when Dr. Brigham

encouraged Daniel to install a telephone. He reasoned that isolation was both unhealthy and dangerous for those of us living in the more remote areas, and I was surprised that my thrifty husband agreed without argument. I was grateful to be only a phone call away from medical help when Daniel struggled with his breathing, and although the phone rang very seldom, I was reassured by a thread of connection that had not been there before. The children had fun listening in on the party line, and it was easier for Dr. Brigham to reach me when he needed my help. I wrote often to Emily about my exploits with the good doctor:

> *". . . He has come to rely on me for simple follow-up visits, dressing changes, and light nursing but recently convinced me to accompany him at a few births so that I might learn midwifery. What do you think of that, my learned friend with the fancy framed diploma? I never imagined I would be delivering babies, but women here must rely upon one another for support of every kind. It can be a dreadfully lonely place at times. What news of your dad? I haven't heard from him in some time . . ."*

I tried to paint a rosy picture in my letters to family back home; I suppose I was not always successful, but I did try. I explained in vague terms about the hardships we faced, all the while exaggerating our ability to overcome them. Emily was the exception, of course. We told each other everything. Mostly, I confided my concerns and grievances to the pages of my journal, and from time to time, I took comfort in re-reading those passages. They reminded me of our successes and of our resilience in overcoming one issue or another. Sometimes it read more like a diary than it should, but mostly, it was a place where I could hide or boast, scream, laugh, and cry aloud without making a sound.

Daniel was a wonderful, caring husband and would have been sickened to know just how lonely I was. His world was the farm from dusk till dawn, spring through fall. It had to be, and he loved it. We raised pigs, chickens, laying hens, and a few cows for milk and boasted four indispensable horses. When he wasn't seeding or breaking new ground, he was cutting hay to feed the animals. He often needed my help in the field, and I became a deft hand at checking the quality of the grain, but I had my own world to tend to. Running the household was a full-time job.

I lugged water from the well, did the cooking and cleaning, and made weekly trips into town with prepared baked goods to sell and eggs to exchange for flour and sugar. I did the milking because neither of the children had quite gotten the hang of it, though they were always on hand as I sat on the milking stool, waiting patiently to dip their tin cups into the bucket of warm milk. In the beginning, they were tasked with gathering the eggs, but as they grew, they were able to help with many of the heavier chores. We churned butter and made ice cream with the wild strawberries that the children picked along the roadside on their way home from school.

My happiest hours were spent nurturing the vegetable garden that was our salvation through the winter. I bordered it with a hearty hedge of caragana to deter critters, and I experimented each spring with herbs and vegetables of all kinds. It was important that I filled our bellies and strengthened our bodies with fresh produce while we were able. I took immense pride at the bounty it provided us at harvest time and filled the root cellar with potatoes, turnips, and carrots, and the shelves with less hearty vegetables (both canned and pickled) to see us through another winter. At harvest, Daniel and the threshing crews worked into the night, as many as two dozen ravenous men were on hand at any given time, and I was responsible for providing them all with two huge meals each day.

Most often, Heather and Ian walked to and from their schoolhouse with lunch pails swinging by their side, but through the worst of the winter, Daniel delivered them on the cutter sleigh, often picking up stragglers on the way.

Dear Mother,

Ian, at twelve, has already grown into a tall, strapping lad and helps his dad a great deal with the farm. He is, of course, still in school, and his studies matter to both of us. You would adore him, I'm sure. He has such a gentle soul with the kind of shyness that lures you in and encourages you to seek him out, like coaxing a turtle to peek out from under its shell. The girls at school pester him relentlessly; he is ridiculously handsome. This morning, as I was lifting the bucket of water from the well, he placed his left hand flat on the small of my back and reached for the handle with the other, muttering, "I'll get it, Ma." Such a small thing but warming to the heart.

His sister, on the other hand, is neither use nor ornament these days. I don't mean to sound unkind, but you know that she's been a constant source of struggle for me. She has decided—and announced, I might add—that since I am not her real mother, she need not heed anything I say. I know how you feel about corporal punishment, but my patience wears thin, and one day she may feel the back of my hand. She is at the age of course when all things blossom, and it seems that her only interest is the next young man she might meet at the community centre or the church. Daniel is of little help in these matters. To be fair, I think she is missing her school chum, although she has not come right out and said so. Lizzie has been her closest friend but is two years older and has recently graduated. She is a dear girl whom we love to have visit; I will encourage Heather to invite her over more often. In the meantime, Heather must complete her studies if she means to graduate next year. She has already been promised an apprentice position with the seamstress in town. She is a keen hand with needle and thread, much like our dear Alice.

Remember me to all the family and give Alice my best love.

As always, your Milly

Daniel made it through the winter without a bout of pneumonia, the farm was doing well, and I was optimistic. We proudly attended Heather's graduation, and with her apprenticeship came a welcome maturity and an easier relationship between us. We strongly encouraged her friendship with Lizzie, who was a wonderful influence and became a fixture in our house just as Heather had clearly become in Lizzie's. They were inseparable. Lizzie, who had a houseful of older brothers, had appeared very shy in the beginning but could not conceal for long the wit and charisma that lay behind her flashing dark eyes. She was ladylike and polite but straightforward. *"If I'm not first to the table in our house, I do without, and if I don't speak up, I'm pretty quickly drowned out."* I liked her. She had wavy auburn hair and a tiny frame that belied the power behind the arms that could carry in as many sticks of wood for the fire as I could in one haul. There was an essence about her, a sparkle that was oh-so-familiar.

I wrote to Alice, *"... I think perhaps I have discovered a sister of the willow, even though there is no willow in sight. There is a 'bree' that radiates from Heather's young friend, a tangible stillness behind a quiet smile that seems to acknowledge a message only she can hear."*

I watched as the girls lay together on the new front-room carpet, flipping through the pages of the Eaton's mail-order catalogue, tittering about the caption: *"If you can't find what you want on our pages, it hasn't been made or you don't need it."* Their camaraderie made me long for Emily, my Emily, who had written only a few months before with the sad news of her father's sudden passing. She was, of course, characteristically more concerned about my feelings than her own, but I felt the depths of her sadness in every sentence. I left the giggling girls to their ministrations and went in search of pen and paper.

Dearest Em,

There have been so many months and equally as many letters since your dad passed, and still I wonder every day how you are getting on. I have changed my "Dear Journal" salutation to "Dear Dr. D." It helps me to feel connected to him somehow, and I do believe he is still listening and giving me the hairy eyeball whenever I'm being ridiculous. I know you miss him terribly.

Just as I miss you, my sweet friend. Never more than when I am made to suffer through one social activity or another—the bane of my existence as you know, especially in your absence. I attend them because I want to feel part of a community, but then I find no joy in the chattering of female voices and cannot make out what to say most of the time. My head is filled to overflowing with a cacophony of dialogue that cannot find its way out. I spy around the room looking for Daniel who is completely content and comfortable jabbering with a throng of men. The church suppers are not too bad because there is always something to do; I busy myself in the kitchen mostly. But then there are the picnics and the big box socials where everyone knows more than anyone else about politics and religion, and when they tire of those debates, they turn to gossip, which I cannot abide. Most often I'm fine one on one with neighbours or folks that Dr. Brigham asks me to see because there's value in those conversations, and I am not so overwhelmed. I have been such a mess, spending half of my time feeling lonely and the other half fretting over being around people.

There is a silver lining to all of this whining, my dearest friend. It seems that the universe has offered me an olive branch. A small division of the Royal Canadian Legion has opened right here in Star City, and I have found solace there. Daniel and I proudly attended the opening ceremony and have made bi-weekly visits ever since. I take such comfort in chatting with folks who shared similar experiences overseas, and the wives have offered me a glimpse into the struggles they endured on the home front. Small talk is so much easier when the subject matter has substance. We all seem to fit together like the fingers of a glove. How often your face has come to mind as I reminisce with these new acquaintances.

I miss you with all my heart,
Milly

Chapter Eighteen

B y 1929, the world was in economic chaos, wheat prices plummeted, and nature had turned on us and brought an unprecedented decade of drought. Daniel was grateful that he had resisted the temptation to buy up land, and we were fortunate to have savings that many of our neighbours could not boast. There was a parade of farmers seeking work in the city or to line up for aid in order to feed their families. Some pulled up stakes and abandoned their farms altogether; other men went farther west in search of employment. Our family chose to stay the course, but having heard of the ordeal in New York City, Daniel withdrew our money from the local bank in fear that it too might shut the doors. He secreted our savings beneath the trinkets in the little wooden box in the vanity. Everyone in the family sought work where we could. Ian spent that summer at a logging camp farther north, and Heather worked a few hours a day at the general store. All the funds were pooled to keep us afloat, and stored in the yellow canister to be counted at the end of the week for all to see. I was grateful that the vegetable garden was in close proximity to the water supply and proud that its expansion over the years now provided root vegetables for sale as well as consumption. I was more grateful still that Daniel had diversified from growing wheat; he now had barley and oats to sell on the market as well.

Each year, we prayed for an end to the relentless drought and scorching temperatures. The men in the community turned to the *Farmer's Almanac* more often than they did the Bible, determined to find something to hope for. The land was dying a slow death. Daniel's health worsened, his asthma exacerbated by the constant swirling dust. I dared not convey our situation in letters home as I knew that the depression was hitting them extremely hard too, especially in the industrial north of England. Young Patrick had been laid off from his job at the Vulcan Ironworks just as Annie delivered their second son, a baby brother for David. They called him Gordon, and I felt yet another pang of jealousy. *Will this longing for a baby never cease?* Mother and Alice were in good financial stead, and I knew they would help the young family as much as they could. As always, I was forthright with Emily.

Dear Friend,

We are dealing with forces beyond our control. The magazines are calling this the "Dirty Thirties" and with good cause. The swirling dust persists day and night, although it is difficult at times to know which is which. It can be so dark in the afternoon that young children find their way home from school by the light from lamps in the window. There are many who are doing without the bare minimum, and illness and malnutrition run rampant. I am increasingly called upon to assist the good doctor as his time is spread so thin. I see women who do without any food at all so that they might feed their children; we share as much as we dare. The drought is much worse to the south of us, and we are as ever hopeful that next year will see the end of it.

Please do not fear for our safety. Daniel and Ian have both found work in town thanks to connections made at the Legion, and together with my meagre earnings, we are staying afloat. Dr. Brigham has begun paying me a stipend for my assistance; I will be forever indebted to him.

Milly

Heather and Lizzie finished their shifts at the telegraph office in town and were fussing about in the back bedroom in preparation for the winter festival dance in town. Heather had completed her apprenticeship with Mrs. Lund, but sadly, with the economy in such as state, the dear lady had been forced to close her seamstress shop and move away. It was nice though to have a skilled seamstress in the house as evidenced by the two young women who danced excitedly into the room to show off the frocks that Heather had made for the occasion.

With a little twirl, Heather asked, "What do you think, Ma?" She had done a beautiful job of stitching the heavy floral fabric in shades of russet and crimson—remnants that Mrs. Lund had gifted her from the shop. I was pleased that she had chosen a pattern that disguised her ample bosom just a little.

"Well done indeed!" I said as my eye was drawn to Lizzie, swishing her hips from side to side in a periwinkle print. I chose not to offer my opinion on the shoulder pads that were too big for her frame; it was the new style after all.

"You both look lovely. What time will the boys be here to collect you?" Lizzie's brothers (the Friesen boys as we all referred to them) had promised to pick them up in the buggy. We had come to know the family only through occasional community events as they attended a different church. Lizzie commented often about her parent's devout faith and their strict adherence to the book of Methodist disciplines. Originally from Germany, Mr. and Mrs. Friesen had immigrated first to the United States and rented a farm there. The oldest of the boys, Carl, was born in the US, but when the family learned that Canada was giving away land, they'd crossed the border with wagons filled with farming tools, seed, and all that they could carry with them. It gave them an advantage over the immigrants arriving from Europe who had only what they could carry in suitcases and steamer trunks.

Their farm remained a going concern even during the drought due to its proximity to the Carrot River and the installation of an irrigation system. Carl, age thirty-seven, had recently purchased a parcel of his father's acreage and was working the land himself. The other two boys, Peter and Martin, would be collecting the girls, but I knew that their big brother would be waiting at the town hall for Heather to arrive. When we first learned that she was smitten with the man, we assumed it was simply an adolescent crush on her best friend's older brother. We were unable to discourage the match; Heather would do as Heather would do! I was uneasy about their seventeen-year age difference while Daniel was more concerned that he was German "*and a Methodist to boot.*" But the young man had grown on us both. He was a steady, hard-working fellow who genuinely cared for our daughter, and I had little doubt that a proposal was in the offing.

I was spot on. Within a week of the dance, Carl arrived at the door and asked to speak privately to Daniel. They were engaged. The Friesen family welcomed the match wholeheartedly; Heather had been like a member of their family for years and had agreed without reservation to change her allegiance to the Methodist church. I doubted that Carl would insist upon strict adherence to the disciplines in their household; he'd been known to have a nip of whisky with Daniel upon occasion. Lizzie and Heather were over the moon at the prospect of becoming sisters-in-law, and although a year-long engagement was promised, they could talk of nothing but wedding plans.

Several months later, on a temperate June afternoon, I was alone in the house and watching with gratitude as a light sprinkle of rain hit the ground on my newly planted vegetable garden. The girls walked up the path arm in arm, and although it was unusual to see them at that time of the day, I was happy for the diversion. Before they made it to the door, I was at the hob putting the kettle on to boil.

"Hello, ladies, just putting on some tea." I prattled on while the girls settled at the table, but it wasn't until I set the teacups in front of them that I took notice of their low energy and dour expressions. Lizzie had not even bothered to shed her mac, and the usually vivacious girl did not make eye contact with me. Heather sat across from her, quiet and grim. The tension was palpable.

"Right, so what's happened then?" I looked at Heather and asked light-heartedly, "Have you two had a tiff?" The girl simply shook her head. I took a minute to pour the tea, noting that even my cheery daffodil china hadn't helped to alter the mood in the room. Still, neither girl spoke. Left to surmise, I asked, "You and Carl haven't had a quarrel, have you?"

"No, it's nothing like that, Ma."

Starting to get annoyed, I demanded, "Well then, suppose you tell me what's wrong. I'm all through guessing."

The young women looked cautiously at one another. "I've suggested to Lizzie that she should talk to you, Ma," Heather said. "I told her that you have an understanding about these things."

"Lizzie, you know you can talk to me about anything." I could see that the girl was welling up and did not want to push too hard. She opened her mouth to speak but then changed her mind.

"Heather, help me here. What on earth is going on?"

A nod from Lizzie gave Heather permission to respond. "She's . . . She's in the family way." The colour rose in my daughter's neck as she took a long slow breath before continuing more quietly. "She . . . We don't know what to do. We . . ." She looked at the other girl, who had not moved. "She can't tell her family. They'll disown her." Both girls were in tears.

Lizzie finally summoned the courage to speak. "Mrs. Pearse, I understand there are herbs or medicines that may help to . . ." She could not continue.

I finished the sentence for her. "Abort the baby." She began to sob. I had seen so many desperate women like her over the years. Most were married but could not prevent unwanted pregnancies and had not the resources to feed one more child. Many were dying in these rural communities from self-induced abortions, and I was fearful of such a fate for this lovely creature. I took her hand in mine. "I would help if I could, but there are no magic cures, no potions that will help. Perhaps we should talk to Dr. Brigham."

She started shaking her head madly. "No! No! No one must know. Please, no one must know!" She was frantic.

"Darling, you know you can trust me, don't you?" The girl simply nodded without lifting her face. Of all the disasters that I could have anticipated that Tuesday morning, this was not among them. "Lizzie, how far along are you?" She shook her head and shrugged, but as she unbuttoned her coat, I could see the start of a mound pushing against her flimsy cotton dress. The light had gone from behind her eyes as the tears flowed and dripped from her chin. I wanted to weep with her but pushed my tongue up against the roof of my mouth to ward off the tears. "Lizzie, do you want to tell me who the father is?"

When she didn't respond, I looked to Heather whose face told me immediately that she would not betray a trust. "He's moved away, so it makes no difference."

With quiet determination, Lizzie answered. "Clifford Hamilton. He said he loved me, but that he couldn't marry out of his faith."

Heather interrupted abruptly, and with a grimace, muttered, "Irish Catholic." She looked and sounded disgusted.

I was puzzled. *Why such contempt?* She certainly had not learned it in our household. I never understood the juxtaposition between Protestants and Catholics. We pray to the same God; the differences seemed too few to provoke such division and hatred. I maintained a position of neutrality and avoided discussion on the subject whenever possible. I expect it was my upbringing that encouraged a more open-minded philosophy. Shaking it off, I turned my attention to the matter at hand.

"Lizzie, did you tell him about the baby?"

"No. His family sold up and moved back to live with relatives in the States long before I suspected this. I've never heard from him since."

Her hands shook so that she could not lift the teacup to her mouth, and the failed effort in civility only caused her to burst into tears once again. This was grave news indeed, and I acknowledged the seriousness of the situation while doing my best to stay calm and console her. Finally, I said stoically, rubbing my hands together, "Right then, there's a solution to every problem, and together we'll find it." I looked at the skeptical faces staring back at me and understood that the words had an empty ring, but I continued nonetheless.

"Now, Lizzie, I understand that you're fearful about telling your parents, and we can leave that discussion for the moment, but I feel you must speak to Dr. Brigham."

Heather pressed, asking, "You've been doing midwifery. You could look after this. Why should we risk telling anyone else?"

"Because I'm not a doctor, and I don't have any authority to direct you in this situation." I ignored my daughter and directed my message to the pitiful creature shrinking deeper into the chair with every phrase uttered.

Heather hissed, "It could ruin her reputation." Her demanding tone was doing nothing to comfort her friend, and I suspected she was as much concerned about her own reputation since she was about to join Lizzie's family.

I turned my head sharply and snapped, "I'm more concerned about her safety, and you should be as well."

I put my arms around the shivering girl. "I promise you that he will be discreet. He is a good man, and I know you can trust him implicitly." I took her sweet, terrified face in my hands. "You've met him here often enough to know that he won't judge you. It's just not in his nature. His only concern will be for your health and safety. That's my concern as well." And so, it was agreed. I called to set up the appointment but did not offer any details. The doctor agreed to drop by in the morning. I expect he understood the urgency in my voice.

Lizzie spent the night. In the morning, Heather left for work and promised to stay on to cover Lizzie's afternoon shift. After examining the girl, Dr. Brigham determined that she was five months gone, and without invitation, sat down at the table for the brew he knew would be on the stove. Gentle and caring as always, the good doctor listened carefully as the young woman explained her situation. It helped that he knew the family well and understood her concerns.

Finally, he said, "Elizabeth, you are of age to make your own decisions about this. Whatever you decide to do, you will need a support system, and I encourage you to talk to your family."

"You know how strict and devout they are; they will never forgive my behaviour, nor would they ever welcome this child."

He considered this. "Perhaps."

I sat quietly, waiting for one or the other to turn to me for comment. They did not.

The doctor allowed a silence to settle, and the atmosphere relaxed just a little as though he was somehow directing it to do so. Lizzie was composed and thoughtful as she murmured, "I can't keep this baby." I watched as the torment of decision-making played out on her face. "I cannot burden my parents, and I have no way to raise the child on my own."

"You will put the child up for adoption then?"

"Yes, sir," she said, expressionless. Numb. "I have no choice."

"I can help you through the process, but you will have to decide the rest, especially if you wish to keep this secret from your family. I strongly advise against that, and if you wish, I will happily speak to them with you." She did not respond but agreed to the doctor's offer of a lift home.

Once again alone in my tiny kitchen, I sank into a chair and wept for the first in an exceptionally long time. I had not shed a tear through all the terrifying early days in our new surroundings, through the frightening nights when Daniel couldn't breathe or as the farm withered and blew away along with our savings. But now, with Lizzie's face clear in my mind, I cried until there were no more tears. When Daniel and Ian arrived home tired and hungry, they were disappointed to find that no supper had been prepared. It was a first. I had taken to my bed.

Daniel sat next to me and stroked my hair. "What's up, love? Are you ill?" I shook my head. "Come on," he said. "I've got a nip of whisky tucked away in the cupboard. We'll have one, will we?"

I nodded, and by the time he came back into the room, I was sitting up and straightening my clothes. "I'm sorry, Daniel. I'll get supper sorted. You must be starving."

"Never mind about that. Ian is scrambling up some eggs." He handed me the glass that boasted three fingers of the glistening amber liquid and kissed me gently on the cheek. "Tell me what's gone on."

I heaved a sigh. "I'm lonesome, that's all," I mumbled as the tears began to well up again. "I've been lonesome for such a long time, but now that the kids are grown and you're away so much of the time . . ." I stopped long enough to blow my nose into the hanky he offered. I could tell that he was searching for the right words, but in the end, just held me close and let me continue. I looked him square in the face "Daniel, there's something that I want . . . that I need."

"What's that, love?"

I told him about my visitors and explained Lizzie's situation. He was clearly concerned but said nothing. I described her anguish and her desperate plea for help in terminating the pregnancy. "Brigham confirmed what I knew to be true: She is too far along for any kind of termination, not that he would have offered it." I took his hand tightly in mine and closed my eyes. "Daniel, I know that money is tight and that prospects are not brilliant, but we have more than most right now. I know we can make it work. Oh please . . . say something."

"You want to adopt Lizzie's child?"

"Yes. Yes, I do. More than anything."

Dr. Brigham was successful in convincing the girl to confide in her mother, and true to his word, was by her side during the difficult conversation. As predicted, the woman was incensed, but after much discussion, she finally agreed to a few concessions. She would support her daughter as she could but insisted that this disgrace remain secret to the rest of the family and the community.

I asked Lizzie and her mother to meet us at the doctor's office in town where our conversation about adoption and the great deception began. Dr. Brigham started by asking Lizzie how she felt about the Pearse family adopting her baby. She seemed immediately relieved that a solution had presented itself so quickly. "I hated the idea that I would hand my baby over to strangers. At least, this way, I know the child will be loved and cared for."

Mrs. Friesen was stoic, speaking only infrequently in her heavy accent, but managed to make her views known. She was worried about her daughter's welfare and did not speak unkindly to her, but appearances mattered deeply to her.

When Daniel asked if our age would be of consequence in the adoption process, Dr. Brigham was quick to assuage our concerns. "Babies," he maintained, "are being dropped off at orphanages every day, and adoptive parents are few. I will write the recommendation, and I assure you there will be no argument."

And so, it was decided, and a plan took shape. Lizzie would politely ask for a leave of absence from her job to attend to a family matter, and her mother would make an excuse for her absence at home. I had little doubt but that she could be convincing. I was just as certain that the menfolk in her family would be too busy to care one way or the other; it was their busiest time of year. Lizzie would live with us, and the doctor would secure a bed for her at Mrs. Brigg's home for unwed mothers in Tisdale when it came close to her time. Her mother was relieved; Tisdale was just far enough away that it would be unlikely that anyone would know her daughter. We reasoned that I would spend the summer close to home, out of public view, preparing for the newcomer, and then come September, I would be a mother. I was euphoric. I contained my excitement, outwardly at least, in deference to the Friesen ladies and all that they were going through. Still, my mind and body were atingle. It was difficult to hide. *Sometimes we are rewarded. Sometimes the sun comes out.*

We all knew that it would be impossible to keep Lizzie's secret from everyone in the Friesen household. Heather already knew about the pregnancy, and it was doubtful that she would keep it from her fiancé. We sat them both down to explain. It was clear that Carl already knew about his sister's predicament, and although he was surprised to hear about our plans to adopt, he did not offer any argument. Instead, he thanked us for supporting Lizzie and asked how he could help. I was impressed.

Heather (on the other hand) was irate and vehemently against the plan. With bitter sarcasm, she said, "You are too old to be having a baby." Then pointing at her father, she sniped, "And you're too sickly to be thinking of doing this. It's ridiculous."

Trying to defuse her tantrum, I said as calmly as I was able, "Your arguments are valid; we know they are. We have talked it all through a hundred times and more than once with the doctor. We have not come to this decision lightly."

She was having none of it and told me so plainly. "Think about what you're doing to that girl. She will be forced to see that baby; I am marrying her brother for God's sake. We're going to be family."

"We've considered that too. Honestly we have. Lizzie is content to know that the child will be cared for and has told us that she is pleased to be able to watch it grow up." I looked at Carl and said, "Your mother will not have a role to play but has confessed that she too will be glad to see her grandchild from time to time."

Not waiting for Carl to respond, Heather shouted, as though daring me to rise to the challenge, "You'll be rubbing her nose in it every time you bring that child out in public! She's my friend! How dare you do this to her?"

I had no doubt that she was genuinely concerned for her friend, but I had little tolerance left for further abuse. When I refused to be provoked, she became even more belligerent and spiteful. "I'll probably be pregnant in another year!" She did not look at Carl as she continued. "What then? We all just play happy families? You, at your age, pushing a pram down the street and me following along behind with mine? You can't be serious!"

In response and still surprisingly keeping my cool, I replied, "Is it my age that really worries you the most? You do understand that you are about to marry a man only three years my junior. I sincerely hope you will have a nursery full of children and that no one points a finger and tells you or Carl that he's too old for fatherhood."

She'd run out of arguments, but with a harrumph, she offered one last attack: "This is all about you, you miserable old cow. Milly always gets what Milly wants, doesn't she?"

At that, Daniel was on his feet. "That's enough!" he shouted, red in the face. I had never heard him raise his voice before. "You've said your peace! Now I'll say mine!" He moved her toward a chair and pushed down on her shoulders until she was seated. She opened her mouth to contest, but he spat back, "Be quiet and sit still!"

Carl moved forward on the sofa as though to intervene until I lay my hand gently on his leg to discourage the move. "My wife, your mother, has spent the better part of her adult life raising children that weren't hers! She has asked for nothing but respect from you! She has earned it! He turned to me. "She ... *we* have always wanted a child of our own but have not been blessed. The decision to adopt this child is ours to make, and Lizzie's willingness to offer us such a gift is a blessing. I hope you will come to see that. In the meantime, you *will* apologize."

She refused, pushed past her father, grabbed Carl by the hand, and made for the door. Carl's strength of character showed plainly when he denied her the dramatic exit.

"Come on now," he said. "Let's just calm down and talk this through. Nothing can be accomplished in a temper." He directed her back to the sofa where she sulked and sidled up close to him. Little was settled in the time that followed, and no apologies were made, but the conversation was more composed.

In contrast, our brief response from Ian on the matter was simple: "If this is what you want, Ma, it's okay with me." The boy had already made plans to work at a logging camp up north for the summer and so, in his absence, Lizzie would have his room.

In the months that followed, Lizzie and I became ever-so-close as kindred spirits do. We spent every hour of the day together, and although Heather remained distant with me, it was clear that the friendship between the two girls had not suffered. In deference to her friend, Lizzie asserted, "For all her blustering, Milly, I can promise that she sees you as her mother." At my doubtful expression, she continued, "She wouldn't bicker so if she didn't. That's what mothers and daughters do." She smiled. "Perhaps that's why you and I get on so well. We're not related. Just friends. I think it's likely that Heather feels a little jealous of that friendship just now." I still had my doubts but admired the girl for so vehemently defending her friend.

Mrs. Friesen dropped by now and again and brought special treats from her kitchen, but as Lizzie grew bigger, the visits became brief and less frequent. The old woman was uncomfortable, and her daughter seemed to understand. I (on the other hand) watched with enthusiasm and awe at the life growing inside her and was grateful that Lizzie welcomed my desire to rest my hand on her belly and feel the baby (my baby) move. It never grew old for me.

Everything about that summer was sweet. The wild strawberries were sweeter, the dust-clogged air was somehow sweeter, and the hay, the well water, and the atmosphere in the house were all sweeter. When neighbours popped in to see if I was all right, I wore an oversized house dress, grateful that propriety prevented them from asking the obvious questions. Lizzie busied herself in the bedroom, away from prying eyes. Together, we knitted garments and tore up old sheets to make nappies; Daniel built a cradle and brought home odds and ends that we would need like bottles and nipples. Dr. Brigham was resourceful as well. He had something new to contribute each time we saw him.

Without making any concessions of support, Heather returned home from the church hall on occasion with items she had found on the exchange table: a rattle, a scruffy teddy bear, and some cotton nighties that had a drawstring closure at the bottom. Her ruffled feathers softened just a little as the weeks marched on.

By the middle of August though, the scorching heat on the farm was taking its toll on Lizzie; she was uncomfortable and nearing her time. It was a relief when Dr. Brigham called to say that a space had become available for her in Tisdale. I had such mixed emotions. I was grateful, certain that she would find it much less humid and dusty in town, but also desperately concerned that she would feel abandoned or scared. I wished that I could go along or visit with her, just to hold her hand and be a gentle presence, but we both agreed that for a successful conclusion to the ruse, I must stay out of sight. Dr. Brigham promised to call the minute her labours began and that I could be in the room to help her through the birth. I was excited to share that experience with her but conflicted; it wasn't realistic to believe that our relationship could be the same after the baby was born, and I already mourned the loss of my friend.

We had shared a great deal in our three-month internment together and trusted one another with intimate secrets as good friends do. I felt a keen connection to this amazing young woman, and I was going to miss her.

On September 6, 1934, Lizzie gave birth to a healthy baby girl. Within a week, the papers were signed, and I had my baby. The sparkle had not left my young friend, as I feared it might. She seemed resigned and somehow comforted by the outcome. We held each other close for a long time, and I struggled to find sufficient words of gratitude. It was an impossible task. This beautiful girl had given me the gift of life—a dream that I had long since put aside. I placed around her neck a silver chain, dangling from which was the last of my willow pendants. No explanation was needed; she understood the depth of its meaning. Daniel sat in a corner of the room, getting acquainted with his new daughter and looking almost as happy as I felt. I marvelled at my good fortune. I had just experienced love at first sight for the second time.

We took our baby home. I could not take my eyes from her as she nestled warm and trusting in my arms. I breathed in her essence over and over again, enticing her scent deep into my memory. I resisted the impulse to squeeze her closer and closer to me and wondered how long my heart could survive beating outside my chest as it was.

When someone (I don't remember who) finally convinced me to set her in the cradle, I took the opportunity to put pen to paper.

My Dear Emily,

I have the best of all possible news. We have a baby, a darling little girl only one week old. We have named our bonnie dark-haired child "Vivian Millicent," after you, my darling "Emily Vivian" and hope you will agree to be her godmother. We will, of course, invite a surrogate to stand in for you at her christening. If only you could be here in person! Oh Emily, I never imagined happiness such as this. The world seems in chaos all around me, the farm, finances, and certainly the weather, but I am immune to it all. I have never experienced a happier day.

I have written you already about Lizzie and the circumstances leading to this joyous moment but must tell you that she has proven to be a most remarkable young woman. There is nothing to be said or done that will ever repay the gift she has given me.

Daniel is besotted. We made love last night as young people do in the infancy of their relationship as though to imagine we have conceived her. Together, we slipped the tiny gold-link bracelet onto her wrist—the first time it has been out of the box since Daniel gave it to me those many years ago.

Ian has returned home from his summer job in time to help with the
meagre harvest. He is quite smitten with our new arrival, and I find
I must compete for time to cuddle with her. Heather has warmed to
her and is being more helpful with the running of the house. It's good
practice for her I suppose as she will be married in the spring. Her fiancé
has been incredibly supportive of this situation and is eager to help his
sister re-enter her life; he will be Vivian's godfather as well as her uncle.

Lizzie and her mother will keep their distance. Mrs. Friesen will be
happy to put this episode behind them. I understand that this is the
appropriate and practical course of action, but in my heart, I will miss
my young friend very much.

I must go now, my dear. I have a baby to care for.

With much love, Milly

I wrote similar letters to Mother and Alice, knowing that their joy for
me would be immeasurable.

Having avoided community life for many months, I could not wait to
burst out of my self-inflicted prison to attend the church's fall supper with
a baby in my arms. There would be no reason for anyone to suspect she
was anything but mine. She was mine. I admitted to God that I was guilty
of the great sin of pride—an overabundance of it. *If that is what sends me*
to hell, so be it.

Carl arrived at the event with a new camera in his hand and snapped
photos at random. "Come on, Milly; let me take your picture." I held my
daughter snug in my arms and posed for our first photograph together. Weeks
later, he dropped by for a cup of tea and presented me with three copies of
the image; I sent one to Alice and another to Emily. On the reverse of each
one, I wrote, *"Holding Vivian at six weeks old. I finally have my baby. Much*
love, Milly." I folded a piece of tissue around the third copy and placed it in
my little wooden box.

Dr. Brigham stopped by often on his rounds and commented each time,
"You seem to be in your element, my dear." He was right. There were sparkling
white nappies hanging on the line despite the dust, a pristine apron tied

around my waist, and a baby cradled in my left arm while I bustled about the kitchen preparing bottles and pouring tea.

Heather and Carl were married in May, and within a year, were the happy parents of a baby girl they named Muriel, a grandchild for us and a playmate for Vivian, and although they lived a good distance away, we saw each other as often as we could. Time worked its magic on family tensions, but it was circumstance that brought Heather and I closer when her baby suffered a bad bout of croup. I was concerned about the baby, of course, but must confess that I was delighted that Heather called to ask for my help. I packed a few things for an overnight stay and left Vivian in the tender care of her dad and brother. The young mother was surprised and a little hesitant when I bundled little Muriel up in shawls and blankets and trudged out into the snow to sit with her on the stoop. "The cold air will help open those airways, maybe even take a little of the swelling down." The poor exhausted woman offered no argument when I suggested that she get a little sleep. I spent the night taking the child outdoors at intervals and then back into the kitchen where I held her tented under a towel over a steaming pot of water.

During the wee hours and trying to stay awake, I hovered in the kitchen waiting for a much-needed pot of coffee to finish brewing. I strolled back and forth with the baby in my arms, admiring the lovely framed photographs lining the sideboard. Carl, it seemed, had a notable talent with his camera. Discreetly tucked in behind one of their wedding photos was a tiny silver-plated frame with what appeared to be a recent image taken just outside the church hall. Heather, with her frenzied hair, was holding a crying Vivian on her hip. Next to her stood Lizzie, who inconspicuously reached out to touch the child's leg just as the shot was taken. There were two other young friends in the image, and it was a congenial scene but for the look on Lizzie's face. *Is her expression one of longing or regret?*

Her sad eyes pierced through my heart and left me wounded. The girl had been true to her word, avoiding contact with "my daughter" except at occasional, inescapable family functions, and I was certain that in the moment the photo had been snapped, she had been put on the spot. Still, my insecurities brought about a ridiculous, piercing pang of possessiveness. *Shameful. You're shameful, Milly.* After all she had given me, could I not even allow her this one fleeting moment on film with her progeny? How could I deny her that? Yet I did.

Vivian was a beautiful child with a heart-shaped face and a button nose. Her features were delicate and her frame slight. I looked at her image, then at Lizzie, and back again, wondering why people were oblivious to their obvious connection; it stared blatantly back at me in shades of black and white. *Why would anyone believe that I have mothered this lovely creature?* Our skin didn't match. Our faces were shaped differently; she didn't have my eyes or mouth or (thankfully) my nose. Most folks were too busy with their own lives to see it while others simply did not care, but the photograph put a spotlight on it for me.

I desperately wanted to look at her and catch a glimpse of myself as a child. Perhaps the lathered and irate Heather had been correct all those months ago. The child's proximity to her "real mother" was indeed distressing for Lizzie, as evidenced by her expression on film. I had not considered, however, how Lizzie's presence might affect me. Her eyes were haunting. My insecurities, however absurd, were spreading in a slow and steady ache deep into the pit of my stomach. *Vivian is my baby. My daughter.*

By morning, both the barking cough and the fever had subsided. Heather's baby was settled, asleep in her cot.

The next five years were extreme and difficult for everyone and doing without was just a way of life. History would label these the "lean years," the Great Depression, the Dirty Thirties, the Dust Bowl, and Canada's "lost ten years." I journaled daily, reminding myself of all that I had survived before and the battles that I had already won. It was Dr. D. who'd taught me to count at least one blessing on every page, even on days when it was difficult to do so. It was a good exercise. As I flipped back through the pages of this particular volume, I realized that, in some ways, I had more now than I had ever imagined. I could not pretend our troubles away, of course. They existed. I simply held onto a fragment of hope that things would be better. *"Being strong isn't always a matter of choice,"* I wrote and concluded as I had every day for months: *"We've made it through another day."*

Lizzie met and married a nice fellow and was now a mother of two living in Prince Albert. "The distance between us is a blessing," I wrote ashamedly in my journal. She returned to visit with her family from time to time, as Heather was happy to report, but I saw her only on rare occasions. We were strangers. Any previous emotional connection between us was long since buried beneath layers of guilt and shame, enigmatic resentment, and fear. All on my part of course.

Daniel and Ian continued to pivot between a few hours of work in town and tending to what remained of the farm. We had been forced to sell two of the horses and several of the other livestock. I continued to raise chickens and sell eggs. We were not starving, but we had nothing that could be considered extra. I would have loved to dress my little girl in frilly clothes and buy her fancy dolls, but we had no money for such frivolities. Clothing swaps at the church hall had become the best of all community events, where once a month, mothers met to trade items that their children had outgrown.

Coats and boots that fit a child last year would protect someone else's family this year. Gift packages from England were a welcome sight at Christmas and birthdays. Emily was very generous to her godchild, and Alice (who was a grandmother now) took time out to sew for her. Daniel built her a little sleigh, and Ian brought home sweeties whenever he could. He was a doting big brother, and she adored him. He bounced her around on his shoulders and called her his "little blossom." He read to her every night while she sucked her thumb and twisted her hair into a curl around the forefinger of her other hand, and once asleep, he slipped his arm out from under her and placed a kiss on her forehead. She cried every time he left the house without her.

While my loneliness was abated, I knew that hers was fresh and new. She did not have the typical gaggle of siblings to play with, and so the isolation of farm life was more difficult for her than for most children her age. She disappeared into her own fantasy world much as I had done as a child under the willow. She had an imaginary friend named "Dizzy" that she talked to and argued with ad nauseam. Dr. Brigham assured me that it was all completely normal. She loved the radio, music of any kind really, and played dress up with whatever scraps she could find. She sang and danced and watched out the window each evening, squealing in delight when Ian walked through the door.

She was less fond of her father, which was not surprising considering his ever-souring disposition. While I trudged along, enduring but still able to count that one blessing per day, Daniel was not faring as well. His health was failing. The asthma was out of control, and his mood was worse. He sank into depression, and no one could blame him. It seemed that the whole world was in a similar state. In his weakness, I found strength. I suppose that is what teamwork is about, and I was grateful that Ian was making an extra effort. My poor Daniel. An unrelenting gloom hovered over him. I empathized. I had been there before, and I was sure that he would rally in time, but I also knew that it would have to be on his own terms. It seemed an eternity since I had seen him smile.

As it happened, it was my need that brought him out of the abyss. I awoke one morning with such a sense of dread that I could barely pull myself from the bed. I felt hollow, my hands were shaking, and the room spun around me. Daniel said, "Just lie back down; you've obviously got a bout of something coming on." I shook my head.

"That's not it." I pulled myself upright just as the phone rang. Alice's voice was on the other end. I had not spoken to her since she'd called the previous Christmas. *My goodness, was that almost a year ago?* Before she could say the words, I knew that Mother had died. Daniel was wonderful; he made a concerted effort to lift his own spirits to support mine. For days, I suffered in my grief, and the family rallied around me, but it was the dear woman herself who brought me strength.

On a lovely clear night, she visited me in dreaming. She was all aglow in gold and bronze with taut milky skin and silken hair, looking for all the world as though time had never touched her. She bent slowly from the waist to speak to me in the same gentle voice that I knew from childhood. I felt so small. *"The bonds between us have not broken, my Milly. They are simply sleeping in the silence. Remember to listen. Just listen."*

I woke, went to my mirror, and spoke to my own reflection. "I will listen for the *Sonnish, Shuyr my chree.* Goodbye, Mother."

Chapter Nineteen

We trudged through the day to day until 1939 put an end to our monotonous existence. "The war to end all wars" had not lived up to its promise, and Ian was the first to enlist. The day he came through the door in his Saskatoon Light Infantry uniform, I thought I might drown in the wave of nausea that swirled around me. Images, memories, sounds, and smells were so vivid that I lost my footing and slumped into the nearest chair. Sweet, gentle, soft-spoken Ian was every bit the image of his father in uniform all those years ago; his naivety was part of the outfit. He reached for my hand and asked if I was all right, but I couldn't respond. I was already mourning the loss of his starry-eyed innocence; it would surely be the first casualty. I had seen far too many like him, determined and dutiful young men who'd lost that and so much more on the battlefield. Daniel was shaking his son's hand and pumping it in exuberant pride, while I crept into a hiding place of my own making, deep in melancholy. An old song popped into my head and played repeatedly:

> *I didn't raise my boy to be a soldier.*
> *I brought him up to be my pride and joy.*
> *Who dares to put a musket on his shoulder,*
> *To shoot some other mother's darling boy?*
> *Let nations arbitrate their future troubles.*
> *It's time to lay the sword and gun away.*
> *There'd be no war today, if mothers all would say,*
> *I didn't raise my boy to be a soldier.*

We sang it with the Will-o'-the-Wisp during the Great War, the lyrics more poignant now. I was angry, mostly at Daniel in that moment. *How can he be this excited? Has he forgotten how it was?* And just as I was about to lose control, I heard the words, "And I'll be right behind you, my boy."

Daniel still had hold of Ian's hand, but I moved between them, forcing

Daniel to look me in the eye. We quarrelled for the first in a very long time while Ian entertained Vivian in the bedroom; my arguments and feelings were deafly ignored. Ian was young and naïve, following along dutifully behind his peers, but Daniel's motives, I believed, had more to do with proving his virility. *Validating his manliness may well cost him his life!*

Within the year, he too had enlisted. We were forced to consider our options; I would not be able to manage the farm on my own, I harboured no illusions about that. Selling was impossible in the present economic climate, and so, with regret and like many others before us, we simply abandoned our farm. We said our quiet goodbyes to friends and closest neighbours; my tearful exchange with Dr. Brigham was by far the most difficult. We offered the livestock to a grateful Carl, who promised to repay us in installments. Heather, who had not yet forgiven her brother for joining up, was so upset by the whole arrangement that she refused to see us off. We kept the two horses for the time being and the little dog that Vivian had become so attached to. She was a sweet little stray, a mutt aptly named "Happy" for her temperament. I drove the truck, piled high with our belongings, while Vivian played with Happy in the back seat, tucked up in blankets and pillows and with boxes and cases piled high next to her. Daniel followed in the buggy, which was loaded down with furniture and bigger items.

We stole away in the middle of the night, away from prying eyes and resisting the impulse to look back. We trekked one hundred twenty miles to Saskatoon with one overnight stop to rest the horses. Ian was already in Saskatoon on training, and with the help of some Legion connections, had managed to find a small house for us to rent just on the edge of town. We settled in quickly, enrolled Vivian in school, sold the horses and buggy, and set about making Saskatoon our home. We had not been there long before the dreaded day came to say goodbye to Ian who was shipping out with the 1st Battalion for further training somewhere in the United Kingdom. I rehearsed the scene in my mind many times, prepared as best I could to see him off without an uncomfortable public display of emotion. I wanted my expression and my final embrace to say, *"You'll be fine. You'll be back. There's nothing to worry about."*

No manner of rehearsal was likely to make the act believable, but I was hell-bent on trying. I had not considered, however, how the scene would play out with Vivian in it. We explained to her, in terms that a five-year-old could understand, that her brother was going away on a trip and that he would be gone for some time. She'd seemed perfectly content upon learning that he would bring her back a pressie. But on the day she was hysterical to the point of physically sick, and Ian boarded his train distraught and tearful.

Daniel was enrolled into the 2nd Battalion, which served as a reserve force, and I was grateful to learn that he would not be going overseas. His age was a factor, but it was primarily his medical history that led to his limited duty assignment. I voiced no opinion on the matter, understanding that he was disappointed at the decision. He was sent to training camp, and I worried constantly that the rigours of drill and exercise would be his undoing.

Both of my soldiers sent a portion of their pay packet home every month while I took in washing and ironing. I even did some simple mending just to make ends meet. I did not have Alice's talent with a needle and thread, but I could manage hems and seams. Our house was a duplex, which took some getting used to. I was spoiled by the quiet and privacy of country living. There seemed to be a lot of coming and going from the other unit, but we soon learned that our neighbour, Anita Peppler, was a hairdresser with a small studio set up in the back bedroom. She was a fiery redhead with a bizarre accent that I had never come across before.

She and her husband, Sam, were originally from Newfoundland, hence the accent. They'd settled in Saskatoon when he was offered a position at the university. He was a football coach. Like Ian, he was away with the 1st Battalion. It gave us an immediate connection, but moreover, it gave Vivian something in common with their daughter. Patsy Peppler (two years older and much, much wiser by all accounts) always had plenty to say and buckets of energy. Like her mother, she had silky red hair that ran down her back in two tightly braided plaits, and her knees were perpetually skinned. She was a wonderful companion for Vivian, walking her to and from school and never letting the younger child out of her sight. Patsy consoled her little friend. "My daddy will watch out for Ian. You'll see. They'll be home in no time."

With the bulk of the training behind him, Daniel was able to come home on occasional weekend furloughs, but he did so begrudgingly, each time looking more tired and depressed. "I'm too old to be in the thick of it and too restless to be sitting behind a desk." I had run out of appropriate responses and so, to change the subject, went to retrieve an envelope that had come in the post.

"Look now, love, good news." I waved the envelope in front of him. "It's our transfer to the Saskatoon Legion and an invite to attend a function tomorrow night. That'll do us both good now, won't it?"

The news landed with something of a thud but, in the end, the outing did have the desired effect. He took some comfort in knowing that there were many like him who had already served and were being sidelined for one reason or another. He found a community, and while it was helpful therapy for him, it was serendipitous for me. I loved it there. I loved the people, the comradeship, the sense of purpose, and the positive energy. I dove in with both oversized boots to do whatever was necessary to help the Legion in its unfailing effort to support the troops. Month after month, I worked alongside an ever-growing number of volunteers. We organized care packages and mailed parcels. We prepared sandwiches and tea for the troops returning home on the Red Cross trains. It was the same at every station across the country, with Legion women there to greet them and feed them as the great locomotives delivered the wounded home.

Letters from Ian were regular as clockwork and, although short on substance, they served to ease our minds. He spoke about ongoing training, but details were blacked out on the page. For over a year, he was in Aldershot, but then in June of 1940, the return address changed to Northampton. After that, they seemed to be constantly on the move through England, Borden, Oakley, Surrey, and then Sussex.

December 25, 1940

Dear Ma,

Merry Christmas to you all. Looking festive here, lots of decorations in the mess hall, and the officers served us a smashing dinner. It's a tradition.

Went with the lads on leave for a few days again. Got up to a bit of no good, but we're deep into training again. Lots of manoeuvres and moving about. Seems that new vehicles and equipment arrive daily, we saw them bring in XXXXXXXXXXXXXXXXXXXXXXXXXXXXXXXXX.

We witnessed an aerial battle, and air-raid warnings keep us up some nights, but we don't come to any harm. We did hear that London is having a time of it.

I hope that Vivian received her Christmas box in time and that she likes her new doll.

Love to Dad . . . I'm sorry to hear he's been unwell.

Ian

Daniel was indeed unwell. The worst bout of pneumonia yet hit him in late November, putting him into hospital and in an oxygen tent for several days. Within months, he was home for good, thin, sickly, and defeated. In his forty-fifth year, he looked like a frail old man. The discharge certificate stated, "*. . . by reason of being unable to meet the required military physical standards.*" Surprisingly, it also noted the clubbed fingers on his right hand. Dr. Brigham had explained long ago that they were the result of his lung injury and the mustard gas that had left so much agony in its wake. I was happy to have him home but unequipped to deal with his ever-worsening disposition. I encouraged Daniel to begin a journal as I had done, but he would have none of it. I desperately wished Dr. D. were here to advise me and comfort him.

He was forced to snap out of his doldrums a few months later when Vivian became ill. I seemed always to be nursing someone, and this time it was my daughter. What started as a sore throat and lethargy progressed over a period of weeks to muscle spasms and high fever. I knew there was more going on than I could care for. I was beside myself with worry, certain that I would lose her, and promised God whatever he wanted if he would only see her through this. She was diagnosed with rheumatic fever at the Salvation Army Hospital where I fought with the nurses until they allowed me to stay with her. Even when we were finally able to bring her home, she was weak and needed round-the-clock care. I did not leave her side, and Patsy Peppler was my wing man. Each day, my redheaded helper brought home schoolwork for her friend, diligently overseeing its completion so that Vivian might keep up her grades. She was a treasure, as was her mother, my precious new indispensable and devoted friend.

"She's been left with a heart murmur," I said to Anita over coffee one morning. "That's what the doctor told us at her last appointment. She's well on the mend, but he can't say whether or not the damage will be cause for concern in the future." I was still wearing my nerves on the outside of my skin.

Anita, rarely short on words, simply nodded her concern. "So, 'ave you written Ian about this episode?" In one swift movement, she got up from her chair and moved behind me where she began brushing my hair in long strokes; she always had brushes and combs tucked into the pocket of her apron. It was the most delicious feeling. She wound my hair around the back of her hand like a sausage roll and secured it into place with a few pins. I felt like a new woman.

With eyes still closed in contented relaxation, I finally responded. "No, I've chosen not to burden him with it. I like to keep our letters as light and hopeful as I can. Please ask your Sam not to mention it, will you?" I knew that the two men had bonded and would be likely to share news of home.

"My Sam knows better; don't you be worryin' 'bout that." She sat back down, sipped at her coffee, then changed the subject. "Sam's letter last week said that Southampton has been badly bombed. 'Ow is your British family faring? They're in the north, aren't they?"

"Yes, Lancashire. I receive news from home every week or so. They are coping, although fearful of course. Many of them are involved in the war effort in one way or another." Anita followed me with her eyes as I retrieved the coffee pot and poured another cup. She had the most marvellous way of making you feel as though you always had her full attention. "My favourite nephew, Harry, is in France, and I pray for him daily. My great nephew David, a very clever lad, has begun pilot training, although he's too young to enlist just yet, thank goodness."

As though to lighten the mood, she asked, "And 'as Ian told you that the battalion 'ad a visit from the king no less?" He hadn't. "Sam was quite impressed, so he was. The king presented colours to several of the regiments, and it seems they 'ad quite a day of it, parades and celebrations and a fair bit of drinking I'll bet." I had never met Sam, of course, but Anita spoke of him with such adoration and so often that I felt as though I knew him. She described him as a great sexy lout with a gregarious sense of humour. "*E's got 'ands near as big as 'is 'ead. Should be playin' baseball; 'e'd not need a mitt.*"

It took me some time to get used to the dialect; dropping the "h" on some words and adding it where it had no business being on others. I pictured him in my mind's eye as she continued with other news and babbled on, as was her custom. I had grown used to it and could not fault the woman on her kindness of spirit. I simply learned to tune some of it out and jump in quickly when she took a breath.

"Are you coming to the concert at the end of the month?" I asked during just such an opening.

"We already 'ave our tickets. Can't wait."

"Now that Vivian's on the mend and back to school, I'll have a little more time and energy to put into it." I looked forward to it with every fibre.

Daniel held the office of vice president at the Legion, and I quickly climbed the ladder to entertainment chairman on a special committee designed to help the wounded on their return home. I revisited my days with the Will-o'-the-Wisp fondly. I organized concerts and events designed to lift spirits as the war dragged on, and to raise funds of course. I especially loved my new role as mistress of ceremonies. *There is nothing like the feel of a microphone in one's hand.* Together, Daniel and I did a little performing, although his voice was not what it used to be. He struggled for breath much of the time. I was encouraged, but it didn't really require much convincing for me to agree to close each show with a song. I was no virtuoso, but I was able to lend an air of authenticity to the message of each war song. I tried each one on for size as though fitting a new shoe but had yet to find that one vehicle that I could own as my signature song.

Always by my side, Vivian attended the rehearsals and sat off to the sidelines during the shows, singing along to every word. After one of the rehearsals, while I was busy chatting with some fellows who were helping build a new set, our pianist stayed behind to practise a few of the newer tunes. When I went back into the hall, Vivian was sitting next to her on the bench happily singing her heart out. The woman stopped playing long enough to look at me and say, "The girl has some pipes," to which I nodded my agreement. I looked at the child's animated face. She had been singing practically since the day we'd first brought her home, and I suppose I was simply used to hearing it. It simply had not occurred to me that she might have real talent. Nevertheless, I enrolled her in the church choir the following Sunday.

Dearest Milly,

Thank you for the recent snapshot of Vivian. She is a beauty. Oh, how I do hope to meet her someday.

I write to tell you, dear friend, that I have taken my commission with the QARANC (Queen Alexandra Army Nursing Corp), not that I need explain the acronym to you. They've bumped me up to 1st lieutenant, due to my advanced age and experience no doubt, and I am bound abroad very soon. They are in much need of senior nurses as this horror continues. I'm told I will be working in conjunction with the Red Cross and may be moving about a fair bit, helping to build a nursing staff as each new hospital and clearing station is established. I will no doubt be herding a gaggle of newbies at each location and will do well to remember the dour old matrons of our youth; I must try not to emulate them too closely.

I will let you know when I am situated, and in the meanwhile, I send you my very best love, dear friend. I miss you now more than ever and hope that we will have occasion to meet when this mess is behind us.

Yours always and always,
Em

My heart hit the floor with a thud. My darling Em was putting herself in harm's way and doing so without me. I was not surprised. In fact, I might have predicted it, if I hadn't been so wrapped up in my own struggles. My feelings were all over the place. I questioned whether I was more concerned for her safety or jealous of her adventure. I finally landed on the former.

The next letter came from Ian, who was now in Doune, Scotland. He had been away from home for over three years and thankfully had not seen any action; it seemed that my prayers were working.

18 May 1943

Hi Ma,

It's beautiful here. Lord Muir has invited us to fish in the local river if we wish. Locals seem nice, and there's a dance tonight in Muir Hall in aid of the "Wings for Victory fund."

Training started even before the site was up and right through Sunday church parade. We have all been marched through for fingerprinting in recent days, makes us believe that we're finally gearing up to something. There are a lot of lonesome lads who just want to get on with it or go home. Sam says to say, "Hello to his girls."

Give my love to "Blossom" . . . I know she hates that name now she's getting all grown up. She said so in her last letter. Give her a brotherly hug, won't you?

Your loving son,
Ian

That was his last letter before the 1st Battalion left the British Isles bound for Sicily, and we didn't hear from him again for almost two months. There was little information coming out in the press about their campaign, which was later called "Operation Husky." It was a distressing time for us and for the girls next door awaiting word from Sam. We were glued each evening to the radio and poured over the casualty lists in the newspaper every day, heaving a great sigh as we glossed over where their names would be. It was selfish, we knew; there were so many to mourn. It seemed that the war had spread all over the map, and it was difficult to keep up. All we could do was hope. It became a race to the mailbox each day for Vivian and Patsy, who returned each time looking glummer than the day before.

Finally, letters arrived for us and for the Pepplers, both on the same day and written in the same hand; a jolt of panic surged through my body.

Dear Mrs. Pearse,

First off, let me assure you that Ian is alive and well. I am sitting beside him at a field hospital here in Messina where he's lounging back like a lazy sot with his wrist in a cast. He's telling me what to write, and I'm ignoring him of course. He'll be right as rain in no time. Fell over some Kraut or other in a foxhole and landed nasty on his arm just as a tank was blown up. He's got a bump on his head and a shiner, but I expect he got that from one of the pretty nurses he's been flirtin' with.

Not sure how much they'll let us tell you, I expect half of this will be penned out, but you should know at least that we were successful. Conquered Sicily and drove out the Jerrys in thirty-eight days, so we did. It was tough going, four hundred miles of marching up through the mountains in full gear in melting heat; we'll never complain about the cold in Canada again.

We're not sure what's next. We never do until it happens. Ian will write just as soon as they get this cast off him in a few weeks. Not to worry; your boy will be fine. Lots of our lads here in Sicily weren't so lucky.

I'm off to write now to my girls. I'll try to sneak in a few more details. I know you'll compare notes.

Ian says, "He loves you all."

Fond regards, Sam & Ian

PS. As I'm sure you've heard Patsy say more than once, "Stay where you're at till we comes where you're to."

Our two families shared the supper meal together that night as we often did, comparing notes and breathing a joint sigh of relief. Sam did manage to sneak in a few more tidbits of information in his letter to Anita. They had started via amphibious landing (attached to the British 8th Army) on the southeast coast and worked their way up through the mountains to

Messina on the northeast coast. The lads had survived twenty days of non-stop fighting (lost more than five hundred Canadians in the process) but pushed through until the remainder of the Germans fled across the strait into Italy. The Americans were involved as well, coming in from the west under General Patton.

Neither of our letters had suffered any redaction. I supposed that the details were a matter of historical record at that point. In the months that followed, we had several communications back and forth before Ian shipped out to join his unit; they had already crossed the Strait of Messina into Italy. Once there, Ian wrote that he was well rested and in good spirits; he and the lads had even had opportunity to swim in the Ionian Sea. He described the mainland as an odd mixture of olive groves and mine fields, but the rest of his letter was blacked out.

In august of 1944, Sam wrote home.

". . . We saw the famous 'V' sign in person yesterday. Prime Minister Churchill in the flesh came over the River at Metauro and visited our twelve platoon. It was a great boost for morale. We're losing as many lads to malaria as we are to the Jerrys. Lots of activity in the sky tonight, dropping flares and incendiary bombs; we're hunkered down though with some civilians who are taking refuge with us. It's incredibly sad to see these women and children so hungry; we share our rations with them as we can, biscuits mostly. I am grateful every day to know that you are safe.

Give each other kisses from me. I miss you more than I can say."

Matthew Halton of the Canadian Broadcasting Corporation spoke to us directly over the wireless from an observation post in Italy on December 8. His words tore through us like shrapnel in their descriptive detail.

Soaking wet, in a morass of mud, against an enemy fighting harder than
he's fought before, the Canadians attack, attack, and attack. The enemy
is now fighting like the very devil to hold us, but he can't do it. He brings
in more and more guns, more and more troops, and the hillsides and
farmlands and orchards are a ghastly brew of fire, and our roads for
four miles behind the forward infantry are under heavy shelling . . .
sometimes a battlefield looks like a film of a battlefield, but not this. It's
too grim.

The telegrams came three days apart. Ours arrived first. Alone in the front
room, I watched the messenger walk back down the lane, hat still under
his arm. How often he must have seen the same look on a mother's face. I
couldn't open it; it was for Daniel to do, and I was grateful for my solitude
in that moment. The shaking started first in my arms and then up my back
and right through my body. I reached for a glass of sherry, determined to
save what was left of the bottle for Daniel. He would need it. I watched from
the window as he sauntered toward the house beleaguered and weary. *This
might kill him.* My expression registered with him before he even noticed
the envelope in my hand, and I watched his frame straighten as he stepped
into his protective suit of armour. I laid the telegram into his outstretched
hand and waited until he had collected himself sufficiently to read the words
aloud. He couldn't. He laid the scrap of paper on the table in front of me
and turned to walk into the bedroom.

Canadian National Telegraphs
8 December 1943
Ian Pearse
Saskatoon, Saskatchewan
Deeply regret to inform you that Pte. Ian Pearse has officially
been reported missing in action (Stop)
Director of Records

I had no place to put my emotions. I was prepared to grieve his death but
not this . . . not this cryptic teaser. He's alive or maybe not. He's wounded or
maybe not. He's a prisoner of war or maybe not. I wanted to go to Daniel,
to comfort him, but I had no words. Why had I not considered this? I

was shaken back to consciousness by Vivian and Patsy who bounced into the room carrying a card they had made at school for my birthday. I had forgotten. I lost my composure. I don't think the child had ever seen me cry before—really cry.

The pervasive textures of fear and gloom hung in the air. There was little to talk about and no more tears to be shed. I dreaded picking up the telephone to call Heather. She and the family had never made the journey to see us, but she had softened over time and made the effort to call her father once a month. After many letters and conversations, she had finally acquiesced to Ian's enlistment and was genuinely concerned about her dad's health. I think she was also lonesome for family. Germans and those of German descent were having a tough time of it in Canada by that time; she and Carl had been shunned by some radicals in the community. She would not take this news well. Of that I was sure. *Dreading, dreading, dreading. .*

Within days, the same telegraph messenger knocked on Anita's door, and before he was back at the road, I could hear her screams. Her telegram read:

*Deeply regret to inform you that Private Samuel Peppler officially
reported died of his wounds* (Stop)
*You will receive further details and burial report from the
unit in the theatre of war* (Stop)

There was no consolation for our combined grief, and I wondered at how each of us seemed to cope with sorrow in a different way. Misery seemed to bring Vivian and Patsy closer than ever, and we were all relieved that they were comforting one another. Anita was stalwart in her acceptance of Sam's demise, resisting tears and hiding behind a tough outer shell. She had a child to consider, of course, but I knew the consequences of smothering one's sorrow. She pushed away at even small gestures of kindness as though they might send her into a state of collapse. Sadly, I did not yet have the strength to argue the point; my well-meaning lecture would have to wait. Daniel was simply lost. He slumped about, his shoulders weighed down under invisible bags of cement. Engulfed in fear, he burst into tears at the mention of his son. I could not reach him, my voice echoing unheard.

My sadness, on the other hand, manifested in rage, I was angry—angry and overwhelmed. I desperately wanted to protect all the tormented souls around me but knew that first I must struggle through my own hurt. I was bitterly angry at God and intolerant of the morons on the street who dared sing songs of joy and peace. I wrote several times a day in my journal, confiding my fears to Dr. D. and eventually taking my own good advice. *Grieve, Milly. Tears are not a sign of weakness.* When I was finally able, I shared that wisdom with Anita.

"Sweetheart, you must not let this wound fester unattended. You must process it." This dear woman, Trojan in her movements, looked toward the door of her daughter's bedroom. "Patsy will be the better for it. That I can promise you." She was not persuaded. I caught her attention again. "Anita, this grief is not fleeting. It will be with you forever. I know that is not what you want to hear, but it is the truth. The open wounds will heal over, but the scars remain." I waited while she processed the words.

When she finally responded, it was through tiny tears, the little ones that escape just before the dam breaks. "I seem to be losing 'im in pieces," she said in a whisper. "There's a scent hanging on 'is clothes in the cupboard that disappears a little more every day. I see a little less of 'is profile in Patsy, and I've forgotten what it feels like to 'ave 'im next to me in the bed." The dam burst, and I held her close for a long, long time.

Once home, I glanced over at the small box of Christmas decorations tipped over in the corner of the room as though daring us to find something joyful in the occasion. I was secretly pleased when Vivian had kicked it over on her way out the door to school in a display of pique that I envied and chose not to address. Black was the colour of Christmas that year.

Letters arrived from England, each one carrying the same prayerful message of hope. Still angry at the world, I dismissed them as trite and was especially annoyed by the ethereal note from Alice. The missive from Emily offered a little more substance; I could always count on her to affect a change in my disposition.

Milly Dearest,

I am desperately sorry to hear your news. Your fearfulness and anger are understandable, and I share those emotions with you. The unknown is always the most fearful place, is it not? I regret that Daniel is in such a bad way and know how difficult that must be for you. As ridiculous as these words will sound, my friend, I will say them anyway: "Please try to remain hopeful." If Ian has been taken prisoner, he will be cared for under the Geneva Convention and humanitarian law. I will put feelers out through my connections with the Red Cross to see if we cannot find him. I will add my prayers to yours that he remains alive and that he will be returned home to you when this dreadfulness ends. Take a care for yourself during these distressing days; he may need your strength in the future.

I remain as always,
Your devoted Em

We walked through the pain to the next day and the next, amazed each morning when the sun came up. After a year with no word, we reconciled ourselves to Ian's death. Daniel was consumed in grief, irritable and wasting away physically as well as mentally. I threw myself ever deeper into Legion work; it was my solace and proved a similar refuge for Anita, who was an amazing artisan in hair and makeup for our shows. I missed many things about the farm, fresh eggs and my vegetable garden most especially, but I had come to appreciate the convenience of a store on the corner and a short walk to town. We struggled as all families did, gathering ration stamps and doing without luxuries, but the combined efforts of our two families made it much easier to make ends meet. Letters came regularly from Em, who seemed always to be on the move—France, Malta, Algeria, and back to the coast of France—setting up hospitals as they were needed. She spoke highly of the efforts of all the Allied forces working together to care for the quantity of casualties in every theatre of operation. It was interesting to hear her description of the differences in medical care since "our war," the advent of penicillin being the most advantageous advancement by far. I wondered how many lives and limbs might have been saved if only antibiotics had been discovered sooner.

In March of 1945, a courier brought us a telegram of a different sort, unexpected and cryptic.

Milly
I believe we have found him (Stop)
Cannot relay details at this time (Stop)
Will travel to investigate (Stop)
There is reason to hope (Stop)
Will write soonest (Stop)
Lt. Davidson

I was buoyant; I knew that Emily would not offer a crumb of optimism without evidence and faith in her sources. Daniel was not persuaded, but I would not allow his pessimism to bring me down. He insisted, and rightfully so, that we refrain from mentioning anything to Vivian or the Peppler girls until we were certain of the facts. It was a difficult two weeks though. I wanted desperately to share this news with anyone who would listen and especially hated keeping the truth from Anita. My jubilant mood almost gave me away.

With one suspicious eyebrow raised, she asked me, "What's after happenin' now?" We knew each other too well for anything to remain secret for long, but I managed to fob her off with some nonsense about an upcoming show. She wasn't convinced. I marvelled at her. Grief had only been a visitor in her home. She simply would not allow it to take up residence. "*Right then, time to get on wi' it,*" she'd said only a few weeks after becoming a widow and then asked if I would help her clean out the closet and take Sam's clothes to the church. If she had bad days, she didn't declare them; she talked about Sam fondly but would not harbour maudlin conversations. I was certain that she would be as happy and relieved by good news of Ian as I was.

Dear Milly,

I am at the 98th BHS in Naples and sitting next to Ian. Milly, he's in a bad way, but he is alive, and I am doing my best to expedite his transfer to a British hospital. It is difficult to explain what has happened in terms that the authorities will not redact. To that end, I am sending this with my own private courier, a nurse friend who is heading home to Britain on leave today. She will post it from there. I regret that it will take a few additional days to reach you.

The Red Cross received a letter from a farm family near Ortona, in Italy, who had been harbouring a wounded soldier for over a year. He was non-verbal and had no dog tags; his uniform was all but destroyed. They found him half dead in their field and had no idea if he was friend or foe. They simply couldn't leave him there to suffer. The woman "whose name they will not disclose" sewed up his wounds as best she could and has fed and cared for him all this time. She feared that he may be German because of his light hair and eyes and was frightened of reprisals even from their own Italian authorities. These peasant people have been through so much, and I suspect that for a long time they didn't know who they could trust. According to her letter, it was well over a month before he regained consciousness, but to this day has still not uttered a word. The couple finally found the courage to sneak a letter out to the Red Cross, who liberated him almost immediately to this base hospital. Sadly, fingerprint identification has taken some time.

It appears that Ian suffered a traumatic blow to the head and also severe wounds to the upper arm and shoulder; there is still evidence of infection. To say that the lacerations were stitched unskilfully is being generous to the extreme, but I expect these amateur sutures suspended further hemorrhage and saved his life. Further surgery will no doubt be necessary. It seems unlikely that his head wound is the cause of his mental state; I've seen enough shell shock to recognize the symptoms.

Milly, I know I need not explain to you that these people risked their own lives to shelter your son. They did the best they could with what they had, offered him food they surely couldn't spare, and it was fear that kept them from reaching out sooner. As I write the words, I find I am profoundly amazed at the inherent goodness of people even in the midst of this nightmare.

You will soon receive official word, and in the meantime, I will do all that I can to get him home to you.

As always, your Em

Letters by the dozen crossed the ocean between us until Ian was finally fit for travel, first to England for surgery and then home. Em stayed with him in Naples for as long as she was able but worked her magic behind the scenes to expedite his transfer.

My dearest darling Emily,

After all that you have done, I had hesitated to ask that you might travel with Ian as far as England and to see him safely aboard his hospital ship to Canada. I am comforted that you will be with him and grateful to the authorities who give you leave to do so. If only it were possible for you to escort him all the way home so that I might wrap my arms around you, I would never let you go.

How will I ever be able to convey to you the depths of my gratitude and devotion? You have showered me with your affection for what seems already a lifetime, always there, always my precious friend. When I was alone, you were there. When I cried, you were there. And now, in this moment to rejoice, you are there. In my whole life, I will never love anyone more.

Milly

Standing in the hallway of the hospital ward in Saskatoon, the doctor spoke in serious tones, trying to convey the nature and seriousness of Ian's injuries. His shoulder had been all but blown off, and the repairs had been primitive at best. It was difficult to diagnose his head injury after so long, but the exterior wounds seemed to have healed well enough. His greater concern was about what was happening under the surface. *Emily's words from someone else's lips.*

"Your son," he said, "by all accounts, has never spoken. He is awake and aware but not able to communicate or participate in his own care. Automatic body responses like breathing and swallowing are functioning, but he has to be fed, cleaned, and rolled over." As he reached forward to swing open the door, he warned, "Be prepared, both of you. You may not recognize him." He was right. The broken and emaciated body lying in the bed looked nothing like the boy who had left the farm six years ago. His hair had gone snow white in places, and although his eyes were open, it was clear that he was lost deep inside himself.

I approached first and sat close to him on the bed, gently stroking his hand. I repeated his name over and over, touched his face, and talked about home. Daniel said nothing, just sat in the chair with his head in his hands. The doctor stood in the doorway, and said, "Mr. and Mrs. Pearse, we'll continue to care for his physical needs, but his overall recovery will depend a great deal on you. You are already doing all the right things, Mrs. Pearse. I can see that your instincts are correct, but make no mistake, it will be a long, hard road." He walked over to Daniel and rested a hand on his shoulder before exiting the room; I looked up just in time to see his white coat swish through the door.

"Thank you," I called after him, but he was gone.

We agreed that Vivian should not see Ian in his current physical state but that Anita would be permitted to help as I knew she would want to do. We began our vigil, one or both of us spent hours every day by his bedside. The nurses, who were desperately overworked, were grateful to learn that I had some experience and was able to take over some of their duties, feeding and bathing him, changing his bedding, and propping him up in various positions. I was not permitted to change his dressings or administer meds of course, but I was most often present while the nurses tended to his shoulder wounds. I thought I had prepared myself sufficiently the first time they removed his bandages. I'd thought I had seen it all, but this was beyond my imagining.

The wound, which started at his upper chest, coiled up and over the clavicle, over the shoulder, under the arm, and then back to where it started on his chest. It looked as though it had been sewn together with knitting needles, and perhaps it had. A set of X-rays showed that there were fractures of the upper-arm bones that had been set correctly, and that a large crack through the scapula was healing. Pockmark scars were evident all over the scapula, where shrapnel had been removed, and one piece remained, lodged deep in the bone. The surgeon determined that it was better left alone but indicated that much attention had to be paid to the severely damaged muscles and tendons. A physiotherapist showed me how to help him exercise the arm several times a day, and I did so, all the while talking and coaxing him to find his way to the surface. I looked deep into his empty eyes, searching for any spark of life. There was nothing. They were dead. Motionless. Sometimes I challenged and ordered him to answer in the hopes that he would sit up and argue. He didn't.

Anita was hesitant at first, afraid to do or say something wrong, but she proved a dependable soldier in our battle to bring Ian home—properly home. I walked in one day as she was talking away to him, sweetly and reassuringly. "You're just afraid to peek out and find that the world is still ugly, aren't you, luv?"

She's spot on, I thought. She attended to him in the hospital for an hour every day, continued to run her business, had a meal prepared for us every night, and saw to the girls. "She's a rosy, red-haired marvel in high-heeled pumps," I wrote to Em. I hadn't had a letter from her in some time and wondered where on earth they had shipped her off to now.

Daniel, who had secured a position at the nearby veterans affairs office, had also stepped up to spend time with his son. Before heading home each day, he dropped in to the hospital and read to Ian from the evening paper, being careful to leave out any news of the war.

Just around the time that Ian started to show some sign of physical improvement, I began worrying in earnest about Emily. Long stretches of time between letters were not unusual, as she was moving from one post to another, but never so long as this. I had been busy and preoccupied but still I had written many times with updates on Ian's progress. Were my letters were lost in transit? I just didn't know. I chatted with a friend at the Legion about my concerns, and he offered to make some inquiries.

Ian's colour was better, his hollow cheeks were beginning to fill out, and best of all, he was starting to turn his head and follow movement in the room with his eyes. He was ambulatory, which allowed me to take him out in the wheelchair for a walk around the grounds. I was sure I heard him take in a long deliberate cleansing breath on our first day out and about. *The fresh air was just what he needed,* I'd thought as I wrapped the blankets more tightly around his legs.

Ian's care was occupying a great deal of my time; I was singularly and obsessively focused, which was brought gently to my attention over coffee one morning with Anita. She hesitantly suggested that Vivian might be in need of a little attention. The ten-year-old child was starting to act out and had complained to Patsy that "I'm doing my best to be helpful around the house, but nobody notices. I'm not sure they care that I'm here at all."

Anita said, "I'm betraying a trust 'ere, and I'd rather the girls don't know I spoke to you about it. Right?"

I nodded. "Of course." I could see that my friend was treading carefully; it is a touchy thing to sound like you're criticizing someone's parenting.

And then, to plead her case, she said, "The girls 'ave been so good, don't ya think? They get themselves off to school without argument. Every day, they take their bicycles to do their paper route, so they don't 'ave to pester about pocket money. I know they spend it at the cinema, but that's as it should be. Right?" she asked again, through a bright-red lipstick grin.

I knew she was correct and felt terrible that I had not taken my daughter's feelings into consideration. I had an idea that might appease but wanted to discuss it with Daniel first. That weekend, I called Vivian into the front room, and while I untangled the rags from her hair and brushed the waves of auburn silk down her back, I said, "How nice it is that I don't have to polish the furniture in here today, Vivian. I must have a helpful elf around here somewhere." The girl giggled. I pressed a few coins into the palm of her hand, and said, "Maybe my helpful elf would like to take Patsy to the pictures this afternoon."

Vivian beamed and made for the door, but I called her back. "I'm not finished just yet." She looked concerned as though news had just reached me about her talking back to the teacher the previous week. Instead, I smiled. "You know that twenty-five cents a week is a lot of money, don't you?" She nodded, looking suspicious. "Dad is working now, so there's a little extra coming in. We've decided to let you have those voice lessons you've been pestering about."

Vivian danced around the room excitedly. "I have to tell Patsy! Oh, won't she be surprised? Can I go now?" She was out the door before I could respond but came back a moment later, threw her arms around my neck, and said, "Thanks, Ma."

It was a massive amount of money for something so impractical, and I was not given to extravagances, but the child did appear to have some talent. It couldn't do any harm. Mrs. Calles who played the organ and led the church choir was to be her teacher and was quite enthusiastic about the girl's natural ability. Vivian was growing up fast and was prettier than I was comfortable with. *The busier I can keep the lass, the better for all concerned.*

As Ian's physical health improved, we decided it was time to allow Vivian a visit with him as she had been nagging daily, and I had run out of excuses. We were still concerned that the sight of him might upset her. We explained his injuries in as little detail as possible, simply hoping to soften the blow, and carefully chose the location for her first visit. I did not want her to see him in his stark, clinical hospital room. Daniel parked the vehicle and walked with Vivian across the hospital grounds to where I was sitting with Ian in his wheelchair. The child approached cautiously at first but surprised both of us with her strength of character as she crouched down and took hold of her brother's hand. She didn't flinch; she just talked to him as though not a day had passed since they'd last seen each other. It had in fact been almost six years.

Daniel turned his head, sniffed, and wiped away tears, and I swallowed hard. Ian stared straight ahead while the girl prattled on about the film she had just seen and didn't seem at all rattled that her words landed on deaf ears. Finally, I said, "I think Ian may be tired. Perhaps I should take him back to the ward. You can visit with him again soon. I promise." She was satisfied. She kissed him on the cheek as I tucked the blanket snuggly around his legs, and then she bounced toward her father.

I turned the chair toward the door. I heard a raspy voice ask, "Blossom?"

With happy tears wiped away and farewells still echoing behind me, I gently moved the chair through the hospital doors, lost in my own thoughts. *He couldn't have known her. She was just about to start school when he left, and she's almost in her teens now. She's changed so much.* I was in a daze and almost knocked over the nurse who was waiting by the bed with Ian's medication. I explained what had taken place, still shaking my head in disbelief. He had only spoken one word, but I knew that we had made a start. "Perhaps it was her voice, a simple recognition of his sister's voice that touched his consciousness." I was talking more to myself than to the nurse who was busily jotting down notes for the doctor and paying little attention as I wobbled, slumped into the waiting chair, and evaporated into a deluge of tears. Tears of relief and joy.

Chapter Twenty

Never, Oh! Never, Nothing will die;
The stream flows, The wind blows,
The cloud fleets, The heart beats,
Nothing will die.

ALFRED LORD TENNYSON

I stepped through each day with leaden feet and with no other purpose but to get to the next one. I had no wish to see the next one; I just knew that I would be needed when I got there. Ian was home now, making real progress although lost in his own little world much of the time, like a ghost who peeked out from behind the closet door now and again. I was his daily chauffeur to and from clinic visits and his interpreter when people asked questions or dared to involve him in conversation. Daniel's health was on a steady decline, as was his mood and our relationship in general. I was no more than a crutch that he leaned on, but I relished the isolation of it. It was a fitting punishment.

The war was over, and the courageous limped home, but I was numb to the rejoicing. I held the letter in my hand from Rankin and Sons Solicitors of Manchester England, the bank draft still mockingly peeking at me from within the engraved envelope. I read every third or fourth word again: "Probate complete . . . assets dissolved . . . inherit . . . sole beneficiary . . . no living relatives . . . no contest to the estate . . . specific items enclosed as per instruction."

The letter was brimming with legalese that I didn't understand, all very cold and formal as though penned by an efficient office worker who clearly had never met the warm, sweet creature who had hired the firm to do her bidding: my Emily.

It had been months since the fateful telegram arrived, explaining that she had been killed in an explosion at the dockyard while awaiting transport from England back to France. I was recorded as her next of kin; otherwise, I might never have known why her letters had simply stopped. It was my undoing, the final blow that sent my consciousness swirling in a revolving door of grief and guilt. The two emotions seemed inextricably linked, one fuelling the other in a vicious feud, woven together by the common thread of relentless, gnawing pain.

How arrogant and self-serving I had been to suggest that she accompany Ian to England. Had she remained at her post, she would be celebrating now with her comrades, tipping back a glass, and sharing that infectious laugh with all those fortunate enough to be in her orbit. Guilt was the strangling demon that haunted my wakefulness and chewed at my insides. Emily's death was my fault, and no amount of talking or sermonizing could change that. Lord knows, many tried. Alice was on the phone weekly, and I was grateful to speak about my friend to someone who knew and cared about her. Daniel was attentive at first, but he had no stamina for my despair. Anita was on a mission to see me through the crisis, but what I had previously found endearing in her character irritated my raw nerves, and I found her energy exhausting. The new minister at the church had run out of scripture and platitudes at about the same time I had explained what he could do with "his God." Vivian simply stayed out of my way.

Heather, who finally made the obligatory journey to visit her father and brother, arrived with two of her children (our grandchildren) in tow. We should have been delighted to see them, these young strangers, but her timing was poor, and she brought no relief to the sour atmosphere that pervaded the house. She spent the better part of a week shouting the odds about what should and should not be done for Ian, sending my hackles into frenzy. To say that we did not get along would be an outrageous understatement. Anita tried to intervene and soften the tensions in the household, driving the children to the pictures and offering to perform miracles on Heather's tangled mass of frizzy hair. In her youth, Heather had been attractive if not pretty, but her appearance as well as her temperament had hardened; her frantic mop of hair encapsulated her personality perfectly. She was overt in her distaste for Vivian and cruel in her observations about the grief I suffered. "Women have lost children and husbands, for God's sake," she sniped on what would be her last day with us. "You're wallowing and enjoying the attention a bit too much. Emily was a friend. That's all. Isn't it time you got over it?"

A part of me felt sorry for her, that she could be so cold and have so little empathy. *How can this wretched woman not see that I am crushed beneath the weight of guilt and paralyzed in sorrow?* I thought about the ebb and flow of the pain, how it felt sharper some days and more of a dull ache on others. Every day was a tragic dance of emotions where the fog blinded me on one day and cleared into a mist the next. *How cruel and ignorant she is to make comparisons about sorrow.*

"How dare you!" I finally responded, having swallowed my anger deep into my gut. "I pray that you never suffer the pain of having your heart torn from your body as I have. There's no 'getting over it,' you stupid, stupid girl!" I could see by her expression that there was little point in trying to enlighten her. She would never understand. When she turned her attentions to Ian and demanded that he return with her to the farm, I wasted no energy explaining the obvious; I simply told her it was time she went home. We did not part well.

Pandora's box lay unopened at my feet, a bridge of regret between it and me. My thoughts were disorganized, always circling back to what was and what could have been, and a huge part of me wanted never to open the parcel. Emily was having none of it though; she coaxed gingerly at first and then more adamantly, like an irritating sibling poking at my shoulder. *"Come on, Milly, I'm in here."* Even in death, she was pulling me up, dragging me out of the mire.

When I finally broke the seal and lifted the first flap, I was immediately transported to a musty tent in France. The odour sent a shiver through me. I closed my eyes and pictured our shadow puppets dancing in the lantern light. I may even have smiled for a moment. Each item was carefully wrapped but the edges of a familiar canvas box peeked out from beneath the mound of newsprint. "Sergeant Miller," I said aloud, surprised to hear my own voice in the moment. Amazed that I had remembered the young soldier's name, I lifted out the camera that he had so proudly given to Emily on the day he left the hospital. I had forgotten all about it. I opened the case and ran my fingers around the brass, admiring the workmanship and surprised at its pristine condition considering the life it had led. An envelope tucked into the case held our images, the ones that the young man had taken of me and Emily before he lost his sight. We were so young, so alive. Behind the serious pose were dancing eyes and a little grin. Had we been laughing? Had we been mischievous? I could not remember. Oh, how I wanted to remember every detail of that day. I pressed the photographs into my chest while the tears I'd thought had all dried up spilled down over my cheek.

I tripped clumsily down memory lane toward the next item in the box. Wrapped in plastic was the little porcelain doll with the missing arm that Em had found in the rubble during our visit to London. I shook my head in disbelief that she had kept it all this time. The small packet that remained was adorned in a blue ribbon and attached to a square alabaster envelope. I held it gently, summoning Emily's voice, which I was sure would be on the pages within. The envelope wasn't sealed, simply folded closed as though she might add to it at a later date. I eased it open, reminding myself to breathe, and gazed longingly at her handwriting. These would be her last words to me. My eyes were a blur of tears as her voice spoke the words for me:

My Milly,

I hold you close in my heart as you read this. I cannot begin to imagine the sadness you are feeling. I will walk through it with you, my darling; it is but one more chapter in the book of your life. You can't skip it; you must move on to the next. Whatever the cause of my demise, know that I have lived a full life, and I regret nothing. I have been loved, deeply loved, and it is you I have to thank for that.

As you know by now, most of my possessions and Dad's house have been sold with instructions that the proceeds go to you and your family. It is my fervent hope that whatever funds remain will offer some peace of mind. You will be pragmatic and sensible, of that I am sure, but I urge you to permit yourself a luxury or two. I ask also that you spend a little on my godchild and remember me to her. I do wish, as I write this note, that I would have had the opportunity to meet my namesake; she is yet another precious gift that you have given me. In this little parcel are a few of my most treasured belongings. The amulet that you pinned on me when I was so ill at Royaumont; until now it has never left my person. The signet ring that you gave me at my graduation and the pendant that Dad presented that day. Lastly, my friend, I bequeath to you a choker

*of pearls that belonged to my mother. It is the only piece of her that
remains, and I know that you will cherish it as I have.*

*My dearest Milly, I know that you are hurting and for that I am sorry.
Let those feelings wash over you like waves and reach out to those who
love you as I do. Choose to allow them in. Rejoice with me in the marvellous moments we have shared and allow me the privilege of living on
through you in the warmth of your heart. I am with you now as I have
always been, in mind and spirit. You will find me smiling back at you
from behind the laughing eyes of your daughter, my kiss will dance on
the breeze and rest upon your cheek, and you will find me in that misty
moment between wakefulness and sleep. I will watch over you among
the angels and wait for you at the gates of heaven.*

Your Em

Time, I learned, was no great healer. I walked through all the stages,
listened to the psycho-babble, and did my best to respect everyone's advice
and wishes, especially Emily's. I reached out to loved ones, consciously
chose to lay bare my vulnerability only to find Daniel empty and Ian absent.
I wrote volumes in my journal and went in search of a spiritual connection
to those I was sure would listen. We lived near a lovely park on the South
Saskatchewan River where willow trees were abundant, and I spent more than
one fruitless afternoon there. I found an incredibly old tree and wrapped my
arms around it in an invitation to converse. I felt no movement, no vibration
or life force; there was no heartbeat for me in its mighty trunk. There were
no whispers. Not from my mother or Alice or even my Emily. Or if there
were, I was deaf to them. If the trees all around me were chattering to one
another as I had been taught, I was no longer welcome in the conversation.

My personal journey ended that day. I had no wish to die but no desire to
grow. Limbo, a purgatory of my own making. I had to accept that the Milly
before Emily's death no longer existed. Imprisoned in a fortress of blame, I
was closed up, every pore on my body cinched tight against an icy bath. Alice
had warned, "*Move forward, Milly, and resist the urge to become hardened to
the world.*" I failed at that. Determined never to open myself to hurt again, I
put one soldierly foot in front of the other and simply got on with it.

Once home, I retrieved the wooden box from the dresser, taking one last glance at the treasures within before adding Emily's ring, amulet, a few other trinkets, and our photos. I kissed her image before closing the lid. The wood-burned image of the triskelion stared back at me, taunting me: *"Always land on your feet."* With it tucked back into its hiding place, I moved on to the next order of business and reached into the closet for the carpet bag that housed my stack of journals. After flipping cavalierly through them, I tossed each one into a growing inferno in the big steel drum in the backyard, and then I moved on.

Daniel's words from long ago found their way to my consciousness: "Like twin flames keeping each other alight; if one were to be extinguished, it would surely douse the other."

Chapter Twenty-one

A vision of loveliness glided confidently into the room and swished into place on the awaiting pedestal as though she had done it a hundred times before. She took my breath away. Luminescent clouds of chiffon floated around her heart-shaped face and perfectly matched to the kiss of pink in her cheeks. She was a classic beauty, radiant and bewitching with delicate features and flashing chestnut-brown eyes. The glamorous organza gown that we had chosen together was cinched in at her tiny waist, the perfect shade of rose-petal pink to compliment her shiny auburn hair and creamy porcelain complexion.

She charmed the good-looking photographer in an instant with her dazzling smile as he adjusted the lights and asked her to turn this way and that. He fussed a moment with the chiffon fabric around her neck, and I felt myself instinctively lean in to object to his overt familiarity. The bristles on my arm settled when she peered past him and gave me her customary coquettish wink.

She put me in mind of Annie, my sweet niece who'd looked so fragile the day she walked down the aisle in her lace wedding gown. They had similar features and colouring, but their personalities could not be more different. Annie was modest and shy while my daughter had abundant poise and self-assurance; in truth, a dose of humility would not have gone amiss. Still, I likened her to a china doll that I polished and protected; she was too lovely not to be displayed, but I lived in fear that she might fall from the shelf and break. I was possessive, at times to the extreme, and I indulged her.

Finally, the photographer snapped the shot, and her image was captured, feminine and fair, a moment in time. I wondered, as I had so often over the years, how anyone could believe that this incredible creature was mine. *She is mine!* Something repeated often enough eventually becomes truth.

The portrait sitting was a gift for her sixteenth birthday—an expensive gift from the godmother she never met and one that seemed to drag on over a period of weeks. The gift had become an event; Anita and Patsy had joined us for a preliminary shopping trip to find the perfect gown and accessories, followed by a lovely lunch in a fine restaurant at the big hotel downtown. Patsy had presented her friend with a delicate crystal bracelet, and when a smiling Vivian had slipped it onto her tiny wrist, it picked up the colours of green in her outfit and sent little rainbow prisms of light all around the table. Anita had given her a beautiful card with an inspirational message and promised to work her magic on Vivian's hair and makeup on the day of the sitting. It had been a charming day, less like mothers and daughters on an errand and more like four girlfriends out on an escapade.

The portrait was the only thing the girl had requested for her special birthday. Its purpose, she made clear, was not ornamental; it was *"one more item for my toolkit to success!"* I admired her singular focus and determination; she reminded me just a little of my adventurous sixteen-year-old self. Her aspirations, however, were considerable compared to mine. She believed that a career on the stage as a singer was her calling, and it seemed that nothing was going to get in her way. The photograph, the "head shot" as she called it—no doubt a term she'd learned in one of the movie magazines—would bring her one step closer to that goal.

She had earned the right to try, and although I had misgivings, I was proud of her conviction and of her successes. The little girl who'd shadowed my every move at Legion shows and rehearsals year after year had blossomed and come into her own. She became a feature solo voice on every production and was a natural performer with no inhibitions, one who could dance almost as well as she could sing. She never missed an opportunity to learn new steps and was always pestering someone to get up and dance with her at Legion functions. She was proficient at the foxtrot, waltz, and polka and learned many of the Scottish reels and country dances, her favourite by far being the Gay Gordons.

After years of lessons with Mrs. Calles, she began competing in local singing contests where she seemed always to be the youngest of the competitors. The judges were smitten with her maturity and poise on the stage and were consistent in their praises. Her pretty voice earned her many successes and a few dollars in prize money. I watched from the wings at each event, amazed at her composure and gently taking stock as her talent and her ego grew in equal measure.

"I have ambitions to sing on a much grander stage than this!" I overheard

her say arrogantly to her cast mates at the Legion. I cautioned my little starlet against unrealistic illusions of grandeur but lost the battle when she took second place at the next local contest. Shortly thereafter, the Lions Club awarded her a grant to pay for additional lessons with Mrs. Calles, and it was then that she announced, at the tender age of fourteen, "I want to leave school." Before I could turn on my heels and form the argument, she continued in one long breath and in one long sentence, as though she had been rehearsing it for days: "I'm not doing well in my studies anyway; I have no interest in them at all, and I can put much more time and energy into my singing; you must see that I'm right." She was right about one thing: Her grades were poor. The girl continued. "Mrs. Calles feels that there is a career for me in singing, and I agree." She was determined.

Daniel entered the room at that precise moment and stated simply, "Well, if you've a mind to make your own decisions, you best start paying for your keep." With that, he simply turned on his heels and back through the door to the bedroom. He had not raised his voice or offered any argument. He was always strict with the girl about her dress and decorum but rarely found reason to reprimand her, and I did not feel compelled to challenge him; in fact, I thought he made a valid point. Her head was full of fantastical ideas, and it would not hurt for her to work at a real job for a little while at least. She spent far too much time giggling in her room, star-struck over the latest movie magazine pilfered from Anita's waiting room. I often heard her prattle on to Patsy about becoming the next big discovery. *"Kathryn Grayson and Jane Powell were both discovered while on vacation in Hollywood with their parents. Honestly, Patsy, look here. There's a radio show called* Hollywood Showcase: Stars Over Hollywood. *It's a contest and Jane Powell took first prize. MGM signed her up and look at her now!"*

Patsy, on the other hand, had grown up; she was a studious and sensible young woman who had her feet firmly planted in reality. She earned a scholarship and was enrolled in a literary arts program; her studies were to begin at the university in the fall. We were all immensely proud of her accomplishments and pleased that she would be close enough to continue living at home. Tall and skinny, her flowing red hair turned heads, but she was not what could be described as pretty. The outgoing personality she had worn as child became quietly serious as she matured, and while she attended the Legion shows with her mother, she rarely stayed for the dances.

I was always amazed that the two girls remained such good friends; they were really nothing at all alike. Still, she seemed to enjoy their girlish banter, and although exuberant in her praise whenever her young friend sang, she tempered her encouragement of Vivian's ambitions.

I enjoyed the movies just as my daughter did, although I saw fewer of them. I could even lose myself in one of her frivolous magazines from time to time, but I shuddered at the opulence of it all. Fame and all its trappings were a contagion. Actors were paid ridiculous fortunes, lived extravagant lifestyles, and sat atop pedestals that should have been reserved for true heroes. On the other hand, a solid day of hard work by real people carried less value. *This can't be what a generation fought and died for.* The whole idea made me cringe.

I wanted to support my girl and to offer encouragement; she had a lovely voice and many other wonderful qualities. She was helpful around the house, respectful to her parents, and was a godsend with her brother. Whenever Ian disappeared into himself, sometimes for days on end, it was Vivian who seemed best able to bring him back. She was gentle and caring, talking to him as she used to prattle on to her dolls. I supposed hers was a talent born of loneliness. When he finally came around, she would give him a big peck on the cheek and say, "So, where've you been this time, sailor?" There was rarely a response but always love behind those hauntingly gorgeous eyes.

I commented one day, as much to me as to her, "You, madame, would be just the ticket for some of those poor blokes at the clinic; now that would be a worthwhile career." She grunted back and shook her head in a vehement negative.

I wondered if she had the temperament for a career in the cutthroat industry that I imagined show business to be. Could her delicate shoulders bear the weight of criticism and rejection? I wondered. She certainly lacked humility. She was an only child, indulged at times but never spoiled. She was, however, the centre of attention. Our little china doll.

On the day that the finished portrait arrived in the post, I was sitting with Anita and bragging that the Legion had once again asked me to stay on as entertainment chair. The always expressive face before me cautioned playfully against indulgent self-praise. My dear friend was a prodigious talker, but there were times when words were unnecessary to make her point. I shrugged it off, took a sip of the lovely, sweet tea, and reflected only momentarily on my self-gratifying pat on the back. The Legion was a continual source of comfort and gratification for me; its members were the surrogate family that hoisted me from despair in the years following Emily's death and continued to be the best therapy for Daniel and Ian. I worried in vain that our shows would be deemed unnecessary after the war, but instead, they remained a source of pride and revenue for the organization. The biannual productions became better funded and more elaborate, and I was in my element. Those shows were my baby as evidenced by the carpet bag at my feet, overflowing with music and fabric swatches for the new show we were rehearsing.

Anita broke into my thoughts. "We're not gonna start puttin' on airs, are we now?" she asked, raising one eyebrow in an alarmingly sharp angle.

I laughed her off and reached in the bag to show her a Butterick pattern I had found. *Might do for a costume idea.* As I pulled it out, a photograph fell from the bag. It was a postcard really, and one that I had forgotten was in there. I poured over it for a moment and then asked, "Anita, did I ever tell you about The Dumbells?" She cocked the other eyebrow and was about to make a smart remark when I jumped in to continue. I explained a little about the troupe and showed her the image. "They were wonderful," I said, leaning in to look at it again. "They filled a very great need during the Great War, just as we're trying to do at the Legion in our small way. They were a diversion from the horrific realities we faced every day."

"Were they professional entertainers?"

"Some were, and others were soldiers with some talent who they found along the way. Daniel sang with them for a little while. I can't believe I've never told you that."

With a huge grin, she said, "All the times we've nattered on 'bout nothing at all, and you've managed to keep this little tidbit to yourself you, cheeky mare."

I smiled back at her. "They look primped and pristine here, funny too, I know. Men dressed in women's clothing and slathered in makeup. But picture them also with boots, thick with mud that they had just dragged in from the trenches, and army helmets waiting at the edge of the makeshift stage should the shelling start again." She nodded her understanding. "They were heroes really; they were as mired in the cold bloody muck as the rest of us and never backed away from an opportunity to perform for the lads. They were a marvel."

"Sounds to me that your motives are the same, and you've every reason to be proud of what you're doing."

I acknowledged her compliment but added sheepishly, "Oh, I like the limelight; I can't deny that. And I like being in charge. Cannot deny that either. But I do think we make a difference. I hope we do."

The postman tucked his head in and around the door. "Anybody in?" He handed me a large envelope, tipped his cap, winked at Anita, and was off.

The eight-by-twelve portrait was sandwiched between corrugated cardboard and wrapped in tissue for protection. I took in a deep breath as I carefully uncovered it and breathed out in one long warm stream as I drank in the image of my beautiful girl. Vivian was aglow; the rich sepia tones could not conceal the blush of pink in her cheeks. Luminous eyes looked directly, unabashedly into the camera lens, haunting and alluring. Anita came around the back of my chair, and with hands resting on my shoulders, she kissed my cheek and said, "Ravishing. She's simply ravishing."

Vivian hated her job at the bakery but dutifully gave her father a small sum for her keep each month. She was not aware that he tucked the money away, fully intending to return it to her as a wedding gift when the day came. The demanding work did not suit her well, but it gave her pocket money and was a means to an end. She purchased additional copies of her portrait, captured her voice on vinyl at the music store on Main Street, and set about the task of acting as her own agent, sending her "portfolio" to talent scouts and radio stations. She was driven and tireless, but as luck would have it, success at another local contest was the catalyst to her first significant opportunity. She was hired to sing two songs on the local talent-spotlight segment on the CFQC radio station every second week: one gospel piece and a signature selection of her choice. Mrs. Calles suggested that "Vilia" from *The Merry Widow* operetta would make a wonderful signature song for her, and so it was decided. She arrived at the radio station in full regalia, as though she could be seen as well as heard, and sang confidently into the microphone for all of Saskatoon to hear. She was exhilarated and convinced that this was just the exposure that she needed. The community, friends, and family were enthusiastic in their praise, and she was on cloud nine.

She quit her job at the bakery when a cashier position opened up at the Famous Players Theatre. "How wonderful," she said as I drove her to the cinema for her first shift. "I'll be getting paid for doing an easier job, and I'll get to see all the new movies for free."

The road was icy, and I dared not take my eyes from it, though I glanced at her sideways. "I'll pick you up at eleven. You stay right there and wait for me."

"Thanks, Ma."

When I arrived, she was standing outside in the shivering cold with several attentive young men, and I realized to my dismay that I had more to worry about than her career ambitions. In the months that followed, she dated many nice young men, each one subjected to interview in the front room by a stern-faced father and a much older brother who said nothing but stared daggers at each would-be beau. As soon as the young couple were out the door, we'd burst into laughter as I applauded the men in my life. "Well done, you two!" Whether it was for that reason or not, the poor girl rarely went out with the same fellow more than once. I need not have worried; dating was all just a bit of fun for her. She was a charming, skilled flirt who knew the boundaries that must not be crossed and thoroughly enjoyed the attention. She remained focused, and I was proud of her resolve.

Vivian was over the moon to be hired as an entertainer at an important Red Cross benefit dinner along with many local celebrities and performers. She had such high hopes. "Someone of importance will notice me!" Although she sang beautifully, there was no mention of her in the newspaper article the next morning. It was a huge disappointment.

When ten months passed without another invitation to sing, I confessed my thoughts to Daniel in a quiet conversation. "A fourteen-year-old singing star on the brink was newsworthy a few years ago, but I don't think she's a novelty anymore. She may be just another lyric soprano with a pretty face; there are thousands just like her."

Still, we pressed on. Vivian auditioned for several musical theatre productions, even taking a few acting lessons, but in each case suffered rejection for one reason or another. We travelled as far as Regina for one such opportunity and stayed in a hotel overnight because she was invited to return for the final round of auditions. She was so excited. The role seemed like a perfect fit, but sadly, the part went to another young hopeful. I watched her expression turn from hopeful to disheartened in a matter of moments, and my heart ached for her. The rejection was yet another difficult blow to her self-esteem; her contract at the radio station came to an end, and at the ripe old age of seventeen, she was too old for most of the local singing contests. ,

She was deflated. Even Patsy's ministrations could not bring the distraught girl out of her slump. Home for the holidays, and in deference to Vivian's feelings, Patsy hesitated at first to share her own good news. She chatted and consoled at length, offering her younger friend a shoulder to cry on throughout a whole evening before Vivian caught sight of the ring.

"Why on earth did you not say anything, you devil?" It was the first time in as many days that I had seen some animation in my daughter's face. Her attention was diverted for a time to all things wedding, and the following day we were introduced to Kevin, the groom to be. He was a squat, plain little fellow with a gregarious personality and infectious laugh. The couple, mismatched in appearance and personality, seemed oddly perfect for one another. Anita was completely taken with him, as were we. Vivian accepted her role as maid of honour and happily agreed to sing at the ceremony. In conversation with Patsy and Kevin about song choice, the subject of her career came up again, and it was the attentive young man who suggested that she consider going back to school.

"You're not giving up on your dreams if you simply prepare a contingency plan," he said. "Study toward a secondary vocation, and when your singing career takes off, you'll be none the worse for it." These were not new sentiments—Lord knows I had offered the same suggestion many times—but because Kevin was a new source of wisdom, she relented. The high school offered secretarial classes two nights a week, the manager at the theatre agreed to adjust her shifts, and a more mature Vivian began learning to type and take dictation.

It was a turning point for her just as that winter marked a crossroad for the rest of us. Daniel suffered dreadful chest pain and was confined to his bed much of the time, every breath a struggle. His boss at Veterans Affairs had been very understanding, but we all came to the realization that it was time for the poor man to retire. Drugs and therapy had carried him for years, but new X-rays exposed the dreaded reality: He had developed lung cancer. The doctor, matter of fact in his delivery of the news and with only a modicum of compassion, stated, "The damage caused all those years ago by the mustard gas is the likely culprit, but I'm afraid that at this point there's little to be done."

I brushed past his dismissive tone and interjected, "How long do you think?"

"I can't be certain, but I would suggest eighteen months at most." He shifted in his chair to face us, and his manner changed a little; he removed his glasses and his posture softened. "Mr. Pearse, you will soon need to be in hospital. We can help to ease your suffering and lift some of the burden from your wife and family."

I clung to Daniel's arm as we left the hospital but neither of us spoke until we were comfortably seated in our tiny living room. Daniel was worn out, but he refused to lie down until we'd had a chance to properly talk things through. I adjusted a blanket around him and put the gas fire up to full whack. He was so cold; I rubbed his hands between mine and blew warm air into them. We were not really surprised. I suppose we had anticipated what the doctor was likely to say, but still, news like that never comes easily. Daniel seemed more resigned to it than I was. In my bones, I could feel a battle brewing, a coping mechanism I often adopted in demanding situations, and I was the first to break the silence.

"First of all, you are no burden to me. The nerve of him to suggest otherwise. And secondly, that old coot could have it all wrong." I preened my feathers and announced, "I'm going to give Dr. Brigham a call. Let's see what he has to say." I had kept in regular contact with the good doctor, my friend, who had even made the journey to visit with me during those dark days following Emily's death. Daniel tried to argue the point but didn't have the wind. I tucked a pillow under his head, kissed the top of his head, and whispered, "You have a wee nap, and I'll check on you shortly." With a pivot, I made directly for the telephone.

An hour later, I returned to find Daniel sitting up and anxious to talk. I did not give him a chance. "We must go to Toronto. We should have taken you there right after the war, Ian too for that matter." I did not pause for a breath. "Now, Dr. Brigham wouldn't dispute the diagnosis of course but did suggest that they're doing amazing things with cancer at Sunnybrook Hospital in Toronto." Daniel waited patiently and made no effort to interrupt. "I read all about that place when the Queen and Prince Philip visited there last year; it's just the ticket, and that's where we're going to go." Still, he said nothing; he knew all too well that I wasn't through.

"Apparently, there's a place attached to the hospital called the Red Cross

Lodge, and I'm sure I can find accommodation there. Vivian can stay here with Ian while we get you looked after." I ran out of steam and sat down with a thump, feeling the colour high in my cheeks. "We'll all be just fine." Tearful spasms took over my body, my energy drained.

His voice calm and his affect composed, Daniel waited until I regained a degree of composure. "I'll not talk you out of your mission, I know from experience, but I have a thought or two of my own." He took a moment to fill his lungs before continuing. "Milly, I want to go home while I still can. I want to set foot in my birthplace, see the face of my sister, and say goodbye in my own way." He waited a moment while I reached into my apron for a hanky and wiped my nose, then found the strength to continue. "We can't leave Vivian to be responsible for everything here, including Ian."

After another pause, longer this time, he said, "I think we should sell up. Take them both with us to England for a visit. It's time they met their British relations anyway." He grinned. "If we have to dip into that sacred vault of cash from dear Emily, it would be money well spent. And my dear, if I should die there, so be it."

I moved to the couch and held his hands. I attempted to debate the issue, but the look on his face precluded argument. He continued. "I promise that, if I make it back to Canada, we four will move to Toronto, and I'll go to your Sunnybrook Hospital." With that said, he collapsed against the cushions.

Chapter Twenty-two

It was the summer of 1952. The Pearse family were bound for England aboard the *Empress of Australia*, and no expense was to be spared. Daniel's wish was months in the making and not orchestrated exactly as he had envisioned. I preferred instead that we organize our move to Toronto before the holiday, and we did just that with a preliminary train trip to Ontario. Daniel had been given a complete workup at Sunnybrook, and I was surprised that doctors encouraged our planned journey overseas. While they agreed with his diagnosis, they seemed more optimistic in terms of his life expectancy.

"Have a good holiday, Mr. Pearse. Rest as often as you can, and when you return, we will begin therapies that we are confident will ease your discomfort and perhaps prolong your life by a year or two. It is imperative though that you cease smoking immediately." Daniel immediately took on a defiant posture, but the doctor reiterated, "The poison that you've been taking into your lungs for so long has already shortened your life by years; every puff that you inhale, Mr. Pearse, is another nail in your coffin. It really is a choice you will have to make." He turned pointedly to me and said, "There should be no smoking at all in the house, Mrs. Pearse."

I assured him that we would follow his directions, although I was apprehensive about the moodiness we would all suffer as Daniel withdrew from the habit. I was only a casual social smoker and had no concerns about giving it up, but Ian would have to be confined to his room. With my husband comfortably settled into a hotel room, it took me only a matter of days to settle the rest of our affairs with the assistance of our comrades at the Legion. Our bank transfer complete, I found and put a deposit down on a small house in the city. After that, I met with folks at the nearby Thistletown Legion branch who assured me of further assistance in finding a job for Ian. Vivian, I was certain, would have no difficulty in securing secretarial work. She was unpredictably open to the whole notion of moving and thrilled at the prospect of sailing to England. When our sojourn to the old country was over, we would have no reason to return to Saskatoon.

Our excitement intensified as we began the process of packing up our lives, and letters flew feverishly back and forth across the Atlantic. At one point, while wrapping newsprint around cups and saucers before placing them in the china bin, Anita said, "It's all sounding grand, isn't it? Like a great royal visit." She'd been stoic when I'd first explained our plans but had come around when Patsy and her husband announced they were pregnant and could take over the lease on our half of the house.

My friend was spot on. The itinerary for the trip had taken on a life of its own with parties planned and relatives coming from near and far to see us. "It's been twenty-six years since I've seen my family, a lifetime really. I suppose it is a bit like a royal visit." With only a note of dramatic sarcasm, I added, "We're the brave adventurers who travelled off to the land of milk and honey." I looked around me at the tiny room and the stack of unimpressive boxes, and we both laughed. "Most of my relatives, except for the fellows who fought in the war of course, have never so much as left their little communities for an overnight stay in a B&B."

Joking and kibitzing became a coping mechanism between us; she pretended to rifle through one of the boxes. "I'll see if your crown and sceptre are in this lot somewhere, shall I? Don't be expecting me to curtsy now, will ya?" With most of the kitchen packed up, Anita made it her mission to see us fed and pampered. "It's right what you're doing. I don't 'ave to like it, but it's the right thing."

Heather, on the other hand, would not listen to any argument in favour of our move and, in the end, slammed down the phone and refused to attend our going-away bash. I had neither the energy nor the inclination to fight with her. The Legion threw us a brilliant party; Dr. Brigham was there along with all our Legion family, Vivian's friends, and our darling neighbours. It was a difficult but necessary farewell made minutely easier by the anticipation of our overseas holiday. On our final day, with suitcases at the door and all our possessions sent by moving van to Toronto, where Legionnaires would be on hand to receive them, I knocked on Anita's door.

I found her sitting on the bottom step of her staircase in tears and uncommonly quiet. My knees creaked as I plunked down next to her and began the speech that I had rehearsed all morning: "I've been lucky to have had two best friends in my lifetime." I put a little box into her hand and said, "This belonged to my darling Emily, and now I want you to have it." Without a word, she flipped up the lid and sobbed. I reached in to retrieve the delicate little pearl pendant and clasped the chain around her neck while she screwed the little earbobs onto her lobes.

"They are a treasure . . . and so, my friend, are you."

I kissed her cheek and lingered there until her hug came around to catch mine.

Daniel and I walked arm in arm around the deck, both remembering in our own way the last time we'd felt enlivened by the sea air; it was like a tonic. My hair, now white with age, was swept back from my lined face by the gentle breeze; I wished that it could carry the years away with it. How would I find my family? I felt every bit of my fifty-eight years and realized with a start, for the first time, that Alice was nearing eighty. *Dear God, how did we get so old, so fast?*

Daniel wore a weighty expression and I wondered what he was thinking but did not want to disturb him. Ian was somewhere about, content to walk alone and investigate the workings of the vessel, and a jubilant Vivian was already dressed and ready for another evening of dancing; she was in her element. We chose to take meals in our room most of the time to avoid smokers more than anything but also to appease Ian's sensibilities. Once my husband and son were happily tucked in for the night, I drifted down to the ballroom to listen to the music, take in the beauty of the ball gowns, and keep one doting eye on my daughter. She was in every respect the belle of the ball, dancing every dance, flirting and cavorting with the bachelors on board, and even secured an invitation to sing. She was as happy as I had ever seen her.

Sandra met us at the dockyard in Liverpool and nearly knocked Daniel over in a sisterly embrace that lasted some minutes. Vivian and I were given an equally warm reception, though she was careful not to overwhelm Ian, and I admired her restraint. She was a widow now living in a tidy compact cottage on the coast in the quaint small town of Crosby only a short drive from Liverpool. In her thoughtful letters, she'd boasted of plenty of room and had invited us to stay for the duration. Since it was his family Daniel most wanted to see, it seemed logical that he and Ian spend the holiday with her, and I was certain that the sea air would be of great benefit.

Sandra was shocked at first by her brother's appearance but shook it off in good order, making us all wonderfully comfortable in her company. An exhausted Daniel took to his bed for the first few days while Ian simply disappeared into himself. Even Vivian was unable to coax him out of his fog, and so we decided to just let him be. "He'll come around in his own good time," I promised Sandra as she flitted about the kitchen preparing plates of food for the table. We had a lengthy conversation about the different issues and needs of our two men, going into greater detail than I had been able to accomplish in my letters. She welcomed any instruction that would set my mind at ease and seemed to have an excellent grasp on it all.

"Are you sure you'll be able to manage the two of them when Vivian and I go to Warrington?" We were only planning to stay with Sandra a few days.

"I'll be just fine and so will they. Do not worry your head about a thing; you will only be a phone call away. You must be so anxious to see your family, Milly, and I know they will be chomping at the bit to meet this young lady." She was squeezing Vivian's cheek for the third time that day, and the expression on the girl's face told me that the novelty had worn off.

We enjoyed a few leisurely days walking the beach and visiting with Aunty Sandra's friends, but with the boys settled and content in their surroundings, it was time for me and Vivian to take flight. And so, the next morning, we said our goodbyes and were off like giddy schoolgirls in search of adventure, loaded down with gifts of maple syrup and trinkets from home. As the train pulled into the station, my heart pulsed madly in my throat while the dignified façade that I had hoped to present began to dissolve.

"It's alright, Ma. You're allowed to be excited you know," said an observant Vivian. As the taxi turned into the street, my body relaxed into itself, and I realized I'd been wearing my shoulders up around my ears for some time. I cried, for no particular reason. I just cried. The taxi driver gave me a minute to compose myself, but I started all over again the minute Alice opened the door. She greeted us with a giant joint hug that nearly knocked Vivian off the stoop, and amid tears and squeals of delight, she managed to usher us into what was already a crowded house. She was much changed and yet not at all. She wore her hair piled high on her head, and she had put on six or seven stone, but her smile still bounced around a room like candlelight, and she radiated warmth with every word and touch.

Many Aspinall family members were there, all gaily speaking at once, and by the time the introductions and hugs went around the entire room, no one could remember where the receiving line had begun. I watched as Vivian's hand was pumped by this one and that, and I could tell by the look on her face that she understood only about half of what they were saying. It was interesting to hear them through her ears. I had never really thought of my family as having an accent, but after so long away, they sounded like foreigners even to me now. Viv had confessed in the taxi that she was terrible at remembering names and worried that she might offend someone. She had no need for concern; they loved her from the first moment as though they had known her forever. In a way, they had. Throughout the afternoon, the conversations and questions continued, and she glanced over at her me with a smile. She had not realized just how much and how often I had written about *"my Vivian."*

I felt like queen for a day and thought with a smile about Anita; she'd been dead right, and I lapped up the attention like a thirsty puppy. In the run of an afternoon, I learned that I was something of an urban legend, and I liked it.

"This is your Aunty Milly who moved all the way to Canada and braved the elements to work on a farm . . ."

"Did ya know Aunty Mil served in the Great War and put on shows for the soldiers?"

"Did ya live with the Indians, Aunty Mil?"

"Does everyone in America live in a big mansion, Aunty Milly?"

On and on it went. It was fun, and I realized that, for some of them, what they knew of North America came solely from the movies.

On the other side of the room, I could see that my daughter was enjoying the limelight as well. The room was smoky, and I was relieved that Daniel had not come with us. The noise level increased as the liquor flowed, and everyone had a marvellous time. I was home, anxious to spend some time alone with Alice but content to wait.

Next, it was off to the local for a pint and then supper. No less smoky but a little less crowded, the pub was just the place for our cheery gaggle to continue merrymaking. Alice, who had been cleaning and planning for weeks, found a much-deserved comfy chair in the corner. At seventy-seven, the family matriarch had amazing energy and charisma; I was the visiting dignitary, but she was the queen bee with a family that constantly buzzed around her. I watched and wished that I could capture the moment in a gilded frame. This woman had lived an ordinary life, learned a valuable trade, and raised a family through tough times. She had not chosen adventure or travel but had earned the devotion and respect of everyone around her. I was a little jealous.

Annie and Patrick arrived at the pub and were hovering around, waiting for their chance to visit. I listened attentively as they talked about their three boys. The couple apologized that they could not stay longer as their youngest was only five and would be asking for them. In departing, they proudly announced that all three of their sons would be at the "do" tomorrow night and could not wait to say hello to their great-aunty Milly. Oh, how old that made me feel! I had always been "Aunty Milly," even as a child, but "Great-Aunty Milly" had a different ring to it altogether. I felt ancient under the weight of it.

Supper arrived in the form of great platters of sandwiches, cheese and pickles, sausage rolls and mince pies, and cakes and pastries, and the crowd tucked in as buzzards to a carcass. Vivian, who had not eaten a bite all day but had been imbibing a little, was beginning to swoon. It was her cousin Kate, Alice's eldest, who pitched her into a chair and tucked a plate onto her lap.

"You get some of that down you, lass, and 'ave a butty," she insisted. "You're altogether too skinny." Then she smiled a great smile.

Vivian liked all of Alice's children but, so far at least, Kate was in the running for her favourite. She was a naughty character with blonde hair piled high, one hand on her hip and the other jauntily flourishing a cigarette. She was buxom and dressed to show off her assets. She smelled of expensive perfume and tossed her head back with fervour whenever she laughed, which was often and gregarious. This was a woman who knew how to have fun. Her husband Henry was sweet as could be and enormously proud that their only child was away at military college in pilot training.

One of the second cousins was pointing to Kate, telling Viv, "They own an antique shop and a lovely cottage in Wales, do ya know? Lots of money there, by gum." He gave a wink before moving on.

Vivian moved into the booth next to me for a moment. "They must think I'm thick," she said. "I'm constantly asking people to repeat what they've said;

it's like another language." She was only partly kidding. "Nobody seems to use the word 'the' at all. Have you noticed?"

"Shhh," I said with a grin and then whispered, "I suppose every sentence sounds like a question?" She nodded furiously. I'd noticed it too and wondered if I sounded like a foreigner to my family after so many years away. I didn't remember ever having had such a thick accent, but I suppose I did. My upbringing had been different though, influenced by Mother's Celtic lilt and her insistence on proper diction. It was probably why Alice sounded less like many of the others, although she too had her moments.

Vivian whispered, "Everyone calls everyone else 'luv.' It was 'Chuffed to meet you, luv.' 'Must be off now, luv.' 'Have a wee dram won't ya, luv.'" I nodded my acknowledgment, and she added, "I hear three or four sentences, and it always ends in 'ya know,' and I'm never sure if I'm meant to answer a question."

With that, she was hoisted from the seat next to me by her dizzyingly handsome cousin Jack. Like his sister Kate, he had a bit of the devil in him, devilishly playful. He'd overheard part of our conversation, so he leaned up against the bar and put on the broadest, thickest old Yorkshire accent he could muster. He watched her eyes widen in horror when he summed up with "Ya know?" He didn't leave her dangling for long. "Well, lass, I'll let ya get on. Your mam is likely lookin' for ya, and so is my missus." He lifted her off the bar stool. "Oh, wait now, you've not met my Eliza?" And they were off.

A few folks were donning hats and readying to go, saying, "Ta-rah," with a promise that they would see us at the party the next evening. Alice apologized that her sons, Arthur and Sam, were away on business but would be back to meet us before the end of our holiday. Joining us at the table were Kate and my sister's sixth child, Paula. The latter was elegant and charming and had a stillness that was contagious. As they chatted away, I thought, *This girl is the image of her mother years ago, inside and out. A sister of the willow for certain.* As though reading my thoughts, Paula simply patted my hand.

Finally, there was Betty, Alice's youngest. At thirty-two, she was much closer to Vivian's age than most in the room. She was a wide-eyed flirty redhead who was as fun-loving as Kate but unique and quirky. She was married with one son but had attended this gathering on her own. As the evening began to wind down, she latched on to Vivian, and I overheard her say, "My guys are away in Ireland, and I've lots of room. "Now't to stop ya stayin' with me if you like. Bloomin' 'eck, won't be much fun hangin' about with these old crones." She flicked her cigarette onto the floor and in a flourish was off to sit on a vacant lap. No one seemed to pay her behaviour much mind, Vivian included.

The festivities ended abruptly once Alice rose to leave, as though her unspoken orchestrations were always heeded. We followed her out the door amid shouts of "Ta-rah" as we walked down the street and into the quiet of her living room. Viv (as everyone seemed to have labelled her) was so glad to take her heels off that she plunked down in the first chair she saw and absentmindedly flicked them across the room, an action that brought a stern reprimand from me.

Alice chuckled and said, "Make yourself at home. We'll not stand on ceremony here." She looked at me with a grin. "You're on holiday. Now relax and do as you're told." We three sank deep into our chairs with our feet up, comfortable enough already in each other's company not to converse.

The sun was not yet up in the sky when I tiptoed quietly down the stairs only to find Alice already sitting at the kitchen table with a pot of tea and an empty cup across from her just waiting for me. She made to rise, but I motioned for her to stay seated, placing a tender kiss on her wrinkled cheek. "That was the best night's sleep I've had in ages."

She smiled and reached for the pot with arthritic fingers that I had not noticed the day before, "They must hurt," I said as I brushed my hand across them.

"Only a little."

"How do you manage here on your own?"

She replied with a laugh in her voice. "Oh, my dear, I am rarely alone. I have lots of help and an abundance of company. It's the very reason I get up so early in the morning: a little peace and quiet before all my little helpers arrive."

We spoke of trivial things at first and then about the men in my life and the trials that our family would be facing in the months and years to come. "Ian, the doctors have told us, may never really recover. He'll be able to manage a little job with some support, but he'll likely live out his days with us. With me." Alice understood what I meant. I had been clear in my letters about Daniel's diagnosis. We spoke a while about Mother and others in the family who were no longer with us, including her husband, Philip.

She got up to put the kettle on for another brew and glanced up the stairs before resting her hand on my shoulder. "She's lovely, Mil. Just lovely. A real credit to you." I thanked her and nodded agreement.

"She's a spitfire and likes to get her own way."

Alice, wearing a wide grin, was quick to respond. "Much like her mother then."

The morning air was crisp and familiar; the gentle patter of light rain on the roof took on a hypnotic rhythm. I closed my eyes and cradled the hot liquid in my hands, elbows resting comfortably on the table. An easy silence fell between us, the rare kind born of trust. The tension unravelled in my neck as I eased myself back into the chair. Alice lifted the cup out of my hands and said softly, "Just relax, breathe, and let your mind be empty for a little while." I did not argue.

Gently, she asked, "Would you like to spend some time at the willow, my dear? I will go with you if you'd like?"

With eyes still closed, I answered, "No, Alice. It's not for me anymore. It died, and the whispers with it, a long time ago." She was silent. I turned to face her. "Did I tell you about the dream I had the day I learned of Emily's death?" Her expression was a heartwarming mix of concern and pity. "It was a nightmare really. You and Mother and I sat together in what could only be described as a picturesque tabloid; I believe there may even have been parasols." She smiled as I continued. "Lightning hit the willow in an electrical charge of white fingers that turned a bright fuchsia pink as it travelled down the trunk. When the charge hit the ground, we watched as the flames burned blue and followed the roots out in all directions and along the ground to where we were sitting. We didn't move. It was mesmerizing, dangerous, and destructive, and we didn't move."

She hesitated, and it was clear that she was searching her mind for the right words. "I don't know what your dream was telling you. I wish I did. Despair can lead our minds in many directions; perhaps yours was searching for a path away from the hurt."

When I did not respond, she faltered momentarily and then continued. "When I lost my way many years ago, it was you that helped me back to a consciousness of spirit."

I looked quizzically into her eyes. "When was that? I have no recollection of you ever having doubts."

"It's a part of my journey that I've kept to myself. Perhaps that was a mistake." She examined my face for an invitation to continue. "Kate, as it happens, was not my first child." She waited for my reaction and then went on. "I was heavy with child when I married Philip, and yes, it was quite a scandal in its day." I struggled to contain my shock. "I hid the pregnancy for many months, and in the end, I was fortunate to have a mother and father who didn't throw me out on my ear and a young man who met his obligations."

"I had no idea. What happened to the baby?"

"Evelyn was a healthy infant until dysentery took her in her second year. We never learned the source of the virus."

"Oh Alice, I'm so sorry. How terrible that must have been for you."

"It was a tragic loss that far too many experienced in those days; infant mortality was a great problem. I was already pregnant with Kate when she died, and while her father and grandparents suffered grief at her loss, I was mired in guilt and shame. I was convinced that I had done something wrong or that my promiscuity was finally being punished. I was inconsolable and turned away from all those I loved, including my spiritual friends, all except you, my sweet little sister with the abundance of blonde curls." She touched my white hair. "You were only about four at the time."

I finally responded. "We are so different, you and me. I look in a mirror and see a bitter woman with shields up all around. I recognize it, I feel it, but I honestly have no desire for change. I need those defences." She nodded her understanding. "Alice, I admire you, I truly do. I suppose I envy your serenity; I don't know how you've managed to hold on to it all this time, even after Philip's death."

"It's been important for me to stay connected to something greater than myself. I don't mean to preach. I think everyone must find it in their own way. I was lucky that our family gave us a unique avenue to spirituality through nature and our roots; it was something to cling to during difficult times. Philip went to church every Sunday; that was his crutch, and our boys have followed suit. Organized religion wasn't for me though. I cannot find what I need in a building mired with shiny objects or in a book for that matter. I suppose I resented anyone telling me their interpretation of what my creator thinks. My path leads backward to the women who came before and to the nature that connects us all."

"What brought you back to the *Brie* after your baby died?"

"You, my darling; I dropped by to see you on the very afternoon that you first felt the shivers. Mother was whispering to you about the faerie folk, and I watched as the hairs rose on your tiny arms."

I had a vague recollection of that day and suddenly felt a need to be closer to her; I pulled my squeaky kitchen chair close enough that I could rest my head against her shoulder as she continued. "You were so inquisitive, Milly. I visited every day to sit with you and share the stories. It was a wondrous and magical connection that we three shared, and you loved our little secret."

I laughed. "I remember pouring over the pages of the atlas looking for the little island in the Irish Sea between Ireland and England."

"You were so impressed that the Vikings used to live there. Do you remember?"

"I do. The magical Isle of Man and all of Mother's Gaelic ancestors. Oh, my goodness what was the Manx word for island, let me think . . ." She waited with the same patient smile that she had worn when I was a child. *"Ellan Vannin."*

"Well remembered, my dear," she said in a schoolmarm manner.

"Why did it all need to be such a great secret, do you think?"

"Fear, I suppose. As in all things, fear is the great divider. We must not appear strange or odd or different, must we? Witches, pagans . . . I suppose our ancestors wore all those titles and suffered for them. It was safer simply to blend in. Now though, I think an air of secrecy helps to preserve our unique gifts. There are far too many skeptics who sit in wait with a critical eye bent on challenging that which is special."

There was a momentary pause in the conversation while she went in search of the biscuit tin. She popped one into her mouth and pushed the container toward me. "Do you remember the name for women charmers in the old language?"

"No, I've forgotten so many of your teachings," I responded sadly.

"'Ben-Obbee' the women charmers who were akin to nature but particularly skilled in the art of listening. Mostly, they were herbalists and healers, just like you my, dear girl." She stroked my hair just as she had done all those years ago. Her dulcet tones gently transported me to another time. Soft and genuine, she continued. "They harnessed the compassion of the sun, the wisdom of the moon, and learned to feel the lifeblood flow beneath the earth. But it was the wind, the *'gheay'* that was the most powerful because it brought with it the whispers that connected the women as sisters even after death. Some felt its power through the sea and others felt it surge more strongly through the trees, but all were connected in some way through those whispers, the *Sonnish*."

It took me a moment, but a phrase came to mind, my pronunciation childlike: "*Cheayll mee sonnish ny shellagh.*" I surprised myself. "I heard the whisper of the willow."

"You remember more than you think."

"What about your girls? Paula certainly."

"Yes, and Kate as well. If Annie feels charmed at all, she has never given in to it that I'm aware of, and Betty couldn't be still for five minutes to save her soul. I expect your Vivian is the same."

After a moment's hesitation, I reduced my volume to just above no sound at all and said, "Perhaps, but we both know that she's not a blood relation, so it wouldn't apply anyway."

"Oh sweetheart, it has nothing to do with our particular family line. Women, all women, have the potential to hear the whispers and bond with their ancestors. Vivian might not connect to the same spirits as you and me, but that's not to say that she can't feel the enchantment."

I had all but forgotten about Lizzie, put her out of my mind entirely I suppose. The green veil of jealousy drifted by at the thought that Vivian might someday reach out to her "real" mother, even if it were in the afterlife.

Alice caught my eye then. "So, my Milly, if not at the willow or in the whispers, where do you go to find your solace?"

"I suppose I feel most comforted at the Legion and in the work we do. The members share a special connection that many people could never understand. In a small way, it brings me closer to Emily."

"She was an extraordinary woman."

"She was indeed."

"Remind me, when do you leave for London?"

"Day after tomorrow. Vivian and I will go back to Crosby to give Sandra a respite from the boys, and then at the weekend, Viv will stay there to help while I go down to London for the memorial service. We'll be gone about ten days in all, but we'll be back to spend at least another week with you." I had written to her with a detailed account of our itinerary, but I wanted her to understand that we would do our best to share equal time with our families. "Did I tell you that my old friend Squeak is coming up for the memorial service as well?"

"No, but that sounds lovely. I'm glad you've been able to connect with Emily's comrades and organize this tribute for her. I hope it will offer you some closure."

"The hospital has been very accommodating, and a few of her old friends have gone out of their way to put the plan into motion. One of the nurses has very kindly offered those of us from out of town a place to stay."

The quiet conversation between sisters came to an end as the house stirred, and Vivian made her way down the stairs.

The family and the extended family, including children, neighbours, and friends, were all invited to the welcome-home bash at the golf club. It started with a sit-down dinner complete with a very formal head table and a few speeches that bordered on a roast of Aunty Milly. I didn't mind. I enjoyed being the main attraction; my ego was well fed. Band members were setting up their instruments in the corner just as the tables were cleared and rear-ranged around a sizeable dance floor. Vivian, who looked stunning in her "portrait" gown, was happily milling around and involved in animated conversation; she made it look so easy. Annie's in-laws, the Turner family, many of whom I had only met at her wedding, were well represented. I was happy that Vivian would have some dancing partners more her own age. Once the music started, she was on her feet the entire evening.

Alice gravitated toward a particular table far enough from the music to make conversation possible but still in full view of the festivities. After circumnavigating the room and making the compulsory greetings, I found my way back to her and happily plunked down in a chair, wishing all the while that my new girdle had had more of a breaking-in period. My floor-length dress and embroidered jacket, a creamy custard colour, was set off beautifully by the three-strand pearl choker with the faux-ruby clasp that had belonged to Emily's mother. I wore it often and with great pride, touching it every so often to feel her presence. I was royalty for a day, without a crown of course but with all the other trappings, and I happily held court throughout the evening.

Vivian tore herself away from the dance floor when I crooked my finger in a motherly command for a royal audience. Annie stood at the table with her husband Patrick and proudly introduced their three handsome sons. Paul, the youngest (only five years old) peeked from around his mother's skirts. He was dressed in short pants, a blazer and tie, a devilish grin, and ears too big for his young face. He was seventeen years younger than his nearest sibling, extremely attached to his attentive mother, and appeared full of mischief. At twenty-two, Gordon was a fine-looking young man with a thick shock of wavy hair and a twinkle in his eye. He was the first to extend his hand. "How ja do, Aunty Mil. Heard a lot 'bout you."

All the while he was speaking to me though, he was looking directly at Vivian, and I watched as he shook her hand and drew her in for a peck on the cheek. "Well, lass, you're a sight for sore eyes." A lady's man no doubt, he was charismatic, free-spirited, and funny, and I warmed to him immediately even though he had clearly charmed my daughter. I was grateful that they were cousins. David, shy and introverted, was the baby I had rocked on my knee the year before we'd immigrated to Canada. Now twenty-eight, he smiled and greeted me warmly, nodded a hello to Vivian, and with a gentlemanly manner asked if we were enjoying our visit so far.

"Come on, darlin', let's have a dance," said Gordon as he steered Vivian out of her seat and into the swirl of bodies. Paul was already off in search of other children, and David made his way toward an empty seat at the bar. I watched as he took a pipe out of his pocket, lit it, and puffed on it. He wasn't exactly handsome. He and his closest brother had similarly pronounced noses (an Aspinall trait) and the same dark-brown eyes, but his hair was darker and slicked back. He had a widow's peak, an unusual hairline for one so young. Still, there was something distinguished and intelligent-looking about him. Perhaps it was the pipe.

The music went quiet, and someone was demanding attention with a "tink, tink, tink" of their glass. It was my nephew Jack, with drink in hand. He spoke loudly enough for everyone to hear. "I'll not break up the festivities by making a speech, but I would like to propose a toast." He raised his glass high. "To Aunt Milly, we welcome you home; we are pleased to see you so well after all these years and hope that it'll not be so long before you make th' journey to see us again."

The crowd responded. "Hear, hear!"

He continued. "And to Vivian, we are so happy, my dear, to meet you at last and to welcome you home to your family."

The faces in the room turned toward Vivian. "Hear, hear!"

Jack concluded with a beaming smile. "I ask you now, who could ever say they don't make them out of good stuff, those lasses from Lancashire? Cheers!"

Glasses were raised higher still with a resounding "Cheers!"

He stepped down from the chair he had been using as a platform, and as the music filled the room once again, he made his way over to our table. He placed an affectionate kiss on his mother's cheek before turning to me. "We really are delighted you've come home." I was moved.

The evening continued much as it had started: with dancing and merriment and a good deal of liquor. The older folk gathered around tables to talk while the younger adults, mostly Annie's clan, either held up the bar or did their best to stay upright on the dance floor. Vivian, who was a light drinker, was still dancing and one of the few who still had her shoes on. It seemed that every time I glanced in her direction, Gordon, who was an excellent dancer, had her by the hand and around the waist. I watched with a grin as she coaxed and finally persuaded David onto the floor. He lacked his younger brother's proficiency but did his best to lead her around the room without stepping on her toes. When the foxtrot was over and the band began playing a polka, David shook his head in an obvious refusal to continue, and as the two made their way toward the bar, I watched as Betty grabbed Vivian's hands and drew her back for another twirl around the room. They were an uninhibited and peppy twosome who brought about raves and laughter as they made a show of themselves. They were having a marvellous time.

Vivian and her vibrant cousin skipped toward us, still laughing and with their arms linked around each other's waists. Alice beamed and said to her daughter, "Seems you've met your match for staying power."

"Well now, that's th' truth of it," she replied. "And my mate Vivian and I have a proposal to make." They glanced at each other with a girlish titter. "I know you're heading away for a few days, but I'd love it if Viv could stay here with me. I can show her around and take her to the pictures. I'm on my own, and I could use the company." My hesitant expression was all that she needed to continue. Looking to Alice for support, she prodded, "Come on, Mam, convince her that she needn't worry. Viv will have a much better time with me."

Arguments were made for and against, but Betty made a convincing case, and with Alice on her side, I finally relented. "I will call your aunty Sandra in the morning and ask her thoughts on the matter. If she can manage without you while I'm in London, I see no reason why you shouldn't stay and have some fun."

Alice seemed pleased, and as the girls danced back toward their young friends at the bar, I wondered if I was doing the right thing. As though reading my mind, she said, "Can't have been easy for her growing up without siblings her age." I hadn't really thought about it in a long time. "And I expect that life with her dad so ill and Ian in his state can't have been much fun for her either." I couldn't tell if she was being critical or simply pleading the girl's case.

"I've done my best to see that she is happy."

"And a fine job you've done too. At a glance, you can see that she's confident and full of joy. It's exciting to watch your children at this stage, standing on the precipice of what life has in store for them."

On my return to the coast, I found Daniel much improved and holding court in a deck chair much as I had done in a party hall. Ian was comfortably out of his shell and taking daily walks into town, spending time at the pub and fending off a few pretty girls. Sandra was ruthless about her no-smoking rules and earnest in her care for her brother. Her family doctor, who was a supper guest on my first night back, promised to be on hand should the need arise, and after a few days of rest and relaxation, I had no concerns about leaving for London.

My pilgrimage began and ended with thoughts that flooded back to the first time I met that sweet creature in a train station. Had it not been for Emily, I may never have survived our ambitious foray into the "Great War." *What a ridiculous way to describe it . . . utter carnage . . . what a waste.* I would most certainly have succumbed to depression in the years that followed were it not for her and her father. It was she who had orchestrated my reunion with Daniel, and without her intervention, Ian may never have returned to us.

Her memorial service was small and respectful, honouring her work and the lives she had saved. Each of us in attendance shared short stories about our connection to her life. I struggled to sum up my Emily in a few brief sentences. I reached over to place on her headstone the rosary that I had discovered in the rubble during our oh-so-memorable holiday in London. We continued our celebration of her life for several days, through laughter and tears. And among people who had been close to her, I was finally able to say goodbye. The guilt remained (the guilt would always remain), but I allowed her to rest a little more peacefully.

The train sped along the countryside toward the coast with the morning sun piercing intermittently through the trees. I considered, and not for the first time, how different my life would have been if I had stepped over the threshold into Emily's arms all those years ago. There would have been love and adventure, but there would not have been a Vivian. Still, the thought rested deep and unspoken. I felt closer to her than I imagined possible. Stronger and yet sad, connected but terribly, terribly lonely. Lucky to have a compartment all to myself, I relaxed into the rhythm and sway of the train and sang quietly.

I'll be loving you always
With a love that's true always
When the things you've planned need a helping hand
I will understand always, always

Days may not be fair always
That's when I'll be there always
Not for just an hour, not for just a day

Not for just a year, but always

The song would become my signature—the solo piece that would end every performance. Em smiled back at me from the front row of every show from then on.

I looked forward to a few days in the sea air and an opportunity to regroup before heading back to the Aspinall, Simpson, and Turner clans and their well-meaning social agenda. As promised, Sandra was waiting for me at the station but, astute in her assessment of my mood, she refrained from asking about the trip as we drove to the cottage in comfortable silence.

I was thrilled to see a little pink colour in Daniel's sunken cheeks and happy to find him puttering in the vegetable garden. If it were not for his pension, Ian's too for that matter, I could have envisioned living the rest of our lives in this peaceful existence. We had budgeted carefully for this holiday, but it was only that: a holiday. I was determined to enjoy it. I found a deck chair and soaked in some sun.

Chapter Twenty-three

I returned to Warrington after my ten-day sojourn feeling rested and ready for anything. Once again, Alice greeted me at the door and ushered me into the front room where my nieces Kate, Paula, and Betty were tipping back a sherry. Eliza, Jack's wife, was pouring one from the decanter for me and pointed toward the comfiest chair while Alice picked up her glass and scrunched into the vacant spot on the couch next to her youngest. Kate raised her glass. "Cheers, ladies."

"What a pleasant surprise it is to have an all-women gathering," I said. "Was Annie not able to join us?" There was a momentary glance between sisters on the other side of the room, and I thought, *Okay, that's a question better left alone.* "Never mind, this is just lovely. Thank you all." They asked about my trip and inquired after Daniel and Ian, but I sensed some tension in the air. I had the sinking feeling that something was amiss.

As though detecting my concern, Alice cleared her throat. "Now, Milly, we have something we need to talk over with you." Her expression conveyed no need for alarm but there was a note of seriousness in her voice, "Vivian—"

"Oh my God!" Just her name was enough for me to jump in, panicked. "Is she alright?"

Betty immediately chimed in. "She's just fine, right as rain—" but stopped talking after a sharp look from her mother.

Alice concurred. "She is absolutely fine, I assure you. We just wanted to give you fair warning about events that have transpired in your absence." She sounded as though she was giving dictation instead of telling me what I needed to know about my daughter.

Once again, I interrupted, "Oh no, what has she done? Has she been making a show of herself?"

"Nothing of the sort, Milly, and now if you'll just give me a minute, I'll try to explain." I felt chided but chose to do as I was told.

"It seems that she has been spending a lot of time with one of Annie's boys, and they've formed quite an attachment in this very short while."

Once again, I let my impatience get the better of me and jumped in angrily with both size nines. "I had a feeling about that Gordon at the party. He was buzzing around her all evening, a proper ladies' man."

The girls all looked at each other; Betty was chomping at the bit to say her piece but deferred to the family matriarch who was clearly in charge. Alice orchestrated a silent moment to bring the conversation back to a civil tone. I settled, and she responded calmly but with purpose. "I would remind you that these are my grandsons we're talking about . . . your great-nephews," she said pointedly. "We should tread cautiously. We, none of us, want to say anything we may later regret."

I opened my mouth to speak, but she did not give me a chance "As it happens, it's the older boy, David, that she's fallen for, and he for her, as I understand it."

My mind reeling, I sniped at Betty, "I thought you were meant to be taking care of her; you were supposed to be her hostess, not her dating service."

Alice didn't try to step in; she knew that Betty would stand up for herself, and she did. "Now see here, Aunty Mil, I don't want to be disrespectful," she looked at her mother and added sarcastically, "or God forbid, impolite," she took a big sip of her drink and got up for another, "but your daughter is no child. She has a mind of her own. She's a grown woman, and I did not agree to be her keeper."

A calmer voice was interjected by Paula, who, like her mother, was less inclined toward the colloquial Lancashire slang. "I had a lovely sit-down conversation with Viv. She told me that she was drawn to David because he did not behave as most lads do around her. He was shy, and she found that attractive. He didn't feel the need to boast or ruffle his feathers; he was just quietly confident and seemed more interested in what she had to say. They talked well into the evening the night of the party, and she said she'd never felt more special." Her patronizing tone was only half as irritating as her oh-so-pleasant expression. She was talking as though her words would meet with my approval and that I would miraculously be overjoyed at this news. I was numb.

Betty finally calmed down under her mother's stern glare and made an effort toward civility. "Viv and I have had a wonderful time. We've been to the pictures and shopping, and we've had loads of girlie chats. We did now't wrong." Her tone took on more of an edge now. "But like a good waiter who doesn't hover about until he can see ya need somethin', I believe a good hostess does th' same. When David called to ask her if she would like a tour guide, she jumped at th' chance." With a smirk, she then added, "And right onto th' back of his motorbike, I might add."

Alice chided her. "Not helpful, Betty. Please sit down now."

I was losing control, and I hated the sensation of it. My skin was alive, my heart was beating rapidly, and there was a twitch vibrating in my cheek. With my voice sounding higher than I intended, I asked, "So this has been going on since even before I left? Why didn't someone call me?"

Kate, who had remained silent until that point, challenged me in her low sultry voice. "Call you about what?" All her vowels sounded longer than they needed to be. With Betty Davis flair, she smirked. "For goodness' sake, they're two young adults who enjoy each other's company. Why on earth would we ring alarm bells over that?" She flourished her cigarette in a crazy eight and after a big breath said, "Now, Aunty Mil, be reasonable. There's now't to myther about here."

Eliza nodded her agreement and nervously added, "They are two lovely young people having a holiday romance; surely there isn't anything wrong with that? They live an ocean apart, and when the holiday is over, they'll write a few letters and that will be that."

Alice acknowledged her but calmly returned to the conversation. "Perhaps, but Milly, I think you should be aware that what began as friendship *has* bloomed into a romance. Quickly, I'll grant you, but a romance nonetheless. I see nothing amiss. They will sort out how to deal with it, and Eliza may be right that a long-distance relationship will fizzle out if it's not meant to be."

The pressure and friction were too great to hold back any longer and with a silent "pop," the cork flew. I rose from my seat, enraged. "They're cousins! You are all out of your minds if you think I'm going to sit back and watch this play out!"

A now drunken Betty snickered and scoffed. "My God, people in small towns like ours have been marrying their cousins for centuries and none of us have webbed feet."

I stomped from the room, leaving the chattering hens behind me. It was little wonder that Annie had not appeared at this summit, and I briefly considered how difficult all of this must be for her and Patrick. I picked up the telephone receiver, determined to find my daughter, but really had no idea where to call. Alice's gentle hand reached past me, took the handset, and placed it back down on its cradle. With the other hand, she rubbed small circles on my back. "Come on, luv, let's you and I go upstairs for a quiet minute."

I pleaded, "Where is she?"

"She and David are spending the afternoon with Jack. Milly, she was so very apprehensive about confronting you with any of this. That's why we tried to break things to you gently." She shook her head. "I suppose we weren't terribly successful at that, and I am sorry."

"I'm going over there right now!"

She could see that I was past the point of reason or argument. "Alright but I'll come along. Wait here; I'll get Eliza. I expect her husband will need some moral support."

Jack met us at the door and sized up the situation immediately, urging caution. "If you try to drive a wedge between them, Aunty Mil, you may just push them closer together. Go easy, won't you?" I didn't.

What followed was a one-sided shouting match that ended with my demand that Vivian come with me that instant. She was in tears but stood her ground. "No, Ma, I'm not going anywhere. I'm a grown woman, and if this is a mistake, it's mine to make." She was defiant but maintained her decorum; in any other set of circumstances, I might have been proud.

David, who had been quietly steadfast throughout my tirade, displayed a hint of temper at the sight of Vivian in tears. "This is no one else's concern but ours. I appreciate that you are surprised, but we are adults and know our own minds." His arm, already around the girl, defiantly pulled her in closer.

"Do not challenge me, young man. You may be of age, but she is not. You are ten years her senior, and I would think you'd have a little common sense." I looked at Vivian, and in my anger, used her father's illness against her. "Do you have any idea what all of this will do to your dad? Have you given that even a moment's consideration?"

She did not rise to the bait but calmly removed herself from David's embrace and crossed the room, taking my arm gently and turning me toward to door. "I think it's time you and Aunty Alice go home. There's no more to be said here today, and I think Jack and Eliza have put up with quite enough." I was shocked by her easy dismissal and inwardly impressed by the maturity of her actions.

She was right. There was no more to be said. When I returned to Alice's home, I would not entertain any conversation from her or her daughters and chose to secret myself in my room for the short term.

I chose not to worry Daniel with any of this nonsense until I was able to talk some sense into my daughter. I stewed for a couple of days, escaping downstairs for a whisky-laced cup of tea and a bite to eat now and again. Alice made no attempt to debate the issue but knocked on my door and handed me a letter that had just been delivered. I recognized Vivian's atrocious penmanship at once and closed the door without a word. Every fibre of my being wanted to rip the envelope in half, but I simply couldn't do it.

Dear Ma,

Funny, isn't it? I don't think I've ever written a letter to you before. I'm sorry you've been upset, and I hope that you are okay. None of this was planned; some things just happen I suppose. I want to explain how innocently it came about and just how wonderful David is. I thought maybe if I tell you a little bit about him, it'll help you to see why I feel as I do.

After you left for Aunty Sandra's, David called to ask if I would like to see some of the sites with him. I was surprised because he seemed so shy at the party, and to be honest, I thought it was his brother who would be asking me out. We spent a wonderful day touring around, and he took me for a lovely picnic in the country. He was a perfect gentleman. He's had so many accomplishments and adventures but never boasts about any of them. I had to drag information out of him. We met with some of the other Turner clan for supper, and he even made the effort to take me dancing at a club in Manchester; it is not his strong suit.

I was invited to "tea" at his house the next day and was made so very welcome. His mother, your Annie, was so proud to tell me about his graduation from the Royal Institute of Chemistry in Liverpool. Now he's employed as a chemist at the Shell Oil Refinery laboratory in Ellesmere Port. She pulled out an album of photographs of David's mountain-climbing expeditions in Wales and Norway. He and a friend spent a

*month travelling the Norwegian countryside on their motorbikes, and
there are all sorts of pictures of him hanging onto the side of a cliff with
a pickaxe or scaling a steep rock face with ropes and harnesses, frightening really. Photography is one of his great hobbies as well. I'll bet you
didn't know that either. Honestly, he has always got to be busy; I suppose
it's one of the few things we actually have in common. He seems a little
uncomfortable in social situations and content to let characters like his
brother steal the limelight. I know that I'm like Gordon in that way. He
describes me as petite and perky. He has given me a nickname: "Titch."
Silly, isn't it?*

*I found myself waiting for the phone to ring; couldn't wait to see him at
the door. I've never felt that way before. Oh Ma, if you ever felt that way
about Dad, you'll have to understand. It isn't something that happened
on purpose or to distress anyone.*

*We went to Wales and spent an overnight with Kate and Henry and
that's when I knew I was in love with him. I didn't know where it would
lead, and I didn't care. We are second cousins. I know that. He's a good
deal older, and I know that too. There's nothing wrong in our being
together, and I have no idea how it will all work out, but I so want you
to be on my side, Ma, please understand.*

I love you,
Vivian

I didn't, and I couldn't. I was hateful and unbending. All that I could see
in front of me was a scenario where Vivian was going to be taken away; she
would stay in England, and I would lose her. I made it my mission to dispar-
age their romance to anyone who would listen. Everyone had an opinion.
Some of the older relations were on my side, disgusted that cousins should
be carrying on like that. They fuelled me. My attacks became more hostile.
*"She's only a child and him a grown man; he's taken advantage . . . If he gets
her in the family way, their children would be mongrels. Mongrels!"* I cringed
at the words even as they flew out of my mouth; I hated the sound of them
and detested the person who spewed them out. She and her hateful dramatic

rhetoric were everything I had loathed all my life. Mostly, my daggers missed their mark, as David was highly regarded. Eager to help, family members tried to assure me of his character, but I dug in, stubborn and unyielding. *"This will kill her father!"* This was always my fall-back position.

"When we're home safely in Canada, we can put this whole sordid mess behind us."

Alice refused to be drawn in; she understood that taking sides in a family drama was a dangerous game that would end badly. She watched and listened carefully to all that was said and held out hope that the situation would resolve itself in a compromise. There had been squabbles before, and there would be squabbles again; she was astute enough never to give her opinion lightly or involve herself without invitation. It was a common-sense approach that had served her well, but she made an exception on the evening when I made a public spectacle of myself.

Vivian and David arrived at the local with a few of the other young folks after an evening of clubbing; their boisterous and giddy celebrations continued with a drink at the bar. They had no idea that Alice and a few of the other old cronies were sitting at a corner table with me. The bell rang behind the bar, the room quieted, and our attention was drawn to a gentleman who held his glass high in the air and asked for everyone to raise their glasses in a toast to the newly engaged couple. I watched as Vivian kissed David passionately and flashed her ring to the young woman beside her.

The rest played out like a scene from a bad melodrama. I flew into a rage, knocking over glasses as I hurled myself toward them, all the while screeching like a banshee with hateful snipes and accusations loud enough for the entire building to hear. David took Vivian by the hand and escorted her toward the door. "Come on, let's go."

I envisioned them heading directly to a registrar's office. "You can't marry her! She's not of age!" My temper spiralled out of control. "I suppose you've knocked her up already, have you?" I heard the audible gasp from the crowd around me, but I didn't stop. "You need parental consent, and you won't get it from me! You cannot stay in England; you need a visa, and I will not sign for that either! You, madam, are coming back to Canada with me and that's an end to it!" I grabbed at her arm, but David steered her away and stood between us. His stance, defensive and angry, was in sharp contrast to the look of shock and disbelief on his face. He was wounded but still he said nothing. Jack dragged me back to the table while the young couple made their escape, and several others followed them. The room was abuzz, but most of the irritated faces refused to make eye contact with me.

I do not remember returning to the house, but it was just as the door closed behind us that Alice placed herself squarely into the middle of the situation. I was nonsensical, still snorting and blustering, when she spun around, pointed one bony finger, and demanded that I sit down and listen. I faltered for a split second, opening my mouth to speak only to be silenced by an angry, much-older sister.

Emphatically, Alice stated, "Your behaviour is outrageous." She gave me no chance to respond. "I've listened to your ridiculous mean-spirited accusations and this self-serving nonsense for quite long enough." I was stunned into silence; I had never heard Alice speak with such disdain. She didn't let up. "Whatever has come over you? You're out of control, and I believe you are enjoying the spectacle!"

I found my legs after this accusation. "I'm not a child, and I won't be spoken to that way."

Incensed, I made for the stairs, but Alice shouted and then threatened, "If you leave now, I will break my promise to you, Milly. I will march right back to that pub, and before morning everyone will know that Vivian was adopted."

There was no sound but for the clock on the mantel and the hum of the fire behind the grate. I turned slowly and moved toward the living room with deliberate and measured steps. Alice waited, taking a moment to rein in her own temper and allow the quiet of the room to wash over us both. Finally, she broke the silence, controlled and just above a whisper. "There is no biological reason those children should not be wed, and we both know it. Is keeping your secret so important that you would forsake your daughter's happiness and slander a young man's good name?"

I stared at the wall directly in front of me, feeling the colour drain from my face as my temper abated. I discarded one sentence after another as they came to me. I formed arguments that held no merit even to me. Then finally, painfully, the true source of my upset, so long denied, was given voice.

"She was so tiny when they laid her in my arms . . . it was as though she were actually mine." My voice was almost inaudible. Tears were streaming down my face as I continued, never taking my eyes from the wall. "The babe that was taken from me all those years ago was my penance for loving a married man. I paid the price. I suffered." I drew breath and blinked away tears. "I gave up my home and my family. I raised another woman's children, and God rewarded my sacrifices with Vivian. She is mine. She's all that I have that is really mine."

Alice released a long slow breath. "None of us belong to anyone, Milly. We steal a little time together, but in the grand scheme we stand alone. You don't own her."

"If I allow this marriage, I may never see her again. If I agree to cousins being married," I turned to look at her and conceded sheepishly, "especially after my tirade . . . everyone will suspect she is not mine. She may suspect the same, and I cannot live with that."

"You've been a wonderful mother to her, saved her from what might have been a retched life, and she will see that in the end. There's no shame in being adopted, and there's no shame in being childless."

"Please, Alice . . . don't take her from me."

"Milly, what are you really afraid of?"

I searched deep in my soul for the answer. "Being alone, I suppose. I will lose Daniel very soon; we all know that to be true, as hard as I have tried to deny it. And Ian . . . oh Ian, that sweet boy, he's already gone, lost to me long ago. I have only my daughter to see me through my old age."

She consoled me as best she could and spoke all the appropriate platitudes, but nothing penetrated. "Come now, we're both exhausted. This will not resolve quickly or without careful thought." She guided me toward the stairs. "A good night's sleep. That's what we need now; we'll talk more about this tomorrow." She slowed to a stop. "But Milly, of this I am certain: If you do not adjust your thinking, you *will* lose her." That arrow hit its mark.

The telephone rang. It was Annie, asking if her mother could please drop over. I promised to behave myself and go to bed while my sister, looking every bit her age in that moment, donned her hat and closed the door behind her. I spent a fitful night. We all did. The next morning though, once again, Alice was up and about in the kitchen before I rubbed the sleep from my eyes. I motioned for her to sit while I prepared a brew and dared to ask, "Are they okay?"

The depth of her concern for me echoed in her words. "Everyone is okay."

I sat beside her and made a feeble attempt at an apology. The words sounded flat even to my ear. She listened and then looked at me. "I understand your struggle, Milly. We are all afraid of being alone. It's human nature, I suppose. Unfortunately, you have caused damage here that will not mend quickly or easily."

"I know."

"David took Vivian back to his house last night where they had a good talk with his parents. That's why Annie called to invite me over."

"I assumed that would be the case."

"Both Patrick and Annie are very quiet people, passive some might call them, and while they've kept their distance through all of this, they have detested the conflict." I hung my head just a little as she continued. "They like Viv very much, but they have concerns as well. When they asked David what he planned to do, he announced that, if necessary, he would immigrate to Canada." I felt bristles growing on my neck, but I remained still. "His father questioned the logic of leaving a good job. Those of us who've lived through war and depression don't make decisions like that lightly, do we?" She added the question as if to ensure she still had my attention. Without waiting for a response, she went on. "His mother, who is well aware of *all* that has been said, questioned the legality of cousins marrying. David assured her that no such rule or law applies to second cousins. He promised that they would consult a physician and get expert advice regarding genetics before they would consider having a family. He told her that, if they must, they would simply adopt."

When it sounded as though she was ready for me to enter the conversation, I said, "It seems that they have it all thought out, doesn't it?"

"I know this has all come about quickly, and I understand your concerns, but I really do believe they are committed to one another, and that they will make it work. You can choose to play a part in their new little family, or you can dig your heels in. I fear that you will be the one to lose if you choose the latter."

"What have you told them?"

She understood my meaning. "I have not betrayed your trust, Milly. Viv need not know the truth of her birth until you are ready to tell her, but I do believe that you should be honest with her. In the meantime, if you cannot yet find it in your heart to encourage their union," she looked more closely into my eyes, "and I can see that it may still be too soon for you to do that, I strongly recommend restraint in your language and your actions." Her momentary pause begged for an affirmative response. I simply bobbed my head in agreement. Satisfied, she continued. "Good, I promised Vivian that everything would be all right." Once again, she looked at me for confirmation. "I am sorry, Alice, that you are bearing this burden."

Tenderly, she confessed, "It is the sadness in my own daughter's eyes that worries me most." At my puzzled expression, she explained, "She is the one whose eldest child may be moving to another continent. You hadn't considered that, had you, Milly?"

I felt only a momentary pang of guilt. "Leaving England would be David's choice, not mine. It is not my doing."

"No one is accusing you of orchestrating their love affair, but I ask you this, Milly, could anyone have dissuaded you from marrying Daniel?"

"It's not the same. We were much older. Vivian is just a child."

She bristled. "She's a grown woman who is entitled to make mistakes and learn from them as we all have. I believe, though, that serendipity has played a huge role here, and I am optimistic about the outcome. Milly . . . I will do everything I can to ensure that her *mother* makes no more trouble." Her body language negated further debate. "I told Vivian that you love her more than she'll ever know or understand, and that while unattractive and hurtful, your actions were not born of malice but out of love and concern."

"Thank you, Alice, that was very kind, and probably more than I deserve."

"We'll leave it alone for today. We must give our nerves a chance to quiet a little, but then we'll have to sit down and discuss all of this as adults, don't you agree?" I did, but my expression was unconvincing. "I mean it, Milly. It must remain civil."

Tensions ran high as family members licked their wounds. I chose a cool and detached exterior—a highly polished suit of armour—but as promised, I refrained from any further abuse. Annie greeted me warmly at the door and Patrick shook my hand, their noble generosity making me more contrite than I had planned to be at our meeting with "the kids." Vivian and David stood together, but she crossed the room to give me a stingy hug, and I realized too late that I did not hug her back. David shook my hand and greeted me sparingly. "Aunty Mil." I considered for a moment that he was dreading the notion of having me as a mother-in-law. Annie poured coffee, and it was a well-orchestrated *tête-à-tête*, with no alcohol on offer. Alice affectionately embraced her grandson and hugged Vivian before taking the perfect seat to facilitate the meeting. Vivian nervously twisted the ring on her finger until David rested his hand over hers, and I watched as they threaded their fingers together in a show of unity.

Breaking through the silent tension, Alice began. "We have much to talk about, but also much to be grateful for and to celebrate. There are things to be considered, of course, and I am certain that if we discuss our concerns rationally we will all be the better for it. To begin, I believe David would like to say something."

His deep voice trembled just a little. "Aunty Mil, or perhaps I should call you Mrs. Pearse, your daughter and I wish to be married. I understand that you prefer she remain in Canada, and to be with her, I am willing to immigrate. I assure you that I will never see her want for anything, and I would very much like to speak to her father face to face about our future."

Alice, the director of the scene, looked towards me for response. I began hesitantly. "I can't pretend to be happy about this. I'm sorry to you both for my behaviour, but you must understand that all of this has come as quite a shock." I looked around the room at the faces, pleading for me to be kind, and focused on Annie's pitiful expression. "I apologize to all of you for my offensive conduct."

Alice nodded. "Well then, that makes a good start."

Quiet-spoken Patrick weighed in. "We welcome Vivian whole-heartedly into our family, but it would be nice to know that our son would be welcome in yours, Aunty Mil. He'll be a long way from home."

"Well, there's not much family to speak of really, just we three and Vivian." I looked directly at my girl. "But we'll do our best."

Patrick, still puffing on his pipe, dipped his head, satisfied with my answer.

I felt the need for some control, to feel as though I had a say in something. "I must insist that Vivian wait until she's twenty-one before they are wed. She's only eighteen . . . *far* too young."

Vivian opened her mouth to argue but Alice jumped in. "Vivian, it is important that you see your mother's point of view, and perhaps you will come to a compromise. We have no way of knowing at this point how long it will be before David can join you in Canada. A visa and a new job may take some time. By then, you and your mother will have had a better opportunity to reconcile to all of this."

The girl agreed, albeit reluctantly. "It will give me time to find a job in

Toronto and start putting some money aside."

"I will begin sending resumes right away but won't give notice at the refinery until something promising comes along," advised David as he glanced lovingly at his parents. He paused a moment and then turned to address me. "As far as the wedding goes, I will wait as long as necessary." He pressed his lips into Vivian's hand in a tender kiss.

The young couple seemed satisfied. His parents surrendered to a future far from their son, and I (ever the miserable bitch) remained hopeful that a long-distance relationship would fizzle out over time and come to nothing. We managed to continue a civilized conversation while Vivian made a call to speak to her father. After a healthy length of time, she returned to the room and spoke first to David. "I've explained everything," she turned to me with a subdued glare, "well, almost everything." I did not rise to the challenge; I had it coming. She continued quietly. "Dad was very understanding and wishes us every happiness in our future." She sat gingerly on David's knee and added, "He looks forward to meeting you next week."

And so, it was decided. I would leave for the coast at the end of the week, and they would follow a few days later. Sandra had insisted that she could make room for David, who would stay for the last two days of our holiday and see us aboard the ship. I did not look forward to any of it and dreaded their tearful farewell scene at the dockyard.

Alice decided it best to forego my "leaving party" as nerves among family members were frayed. Instead, she hosted a low-key open house for those brave souls who wanted to say goodbye. My relationship with Alice was, for the first time, fractured. Hers was the only opinion that mattered to me, but I knew that the fissure would take some time to mend. Still, my perfect big sister saw me off at the station. Her final words were gentler than I deserved: "Open your heart, Milly. There's so much love to be had if you're open to receive it." She reached up to kiss me on the forehead as she had done when I was a child and brushed my cheek with the back of her hand. "Be kind. Be happy."

When I looked back at the events of my life, I likened that episode to a volcanic eruption. The spewing of hatred and derision left burned soil and ash in its wake that took many years to heal. Magnanimous relatives found their way to forgive me over time but very few forgot. I was an overbearing manipulative shrew, tried and convicted by a jury of my peers; it was a life sentence. It was a reputation well-earned and one that I defiantly, stubbornly, wore as a mantle for far too long a time. It simply did not matter. The only rift that was of any consequence had no time to heal because Alice died only months after our return to Canada. I was haunted by the insurmountable chasm of my own making.

Chapter Twenty-four

The voyage home was a long, lonely one; tensions ran high, and I suppose it was inevitable that a tearful Vivian would explain the whole sordid story to her father. Daniel, who was looking healthier and had a little of his old feistiness back, was extremely cross with me. The months that followed were lonelier still. Vivian made it her mission to prove me wrong in all my assertions and predictions and avoided me whenever possible. She found work in a typing pool at a busy downtown office and spent her free time tucked away in her gabled bedroom, writing letters to England. She was offered an opportunity to share a flat with two of her co-workers but chose instead to stay home and save every penny. Daniel would not allow her to pay anything toward room and board. We were, by then, well established in our new Toronto home, and Daniel was an outpatient at Sunnybrook Hospital. The doctors were enthusiastic about the state of his health and acknowledged that the healing properties of the sea air may have contributed as much as his cessation of smoking.

I was pleased with our little gabled house on the corner with its full acre lot, the mature gardens, and the magnificent willow tree on the front lawn. We had a small mortgage, but we were able to manage. The folks from the Legion helped Ian to find a job at a tool and die factory only a quick bus ride from home. His employer, an air force veteran, was sympathetic to his circumstance and disability, and Ian seemed satisfied with the work. The decent wage gave him pocket money for booze and cigarettes, while we collected his pension for room and board. His smoky room at the top of the stairs was a bastion where he could vanish into the wallpaper for days on end. Once again, we were fixtures at the Legion, and in no time at all I was organizing shows as their new entertainment chairman.

Ten months and several hundred letters later, Vivian finally got word that David had secured a position with the Swift Canada Co. in Toronto. It would mean a demotion for him. A laboratory assistant was markedly lower on the totem pole than the operations manager title he currently held at the refinery, but it was a starting point. She was ecstatic. He booked passage to Canada, and she set about finding a small apartment for him.

They were wed on March 4, 1954, with full regalia; she walked down the aisle looking every bit the fairy princess on her father's arm; she was not yet twenty-one. The event and all the trappings were courtesy of money that Daniel had been saving for the occasion: a savings bond that he had wisely invested from the funds Vivian had paid for her board in Saskatoon. Over the years, he had matched her dollar for dollar. Her extravagant dress, flowing with lace and tiny red silk roses, was a gift from her godmother. The photographer was Ian's contribution, and their honeymoon in New York City was funded by their British relations.

With the festivities behind us and the couple embarking on their new life together, I found the house particularly empty. It didn't help that winter was dragging on. The walls were closing in. Spring could not come too soon, and at the first glimpse of new life in the garden, I drew up a chair and sat once again beneath the willow. I made many attempts to find my way back to the *Brigh* without success. There were no whispers. Still, I found it a comforting place to talk to Emily and Alice—a church in its own way, I suppose, surrounded by peonies and hydrangeas. I did have a visitor from time to time: a rather large snake, harmless but sinister-looking. I named him "Cody." I had vague recollections of snakes in the stories and myths that Mother used to tell and remembered them as the guardians of the spirit world. *"Coadagh"* was the Manx word for protector. I am not sure why or how I remembered that, but I simplified this big fellow's name to Cody and chose to see him as beneficial.

On that day, I leaned back gingerly in a folding lawn chair with its red and white webbing beginning to fray. I spoke aloud to Cody, who had not yet made an appearance. "Will it hold I wonder?" The air was crisp and fragrant, and I let my mind drift into the restorative freshness of it.

Hello, Alice.

My girl is married. I rejoice in her happiness, honestly, I do. But I think also that I might drown in sadness. How can I be lonely for her now when she's really been lost to me ever since our return from England? I have never been forgiven. Tolerated perhaps but held in contempt. I am looking up into the branches of my willow, not so old as the one in our youth but still grand and sweeping. Can you see me? I listen closely and seek healing, but even these quiet buds of spring have brought me no peace. What, I wonder, would you say to me if you were here? Something wise and ethereal, no doubt.

The sky was clearest blue with just one swath of bright-pink cloud painted across, as though Alice had signed the splendour with her own brush. *I love you too.*

Just over a year later, I was a widow and also a grandmother.

Chapter Twenty-five

Forever

With you in waking and dream I shall be,
In the place of shadow and memory,
Under young springtime moons,
And on harvest noons,
And when the stars are withdrawn
From the white pathway of dawn.

LUCY MAUD MONTGOMERY

My darling Beth, this is where my story nears its end and yours begins. In 1956, your mother placed you into my arms and said, "Her other grandmother is too far away to play a big part in her life. Beth is going to need you."

It was a magnanimous speech and a heartfelt one. As I held your warm little body close to me, I felt a deep and resonating connection to something greater. I leaned in and whispered quietly against your sweet breath, "We share something that your mother and I do not: a bloodline. I may not be your grandmother, but I am your great-great-aunt. You have an abundance of Aspinall blood coursing through your veins; both of the grandmothers that you will know are of the same blood."

You wriggled and tried to stretch within the confines of your swaddling blankets, and I felt a pang of guilt as I considered your other "real" grandmother somewhere in Saskatchewan, the one you would never come to know. I wondered, *Will this sleeping babe be a sister of the willow? What have you inherited from me? None of my crusty disposition, I hope.* I cradled you close and whispered, "Listen, child; listen well."

I was grateful for the circle of life that had gifted me with a small spark of hope. The months of sitting by Daniel's bedside at Sunnybrook Hospital had taken their toll on all of us, and although I was relieved when his suffering was over, there was a void. I was alone. There was Ian of course, but as I watched him slump in his easy chair with the same blank expression night after night, the hollow emptiness inside me echoed louder and louder. I suppose I envied his numbness in a way. I confessed to Emily, *I am beginning to hate the sight of him. This will be my life, moving through each day with no conversation, no company, no destination or purpose . . .*

After talking it through with Emily, I determined that a destination was something to work towards and that I would continue to make the Legion my purpose. *For every problem, there is a solution. Thanks, Em.*

Getting older had many limitations. I was no longer permitted to drive due to failing eyesight. Oh, how I missed my independence. I had been behind the wheel or under the hood of a vehicle since I was fifteen, and I felt as though a limb had been amputated. I sold off parcels of the property to pay off the mortgage and took in a border that lived for a time in the gabled room across from Ian. I was frugal and managed to add a little to my travel fund each month. I wanted desperately to return to England while I was still able; there were fences to be mended. I envied your mom and dad when they made the trip overseas, on a Pan Am flight, to introduce you to your British relatives on your first birthday. What an adventure. I could not wait to board my first airplane.

Two years later, your pretty, dark-haired sister was born. Oh my, how you loved your Julie. You coddled and petted her as though she were one of your little dolls, wrapping your hair around her shoulders like a blanket. You were very sweet together. Your dad found success in his new job at Canadian General Electric, and you girls wanted for nothing. You were a typical two-car family living in a big new house. Your mother, always the social creature, enjoyed the trappings of prosperity, and true to his word, your father worshipped her.

We were such a small family unit; I suppose it would have been impossible to ignore me. I was included but at arm's length, made welcome but not warmly. Your mother considered me her responsibility. She took it seriously, and I let her. Your dad, ever the gentleman, was polite and pleasant but measured; he had never forgotten or forgiven past hurt. He did, however, give particular attention to Ian, and for that, I was incredibly grateful. He tried everything to connect with his brother-in-law, and there were times when I thought he had made some headway, but it was a losing battle.

I journeyed back to the old country many times in the years that followed and made my peace with those that mattered. I dove headlong into Legion work and revelled in the accolades that I received from the membership. It went to my head; there is no denying that. I needed the attention and the tributes. They kept me up.

When you were old enough to be left in my care, I sat with you beneath the willow and watched as my mother had done with me. I observed from the start that you, who loved your dolls and books, had a natural stillness that I thought might be fertile soil for the *Brigh*. It was clear from the start that your energetic sister, who was rarely still, would be more likely to dance with the faeries without ever hearing them. There were no obvious signs, no gentle hairs rising on your chubby little arms, but you did, many times, lift your attention from a storybook in seemingly quiet scrutiny of your surroundings.

"*It's possible,*" I declared to Alice. "*I think it may be possible. I will keep a distant but mindful eye.*"

Tiny silver particles of glass sparkled on the surface of the vanity; the early evening sun peeking through the window cast a pink and orange glow over them. The mirror had shattered into a thousand fragments and yet held firm in its frame, balancing precariously in its desire to remain whole, all at once fragile and strong. What better metaphor for my life? I don't know how long I had been sitting there. I was mesmerized by the distorted face staring back at me, freakishly Picasso in nature, both grotesque and beautiful. It made a nice change from the sour old crone that had been reflected there for so long. Flashes of blinking, all-seeing eyes stared off in different directions, behind them a maze of personalities and tortured thoughts stood as witness to my own brokenness. The icy splinters of this composite portrait wore my sharp edges and prickly bits, as evidenced by the blood on my finger as I traced the wrinkles and crevices of the haggard old face. The light danced from place to place, casting a prism of colour around the room, chastising and reminding me that I had also known moments of joy and contentment. The mirror could be repaired, of course, but it was too late for me.

I had not been ready for this last lonely chapter of my life. I walked through each day, keeping to routine and providing the necessities, but I had no energy left for Ian who had become more miserable and cantankerous with age. Violent fits of fury spewed from him some days, and I was no longer able to reach him. The little swordfish on the mantel, its three broken pieces once healed with cement, now lay shattered into a hundred fragments on the floor. The beer bottle that shattered the vanity mirror was the last straw.

I spoke when he spoke, but I did nothing to encourage life into the silences. I had been caring for him for more than fifty years, and I had nothing left to give. I soured like milk left out in the sun; I was the one in need of nurturing. An understanding hand to hold and an ear to listen might have made the difference, but your mother was too wrapped up in her own life to notice. She was dutiful, made sure that I made it to appointments and that the refrigerator was full, but never once simply stopped to talk. I felt even more alone when she was right there in the room. It was unbearable.

I had long since given up conversing with Emily or Alice. I puttered in the garden when I could manage it but gave the willow a wide berth. I was ever-so-old, and I had burned ever-so-many bridges. Heather's children had children who would never know anything about me; I realized too late that I should have made a greater effort with her.

I have feared little in my life. I've met most every obstacle with courage and confidence but for two. The fear of being alone festered into anger and hate, and rather than facing it, I have allowed it to consume me. It is my greatest regret. The fear of being forgotten is yet to be resolved and has led me to you, our Beth.

The tragedy is that, when old people die, a library of knowledge closes behind them, great volumes of wisdom and details of history that you cannot find in any book. Our stories should be spoken with passion through voices that convey the message in such a way that the listener feels the struggle, the joy, the essence, and the impact of each moment. They are a legacy. What greater gift to share from generation to generation?

Beth, you have heard the whispers with your heart just as I knew you would from the day that I caught you snooping in the vanity. You asked about the "skeleton box" as you called it, and I told you about the three-legged man, Triskelion, *Ny Tree Cassyn,* who always lands on his feet and guards the *Sonnish*. Your curiosity was captured that day, and my suspicions were confirmed that you had the ability to connect with the spirit world. I told you that the box was filled with my treasures, the whispers of my life, and that you couldn't see them because my story was not yet finished. Do you remember what I said to you that day? *"Perhaps, if you learn to listen very closely, you will hear the Sonnish, and one day, these treasures may belong to you."*

Beth, my darling girl, you have freed my soul, and peace—*Shee*—rests within me; it is the first word you heard among the whispers. My most treasured secrets and thoughts now belong to you. I know they are in good keeping, *Shuyr my chree*. Sister of my heart.

Listening

'Tis you that are the music, not your song.
The song is but a door which, opening wide,
Lets forth the pent-up melody inside,

Your spirit's harmony, which clear and strong

Sings but of you.
Throughout your whole life long.

AMY LOWELL

Chapter Twenty-six

I floated toward consciousness, my body heavy but suspended, buoyant as in a heavily salted bath. My arms, like wings, stretched out freely from my body, weightless and unencumbered. The hypnotic sound of water lapping gently against my face was interrupted by the distant song of a goldfinch. Entranced and content in my lucid dream, I resented the mounting stimuli of sounds and scents that brought me nearer to wakefulness. The bird's song was closer now and more insistent; I felt the rigid ground beneath my back. A perfume of wildflowers mingled effortlessly with their neighbours, and my nostrils gave an involuntary twitch. I hesitantly opened my eyes to confirm what the soft chirp of the crickets and the cool cleanliness of the air was telling me: that it was night. With eyelids still heavy, I gazed upward into a sea of stars as each one winked her hello. I smiled back at them. I called out to them, "Hello, Grandma. Hello, Milly." Faint and shadowy images appeared, like the clouds of light that drift behind your eyelids just before you submit to waking, elders with stories yet to be revealed.

Much to my surprise, I was able to sit up without discomfort; still I stretched and eased my way into wakefulness. The skeleton box beckoned to me from within the basket where it lay nestled and safe. It was of no value to anyone else; I knew that it was empty to all but me. I had no doubt what I would find inside. With her story resonating deep within me, I struggled to imagine that a life so large could be summed up in the few trinkets housed in this antique, nondescript vessel. I lifted it out, childishly gave it a little shake, and smiled as the contents rattled their approval for the first time.

The treasure inside was musty with age, and I took a moment to tiptoe my fingers through the faded black and white photos. I smiled, happy to be reacquainted as with old friends. None of the trinkets came as any surprise to me; I knew the importance of each one. Milly had gifted me her story, and it was mine to share. I was eager to orchestrate the plan of action that was already taking shape in my mind, and as I gathered my belongings together in the basket, I felt the pearl choker rattle in my pocket. I held it in my hand, wrapped my arms as far around the tree trunk as they would go, and rested a kiss on the craggy bark. Its heartbeat breathed energy into my body, and as I hesitantly pulled away from the vibration, I whispered, "You will never be forgotten, Grandma."

Biological or not, that is who she was.

Now retired, Julie was enthusiastic at the suggestion that we spend a sister weekend together and chose a lovely spa hotel in Toronto for the occasion. I wanted to have her all to myself, no distractions, no rush, and no sceptical ears. After a day of pampering and a lovely dinner, we settled into our room with a bottle of wine. Without hesitation or fear of judgement, I shared my story while she listened attentively. I gave her the condensed version, although I remembered every detail of Milly's account as though I had actually lived her story. I watched my sister's face for any hint of doubt, but there was none; she was marvellous. I was a little surprised that she was able to step so far outside her analytical comfort zone and remain open to all that I had to say. She was, after all, the clever sister; she took after Dad while I was more creative like Mom. Still, to add credence to my narrative, I took the skeleton box out of my suitcase and placed it on the table in front of us.

"Wow," she said. "Haven't seen that in a long time." I was surprised to learn that she had seen it at all. "It was always empty."

"Was it?" I looked at her with raised eyebrows.

"I guess not." Before I could open the box, she turned to me. "There was always a connection between you and Milly, and not just music and the military. I didn't feel any of that with her." She was thoughtful for a moment. "I did get to know her in a different way though, when she was much older."

"How's that?"

"Well, after you left home, and whenever Mom and Dad went on one of their three-week holidays to Hawaii or wherever, I was left to hold down the fort. I took her shopping and to appointments, ran errands, and did my best to clean up her mess without letting her know."

"She was proud."

"Yes, and very nearly blind by then. She would have been mortified to know how filthy her house was at times but hated the idea of anyone touching her things. She became quite paranoid toward the end. I would wait until she was watching TV—well, listening really, at God knows what decibel. She was terribly deaf. It was during one of those cleaning binges that I found this box in the dresser."

"I'd suspected you had to help out with her but didn't know the extent of it."

"We still weren't close, but I did get to know her a little better and saw for myself just how combative her relationship with Uncle Ian could be; not a healthy atmosphere at all."

I patted the seat next to me in an invite to sit closer. "I can't believe we've never talked about these things before."

Dressed in our fluffy white bathrobes and huddled together on the sofa, I explained why I'd called it the "skeleton box" and lifted the lid. The treasures were mine to share as I wished. It was the most marvellous feeling to introduce her to her kin. Starting with the photos, I said, "This is Grandma Milly and her friend Emily in their Women's Army Auxiliary Corp uniforms during the Great War. She had such a presence even then, didn't she?" I handed her the next one. "This one is Grandma Annie with Dad. He's about nine years old here."

"Dad! My God, he had that crazy widow's peak even as a kid." We laughed. "And Gran is so lovely; I've never seen a photo of her in her younger years."

"I think you look like her." She gave me a skeptical glance for the first time but smiled. "Wow, poor Dad. It all makes sense now; it always seemed that he had more than the usual mother-in-law distaste for Milly."

"Yeah, you could sense it, but nothing was ever put into words. He never bad-mouthed her, or not that I heard anyway. You?"

She shook her head. "No. That just wasn't in his character though, was it? He didn't speak unkindly about anyone, not ever."

I nodded and smiled softly, missing him deeply at that moment. Sighing, I went on. "I think, with Milly, he just tried to keep his distance. It must have been awfully hard to do at times. Do you remember road trips with her? She could be as annoying as hell, pointing out the obvious and snapping her demanding bony fingers. Dad was always in a dreadful mood by the time we got home. He usually had a Manhattan in his hand before the door closed. She was expert at pressing his buttons, and I never did understand why."

"Right, I had forgotten. Oh my, driving around to see the lights on Christmas Eve was the worst. Poor dad couldn't get away 'cause she and Uncle Ian always stayed at our place for the night. He suffered in silence while Milly babbled on in a futile effort to be social, and in the end, they were both miserable."

Julie changed the subject. Lifting out the next photo, she asked, "Who's this?"

"That is our great-great-grandmother Mary Jane Aspinall. And that adorable blonde child on her hip is Milly, your great-great-aunt, at about age two, I think."

A puff of air escaped her lips. "Whew, I'm going to need to see this mapped out on paper. It's a little confusing."

I showed her the make-shift family tree that I had begun "This may help a little, but it still needs tweaking before we can share it with our kids."

Looking around as though someone might be listening, she said, "Who would ever have imagined the old battle-axe with blonde curls." We shared an irreverent chuckle.

"I know. She was a pretty little thing. Don't you just love Mary Jane's dress and hat? Stunning, don't you think? Like something off a *Vanity Fair* cover circa 1900." She agreed and reached for two more photos. "This one is Grandad Daniel; he looks so much like Uncle Ian, but who's this?"

"That's William Aspinall, Milly's dad."

"This one is Mom on her sled on the farm in Star City; she must have been three or four. And in this one you can see her crying next to her biological mother, Lizzie; our grandmother!"

She held the second faded photo close to her face for several minutes, and with soggy eyes, said, "How sad. I can't imagine being that close to one of my children without being a part of their lives. It had to have been torture."

"I agree. Women had so few choices back then, and they had to make decisions out of desperation, especially during the Great Depression. Mom looked like her, don't you think?"

"I do."

Wiping away a tear, she reached in to retrieve the choker and ran the pearls through her fingers. "I can hardly remember a day that she didn't wear this."

"And we had no idea how much it meant to her. I guess that's really the message, isn't it? Everyone's got a story, and we have to be open enough to listen, maybe even going so as far as to ask."

I showed her the little porcelain doll with the missing arm and explained the story behind it. "I remember the little swordfish and a couple of other nondescript trinkets that used to sit on her phoney mantel."

"I know. I always thought they were just bits of junk. I had no idea how important they were or that she was so sentimental. I have a new appreciation for all the things in her crate. Speaking of that, is there anything out of there you'd like to have?"

She thought for a moment. "Maybe the big green fruit bowl. I always liked that. It took pride of place on her dining-room table for as long as I can remember."

"I'll make sure you get it."

Balanced on my hand were Emily's amulet and her tiny signet ring. I had already explained their significance. "A testament to friendship. if only these little trinkets could talk, right?"

Julie responded, "Apparently, they did."

There was a tiny red-velvet pouch that I had decided belonged with Milly's treasures. In it was the little gold locket that my granddaughter had found in my jewellery box and placed around my neck on that fateful day when we'd first sat beneath the willow. "I have no idea how or why this ended up in my possession; you can see the bit of solder on the back where a clasp used to be attached."

Julie recognized it immediately. "Milly gave you that when you were so sick with appendicitis. Don't you remember?"

"Uh . . . no, no memory of that at all."

"Well, you were a bit out of it I guess, but she was worried and uncharacteristically pleasant as I recall."

I shook my head. "My only recollection of that whole time is that Mom and Dad felt so sorry for me that we ended up with a puppy." She laughed at that, and I shrugged. "Somehow this just ended up at the bottom of my old jewellery box."

Julie gently pried open the hinge with her fingernail to reveal the faded miniatures of a young Milly and her sister, Alice. "Wow, there was such an age difference between them, wasn't there?"

"Yep, and remember, Alice is your great-grandmother, Dad's grandmother."

"Lord, what a family!" she declared.

"I don't want to remove the photos. I expect they're pretty fragile, but I know without looking that there will be a symbol of *Ny Tree Cassyn*, the three-legged man, engraved behind one image and the word "Shee" behind the other.

"And that's why she wanted you to have it, so that you would be encouraged to land on your feet." She kissed my cheek.

Lastly, I showed her the delicate Thumbelina bracelet, each rose-gold link untarnished and held together with a tiny heart-shaped lock. Julie leaned her head against my shoulder, and we wept.

We wept, drank lots of wine, and then talked well into the night, reminiscing and gaining new insights about one another. Milly was responsible for bringing my sister and I closer than we had ever been, and I told her so in a whisper as I finally drifted to sleep: "*I have shared your story with your other granddaughter; I can promise that you will not be forgotten by either of us.*"

Julie and I were committed to it: Our children and theirs would learn about Milly's life, and together we formulated a plan to honour "the old battle-axe."

We slept late, ate a hearty brunch, and treated ourselves to a massage before setting out on our mission. Still slightly hungover, we began by laying flowers on Milly and Daniel's grave. Ian was buried elsewhere. He'd survived Milly and lived the remainder of his life at a retirement community for veterans called Legion Village. We agreed to make a sizeable donation to the Legion in honour of all three.

Next, we made our way to Wallasey Avenue. Thankfully Julie was driving; the cloverleaf of roads had changed the landscape entirely; I would never have found the street. Tall buildings and monstrous homes had replaced the modest dwellings we'd known as children, and as we rounded the corner, Julie pulled off to the side of the road. With a deep sigh, she warned, "I haven't been down here in years, Beth. These are valuable properties now, and I am doubtful that her house is still there. Are you prepared for that?"

"I guess so. I hadn't really considered it. If nothing else, we can see the willow and that will have to do. Go on, let's just see." I encouraged her forward.

She put the car in gear and moved slowly along past great homes with pillars and many with religious statues on the lawn. She murmured, "Pretty Catholic neighbourhood, I would say."

"Yeah. Italian, I think." Most of the mansions stood where two houses had previously been. They were beautiful in their own way, but my heart began to ache as we approached the corner. Julie and I simultaneously stretched our necks to look to the left, and there it was, tucked in off the road: Milly's little gabled house. Dwarfed by all those around her, she sat sweetly confident with well-maintained perennial gardens, new shutters, and a darling bright-red front door. Wooden blinds had replaced the cheap shiny gold synthetic curtains that had once hung in the living-room window, and we watched as a light came on in the gabled bedroom that used to be ours. There was no traffic about at that time of the day, and so we sat at the stop sign without speaking, just taking it in.

Julie reached her arm across and drew circles on my back. "Are you okay?"

I wasn't. Tears were welling up, and I found words difficult. "Why? . . . Why?"

"I don't know, Beth. I'm sorry."

Our beautiful willow was gone. In its place was a lovely stone path lined with hostas, leading to the new steps at the front door. It was charming, but everything about it seemed wrong. A car approached from behind, forcing us to make a move. Julie turned the corner to the left and was set to keep going, but I pleaded for her to pull over again, just for a minute. She immediately did as I asked but teased, "I'm starting to feel like a stalker. Someone might think we're casing the joint." I recognized it as an effort to take the sting out of the moment, but I was feeling too emotional for it to have the desired effect.

"Just a little longer, okay?" She offered no argument. From this side of the house, we could see that the dazzling crabapple tree still stood at the top of the driveway, in which a car was parked.

Julie began to giggle, and Julie never giggled. I slapped her thigh. "What the hell is so funny?"

"I was just thinking about all those tragic wig heads; do you suppose they're still all lined up on the dresser? God, what a fright that would give us."

"They were always facing the door. Do you remember that?"

"Yeah, like they were watching your every move . . . *Whaa-ah-ah.*" The tension broke, and we laughed until I had to cross my legs.

"You know, I've actually thought about those absurd creatures. Imagine if we could paint faces on them, each one a different moment in her life."

"That would definitely put a different spin on things. Come on, pet, we can't sit here much longer."

I finally relented, but just as we were about to pull away, a women exited the backdoor with an infant car seat over her arm. She glanced suspiciously in our direction as she opened the back door of the vehicle and placed the seat inside. "I want to talk to her," I decided as I unbuckled my seatbelt.

"She might not even speak English. What are you going to say to her?"

"Not sure yet."

Julie was still talking as I closed the car door behind me and calmly made my way across the street. "Hello," I said with the sincerest non-threatening smile that I could manage.

The woman closed the car door and responded with a strong East European accent. "Hello, can I help you?" She peeked in at the child and took a defensive stance at the back of her car.

"I'm very sorry to bother you." I pointed over to the car where Julie sat bewildered at my bravado. "I'm here with my sister." Julie gave a timid wave. "This used to be our grandmother's house; we spent much of our childhood here."

"Oh, I see. That's nice." There was still a note of suspicion in her voice.

"We're just visiting and thought we'd take a chance, just to see if the house is still here." I smiled and said, "We're so delighted to find that it is!"

She warmed to me and replied, "We love this little house; it is all that we need." She took a casual glance at the monstrous houses around her.

"Our grandmother would be so pleased to see that her gardens are still beautiful."

She nodded shyly and then reached for the door handle. "I don't want to rude, but I have an appointment. I must go."

"Thank you for taking the time to talk to me. You've been very kind." I pivoted to walk back down the drive but as an afterthought, turned back. "Could I just ask . . . Why did you take down the big willow tree from the front yard?"

She responded sadly. "It was hit by lightning. The limbs that fell caused great damage to the roof."

"Oh, that's too bad. I'm sorry." Then I had a thought. "Do you remember when that was exactly?

She then confirmed what I already knew to be the answer. "Yes, it was over a year ago, June 10. I remember because it's a family birthday, and we had a party here that day."

I reached over to shake her hand. "I wish you great happiness always in your sweet house." At that, I returned to Julie.

As I motioned for her to drive on, I explained, "The tree was struck by lightning on the same day that Milly first whispered to me in the park."

At Julie's bidding, I executed the remainder of our plan on my own. The city council in our town happily agreed to my proposal and assigned two gentlemen, contractors from the parks and recreation department, to assist me. The location I had chosen for the installation of our memorial was specific. The wrought-iron legs of the oak bench that Julie and I had chosen were buried a few inches into the ground and set in cement. The contractors were a little confused when I asked them to dig an additional small hole two feet deep under the bench but didn't argue the point. I suppose they assumed ashes would be buried there. I thanked them for their assistance, but they refused the tip that I tried to offer. One of the gentlemen tipped his hat and said, "Our pleasure, ma'am. I do strongly suggest that you wait a day for the cement to set before attending to any further ceremony." I promised to heed his advice.

The next morning, I arrived at the park long before even the most eager joggers came out for their daily exercise. I was glad to have waited; it was a perfect day. The view of the river from the memorial bench was spectacular, and about five yards to the west side of it was a healthy willow sapling. It was the perfect place for a soul to take root. Not far away, the sweeping branches of the great tree frolicked and danced their approval as I lowered the skeleton box, lightly wrapped in my Legion scarf, deep into the waiting cavity beneath the bench. It was still home to Milly's treasures, except for the photographs, which I kept for my own collection of whispers. I filled the hole and covered it over with some dry leaves before turning my attention to the packet of forget-me-not seeds in my pocket. An early riser passed and gave me a curious glance as I scattered the seeds all around the young sapling.

My mission complete, I took a seat with Milly and chatted quietly with her for a time. I imagined her adding another spoonful of sugar to the already sweet, sweet tea in the china cup with the bright-yellow daffodils while I opened a new packet of Fig Newtons. The taste of them lingered on my tongue as I reached into my pocket for a hanky, and I heard her say, *"Good girl. A lady always has a hanky on her person."* With just a little spittle on the cloth, I polished the shiny brass plaque with its inscription:

"Millicent Cynthia Aspinall"
Veteran of the Great War
Shuyr my chree

Author Bio

Mary Capper is a retired administrator living in Carleton Place, Ontario, just outside Ottawa. She is a history buff and self-described sleuth, particularly when researching the hidden truths behind her own ancestry and genealogy. While doing that research, a picture emerged of a strong, courageous, and resilient woman who did not resemble the grandmother she knew as a child. Sadly, Capper only remembers the broken version of this incredible woman: a miserable old curmudgeon who was often referred to as "the old battle-axe" and for good reason. Piecing together her story became a labour of love for Capper who was inspired to write *Sonnish… whispers through time* to commemorate the grandmother she came to know and appreciate. She hopes to encourage dialogue between generations to preserve stories and familial histories.

Mary shares a great number of similarities with her grandmother; she is a wife, mother, grandmother, and accomplished singer. She is very proud to have served in the Canadian Armed Forces.

Printed in Canada